ROCK, PAPER, SCISSORS

MAXIM OSIPOV (b. 1963) is a Russian writer and cardiologist. In the early 1990s he was a research fellow at the University of California, San Francisco, before returning to Moscow, where he continued to practice medicine and also founded a publishing house that specialized in medical, musical, and theological texts. In 2005, while working at a local hospital in Tarusa, a small town ninety miles from Moscow, Osipov established a charitable foundation to ensure the hospital's survival. Since 2007, he has published short stories, novellas, essays, and plays, and has won a number of literary prizes for his fiction. He has published five collections of prose, and his plays have been staged all across Russia. Osipov's writings have been translated into more than a dozen languages. He lives in Tarusa.

BORIS DRALYUK is the executive editor of the *Los Angeles Review of Books*. His recent translations include Isaac Babel's *Red Cavalry* and *Odessa Stories* and Mikhail Zoshchenko's *Sentimental Tales*. He is the editor of *1917: Stories and Poems from the Russian Revolution* and co-editor of *The Penguin Book of Russian Poetry* and Lev Ozerov's *Portraits Without Frames* (published by NYRB Classics).

ALEX FLEMING is a translator of Swedish and Russian literature and children's fiction. Her previous translations include works by Therése Söderlind and Cilla Naumann, and in

2015 she was awarded the British Centre for Literary Translation's Emerging Translator Mentorship for Russian. She is based in London.

ANNE MARIE JACKSON has lived for extended periods in Russia and Moldova. She is a co-translator, with Robert Chandler and Rose France of *Tolstoy, Rasputin, Others, and Me: The Best of Teffi*, and with Robert Chandler, Elizabeth Chandler, and Irina Steinberg of *Memories: From Moscow to the Black Sea* (both published by NYRB Classics). Her previous translations include works by Alexei Nikitin and Olga Slavnikova.

SVETLANA ALEXIEVICH is a Belarusian journalist, writer, and historian. The daughter of two teachers, she studied journalism at the Belarusian State University in Minsk and went on to work as a teacher and newspaper journalist. She published her first book, *The Unwomanly Face of War*, an oral history of women's experiences in World War II, in 1985, and since then has released five chronicles of Soviet and post-Soviet history, including *Boys in Zinc* (1991) and *Voices from Chernobyl* (1997). In 2015, she was awarded the Nobel Prize in Literature, the first time it had been given to a journalist.

ROCK, PAPER, SCISSORS

and Other Stories

MAXIM OSIPOV

Translated from the Russian by
BORIS DRALYUK, ALEX FLEMING,
and **ANNE MARIE JACKSON**

Edited by
BORIS DRALYUK

Preface by
SVETLANA ALEXIEVICH

NEW YORK REVIEW BOOKS

New York

THIS IS A NEW YORK REVIEW BOOK
PUBLISHED BY THE NEW YORK REVIEW OF BOOKS
435 Hudson Street, New York, NY 10014
www.nyrb.com

Several stories first appeared in the following publications: "Moscow-
Petrozavodsk," translated by Anne Marie Jackson, *The White Review* Online
(September 2012); "Rock, Paper, Scissors" (excerpt), translated by Alex Fleming,
Image, no. 92 (2016); "The Mill," translated by Alex Fleming, *Asymptote* (Janu-
ary 2018); "Objects in Mirror," translated by Boris Dralyuk, *Granta* Online
(February 2019)

Library of Congress Cataloging-in-Publication Data
Names: Osipov, Maksim, author. | Dralyuk, Boris, editor, translator. | Fleming,
    Alexandra, translator. | Jackson, Anne Marie, translator.
Title: Rock, paper, scissors and other stories / by Maxim Osipov ; edited by
    Boris Dralyuk ; translated by Boris Dralyuk, Alexandra Fleming and Anne
    Marie Jackson ; introduction by Svetlana Alexievich.
Description: New York : New York Review Books, 2019. | Series: New York
    Review books classics | Includes bibliographical references.
Identifiers: LCCN 2018036766 (print) | LCCN 2018046038 (ebook) | ISBN
    9781681373331 (epub) | ISBN 9781681373324 (alk. paper)
Subjects: | LCGFT: Short stories.
Classification: LCC PG3492.87.S553 (ebook) | LCC PG3492.87.S553 A2 2019
    (print) | DDC 891.73/5—dc23
LC record available at https://lccn.loc.gov/2018036766

ISBN 978-1-68137-332-4
Available as an electronic book; ISBN 978-1-68137-333-1

Printed in the United States of America on acid-free paper.
10 9 8 7 6 5 4 3 2 1

CONTENTS

PREFACE

I LOVE Maxim Osipov's prose. I started rereading his stories and caught myself thinking that his prose now reads like something of a diagnosis: an accurate, unforgiving diagnosis of Russian life. Although the author is filled with love for a simple, human existence, he is simultaneously struck by how little this existence actually coincides with his own expectations. The drama of those raised by culture, raised by books. Culture normally protects us diligently from reality, but here it is hardly able to do so, because Osipov is a writer with a double vision: First, he is a doctor—a cardiologist—a profession directly related to time, to the impermanence of man; the heart is nothing more than time. And second, when you live in the provinces, it's harder for culture to deceive you, harder for it to mask reality with fashionable ideas and superstitions—that of the "Russian world," for example. Out in the provinces, everything is in full view, more exposed—both human nature and the times beyond the window. And that's why the author isn't moved by the sight of the oh-so-familiar peasant when he sees him running naked through the streets, chasing his mother with an ax, "a crucifix dangling from his neck." In another story, one of his characters (a policeman) explains to a writer—a naïve man, as he sees it—that murderers are "just your average people." These stories tell of people who haven't come to understand the meaning of their existence—what is it all for? Very few of us have, it must be said. The soul is forced to toil night and day. But who has the strength? The author relates to his characters as to patients; he asks them where it hurts and whether... in general, does it hurt in the soul? The Russian soul—yet another myth. In reality, there is but one soul; the real question is: Is there a person?

Russia as a country has overextended itself across an enormous territory, and it lives as though time had stopped. And any attempt to speed up time—the October Revolution, for example—has ended in bloodshed. When you delve into Osipov's texts you see that they are deceptively simple, just like Shalamov's: Behind this childish ordinariness there lies a hidden chasm. The whole time they leave you thinking how difficult it is to love humanity—wonderful, repulsive, and terrifying as it is—but in order to stay human, that's exactly what you must do: You must love man. Your soul is restless—it is thinking. To inspire such thoughts—that's something that only true literature can do.

—Svetlana Alexievich
Translated by Alex Fleming

To a reader, a councilor, a doctor.

THE CRY OF THE DOMESTIC FOWL
In Lieu of a Foreword

THE PROVINCES as home: warm, grubby, ours. But there's another way of looking at them—an external, superficial point of view, yes, but one shared by the many who didn't choose to end up here: the provinces as sludge, the doldrums. That the locals are pitiful is the most flattering thing one can say about them.

The cry of the domestic fowl drives out the dark thoughts that take hold through the night.

Morning at the hospital. On the bed lies a skinny, smoked-out man—a bus driver who's had a heart attack, a bird of the wild. For him the worst has passed, so he watches the medics treat the patient next to him, a trampish-looking old man whose wrist bears the blue sun tattoo of a prison-camp guard. An electric shock, his heart rhythm returns to normal. "Old fella's still ticking," the driver chuckles from behind the screen. He and I exchange glances. Will they let him drive his bus again? And the more burning issue: What if his wife runs into that other woman—the one who brings him shashlik—at his bedside? But this driver could also tell you a thing or two about me. These wild birds are very perceptive.

We're compelled, clearly, to love not only those we are close to—our fellow domestic birds—but our wider surroundings, too: the people and the place. And to do this one must notice, recall, invent.

And so, from my childhood: my father and I are walking somewhere, it's far away, the day is hot. We're out in the countryside and I'm desperate for a drink. My father knocks at a stranger's house, asks for some water. The woman says there is none, but she brings us some cold milk. We drink and we drink, a lot—probably three pints. My father offers her some money, but she just shrugs and asks, straight-faced: "You out of your mind, dear?"

The place could be anywhere with its own kind of appeal—particularly Central Russia. You can fall for this place just as easily as a woman can fall for a loser. "Yes, we love this country, as it rises forth," goes Norway's national anthem. We also extol the virtues of our geography, which, considering our size, is hardly decent. Our anthem was written by our authorities—by *others*—not by little birdies like us.

Another memory: I'm eighteen, driving an old Zaporozhets, when suddenly in the back—where the engine is—I see a cloud of smoke. I'm expecting the worst, an explosion. There are people on the pavement—get back, it's going to blow! "Pop it open," says a man, about thirty, walking by. He takes out a rag and—calm, unhurried—smothers the flames. Then he walks off. Another bird of the wild.

Of cars, of travel more generally, the memories come thick and fast; domestic creatures are prone to trouble on the roads. This is where they cross paths with wild and predatory birds. Such encounters make their mark, through unexpected goodness, through evils previously unimagined. "Killers, they're just your average people," the police chief will say, and then all of a sudden you—you chicklet, you domestic little thing—you'll accept it, you'll get it; it'll become part of you.

While on the subject of the police: the doctors here enjoy their own special relationship with the force. Whether it's getting a patient up the stairs when the elevator's broken down, locking up the drunks till morning so they don't brawl in the wards, or even towing an ambulance out of the mud, they have the police on speed dial. They too wear a uniform and give the local populace the illusion of security.

Just outside the casualty ward there's a policeman with a man in handcuffs. The man is young, a little roughed up, must have done something serious; around here they don't cuff just anyone. "If you'd just played the wife-and-kids card straightaway..." the policeman berates him, "but no, you had to go on about that lawyer of yours and your Moscow thugs."

Suddenly, alongside the guy who put out the flames in my car, I remember a sweaty, unkempt ice-hockey player. "You must be doubly pleased to have beaten the nation that invented the sport in their own backyard?" an interviewer asks. The ice-hockey player smiles a toothless grin, "Like I give a shit!" With an income like his, he could afford some new teeth, but clearly this man can still chew his meat perfectly well, thank you very much. The impression is resounding.

What else? A sermon once heard on the Intercession of the The-otokos: the day on which our pagan forefathers were defeated is now one of our most respected holy days. There's no easier pastime than bad-mouthing the church. Much like bad-mouthing Dostoyevsky: it's true, of course, all true, but it also misses the point. The church is a thing of wonder, Dostoyevsky is a thing of wonder, and the fact that we Russians are still here—that, too, is a thing of wonder.

You out of your mind, dear?

That could easily have been one of our grannies in ward one. *Grannies* is no insult here; it's what they ask to be called. The one who's in the worst health hears and sees things: "Yuri, that you?" she'll ask the patient next to her.

"Nope, not me," she'll reply.

"So who are you?"

"Granny."

"Then who's this—Yuri?" she'll ask the patient on her other side.

"No," Granny Three will reply, "I'm Granny, too."

To these women, there's nothing insulting about the word *granny*, even if they don't in fact have any grandchildren; they view themselves not as sharp-witted ladies of advanced years—like their city-dwelling avian contemporaries do—but as *grannies*.

In the afternoon, two of the orderlies have a loud argument. One of them works here so that she can pocket the food the patients don't eat and take it home to that swine of hers, while the other owns several hectares of land, holidays by turns in Turkey and Europe, and became an orderly just to find a place for herself in society. Apparently it gets messier: Orderly One went on holiday to Europe, and, poor as she is, put it on credit. The bailiffs have already paid her a visit.

Around here, the private comes before the public. A tax official, a twenty-something kid, does our auditing. "Oh," he'll say, "good thing you're a doctor... as it happens, the army have... I'm trying to... you know?" It's not hard to catch his drift. *On compassionate grounds* is a reliable turn of phrase—we're all in one another's hands. But where *Moscow doesn't believe in tears*, as they say, around here tears are the only things we do believe in. When the need is great, we make an exception.

It's ugly—we shouldn't allow ourselves to be touched by it—but this happy-go-lucky collective deceit unites the nation just as well as any good law. Electricity, gas, phone bills unpaid? In the capital, a lack of money is something to be ashamed of; here, it's pretty much the norm. The utility-company employees try to help us out here and there: "These meter readings look way off. Why don't I reset a few values for you here..."

"Thank you, that's just what I thought. And if you or your family ever need a doctor..."

Uncles, goddaughters, nieces; water, electricity, gas. It's familiar, comfortable, benign. And though it may have its drawbacks, as a way of life it's pretty stable. Here nobody has any secrets. Just like in heaven.

The orderlies and the grannies are the afternoon's affairs, and by evening it becomes clear that far too much time and energy have gone into one of the day's tasks, while many are left undone. Twilight sees the return of cruel, exasperated thoughts, specifically: Where did all the bright people go? When we were young there were enough of them around. What, did they all emigrate? One thought latches on to another—it's a vicious cycle. Night and its fears make the spirit more vulnerable to evil. To make matters worse, swallows and tits often fly into the house—a very bad omen. But there's nothing you can do; you can't live your life with your windows closed: either move, if you're afraid, or let go of these superstitions. Such are the thoughts that churn in the mind until dawn arrives, with its brief respite of sleep.

Life is scary, whether you're in Moscow, Saint Petersburg, or the provinces. We can say as much—it *is* scary. There are things in life of which it is impossible to write: the deaths of innocents, young people, children. The terrifying, unnecessary experience of their deaths stays with us. That can't be cried away; no cry can drive it out.

But then day will come, and the birds will still be there—fowls of the air, fowls domestic, wild, all of them. The world doesn't break, no matter what you throw at it. That's just how it's built.

September 2010
Translated by Alex Fleming

MOSCOW–PETROZAVODSK

Mark well, O Job,
hold thy peace, and I will speak.
—Job 33:31

To DELIVER man from his neighbors—isn't that the point of progress? And what are the joys and calamities of humankind to me? That's right—nothing at all. Then why is it that I can't have any time alone, even when I'm traveling?

They asked us: Who's going to Petrozavodsk? A conference. An international conference. Come on, doctors, someone has to go! Yes, we know what these conferences are like. A couple of émigrés— that's the "international" for you. The short bout of drinking, the hotel, the lecture, the long bout of drinking—then back home again. After the lecture, you're still answering questions, but behind your back, brawny little red-faced men are pointing at their watches— time's up. These little men are the local professors—in the provinces these days any fool can be a professor, the same way that in the American South any fool, if he's white, can be a judge or an army officer.

Well then, who's going to Petrozavodsk? So I volunteered: Lake Ladoga? All right, why not?

"Not Ladoga. Onega."

What's the difference? Have you been to Petrozavodsk? Nor have I.

*

The station is a pretty frightening place. For my own protection I assume the air of a veteran traveler. I walk to the carriage pretending I'm bored, so that it's immediately obvious I'm no stranger to railway stations—no point trying to rob someone like me.

The train from Moscow to Petrozavodsk takes fourteen and a half hours, incidentally. Your fellow travelers are almost invariably a source of unpleasantness—beer and *vobla*, cheap cognac, typically Bagration and Kutuzov, pouring out their hearts one moment, picking a fight the next.

The train begins to move. Everything's okay. I'm alone for now.

"Tickets, please."

"Excuse me," I ask the conductor, "but could we reach some sort of... I mean... so I can have the compartment to myself?"

She looks at me. "That depends on what you're going to do in it."

What is there to do in it?

"Read a book."

"In that case, just five hundred rubles."

Suddenly, these two turn up—they had all but missed the train. They take the lower berths. There they sit, panting. Just what I needed. This is not the sort of trip I had in mind. Damn it. Go on, then, make yourselves at home—I won't get in your way. I climb to the upper berth and turn my back to them; they go on busying themselves down below.

The first one is simple, primitive looking. His head, his hands, his boots—everything is big and crude. He sits with his jaw hanging open, like a moron. A sweaty moron. He has his phone out and he's playing a game. *Trrrink-trrink* for wins, and if he loses—*blllum*. He's tugging at the zipper of his jacket with his free hand—another noise. And he's sniffling, too. Still, at least he's probably sober.

Below me, the second one says with disgust: "Take off your jacket, you halfwit." He's irritable. "Stop that *shnuffling*!"

It's hard going. The sound of the train wheels. The phone below me going *trrrink-trrink*. And I'm supposed to read a book in this din? It won't be like this all the way to Petrozavodsk, will it?

I step into the corridor. I can hear them talking in the next compartment. "Russia is one of the oblong countries," says a pleasant young male voice, "unlike, let's say, the USA or Germany, which are round countries. I have, by the way, lived in both for some time." A young woman makes a delighted sound. "Russia," continues the voice, "is like a tadpole. You can go only from east to west and west to east, apart from the body of the tadpole, which is relatively densely populated, and where it's possible to go from north to south and south to north."

This is to the left of my door; to the right, they're drinking. Pulling apart a chicken, splitting tomatoes with their hands, the men are clinking glasses and roaring with laughter.

I return to my own compartment. My God, the time is passing slowly—we've only just left Moscow.

Half an hour passes, then an hour. Soon we'll reach Tver. *Trrrink* goes the moron. The second one springs to life.

"Turn off the sound."

"But To-ol..."

Tolya, apparently. He's tall, probably two meters. Fingers long and white, nails rounded. His face is ordinary enough. Thin lipped. But it's as if he doesn't have a face. I'm not sure how to explain it, but there's something about Tolya I don't like. I'm not picking up any signals from him—that's what. *Anesthesia dolorosa*—the painful loss of sensation. You can brush your hand against something, but you can't tell whether it's smooth or rough. Am I being too critical? He's sober, he's courteous, and he's trying not to bother me.

"Newspapers! Get your newspaper, hot off the press."

Thanks, but no thanks. We know your newspapers. Female tennis star poses nude for journalists. Tragedy in a lady TV anchor's family. Billionaire's daughter abducted. Secrets for a flatter stomach. Crime pages. Color pictures of the dead. Pah! But Tolya takes a paper, rustling its pages down below. After a while he says to the moron: "Let's go."

I'm left alone for a while. Some trip this is.

Before everyone turns in for the night, there are a few other minor incidents.

First, one of the drunks from the compartment next door wanders in with a camera in his hands. He opens the door and starts to take a picture. Tolya lunges at him, but then, suddenly, turns away and hides his face. So that's it—he's FSB. Secret police. Now I get it.

The drunk pulls me to his compartment—I'd just been on my way to brush my teeth. I'm supposed to photograph him with his friends. I take a picture. Is that enough? No, not yet. I've got to listen to the story of his life. He's falling all over me: vodka, sweat, tobacco—there, enjoy, breathe it in! People ought to maintain a certain distance from one another. Like in America.

His mother, back in the day, had given him a hundred rubles to buy himself a camera. Then she'd taken the money back—she'd needed it. But he'd really loved photography, ever since he was little. "Just my luck, eh?" he says.

I express my sympathy. I'm going now.

"Wait!" He'll read me a poem—a really cool poem.

"Pardon me," I say, "Nature calls. I'll be back." I barely make my escape.

"Out o-o-on … the tundra! Out o-o-on … the railroad!" he begins caterwauling, throwing open his arms to embrace anyone who can't dodge him.

Clearly I could have worse traveling companions. So what if Tolya is FSB? At least he's quiet and he doesn't stink. And he keeps his distance—he's squeamish, like me.

Second, we can no longer use the nearest bathroom: someone has stuffed the toilet bowl to the rim with newspapers. Sodden color pictures. Why?

Third, the water for tea is only lukewarm, and possibly not boiled at all.

"Just like the goddamned Soviet Union," mutters Tolya.

No, not FSB.

The overhead light goes out. Try to get some sleep. What's the link between those two? Nothing good, that's for sure. Not relatives, not colleagues. Maybe they're queer? Who knows? And what's it to me? Maybe they are queer. It happens among average folks, more than you would think.

The same sounds, over and over: *tuk-tuk*, *sniff*, *sniff*. I feel sorry for myself. I fall sleep.

I fall into an unexpectedly deep and long sleep, and when I awake, awaiting me are the early sun, the snow, and a very cold morning outside the window, judging by the frost on the spruce trees.

Without looking at my companions, I leave the compartment. The train has come to a stop. We're at Snyt . . . or at least I think so, although I can't quite make out the sign. Another sign reads: "Do not use toilet during stops." Okay, so I've got to wait a while for the bathroom. But it's only a couple more hours until the long-awaited Petrozavodsk, the hotel, the hot water, the dinner with wine. My spirits are much improved. I shouldn't let these little things get to me—life's too short.

My neighbors are ready to go. Tolya clearly never went to bed at all. He's sitting by the window, agitatedly turning his head this way and that.

"What's going on? Why are we just standing here?"

"I think we're at Snyt," I say. "Snyt station."

"What's that? Sery, where are we?"

"Svir. We're here for half an hour." Sery now cuts a far better figure. No sniffling, no juvenile games.

Sery leaves, and the train gets going. Somehow or other I manage to wash my face and drink some hot tea. I begin to feel even more cheerful. I want to live: have my breakfast, play the joker, gossip about the Moscow professors, charm the young women doctors. We aren't running behind schedule, are we? I find the conductor and ask. Apparently not.

But what's up with my neighbor? Now, alone and in the light of day, it's Tolya who is a sorry sight.

"Tolya, are you okay?"

"What?" He turns towards me.

My God, his whole body is trembling. I've seen this many times: towards the end of the first twenty-four hours in the hospital, the patient will begin to tremble. He'll start chasing away devils or make a dive for the window…Delirium tremens. Simple as that. Tolya is an alcoholic.

I yell for the conductor. "This passenger is suffering from delirium tremens. Do you understand? Alcoholic delirium. Have you got a first-aid kit?" No, there's no first-aid kit. It really all is just like the Soviet Union! I'm supposed to go and find the train manager. Fat chance of that—where am I going to find him? "Give him some wine or something. I'll pay—otherwise he'll wreck the whole train!"

"Calm down, passenger," says the conductor. "Where's his friend?"

"He got off at that Sviri, Sveri—whatever it's called."

"Why did he get off there? He has a ticket to Petrozavodsk!" She starts shouting. "He's blocked up the toilet with his newspapers! A whole big bundle! There was plenty of toilet paper…"

What does the bathroom have to do with it? A passenger is unwell. It's her job to assist, not to pitch a fit. By now he's probably banging his head against the wall. But it's too late—she's off on a rant:

"We'll deal with your compartment right now, passenger. We'll have him removed from the train!" She dashes off somewhere. Damn, but I'm afraid to go back into the compartment. I stand by the door and wait.

Pyazh Sielga station, the last stop before Petrozavodsk. A policeman is waiting. Yes, this one will set matters straight. I, with my PhD in medicine, can't deal with the problem, but he will. Yes, Comrade Dzerzhinsky has a nose for the truth.[1]

"Your documents."

He barely even looks at my documents. But there's something awful going on with Tolya: he's climbed onto the little table and begun to pound the window with his boot. It doesn't break with the first blow, but break it does: and there are shards of glass, cold wind, and blood. Everything happens fast. The policeman is beating Tolya's legs with his rubber truncheon, and Tolya is hanging there, hands clamped to the upper berth. Then he crashes to the floor. How they drag him out of there, I don't see—the conductor has led me to the next compartment, to the pleasant young man and the young woman.

For no less than a minute they've been beating Tolya outside our window—a man had run up in a tracksuit, too lightly dressed, it seemed to me, and still more policemen. They're beating him with their black truncheons and they're beating him with their fists. This is how we in Russia treat delirium tremens—not, we have to admit, the most uncommon ailment. Do I have to describe the beating in detail? The police have a name for it—forceful apprehension. At one point I thought I heard the crunch of bone, although what can you hear, really, through double-paned glass?

They're beating him and saying something; it even looks like they're asking him questions. And they've dragged in Sery from somewhere or other and they're beating him, too. Sery immediately falls to the ground and curls up into a ball, tucking his head in. With Sery they're not trying so hard. They've worn themselves out, these servants of law and order.

We observe all this through the window; then the train gets going again.

"How awful!" the girl cries.

Why did we let her watch?

"It's horrible! I do not—I absolutely do not—want to go on living in this country!"

"That's just what I was saying," the young man remarks. "But there's no point weeping and wailing about it. That, in my view, is *counterproductive*."

I do not immediately grasp what I've brought about. It's the same after a fatal mistake at the hospital—for a while you just stare, stupefied, at the patient, at the monitors, at your colleagues.

"They suit each other perfectly," says the young man, continuing the conversation, "both the victims and the perpetrators. If they went and beat up a professor at Berkeley that way, he'd hang himself from the shame of it. But these two, they'll get up, shake the dirt off, and be better in no time."

"What about you?" I ask. "What would you do?"

"Me?" He smiles. "I'd leave the country."

I don't believe the three of us are giving much thought to what we're saying.

"Why not leave," the girl puts in, "before you get beaten up? A normal person shouldn't have to live here."

My new companion smiles again.

"How would I have endured this trip without my sweet fellow traveler? This train hasn't even got a first-class carriage."

I look around. It's strange—the compartment is the same as mine, yet here everything emanates order and well-being. The young man gives off the scent of fine cologne. Yes, he's also bound for the conference. Formerly a doctor, in his present incarnation he's a publisher— he publishes journals ("like Pushkin")—he's president of some association, and much more besides. On the little table stands a half bottle of Napoleon. And the girl really is very sweet.

"You need a glass." The little glasses he has with him are made from some kind of stone. Onyx, perhaps jasper. Stone glasses. Yes, it is very good cognac indeed.

The young man is explaining why he's not yet left. Culture.

"Let me put it this way. For my American friends, the letters AAA suggest 'American Automobile Association.' But what do we associate with three *A*s?" He pauses for a moment. "Anna Andreyevna Akhmatova!" He looks at us triumphantly and adds, "Yes, and *biznesses*." That's what he said. *Biznesses*!

How good it is to warm yourself with a nip of cognac when you've brought about the misfortune of two people!

"You're absolutely right," agrees the young man. "This isn't our country, it's their country." Had I really said something of the kind? "Remember, it's not you and I who hired these people to protect us. What's happening here is a particular kind of negative selection. You won't find a humane cop within the existing system. It isn't possible.

The system would just spit him out. So what can we do? Change the system. Or withdraw into a world of our own—internal emigration. Or, if worse comes to worst," he shrugs his shoulders tragically, "*downshifting.*"

I catch the girl's eye. Hmm, yes . . . *Downshifting.*

There is a rap at the door: "The train will arrive in fifteen minutes." Time to go back to my compartment for my things; the pleasant young man will help me. I thank him.

In the wrecked compartment a very important discovery awaits me: I learn who Tolya and Sery are. Beneath the bench, next to my small suitcase, are two enormous checkered bags, the kind carried by only one type of person—the petty trader. Now I begin to understand the strange friendship of my traveling companions—people of all sorts become petty traders. I also understand their horrific beating.

"The competition was settling scores," the young man agrees. "It was a contract job."

"But why try so hard if it's only a contract?"

"For the soul's delight. I'm telling you, cops aren't human."

Petty traders. My companion has an opinion on their line of business, too.

"They carry out an important social function, you know," he says in his handsome voice. "All of us, everyone in our society, suddenly we all began to want the same things—expensive clothes, Rolex watches, whatever. But if you can't afford a Swiss Rolex"—he flicks his left wrist—"those traders of yours—whatever you call them—they'll sell you a Chinese Rolex, or any other kind you want. They're watches too, after all. They tell time. And they look good."

What heavy bags! And what am I supposed to do with them? Give them to the conductor? No way is that witch going to get anything from me! The young man shrugs his shoulders and I drag the bags into the corridor.

"Could you give me a hand?"

"I've got an idea," he says. "Give me your suitcase. I mean, what would I look like carrying those dreadful sacks?"

Okay, thanks. I want to make him happy, so I say, "You have such a lovely traveling companion!"

"Don't be silly," he says, "Not much to look at. A seven—seven and a half, tops."

Something makes me check: "Is that on a scale from one to ten?"

"No," he laughs, "to seven and a half! And her head is absolutely *topsy-turvy*. You know what I mean? Upside down!"

I'm glad he hadn't gotten anywhere with her. It's strange how it bothers me in a situation like this, but it would have pained me to know that he and I had spent our night as differently as all that.

The conductor lets us off the train without any sign of emotion. Someone comes to meet the young woman and we tell her goodbye and wait for a porter. We follow the porter, only just keeping up with him, and see a banner that says, "Welcome, Delegates!" The conference is beginning to look serious.

We get into a taxi and the young man says, "Listen, just forget about your clobbered companions ... So they lost a little blood? I'm more worried about the page bleed in my journal." A publishing joke.

"But it's my fault that they've had so much trouble. No, trouble's not the word for it—a disaster."

"Ah," he says, waving dismissively, "you're suffering from the intellectual's guilt complex. Cops are busting traders' heads all over the country these days. You should know better by now—life's not fair. Give it a rest."

"No, you vulgar snob," I think, "I'm not going to give it *a rest*."

As we're settling into the hotel, I ask for a telephone directory and begin calling everywhere—to the MVD, the RZD, the USB—a whole heap of abbreviations. To my surprise, I get straight through. "Come on over. The colonel will see you." And an hour or so later, I'm already zipping along in a taxi to one of those dark, impersonal buildings, checkered bags at my side. The colonel is waiting for me.

Printed in black on gold on the colonel's door is SCHATZ, and underneath, SEMYON ISAAKOVICH, and below that, in brackets,

SHLYOMA ITSKOVICH. I've never seen that done before. Very bold.

The occupant of the office has only just gotten up and is still in a somewhat lethargic state. He's sitting on a bare couch, without pillow or blanket, and dressed in a T-shirt and track pants. Semyon Isaakovich has stuffed one of his feet into a boot, but not the other. He's a man of some seventy years, short and completely bald, without mustache or beard, but with hair springing abundantly from his ears and nose—in fact, from everywhere that hair shouldn't be growing from. His hands, his shoulders, his chest are carpeted with salt-and-pepper wool. I think, "A hairy man—like Esau."

What should I call the colonel? Shlyoma suits him, and I would prefer it, but do you have to be one of his friends to call him that?

"Colonel Schatz," he says, hobbling up to the table, still wearing only one boot.

Understood. Comrade Schatz it is.

His stomach is big and his arms are thick, like a weight lifter's. His broad, fleshy nose is pitted with scars, as are his cheeks. It's hard for me to describe his eyes: I'd hardly looked at them. The colonel reaches the table, puts a uniform jacket on top of his T-shirt, and sits down.

I've prepared myself a little: I'm a doctor, a delegate to an international congress.

"A doctor," he says. "A state employee." He is silent. "Sit down."

I sit in a small chair across from him. There's nothing in the room but a large, polished table, the couch, several chairs. It must have been redecorated recently.

"You a Yid?"

I nod. It's funny—a state-employed Yid. Like him. Maybe I should get down to business? I tell him about what has happened: our traveling companions, the traders; their inhumane, to put it mildly, treatment; the settling of scores at the hands of his colleagues. One would hope for an impartial investigation, for justice. At the very least, these things should be returned to their owners.

It's unclear whether the colonel is nodding or his head is faintly trembling.

The phone rings. He picks up the receiver, answers in brief sentences. Mostly foul language. I don't like foul language, or vulgarity in general, but here it seems absolutely natural.

The walls are bare, with no portraits. But on one wall there's a map of the world with little flags sticking out. The scope of claims... Although the system by which the flags have been stuck in is incomprehensible.

"Go on and finish up there." He replaces the receiver and turns back to me. "We had a Party organizer, Vassil Dmitrich—a good man. Every morning he'd polish off a bottle of cognac. By 0800 hours he was tanked."

Why's he going on about this Vassily Dmitrievich? So what?

"He pinched just enough, you see, so that every morning he could have his bottle of cognac. Understand?"

For the moment I'm just listening.

"But here," he nods at the telephone, "the director of a government institution has taken thirteen million dollars—in cash. The employees haven't been paid for half a year. Tell me what that *mothertrucker* is doing with thirteen million dollars?"

Nicely said. But what does that have to do with the unlucky traders?

"Traders? You could say that. Read this."

The colonel passes me the same newspaper I'd previously been offered on the train.

"Wanted on suspicion of double murder," I read, "Police are searching for a man from Petrozavodsk." And a photograph of Tolya, with a mustache. Here he's laughing, celebrating. The victims were a man and a teenager, the man's daughter. They had taken Tolya into their home.

Blunt and simple: a man living alone with his daughter had sold his apartment in order to move to a smaller one; Tolya had sent for his friend...Yes, I understand, it was Sery, Sergei.

"No, not Sergei," says the colonel, "*Sery* comes from his last name. Which, in the interests of the investigation, is not being divulged."

With difficulty I fold the paper and return it to the colonel; my hands are trembling and my voice is trembling too.

"Pardon, Comrade Colonel," I somehow manage to say. "But the yellow press, or any press for that matter, isn't evidence in and of itself. I'm sorry, but it's just not convincing."

"Who are you? A jury that needs convincing?"

The way he says it, I understand that what was published in the papers is true.

The colonel takes out several photographs.

"You say you're a doctor? Look at these."

We'd studied forensic medicine, but it's not the same thing. I begin to feel ill and can't hide it.

"Here," he pours me some water. "Drink this."

Precisely how Tolya and Sery murdered them, I'm not going to say. There really are things that no one should know.

I apologize to the colonel—I've slept poorly, the cognac without food, and, well, in general . . .

"*Farshteyn*," he says in Yiddish, "I understand."

"What are the photographs for?"

"To convince their contacts at this end to talk."

They had identified the murderers on the basis of telephone calls made from the apartment. Automatic telephone exchanges record every number dialed—I didn't realize that. One or both of them had called Petrozavodsk before the crime and, more importantly, afterwards. They had been saving money by not using roaming.

They hadn't left the apartment immediately. They spent the night there with the bodies. That really got to me. When a patient dies, I want the windows wide open, and the sooner I'm away from the unit, the better. But this pair . . . they'd actually spent the night, maybe even two nights.

"My God," I start jabbering, incoherent from fright, "I spent the night with murderers! And I slept well! I didn't sense a thing . . . My God!"

This makes no particular impression on the colonel.

"Don't think about them," he says. "Killers—they're just your average people."

*

Again the telephone; again he listens more than he speaks; again I'm on hold, and for this I'm glad. He puts back the receiver.

"What have you got here? Have you looked?" He's asking about the bags.

No, it hadn't even occurred to me to look. He takes the bags and lifts them easily onto the table. He's very strong.

"Don't touch anything," he says. "Otherwise we'll have to fingerprint you."

Electronics. A PlayStation—for Sery, of course. He opens a small case.

"What's this?"

"A flute."

The girl played the flute? I'm feeling faint again.

"Maybe, maybe not. These things might have come from different places."

There are clothes. They weren't even squeamish about taking their clothes! No, the clothing was for covering icons.

"Icons," says the colonel. "Do you believe in God?" Not waiting for my answer, he goes on, "These days, everyone believes. Even the fancy young Jews wear crosses."

Instinctively I run my hand across my neck: Was the chain visible? I hope the colonel hasn't noticed. Suddenly I don't want to upset him.

Books. No, not books—stamps.

"Do you know anything about stamps?"

No. Why would I? I do know that stamps can be very valuable.

The colonel returns the things to the bags.

"It ain't cheap, this," he says.

"And these two, the murderers, I wonder if they wear crosses."

"It doesn't matter. I'm telling you—they're just your average people."

I get up and walk around the room. How can it be, eh? How can I be such a poor judge of people? Why don't I get it? I take another drink of water. Already I'm starting to get used to this place.

The colonel takes the bags away.

"Have a seat. You did everything right. You've helped the investigation. We'd have had to arrest them in the city otherwise."

I can see now that it was just a fortunate coincidence. It seems there was a detective traveling from Moscow on the same train in order to arrest them. I recall the man in the tracksuit. It was just a fortunate coincidence. They might not have found them at all. The number of cases actually solved is so small it almost doesn't make a difference.

"Doesn't make a difference? What *mothertrucker* told you that?" The colonel grins and affectionately says, "*Shlemazl.*"

There's no such word in my vocabulary. What does it mean?

"Shlemazl," the colonel explains with pleasure, "means an innocent fool, a suckling pig."

For this I'd come to Petrozavodsk—to be called a baby pig. I feel bitter.

"In America," I say, "somehow they get by without clubbing everyone. There are procedures to be followed. I'm not standing up for murderers and their like, but there are procedures..."

"In America," responds the colonel. "Let me tell you a story."

And then the colonel told me about his father.

At the beginning of the war, Schatz Senior, a circumcized Jew, was called up to the front, but he never got to fight: by August of 1941 the army was entirely surrounded and had surrendered. Schatz had taken the documents of a dead Ukrainian, so he wasn't shot immediately, and instead of finding himself in a concentration camp, he was sent to one labor camp and then another. He ended up in a mine in the Ruhr.

"Do you know what Schatz means in German?"

Riches, treasure, a lode. The colonel nods. His father spoke a little German—before the war, everyone studied German. And so he ended up in the mine with only one wish—to live. Although, as you can imagine, there was no telling how and when the war would end, and he had no idea what had become of his family. A labor camp is different from a death camp, but among those who spent the entire war there, only one in ten survived.

Put himself forward as an interpreter? No, that was out. First of all, in order to lose himself in the crowd, he had to be like everyone else; and second, the normal people in the camp had a strictly Soviet mentality. Only the scum had any more business with the Germans than was absolutely necessary. Schatz did things differently: he didn't just fulfill the norm, he doubled it. For that, they handed out bonuses—bread, tobacco. He quit smoking—his only pleasure, you might say—but he quit so that he would have more food and be able to work, to fulfill the norm. He traded the tobacco with his comrades for food, and in this way he always had enough to eat. When he was the first one to come up from the mine, he would steal from the guards—potatoes, eggs, bread. Only food. When they caught him he was beaten, heavily beaten—twenty blows every time. You know how the Germans are—order above all. The whole of his back was black-and-blue from the club. They beat him, but they didn't beat him to death.

"So they didn't find out that your father was a Jew?"

"As long as they were trying to flush them out, no. In the bath, the other prisoners shielded him—for them he had come up with an excuse."

"Phimosis."

"Yes, yes, that was it. Then they found out. They found out from our side."

When it was discovered that Schatz was a Jew, the matter of his survival became far more difficult. He was something of a "useful Jew"—the Germans had a word for it. Now he had not only to fulfill the norm, but to triple it. He got it from both sides. But there were only a handful of real sadists in the camp. The guards too were just ordinary people.

"Your average people," I prompt.

"Yes, average people." The colonel doesn't notice any irony.

There were only a handful of sadists, no more than now, but one of them was the wife of the camp commandant. A fine-looking dame, his father said. She loved to kick them in the groin. She would force them to take off their pants. It amused her, you see. But she came to grief.

The Americans liberated them. It happened like this: they surrounded the camp and waited for the guards to surrender and get butchered by the prisoners. They could wait all day, even two days. They kept their distance. It was a typical American practice. The Germans wanted to be taken prisoner, but what did the Americans want with German prisoners?

"What did he do to her?" I ask.

"He had his way with her. Do you understand? He was the first."

"And then? And then what? Did they kill her?"

"Probably." He shrugs. "They butchered all of the Germans. Hardly anyone survived."

We sit in silence for a time.

"Tell me, how did your father feel about Germans after that?"

"No way in particular. And why 'did'? My father is alive. He's just angry the Germans don't pay him a pension. He doesn't appear in any of their documents as Schatz."

So his father is alive. And what does he do?

"He doesn't do anything. What's there for him to do? He likes to go to the market. He remembers that German dame. Before, when my mother was alive, he didn't say a thing, but now he talks about the German more than he talks about his own wife."

In the office it's almost dark. Suddenly I find myself wanting to show the colonel some kind of support, or at least to look him in the eye, but he's sitting with his back to the window and I can't see his eyes. I try to say something: something about the incontinence of affect, about geriatric sexuality. As if my membership in the medical profession somehow gives me the right to utter words that are more or less devoid of meaning.

"Throughout the entire war," says the colonel, "my father didn't kill one person. And if the Americans had liberated them the way they should have—humanely—then he wouldn't still be thinking about that German dame."

The colonel finishes his story and gradually sinks into lethargy. Perhaps it's time for me to go?

In the end, I ask him, "What do the flags on the map stand for?"

Suddenly he smiles broadly; in the semidarkness I can see his teeth: "They don't stand for anything. The flags are just flags. That's all."

Well, then—should I go?

"And where are you going without a hat?" the colonel asks tenderly. "Have you got a hat?"

"I've even got two. A cap and a warm, woolly hat."

"Put on the woolly one."

Petrozavodsk. Dark. Cold. Ice. Streets barely lit. You can't make out a thing.

In the evening at the congress I run into the young man with the handsome voice, the one from the train. He shares his impressions of the city, "same shit as the rest of the country," and expresses a desire to continue our acquaintance in Moscow. Perhaps we could have dinner together? His treat.

Casually he asks: "So how goes it with your two innocents?"

Well put.

"Did you find out anything?"

"No," I reply. "No."

February 2010
Translated by Anne Marie Jackson

THE GYPSY

HE'S A decent doctor, with a good head on his shoulders—the kind of doctor you want, if you happen to need one.

As a doctor, he has two jobs: one he does for money, the other out of interest. When he's doing the interesting job, he thinks: this is the real thing, doctor's work, but it doesn't pay. And he's a young man, he needs money. He's got to feed his kids, pay for his grandmother's night nurse; the car keeps breaking down; there are things he wants, all sorts of expenses—that goes without saying. But he never thinks about money for more than a few seconds at a time. He just knows he needs it, that's all.

The work he does for money, on the other hand, inspires long reflections. I'm not so hard up, he thinks. I'm young, I've got goals, things to do—why am I wasting my life? He knows what he ought to be doing. It's like Pasternak said: Live, think, feel, love, make discoveries. His father used to tell him, rather solemnly: Live with an eye to eternity. He used to read him poems, by Pasternak and others. But that was a long time ago—it's been more than ten years since his father passed.

The job he does out of interest is easy to imagine: examining patients at the clinic; the happiness he experiences when he manages to help, to do something new, to make a rare diagnosis; and, of course, the heartache he feels when patients die, or when he has to spend hours filling out paperwork. There's plenty of that—the emergency room, nights on call—but, as we said, he's a good doctor.

He gets a little money for the interesting job, too: grateful patients, their relatives. But he never names a price: everyone else might do it, but he's not everyone.

It's harder to explain the job he does for money: escorting sick people across the border. There's this organization—it sends people to America, permanently, under supervision. Jews, Baptists, Armenians from Baku, Kurds, all sorts of strange people. Where are they going? How does it all work? Strange people, strange work—but lucrative, six hundred dollars per flight.

And so this Friday, he'll have to swap shifts with another doctor, pack up his medical equipment, make sure his superiors clap eyes on him, and, at around one o'clock, take off for the airport, to fly to America. How many times has he made this trip? He's lost count. He'll hand over the patient—after another flight, a short one, from New York to Portland, Maine. He has friends there; a two-hour drive, and they'll already be in Boston, and it will still be Friday in the States. He'll get the money in New York, leave the patient in Portland, and his friends— a husband and wife, classmates of his, who'd married early, emigrated early, whom he loves, whom he can count on—won't let him spend a cent. And in the morning they'll drive him straight to New York— they had plans to go anyway; they love New York, they love everything that affirms their friendship with him. That'll be Saturday. He'll return home on Sunday, rest up—and then off to work on Monday, to his primary job, the interesting one. So it goes, month after month.

But this Friday, as he was just about to leave, he ran into an obstacle—Guber. A request to look over a patient, a woman. Guber is the head of the department responsible for patients who pay—a resentful man, listless, vindictive, and, in the minds of the doctors, a thief. Patients who pay are nothing but trouble, and the doctors don't see their money anyway. Notice, Guber didn't ask him himself: he went through a nurse. He himself would have put it differently— something like, you've got nothing better to do, so might as well examine a patient.

He's happy to take a look—a quick one. Where is she? In the corridor.

The nurse says, quietly: "A Gypsy."

He'd treated a Gypsy about two months ago. An odd woman. The nurses had warned him: Be careful with her. She undressed silently, to the waist, as he'd instructed, and didn't ask the usual questions: "Do I take off my bra?" Utter solemnity and contempt. She turned to the left when necessary, also in silence. None of the usual rustling, the feminine chatter, no "Oh, is that my heart making those bubbling sounds?" She took the report on the chin. As he remembers it, she just said: "Thank you." You could feel it: she hated them, all the—the word that came to mind was *wardens*. Well, if they're in uniform, even if it's a lab coat or scrubs, who are they but wardens? Why was she in such a hurry? The nurse explained: She's well known in the neighborhood, sells drugs. The nurses know everything, because they live around here; it's convenient to work near home. So that's why the woman was in a hurry: she had a job to do. And it turned out that her son—a grown boy, nineteen—had died, but not on his watch. This would explain the solemnity. All right, so that was that. She's not a real Gypsy, either. Skinny, short-haired, with an inauthentic name—something Russian sounding. Married, he wondered? The nurses knew that too: the first husband hanged himself, the current one has no legs, begs for change in the street. Truth be told, he was getting fed up with all these hard-luck stories. Of course, a doctor shouldn't think such thoughts, let alone express them.

Today it was a different Gypsy. The other one was relatively young; this one was old.

"What's the deal with Guber and the Gypsies?" the nurse wondered. "We'll never get the whole story."

"Call her in, let's make it quick."

A fussy old dame, mumbling indistinctly. Red hair—a bad dye job—rough hands, swollen fingers, face, and legs. Garish clothing—our old women don't dress like that.

The nurse growls, You're wrapped up tight!

"It's warm these days, Grandmother, April!"

So what if it's April? She's always cold.

All right, what's the trouble? They're in a hurry.

The Gypsy mumbles; it's impossible to understand her. How old is she? She can't even tell him her age.

"Granny, this ain't the Gestapo," the nurse explodes, "talk!"

You can't treat patients that way—especially paying patients, from Guber.

They need her year of birth.

"Write 1920..."

"Why not tell us the truth?"

"Write 1928...1930."

Her papers actually list the year as 1920, but the woman doesn't look seventy-nine. Someone dropped the ball. "Dropped the balls," as Guber puts it. He's from Moldova. No one corrects him; they just laugh behind his back.

Let's ask how old she was when the war broke out. She doesn't remember. "Which war?" She missed the war? Where was she in the forties, under a rock?

She answers: "In the woods."

"In the woods? What were you doing in the woods?"

The nurse looks at him: Doesn't he know what Gypsies do?

The woman says: "Singing songs."

Songs? In the woods? Come on, let's get her undressed.

The nurse is clearly ill at ease.

"Gimme the little pills, the good ones," the woman says.

Come on now, undress. A suffocating smell fills the room.

"We've got to treat the intertrigo," the nurse says, angrily. "What a stench."

Wipe that off. Put some talcum on it. A filthy old woman, what can he say.

He does an ultrasound—the heart is big, clearly visible. She's sick, all right. Probably shouldn't leave. He'll get her a bed. The nurse objects: You just watch—something will go missing. Who's gonna answer for that?

The woman doesn't want to stay, either: "Just gimme the good pills..."

Ah, well, he can spare another fifteen minutes. He'll need iodine, alcohol, a catheter, sterile gloves, anesthetic. He marks her back with a felt-tip pen: "You've got fluid in your lungs. We'll drain it."

The nurse shakes her head: Guber asked you to take a look, nothing more. He won't like this. "But we won't tell your Guber a thing. No need to touch the cash register."

What's she muttering? "She's not Russian, can't stand the pain." She won't have to—just a prick and it's all over.

Let the fluid flow. He'll fill out the papers.

A liter and a half, in total.

"Breathing easier?"

See? She should have trusted him. He finishes up the paperwork. "Gimme the good pills," the Gypsy says, all dressed now. "It'll bring you happiness."

"Happiness?" The nurse frowns.

He knows what she wants to say: There's no happiness with Gypsies. No, he won't frown—not out of superstition, just because.

"The pills," the woman repeats, "that go together, you understand?" She bares gold teeth.

Go together with what? Hashish? Or something stronger? The woman is taken aback: Why talk that way? She likes to have a nip is all, with dinner. "Ah, a nip...Yes, great pills. They go together."

Happiness, he thinks. What a world...

The Gypsy woman tries to shove some crumpled bills into his hand. All tens. He pushes her hand away—she's a strong one—and thinks: It all comes down to denomination; if the bills were thousands, he might have taken them. So his anger is false, and everyone knows it, except, he hopes, the nurse.

"How can you come to see a doctor, smelling like that?" the nurse asks indignantly, escorting the Gypsy out of the room.

His nurse is a sensitive "Western" type. She throws open the windows, sprays the room with an air freshener. All right, he's off.

"You'll forgive me," the nurse says, "but, to be frank, I don't feel sorry for people like that—not one bit. They don't deserve treatment."

Now she'll say that she doesn't approve of Hitler, in principle, but on certain matters... She's no Western type—she's just a fool. Coming out of the hospital, he overtakes the Gypsy. She grabs him by the sleeve: Let me read your fortune. "No, thanks." He already knows what awaits him: a long journey, and all that.

He always takes his car to Sheremetyevo—it's wasteful and takes longer, but he's used to it, and he likes to have all his things at hand: the doctor's bag, a book, a shirt, underwear, and socks. Today he's forgotten everything except the bag, almost intentionally: he never did decide what to read, and his Boston friends will make sure he has a change of clothes. His wardrobe always improves after his visits to Boston. He won't read, he'll listen to music; he has a lot of it, suitable for any state of mind.

Hardships await him at Sheremetyevo. First—and this isn't so terrible, really—the patient is a difficult one: a blind old woman with no feet and a urinary catheter. A diabetic. He'll have to poke her with insulin, pour out urine, order wheelchairs. But she has a husband, who seems to be fairly together—so we'll make it. The second hardship is much worse—he had mixed up his Portlands. The ticket isn't for Portland, Maine, which is less than two hours by car from Boston, but for the other Portland, in Oregon, on the opposite side of the continent.

How could he have missed the mark so badly? He tells the people from the mysterious organization—who were responsible for tickets—and they laugh in response: his misfortune doesn't elicit much sympathy. He should warn his friends, he thinks—they're bound to be disappointed. He'll call them from the layover in New York. It's not a disaster, of course, but it's a shitty situation.

The "security" guys know him well by now—they don't hassle him, don't pat him down, just raise and lower their hands a few inches away from his body: "Carrying explosives, weapons?" they ask with a smile. He tells them about the Portland mess too. "Portland," they say, "that's nothing. There's an Oakland in New Zealand, not in—what's it called?" He chimes in: California. "Yeah, that's it—so this one fella…" They're simple guys, but charming, in their way. He likes to stand around with them for a while, chat. Again, their uniforms seem to have an effect.

Now he'll hear—for the nth time—their story about an American girl who was traveling with a kitty cat—they put them in special carriers, for the belly of the plane—and the kitty cat died. The baggage handlers at Sheremetyevo didn't want any trouble, so they threw the carcass in the trash and replaced it with some cat they caught near the airport. The American girl got into a huff and insisted it wasn't her kitty—because her kitty had been dead, and she was taking her home to bury her. She was returning from some town, maybe Chelyabinsk. Last time the story was different: the American with the dead cat had flown in from Philadelphia. Today's version was more believable, but it was still a lie, of course. The "security" guys call Americans "Americunts" and "Amerifucks"—ridiculous words, and they've never been to America—but he still laughs every time. All right, time to board.

As he walks away, one of the guys says dreamily, "Doc, would I like to trade places with you and take a gander at those skyscrapers they got over there."

Not a chance, my friend—medicine is a calling.

"Farewell, unwashed Russia!" a young man intones from across the aisle.

Lermontov's poem seems to be the standard text for those departing Russia—he's heard it more than once. At first, when he had just started working for the company, he expected to see the full range of human emotions; emigration was a major step, after all. But he soon realized that this was no different from working in a crematorium or at the registry office: there was a limited set of reactions.

The plane takes off and he crosses himself—discreetly, so that other passengers don't think he's scared, so that they don't get scared themselves. Indeed, nothing up here depends on his actions. Behind the wheel, on a slippery road, in the dark—that's much worse.

The plane isn't full, but it isn't empty, either. He has two seats to himself, near a window. Two days in transit. Two days of his life in exchange for six hundred dollars. A friend of his father, a former political prisoner, once told him: It's harder to spend one year in confinement than fifteen. You spend the whole year waiting for your release; you don't actually live. So imagine a two-day trip...

He should probably get up and check on the patient. Maybe it can wait. Not that he's lazy—it's just professional immobility, which he had always despised in ICU docs.

This strange work also affords opportunities for little scams. For example, you can pretend you're just another passenger, minding your own business. Oh, a fellow passenger isn't feeling well? Well, here you are, a Russian doctor, with medicine and everything. A miracle! Stewardesses give such doctors champagne, do other little favors, help any way they can. And if the truth comes out—so what? A little awkwardness never killed anyone. They're foreigners to him, and he's a foreigner to them. If his ward's health allowed it, he could even skip the trip to Portland, put the woman on the plane—bon voyage, have a good flight!—and then hang around New York for an extra day. In truth, he envied those who dared to do such things, but he himself would never pull those tricks: Who knows what might happen? No, there's no shaking the legless old woman. And he was supposed to escort some Baptists to Portland, too. Baptists are easy: they don't complain about anything, don't take pills, somehow don't even get sick. Only they're not too bright, and they have whole broods of children—there they are, near the tail. One group even lost a little one at the airport in New York. Didn't faze them in the least: good people would find him, send him home.

"How do you feel?" He takes the old woman's blood pressure, pulse.

She's half asleep. The husband answers: "How do you put it in these cases? 'Considering the seriousness of the procedure...'"

What procedure?

"Fifteen hours by train from Yoshkar-Ola."

The husband's name is Anatoly. No patronymic.

"They don't use patronymics in America."

It's true, they don't. It's the country of forgetting your father's name, as Garibaldi might have said.[2] And the plane is, for all intents and purposes, American territory.

He'd like to know what drove them from their home—he's interested in people—but he's trying to break the habit of asking these extraneous questions that doctors supposedly have the right to ask: Why have you moved here or there? What do your children do? What does your name mean? He's also afraid he'll get the typical story. We were living just fine, going about our business, but then the wife's sister, say, or some cousin, tells us: Send an application to the embassy, just in case. So we sent the application and forgot all about it, and when we received permission to emigrate, we just ignored it. But then we get that letter in the mail: Now or never. That word always has an effect: *never*.

But Anatoly's story is different: His wife developed renal failure. She'll need dialysis. What else is there to say? Their son, an engineer, is in America.

"The medical care in Yoshkar-Ola—it's terrible. There just isn't any."

He nods and thinks: You should have left sooner... Now the old woman will die with the help of the finest medical technology. There's no helping her. But he says: "You made the right decision."

"Is Portland a real backwater?" asks Anatoly. He has a nice smile.

"Well... In comparison with Yoshkar-Ola..."

"Have you been to Yoshkar-Ola?"

He shakes his head no.

"And to Portland?"

"Not this Portland, no."

"There are twenty-one Portlands in America. I looked it up. Ours is the biggest."

Anatoly strikes up conversations with the stewardesses, trying out his English. It's not so bad. A little old-fashioned, sure, but pretty impressive.

"Thank you. I'm flattered." Turns out he taught English at a university for forty years.

Time for the insulin? No, don't you worry, Anatoly will take care of it himself. He'll handle the insulin, empty the urine-drainage bag. Excellent. If they need him, they know where to find him.

He can see land down below. Canada? He looks at his watch: No, Greenland. Food, a little sleep, some dumb flick about nothing. How are the Baptists back there? Said their prayers, ate—now they're sleeping. That's the life.

At last. The first ten hours are behind him. The plane begins its descent.

New York: a wait for the wheelchair, fussing with the papers, a minor misunderstanding with the immigration officer.

"How long have you been a doctor?" the officer asks.

"Ten years. Since I was twenty-two. No, twenty-three."

"Bullshit," says the officer. He really dropped the balls on that. Would've been too busy at that age. All Russians serve in the Red Army.

He shrugs his shoulders. Some kind of nutjob, clearly. Can he go now?

Anatoly catches up to him in the vestibule: He explained everything to the officer—about military training at medical school, and so on. The officer asked him to pass along an apology. Amazing: an apologetic border guard. Clearly a nutjob.

The rest of it goes smoothly. They retrieve their bags—Anatoly's, the old woman's, the Baptists'—and check them for the next flight, to Portland. It's a three-hour layover. Let them sit for a while; he'll be back—he has to call his friends, change tickets.

It's getting harder and harder to find a pay phone these days. Many Americans, even decent-looking people, have cell phones. Back home, they're still a tasteless luxury, an affectation of wheeler-dealers. Guber has one . . . All right, he's called his friends, let them down; needless to say, they won't be driving down to New York just to say hello. When will they see him next? In a month's time, as usual. He won't disappoint them again.

Now to change his ticket, so that he can sleep on the plane. In the morning he'll take a walk around New York, sit in Central Park, and, if he's not too tired, visit the Met and buy some gifts for his family. He knows from experience that he won't actually make it to the Met.

The two men at the ticket window—one tall, the other very pale— work in shifts; the other doctors who work for the company have taken to calling them Longfellow and Whitman. Longfellow isn't too swift, always screws things up—but today, thank God, he gets Whitman. Easy as pie, and no surcharge: his return flight takes off fifteen minutes after he arrives in Portland. And he doesn't have to worry about missing it: it's the same plane there and back. Lucky. Even better: Whitman can upgrade him to first class, one way, thanks to his frequent-flyer miles. Would he like that? "Sure."

The plane to Portland is almost completely empty. He's the only customer in first class. A male stewardess—is it *steward*? Anatoly suggests: *flight attendant*—welcomes them at the entrance. A handsome fellow, with an earring in his left ear—does that rule apply in America? He smells strongly of cologne. Sure, flight attendant. He's a fragrant steward.

"You know what," the steward offers, "let's seat the lady and her husband next to you."

Great idea.

"You see the treatment we get?" He wants Anatoly to like America.

The steward helps the old woman into her seat—more symbolically than practically, with two fingers, but still. He praises her headscarf: a beautiful color. Things are different at home. If a legless old woman decided to take a plane somewhere, they probably wouldn't let her board: Where is she flying off to? In any case, she wouldn't be able to get on the plane. And first class? Forget about it. That's strictly for spoiled brats.

"How can I harass you today, sir?" the steward asks in English. Evidently he has a sense of humor.

It seems Anatoly, despite his excellent English, didn't understand the joke. Harassment is a sensitive topic in America; that's how it is here—they have campaigns against everything. So the steward changed "How can I help you?" to "How can I harass you?"

"I see, I see. 'What can I do for you?' is a better translation," Anatoly gently corrects him.

That's true too.

It's amazing how these little things can lift one's spirit. So, what shall we drink? He looks at Anatoly, questioningly: He won't condemn him? A doctor on duty, and all that. He orders two Camparis on the rocks, for himself and Anatoly, and an orange juice for Anatoly's wife.

"My first time getting sauced in an airplane," says Anatoly. "You and I are now heavenly drinking buddies."

You won't get sauced on a sip of vermouth, of course.

Outside the window—total darkness; the fried food behind the curtain smells delicious; they've given the old woman her insulin and pills; they've got glasses in hand—here's to your new life! And then there's trouble. For the second time today, after the Portland mix-up, not counting that nutjob of a border guard.

He orders meals for himself, Anatoly, and the old woman, and shows off by describing the dishes and translating their names into Russian. But then their dear steward informs them that since only the doctor's ticket is for first class, his two guests are entitled only to snacks. *Nothing personal*, as they say in America—just *regulations*.

Precisely: nothing personal. He demands three portions of food, along with two extra forks and knives. A stewardess comes over, frowns, shakes her head: Don't they understand?

"Let them be. They're right," Anatoly pleads. A fair-weather friend. What a weakling. "Let's drop it. After the mess we're used to, when something's done according to the rules..."

Oh, no, not this time—he'd show them what Russians are made of!

But, as usual, the Americans wouldn't actually learn what Russians are made of. While shouting his stern words, he slips up and makes some kind of grammatical mistake—he himself doesn't know where, exactly—but, of course, garbled insults, with an accent to boot, are funny. The steward—that son of a bitch—cracks a broad smile; the stewardess turns her back to him, her shoulders shaking with laughter. It's a lost cause.

Everyone settles down. They've lost their appetites, but they're given some food anyway, and they eat it. An hour and a half later, he gets up to relieve himself and, through the curtain that separates first class from coach, hears the steward complain: Why do the Russians always stink? It's a specific smell.

I'd like to see how you fare after a trip from Yoshkar-Ola to Moscow, then Sheremetyevo, seventeen hours in the air... He finds deodorant—you can find anything in first class—and sprays himself. Humiliating. But what does he care?

Portland. Ladies and gentlemen, on behalf of the crew, the captain thanks you... The Baptists head up the aisle. The old woman, Anatoly, and he are the last to disembark. They're waiting for the wheelchair. The old woman—she's not that old, really, just sixty-five—asks her husband for something, quietly. To comb her hair. He takes all their carry-on bags and goes into the hall. And there he is, their only son. A respectable fellow, by the looks of it. Tired. They work people to the bone here.

The reunion. Has the son seen his mother in this state? Blind, no legs. He embraces his father—better to turn away, not to listen in and pry. People don't live with their parents here. Even if the engineer wanted them to move in, his wife wouldn't allow it: the elderly live separately. They'll put them in a good home—you wouldn't dare call it an almshouse. "It's more convenient for us, too," the parents will say. A slow descent, step by step—it's all planned out in America. Of course, his wards have nowhere to descend; they'll start at the very bottom.

"This is our doctor," Anatoly tells his son.

"Nice to meet you." A handshake. A tired, absentminded gaze.

All right, farewell. He doesn't want to waste their time, and besides, he has to board in fifteen minutes. But then, the Baptists: "Doctor, doctor, come on!"

Two young men drag him away, down the escalator—there, there! What happened? He runs into the baggage-claim area and scans the floor for a body: all clear, everyone's on their feet.

Turns out their luggage is lost. Brothers—they're all "brothers"—what was the use of dragging him down here? There are people here to greet them—can't they fill out the paperwork?

The greeters are indistinguishable from the newcomers: the same peaceful, vacant expressions. Nobody speaks English? They can't write their own addresses? Garibaldi was wrong about people forgetting their fatherlands in America. These people hadn't even learned the English alphabet. How long have they been here? "Four years."

"The Americans," explains one of the greeters, "are such nice folk. They treat us like we're deaf and dumb."

The Baptists have thirty-six pieces of luggage; each is entitled to two seats.

While he was filling out the paperwork, his plane departed. The next flight is scheduled for the morning, six and a half hours from now. He again changes his ticket without any difficulty; he was supposed to fly in the morning anyway. But what is he supposed to do now? Get a hotel room? By the time he finds a hotel and goes to bed, it'll be time to get up again. And the room would set him back at least fifty dollars. He'll make do at the airport. It would be great to take a shower, of course, but those are the breaks—and he doesn't have a change of clothes, either.

The other end of the earth—this in itself had long ceased to impress him. So he finds himself in towns with beautiful names—Albuquerque, for example, or Indianapolis. So what? Everywhere he goes, be it New York, Albuquerque, or what have you, he sees the same things: the red floor, the red-and-white walls, perfectly straight lines, harmonious colors, nothing too pleasing to the eye, and certainly nothing offensive. And everywhere, as if part of the design: the soft strains of Mozart's symphonies, piano concertos—not the most famous pieces, and mainly the second, slower parts. Who's playing? The Oregon Symphony, the Portland Philharmonic—what's the difference? As long as it's not trashy pop or street songs, like you hear back at home. But where can he go if he wants total silence? A picky passenger—no one is surprised: Please, this way to the meditation room. He can sit, lie down. Meditation? That's right, thinking. The airports back home now have chapels, but even nonbelievers need a place to think. Again, no one's feelings are offended.

"Can I smoke in the meditation room?" he suddenly asks, to his own surprise.

"Smoke?" Is he crazy? There's no smoking in American airports.

The question about smoking cuts off any possibility of informal conversation; it demonstrates to them that he is a dangerous man. Fine, fine, he'll smoke in the designated areas, outside.

The airport is empty. Can he at least leave his bag here? No, he has to keep his carry-on luggage with him at all times. Really, at all times? Don't even try to smile—*this is no laughing matter.*

Rules are rules, he understands. That's why their hospitals are superb, a hundred times better than the hospitals at home—and yet, it's all rather silly. A black guard, thickset and gray, helps him load his things onto the black conveyor belt without a hint of distaste—just work. The guard even appears to sympathize with him. Maybe he's also a smoker.

"Missed my flight, so I have to wait until morning," he explains to the guard, reentering the building for the second or third time.

"Just one of those days, man . . ." the guard says.

In Russian he would have said: "Happens." The guard has a deep bass voice.

He walks out to a spot where he can see the highway—an occasional car passes, neither fast nor slow, just under the speed limit—and remembers his trips around the Boston area, which he took with his friends or sometimes alone. He knew that all the cars passing by contained people who valued their lives no less than he valued his— their lives and the safety of their vehicles; and so they tended to be cautious, give warning, and not to despise themselves for their willingness to yield. Should he live out his life, or at least a part of it—for some reason, he wants to say the last part—here? Here, where they dispose of their trash properly, park their cars according to certain rules. He could master it; it would be easier than mastering English. And it's not just a question of safety. He imagines himself as an old man, for some reason completely alone—perhaps because he's alone at the moment—in a small town on the coast. His neighbors have crude, red faces, but they themselves aren't crude. They talk about him: a doctor lives around here. They're pleased to know that their neighbor is a doctor. They kept their balance throughout their lives, and he kept his, when they all could have lost it at any point . . .

Tiredness diverts his thoughts: This morning the Gypsy had predicted his happiness. You'll be happy here! Are there Gypsies in America? There are Gypsies everywhere, supposedly. No, here it's the American Indians who provide a connection to the prehistoric past. By the way, in all his years of flying to America, he hasn't laid eyes on a single Indian—all he's seen are bizarre place-names, like Idaho . . . And now he's passed through security again and is already lying on the red floor; in the meditation room, the standard linoleum floor is covered in industrial carpeting. He thinks: I'm engaged in a meaningless activity, while eternity exists—father was right—eternity exists, and the only things that count are those that are projected into eternity, that occupy some part of it. Providing medical treatment to people—no matter which people—is an act projected into eternity, even though his patients don't live forever, and sometimes not for very long at all. And a meeting with his friends, which he missed today—has eternal significance. As does listening to music, and observing nature . . . But the rest of it, like this idiotic job for money— *what a waste*! Why do these English words come to mind first? He doesn't know the language that well, and Russian has plenty of synonyms for *wasted*: useless, fruitless, to no avail, in vain … Many ways of saying it: pointless, hopeless, hollow, empty, futile …

He falls asleep.

He doesn't sleep long, about an hour and a half, and he is awakened by a terrible clamor: the sound of a gigantic vacuum cleaner entering the room. It's operated by a black-haired little man—Hispanic, in all likelihood—wearing earmuffs, so as not to go deaf. The earmuffs are trimmed with artificial pink fur; they make the fellow look like an Indian in a feathered headdress.

He gives a short laugh and then pretends to be asleep. How could he sleep with that terrible roar? Not asleep, then—meditating. That's what the room is for, isn't it? He's loath to get up. All right, get a move on, Indian—the room's plenty clean. The fellow quickly passes by with his horrible machine—no more than a few centimeters away—and then he's all alone again, in silence.

He looks at his watch, closes his eyes, and summons images of those who love him unconditionally. It's a sort of lucid dream, almost entirely controlled by his conscious mind, but not entirely.

He wants to see his father—and there he is, his father. He perceives his father as a whole, not as a collection of properties and qualities. These properties and qualities are well known to him—he's the man's son, after all—but they bear little relation to his father's essence, to the mystery of his personality. Kind, generous, dedicated, sure—but he can say all that about his friends, too.

"How did it turn out this way?" he asks his father. "I have a soul, I have talent—not just for medicine, which you know about, but also for music. I mean, I definitely had musical talent, and I still love music more than anything—that's not so common in our time—so how did this happen? Making these pointless trips because my real job doesn't pay, lying around on a red floor, envying people with stern faces who have their lives figured out?" He must really be tired—his eyes are misting over.

But seriously, what's there to cry about? So he's tired. So he mixed up his Portlands and missed out on seeing his friends. He'll see them next month. A night on the floor? He saved fifty dollars, and it's nice and clean. But the fact that his father is gone . . . It's been eleven years and he still hasn't gotten over it.

The tears actually help. He takes a good, hard look at himself and sees the absurdity of the situation—a grown man in tears, the red floor, the medical bag under his head—and soon falls asleep again. And now he has a real dream: He and his father are sitting next to a broken-down car, near the place where the wheel goes. The thing is broken—what's it called, the hubcap? The rim? It's clear there's no fixing it. They don't have the parts, and they don't know how to do it anyway. They used to find themselves in that position quite often. They're just sitting there on the ground, and his father says: "You're my dear boy." It's not about the words, of course; it's what the words contain, it's the look in his father's eyes, which implies that everything is proceeding as it should, and that he regrets that his son is lonely.

He lingers on the border between dream and reality, then abruptly gets up and washes the best he can in the impeccably clean restroom. He's been in transit so long that his face is covered with stubble, but he hasn't got a razor or a brush. Is there time for coffee? A final smoke? He really did forget himself in the meditation room . . . Security check: the change, the keys, everything out of his pockets. The shift has changed, but the new guards are no less thorough. A detailed examination. What if he misses the morning flight? All right, he's made it—on the plane, Portland to New York. There are about fifteen to twenty passengers in the cabin, and the sleepy, aged stewardess informs them all: "If you've ever taken a plane even once since 1966"—the year of his birth, as it happens—"then you certainly don't need me to show you how to fasten your seat belt." A rather charming, creative departure from the rules.

He looks through the window at the droplets of water on its outer surface, dancing and scattering in the wind. The reunion with his father was not terribly momentous. Not even a reunion, really—just a dream, a purely psychic phenomenon. Nevertheless, he feels like a child who had been crying for a long, long time, until grown-ups turned their attention to him, until they looked at him with gentle eyes, so that he realized that all was forgiven, and then his tears had dried up, though his face still ached a little, and all he wanted was to be active, to play, to eat.

May he have another serving? "No, not unless someone refuses theirs. The meals are determined by the number of passengers." Not a problem, he's full anyway.

With his stubble and two days without a shower, he probably seems suspicious, and possibly smells quite bad. Americans are sensitive to smells. But what can he do? Besides, he doesn't notice his own smell, just as he doesn't perceive his own Russian accent. He sprawls across three seats, wraps his feet in a blanket, puts on his headphones— Mendelssohn's Piano Trio, a flawed recording, but what an inspired performance ... Six hours' rest until he hits New York, the city of the yellow devil ... Who called it that?

On his arrival he is possessed by a spirit of profligacy and buys ridiculous, expensive gifts for his friends and family. And on the plane back to Russia, before it even leaves the ground, he commits an act that will make him feel ashamed.

Here's how it plays out. The plane is stuffed with passengers, and he's seated at the window next to the emergency exit—a rare, valuable seat, with more legroom, which he reserved in advance. Beside him slumps a middle-aged gentleman who weighs around 170 kilograms; you see that kind of obesity only in America. What's more, he's completely drunk, and drenched in sweat; his hot flanks extend far over the edges of his seat. It's clear that this situation won't improve during the flight to Moscow.

He scrambles out past the mountain of flesh and, without even thinking of what he'll say, wends his way to the stewardess and informs her that his neighbor is drunk. In his view, that constitutes a threat to the safety of everyone on board: in the event of an emergency, would the man be able to help his fellow passengers climb out the exit?

"Sir, would you like to be reseated?" the stewardess asks the fat man. "No?" She asks him to speak up. "Well, then we'll just have to call the police. You'll fly to Moscow in the same seat, at the same time, but tomorrow."

Now he feels the need to intervene, to vouch for his neighbor... Having freed himself from the mound of flesh, he has a clearer sense of what he has wrought. Maybe the fellow had simply been nervous before the flight—many people are afraid to fly; he himself has had to resort to alcohol, though in smaller doses. But both parties ignore him, and as soon as the fat man hears the word *police*, he gets up and trudges after the stewardess to the back of the cabin.

He feels ashamed. He's behaved like an American. Oh, well, what's done is done—this isn't a matter of life and death.

A woman takes the place of the fat drunk. She's about forty-five, rather young-looking, freckled. Her hand brushes against his on the armrest, and he feels a pleasant chill through her shirt. Very nice. Now he'll take a sleeping pill, they'll bring him some wine, and he'll doze off and wake up in Moscow. But they don't bring him wine.

"But how will you help your fellow passengers in the event of an emergency?" The beverage cart is operated by that same stewardess: it turns out that not all Americans approve of snitching.

Let's see if the pills work with juice. They would have, if it weren't for his new neighbor. She finishes her Diet Pepsi, rattles the ice in her cup, and talks, talks, talks.

She's from New York, going to Russia for the first time. She wants to know more about the country; he's supposed to enlighten her. Half-asleep, he mutters various inanities, but the neighbor is insatiable. She changes the subject to America, then to the whole world, and finally—to herself. The conversation on the plane with a random fellow traveler is a popular genre. It substitutes for psychoanalysis, for confession. She recently broke up with her lover: he used to bribe her with expensive gifts—the last straw was the Jaguar.

"How would you like it if a woman gave you a Jaguar?"

He'd have to think about that, yes... He closes his eyes, and she prattles on—about her ex-boyfriend's disgusting habits, the restaurants he took her to, the cigars he smoked.

Oh, he has an idea: this ought to stem her eloquent tide.

"A woman is only a woman," he says in English, "but a good Cigar is a Smoke."

But the neighbor just nods, unperturbed: "Kipling."

She knows the poem. She studied "creative writing" at Princeton. Anyway, this Kipling used to buy her cars, but he refused to have children. The radical measure of sterilization is fairly common in the United States. Kipling had a vasectomy, and now she herself is too old to conceive.

That's why she's flying to Russia—to adopt a girl. Russia, Kazakhstan, Romania—the few places left where you can find an orphan of European descent. He looks at his neighbor with new eyes.

She extends her hand: "My name is Jean."

He gives Jean his name and sees a slight change in her expression. A half smile—not mysterious, exactly. Will she say it? Of course she'll say it. No, she keeps mum.

"Tell me—it was your dog's name, wasn't it? Your cat's?"

"My hamster's," Jean confesses.

How sweet. They both laugh.

She tells him about the process of adoption. There will be a court hearing. She shows him a photo of the little girl, eleven months old. There's a lawyer waiting in Moscow. They'll travel to Novosibirsk together. Everything has been arranged, even a Russian nanny. Why a Russian nanny? "What do you mean, why? The girl's only heard Russian her whole life."

There's one thing Jean hasn't arranged. She asks him to fill out her customs declaration, and it turns out one can't bring in more than ten thousand dollars on one's person. Jean brought a bigger sum with her. Well, there are two options: either hide the money deeper, or entrust some of it to him. He'd wait for her at the glass doors; he has no luggage.

"Of course I trust you..." she says, somewhat abstractedly.

So she doesn't trust him, but she really has no other choice. He takes her money: Don't worry, Jean. That's the end of their conversation. They both need sleep.

The plane flies over Tver. There are no clouds. He lets her look out the window: See the wretchedness? He's no longer with Jean. When he exits the plane and the customs inspectors ask, "What are you traveling with?" he'll wave his hand and say: "All kinds of crap." They'll smile the best they can—one of ours, on you go. Jean and he will say their goodbyes at the glass doors; friendships struck up in airplanes don't usually develop, but they'll exchange phone numbers, addresses. He'll get in his car and his mind will again turn to his father. For some reason, car trips give him a fleeting sense of reunion. He'll drive into the city—which is aggressive, barbaric on weekdays, and not so bad, more or less familiar on weekends—and make his way to Manezhnaya Square. A decade ago, the traffic around the square was two-way, now it's one-way—he'll have to tell his father about that too.

He really does arrive at Sheremetyevo; he gets behind the wheel, turns around, and slams his front bumper against a concrete pedestal: it's exactly tall enough not to be noticed. Shit. Greetings, Mother Russia. Every penny he'd earned on the legless old woman—down the drain. The material losses cause him less distress than usual, although the bumper is cracked and some slush from under the hood drips onto the asphalt. He dips his finger into it—green: radiator fluid. The engine is overheating: God forbid it should jam. In the city center, at a traffic light, he turns off the engine. He closes his eyes—no dream this time, almost a dead faint. The honking behind him is deafening. He's not going home—he's going to the mechanic.

He's got an excellent mechanic who doesn't overcharge—doesn't overcharge him, at any rate—and immediately diagnoses the problem; he graduated from a technical college. Well, in this case, you don't need a degree to understand what happened. The mechanic condescends to him a bit: poor little intellectual, doesn't know what real life's all about, and doesn't need to know. He takes a part from another client's car, grumbling—"a French turd"—about his Renault. "Shurik!" he calls to one of his assistants. "Shurik!"

The place employs Kyrgyz—no, not Kyrgyz—what do you call them?—Uighurs, without registration. They call them all Shurik. Like the mechanic himself, they never leave the shop.

The radio blasts awful so-called music. Dirt everywhere. Oil, rags, tools underfoot. Disassembled engines, doors, wheel arches, fenders: man is much more perfectly made than any car, especially on the inside.

"Are rats a problem in here?" He's afraid of rats.

"Nope," the mechanic reassures him. "No rats yet—but they're coming." The cat that lived here croaked last week.

Where should he perch himself? He doesn't want to get in the way, breathe down their necks. He finds a place in the farthest corner, in a collapsed car seat. The mechanic curses a blue streak, with various filigrees, pretentiously, shouting over the radio—only intellectuals curse that way. He puts on his headphones—Mendelssohn, a fragment of the second trio, Mendelssohn has two of them—and suddenly realizes that he's happy.

How can he manage to stay in this state? He knows that, in the best of cases, it will last a few minutes and then dissipate. It's useless to try to hold on to it. The very attempt signals its failure.

But somehow it lasts. Is it the music?

No, the music is over, but he's still happy.

April 2010
Translated by Boris Dralyuk

ROCK, PAPER, SCISSORS

THE TIME: ours. A peaceful life. Small town, Central Russia, away from railways and the highway. There is a river, there is a church.

Ksenia Nikolayevna Knysh's house is in the center of town. It's a bungalow, but a large one. The *pelmennaya*—the dumpling restaurant by the house—belongs to her too. Ksenia is head of the region's legislative assembly. She is fifty-seven years old.

Morning, Tuesday, March 7. Ksenia is on her front porch with Mrs. Pakhomova, principal of the local school. Pakhomova is holding a large, personalized card and a bouquet of yellow flowers.

"Dearest Ksenia Nikolayevna! As it's Women's Day tomorrow we wanted to offer you our sincere, heartfelt thanks and our very warmest wishes. May your work continue to benefit this town for many years to come!"

Ksenia nods, doesn't invite her in. There are some sheets of paper inside the card.

"After money again, Pakhomova?"

"Whatever do you mean? Those are your neighbor's *sacred writings*—they were on the computer in the staff room. But please don't show them to anyone, dear Ksenia Nikolayevna, you know what people here are like..."

Ksenia, sternly:

"We'll look into it."

But she smiles all the same: "Happy Women's Day, Pakhomova. To all of you—all of the women on your team." Then back inside her house, to read. This neighbor is an enemy. *Pray for your enemies.* She does pray, she prays every single day...

I am forty years old, and I feel good, but after forty, death is no longer seen as premature—so it's time for me to get myself together, put it all into words. These thoughts—nagging, unresolved . . . Forty. Faith in humanity dwindles, and—by the same token— faith in God. What's all this for, what? It's as though I'm sitting backwards on a train, looking out the window. And out there: the past. All I see is the past. What is turning forty, if not a reason to make sense of my past?

I am a teacher of Russian language and literature; I am un-married; I have no children. My whole life—except that time at Kalinin University (an ugly dream, now forgotten)—has been lived in this town of ours. It's beautiful here; a joyless, Central Russian sort of beauty. If you ignore everything man-made, it's very beautiful indeed. So here I am, apparently forever: here I was born; here I'll die. When I was younger this thought depressed me, but not anymore. Of course, my life can feel a bit lonely, es-pecially in winter, when it gets dark by five, and all of a sudden you lose sight of the things that help make life feel full: the river, the trees, the neighbors' houses. There's no risk of me turning to alcohol, mind you—I can't stand the stuff—but writing I have tried, as I think, in my position, almost anyone would. They're in for a shock when they read it—such are the sources of my "work." But whom will it actually shock? A couple of male teachers—that's all the intelligentsia we have here. Our doctors, our priest, they can hardly be considered intelligentsia, and the women at school are all featureless beings, usually married to some low-level of-ficial. They have a burdened look about them. "What's earth's diameter?" the geography teacher will ask the children. "Don't you know? That's no good," he'll say, "earth is our mother." He's been doing this same act for the last twenty years, but no one—not even we teachers—has bothered to find out the answer. Why should we? We're not going anywhere; earth doesn't feel round to us. He's dying of cancer anyway: everyone knows everyone else's business here, especially when it's bad.

"First I'll do my time in the army, then I'll do my time inside."

That's what a village boy told me wistfully not long ago—he and I were discussing his future. An apprenticeship, is that what it's called? Hardly any of my first male students who graduated are still alive: drugs, war, "business"... this upset me at first, but now—much as it pains me to say it—I'm tired, tired of pity. I've gotten used to these things. As for the girls, in general they get through unscathed; each year a few of them go on to universities and academies in Tver, Yaroslavl, even Moscow. Girls are more interested in books anyway, and as people, they're eager to please: after all, I'm a single, relatively young man; we organize literature evenings together; I have a big house... We call our evenings Literary Thursdays—all very innocent: tea, poetry, prose. I like to feel happy, and to make others feel happy, too. And even that wretched, utterly wretched business with Verochka Zhidkova hasn't dampened my spirits.

We have a river, but no railway—not for many kilometers around. They say this prevents industrial development here, but railways are really just an evil, an unfreedom. *How Tolstoy despised the railway—and how the Bolsheviks loved it! "Our brave locomotive, steaming forth" and the like. But a braking distance of one and a half kilometers—is that some kind of joke? Now, cars, that's another story. Oh, how I wish I had one! As for driving, I'd figure that out somehow. Then I'd get behind the wheel and drive to Pushkinskiye Gory, even Boldino, and spend hours wandering around these sacred Pushkinian sites, and there, look! Another teacher, and she's single and lonely too. Sometimes I lie awake at night, scripting my conversations with her. Is that childish? So be it. "How are you enjoying your visit?" I'll ask her. She won't answer in a direct way, but in a way that shows she loves Pushkin as much as I do. Soon I'll confess: "I loved you from the moment I saw you." Or perhaps not quite so forward as that, but something along those lines. Then she'll start laughing, as though she doesn't believe me. "It's true, I swear," I'll say. "Swear not, neither by heaven, neither by the earth," she'll mutter with a frown, but I'll have the last word: "Nor by the joyful name of*

Pushkin." *After seeing the sights, we'll drive back to my place, without any long discussions or agreements. On the way we'll play a game: I'll say, "The tale of tales," and she'll reply, "The book of books." I'll continue:*

"The king of kings."

"Nation of nations."

"Vanity of vanities."

"Holy of Holies."

"Crème de la crème."

And then she'll think for a while, and give up.

There's no shortage of things we could play, but I am very much short a car. If I were a bit more on the ball, I'd sell half my land (I have a large plot where, weeds aside, almost nothing grows), then I'd rebuild the house, buy a car, and still have money to spare. Land here is worth fifty times what it was just a few years ago, so I'm set for life, only I don't know how to deal with this wealth. To be completely honest, I haven't really tried all that hard: Poverty is quite becoming of a provincial teacher, isn't it? My life here has warmth. And danger, and dirt, and a whiff of . . . yes, certain aspects of our provincial life stink—of course they do—but let's not drag out this metaphor.

I have amazing parents. That village student of mine (time in the army—time inside) doesn't. It's a rough life: from childhood, he'll steal from shops—not out of hunger, but to prove something. Or he'll get drunk, get into a fight—who are we to judge? And if he rapes one of his classmates? If he kills someone? At what point is a child responsible for his actions—if ever?

Just before New Year's I found a boy at the bus station; he was about six, poorly clothed for winter. He came up to me to beg, for what I assume must have been the first time: he still didn't know how it was done. I took him with me to the New Year's show at one of the dachas. We washed the boy, dressed him, gave him all sorts of gifts, and then I took him back to his place. He pointed out their "apartment," but when I went inside it was just a room— and some room it was: empty, save for a light bulb hanging from the ceiling and an iron bed covered in rags, and on top of that lay a naked man, dirty, drunk, reeking. I covered the guy up, then tried to make him see—see his son, see this bag of things we had given him, see that he needed some order in his life, but he just asked: "You Orthodox?" This threw me—what sort of question was that? Then he sat up, heaving himself towards me: "You a real Russian?"

"Yes," I replied, "I'm Russian."

"So then what do you need all these things, all this order, for? See, me, I don't need no-thing."

But why not? He seemed even to have surprised himself. I met his son again the next day at the bus station. He didn't recognize me, but recounted his story excitedly: "You should've seen the house I was at yesterday! Them Muscovites stay there! They sure are good at stealing!"

That's the kids. As for the adults, they've completely lost the plot too. For example, barely anyone can remember our local phone code: we never give our numbers out to anyone outside of town; we don't feel part of a bigger whole. Buddha, Socrates, Tolstoy, and then me: resident of town X, with phone number Y—that's how things should be. The profound depths of the Russian national consciousness? Nowadays it's only the dacha owners who believe in things like that; the locals just watch TV. Not out of exhaustion, and not because life is tough—it's easy; no one's going hungry—but to fill that void, to keep themselves busy somehow.

Now, back to my own situation. My parents are alive, both retired—my father taught English, my mother was a primary-school teacher. They didn't get any grandchildren from me, so they moved to Moscow. They have theaters there, exhibitions, my younger sister lives there too. My parents love each other and my sister and me. I never really went in for any sort of teenage rebellion when I was growing up. People say a youth without rebellion is incomplete, but I don't agree.

Anyway, my whole family is alive, so of all my losses, losing

Verochka was the greatest; in fact, the only genuine loss I've suf-fered. Three years have passed since we lost her, yet I still remem-ber her every single day—perhaps even every hour. Not to mention every time I come across intelligent, animated girls—which some of my students are. One just recently asked me: "Sir, since our punctuation rules are so rigid, perhaps we don't need to use punc-tuation at all? It's not like it says anything we didn't already know." Why had this question never occurred to me? "I need to think about that," I told her, "I need to think about that." It's clever little girls like these that get me to work in the morning.

To finish what I was saying about the dacha owners: not long before Verochka left here, she and I were sitting on the veranda, helping one of my graduating students, Polina, write an entrance-exam essay for some third-rate university. It was the Academy of Services, and apparently they'll take anyone they can get: they don't even take students' phones from them during exams. So Verochka and I sat there drinking tea and trying to outdo each other with text messages to Polina in the exam hall. The essay title was "The Spiritual World of the Provincial Nobility in Pushkin's Eugene Onegin." *The assumption was that Polina would develop each of the ideas we texted her.*

And so we wrote:

"This world is presented from chapter two of the novel to the beginning of chapter seven. It is to this world that Onegin flees from the big city, from Saint Petersburg." We then continued:

"Unpretentious naivete of Onegin's provincial neighbors:

Into that very room he settled,

Where, forty years, till his demise,

With housekeeper the old man battled,

Looked through the window, swatted flies . . .[3]

"Interests:

Their sensible deliberations

Regarding haymaking, the wine,

The kennels and their kith and kind . . .

"Country dwellers—characterized by simplicity, unrefined

interests, monotonous existence. Brought together by habit, not love.

"*Unstructured days, lots of free time:*
    Alone Tatiana roams within
    The silent woods, armed with a novel
    In which she seeks and finds some marvel...
"*For the passionate, a world of illusions blossoms:*
    She breathes a sigh and, taking over
    Another's grief or ecstasy...
"*A main feature of provincial life: lack of real-life experience, especially among women.*"

Only we wrote future *rather than* feature, *because we were in such a rush.*

"*More?*" *we asked.*

"*Yes plz!*"

"*Serious, principled approach to life: had Tatiana been born in Saint Petersburg, she wouldn't have displayed the sincerity we see in any of her declarations of love to Onegin.*

"*Austerity and simplicity—not valued in city life. Onegin lives by the laws of the city, which presuppose neither sincerity nor depth. Through reckless negligence he kills Lensky, devastates Tatiana.*

"*Yet it certainly seems that—just as in city life—provincial life has its share of arrogance, foolishness, and frivolity, in open and grotesque forms. So it would be misguided,*" *we advised Polina,* "*to idealize country life.*"

She thanked us; it was already time for her to rewrite the final draft. Afterwards Verochka and I sat and thought for a while: Onegin's time in the provinces reads remarkably like the story of our dacha owners.

When it's hot, the less sophisticated among them walk around half-naked. They wouldn't do that in Moscow. And the more cultured ones don't mean to offend us, yet somehow they still do. The Petersburgers are a bit different: they at least introduce themselves by their name and patronymic, whereas the Muscovites seem only to have first names nowadays. Somewhere out in the big cities dissertations are being defended, books are being published; something real is happening, with intellectuals slapping one other in the face, but here—how could anyone take our homely, warm, slightly mud-flecked life seriously? They're flippant: flippant in love, flippant in their behavior. They'll pop in to see me on their way up from the river, then head straight on to the pelmennaya to sit, or—as they say now—hang. Then summer will end, and that'll be it: "Let us know when you plan on visiting us in the Big Smoke."

I know that I myself am prone to terrifying bouts of lethargy in all its forms: emotional, spiritual, physical. I don't wish to be a teacher of morality—my own subject keeps my hands full as it is—but certain memories just make me so angry. And no matter how hard I find this monk's life I lead, no matter how little my life has been touched by the joys of a woman's love, since Verochka came into my life I've turned my back on what I once had. But to go back to being an amusement for the female dacha owners— a provincial teacher of literature, a man with passions, go on, I could go for some of that! Why hasn't someone else snapped him up?—*no. That's not a life I'm sad to leave behind.*

Now. About Verochka. Verochka was so lovely that every single man—except the most common drunkard—would stop, turn his head, sometimes even follow her down the street. In her gestures, her movements—her hands, her head, her shoulders—there wasn't the slightest trace of awkwardness or tension, never. She was in my class from when she was fourteen until she graduated—I only teach the older classes. "Why do we need negatives—at least explain to me why!" was the first thing I heard her say. "Wouldn't it be so much simpler just to say: I unwant, I unlove?" *I looked at her intently, and in that moment I felt a sense of foreboding: here was a classical tragic heroine. Or is what came afterwards interfering with my memory?*

Verochka really wanted to be close to me. And yes, I loved her. Of course I loved her. But even so, it was I who cut her off when she tried to tell me how she felt: she was my student, and then there was our age difference, and besides, perhaps it wasn't really me she wanted to get close to—perhaps it was just the literature, the poetry. "You've got this all from books, Verochka, and books are the cure for it too." That was all I could say. But Verochka didn't stop coming to my house for tea. It was all very simple: we were neighbors, we had our unstructured, provincial days.

Ksenia, her mother, was jealous of her, and she used to send Verochka's father—Communist Zhidkov, as we called him—to parent evenings, though he no longer lived with them by that point. He used to be secretary of the District Party Committee— by our standards, a position of considerable standing. But then Ksenia dumped him, and he got sick, started drinking, turned himself a grayish color—ashen—and it became impossible to talk to him anymore. I imagine he must be dead now.

But Verochka—what essays she wrote on Dostoyevsky! Sometimes a bit far-fetched, perhaps, but they showed a great deal of talent. One of them I remember almost entirely by heart. It was about Porfiry, head of investigations in Crime and Punishment, *he of the liquid glint in his eyes: it talked about the surprise we feel when "they" are revealed to be human; and about how Porfiry is the only character with no surname, yet it is he who saves Raskolnikov, he and Sonia save him—justice and mercy, two divine acts! Verochka's essay on* The Storm *was also one of the most interesting I have ever read on Ostrovsky's play: it was about Katya Kabanova in comparison to Anna Karenina. And about weak, inconsistent men.*

Every teacher of literature dreams of his or her students becoming literary scholars, so I encouraged Verochka: go on, apply to study literature. I had Moscow in mind, but she chose Petersburg, and no matter how much I tried to dissuade her—boredom, granite, bitter cold à la Pushkin[4]—no matter how often I asked her to reread Tolstoy's opinion of the city, she wouldn't listen. She was the daughter of officials, an only child at that—she wasn't used to being refused anything. I like to think that in days gone by it was the Verochkas of this world who became socialist revolutionaries, dissidents . . . whenever I spoke against Petersburg, she would simply laugh and recite Akhmatova: But we would not exchange, not for the world / this splendid granite city of glory and misfortune[5] . . . But for Verochka, as it turned out, Petersburg was a city of only misfortune.

Ksenia didn't approve of Verochka studying literature—she wanted to make a lawyer out of her: good money, work at a big law firm, marriage to a foreigner. Happiness, along the trodden path. *We know, we've heard. Naturally, Verochka never judged her mother; she simply said that Ksenia was "different." Verochka didn't go straight to university (she didn't like to lose or fail at anything): she spent a whole year preparing for it. And of course, when it came to literature, that was with me.*

I do not know, and do not wish to know, the details of her death. Student halls, flats, depraved Petersburg boys—cruel, witty boys—splitting up with someone, getting back together again. The Petersburg cultural underground: an evil crowd. Her letters soon became somehow not hers, not Verochka's. She had moved to Petersburg for high culture, but instead she dropped out of university, and then it all began: helping the deprived, the downtrodden. She got it into her head that she would help the misfortunate discover the splendors of life: music, art, beauty. Those with nowhere left to go—*how could she possibly have coped? Among them there are, apparently, different sorts, but their influence was clearly negative. I've heard there was violence, too. One of her so-called protégés. The versions vary: some said that it was pills she took, others—poison. But how could Verochka have gotten hold of poison?*

I didn't even go to her funeral. Pakhomova, our principal, made sure I wouldn't be able to: she sent me into the city, for professional development. She probably pitied me, in her own way. Father Alexander didn't want to perform the service, given the circumstances, but of course Ksenia got the better of him. Verochka's death served no one. No one. And the crux of it all: life's there to be lived, but I was too concerned about being good.

I should have married her, and only then let her go to Petersburg—or anywhere else.

"Married her... as if," sneers Ksenia, "you'd have had to grow a pair first, you weed. Ugh." She stops reading for a moment, rubs her hand. There is a large mole on it, sprouted over with hair. With all her emotion, it is pulsating, itching. She pulls down her sleeve to cover it.

"Hey, what's wrong?" asks Isaikin—tall, stooping: her current husband.

"Go on, open up, the customers are waiting," Ksenia retorts.

He's a poor man. The auto shop belongs to her too. "The right tires for the right people"—the slogan is the sum of Isaikin's work. The right spark plugs, the right oil. She should send him packing, but their marriage, though a bad one, was made in the eyes of God. And *what God has joined together...* Yes, God owes her a lot. For her daughter. For everything.

Now to finish reading this scumbag.

As I've mentioned Ksenia, I ought to say something about power more generally. All the power in our town has been sucked up by small, unsightly people. They're on edge, the lot of them, not because they're ugly, but because it's only through theft that they have come to wield such power. And yes, we have accepted them—but in this town, is there anyone we wouldn't have accepted? First Communist Zhidkov, now Pasha Tsytsyn and his local self-government—each time all we're thinking is: Maybe this one will actually do something about our roads? Pasha, Ksenia, and the judge have their fingers in every pie. Ksenia is their spiritual leader, their ayatollah, very devout. That fool Pasha was elected at some point, though it's been a long time since we've had any elections here—now it's the local deputies who appoint their leader. And then there's the judge, Yegor Savvich Rukosuyev, quite simply the richest man in town. As his patronymic would suggest, he certainly is savvy: half the land around town is Rukosuyev land, I hardly need say more. But as it happens, I've heard the judge isn't such a bad man. That's more than can be said of Ksenia: rumor is she's sacking her Tajik workers. It's as though she gets a kick out of cruelty, like a teenager who tortures cats.

The school cleaner stole money from our jackets, and it was with great sadness that we let her go: she had been one of us, just like us, but she had changed—she was a thief. But if Pasha came creeping into my pockets, it honestly couldn't make me think any worse of him: Pasha's different, he's one of them. Are elections really any better than theft, when they always end up in power? And that's the way things are here, yet they still care what we're thinking—whether it is about them or in general. Take our priest—he's around five or so years my junior; we call him Alexander the Third because we had two Father Alexanders before him. Anyway, he was ordained according to the rules, and—besides it being impossible to make out a word he says—I imagine he performs his duty by the book. The point is, this Alexander hasn't usurped anything—he's nothing to fear. Or, take me, a teacher: I do my best to do everything by the book. I want to be respected, of course, but when I'm walking past a classroom, do I stop outside the door to listen to what's being said about me? No. But had I gotten my job through theft, I certainly would. And that's precisely what they'll be doing—if they don't already, that is.

Yet, in reality, what are the authorities to me? We have light, we have running water—it may be a bit erratic, but it still runs. It's just this setup they have, it . . . No, enough, I only wrote that to distract myself, to stop myself from thinking about Verochka. What was I so afraid of then? Of committing some crime—some theft— by marrying her? Limp justifications. Our life here, of course, would have been impossible. If I look beyond my self-pity, I was afraid of love—that, and the pain I associate with it. Or worse: I was afraid of all the fuss. That's if I disregard self-pity entirely.

Ksenia turns over the last page. "Go to hell!" she exclaims, then, "Oh Lord, forgive me. But you, you *intellectuals*, you took my daughter, you destroyed our country—that's all that you achieved."

Once there had been Socialism, and Ksenia had done her duty, believing and not believing, like everyone else. She had her country; she had her daughter. They had ideals, and things to respect and fear. Then Socialism was no more; the country fell apart; new standards emerged. She knew what had to be done: she had herself christened— her daughter too—and she helped to restore the old church. *Ye shall know them by their business.* And then? Her daughter died. No daughter, no nation. Some reward. It was beyond all comprehension.

The Heavenly Father owes her; yes, he owes her big-time. As for her, she's aware of her debts. She has worked, and will continue to do so, never relying on any guarantees. She said that she would restore the church—and did just that. She has promised a new chapel—and a new chapel there will be. Whom has she promised, exactly? It hardly matters. She's promised the town, everyone, herself. Ha, the ayatollah, that's who she is, all right.

The plan for the chapel has been agreed on with Alexander the Third. The priest had initially shrugged the plan off: "No one comes to church as it is. We'd be better off buying a bell." But she had gone back to see him again and again, until one day she was met by the scene of her priest parked in front of the TV, eating cabbage and watching a film: swearing, shouting, shooting. He tried to crack a joke: "*Evil shall slay the wicked...*" but she caught his guilty look. "Oh, Father," she thought to herself, "is this what our Fridays have come to?" She then paid a visit to the archpriest and the bishop, both times bearing gifts. And now she has the priest right where she wants him. She clenches her fist. Her mole has started to itch again. Worries, all worries.

The priest is a mumbler. Can't give a clear answer to a single question. *My strength is made perfect in weakness...* So what, does that mean he can relax, do something nice for himself? What sort of strength is to be found in weakness? Nothing could be easier than spouting empty words. People like him can't be relied on for anything—nor can her neighbor, the teacher—no, it's all on her, all on Ksenia.

"So," she thinks, "we'll put the chapel behind the house, right there." Now she knows exactly where it needs to go, "We'll move that neighbor of ours. He's an outsider in this town. Poetry, prose...We'll work out who's been commissioning this prose he's been writing, and then we'll work out something of our own with them. Did Pakhomova read it all, I wonder? Yes, most likely. Damn, I have to be more careful. Reckon with every last one of these monsters. Pasha too, that little shrimp. A meter tall in hat and shoes, yet so conceited! Always talking about himself in the third person: 'The head of the administration promises you...'"

It's all on her, all on Ksenia: the town, the house, her businesses. She doesn't have the strength for it all, but what else can she do? It's her cross to bear.

The pelmennaya works like this: from May to September the dacha owners are in town—lots of them—so Ksenia opens the terrace; from October to April it's a simpler clientele, just locals. They serve Central Asian dishes—*shurpa, manti, plov*—and there are vegetarian options too, for Lent. Now that Lent has started, it's the Lenten menu being pushed. But the main dish is, of course, dumplings—*pelmeni*—straight from the wholesaler. When they're almost past their sell-by date you can get them real cheap.

There are two permanent employees: a cashier and a cook, both elderly Russians, Isaikin's relatives. For everything else there are Tajiks. They too have a sell-by date; good for one season only. Their probation period lasts three months. If there's any cause for complaint: Get your things and off you go, auf Wiedersehen. During the probation period the Tajiks aren't paid, although they do get food and lodging—once Ksenia even called an ambulance for one of them, after he had burnt his hand. More Tajiks are needed in summer, but in winter only one or two. And, as it happens, not all Tajiks are the same. One has stuck around.

Her name is Roxana Ibragimova, thirty-five years of age. Her voice is deep: "In Russian, my name is Roxana." No one has heard her say anything more. Roxana. What sort of name is that? "Roxana, Oksana, Ksana…" Ksenia thinks to herself, "Well, how about that—we're almost namesakes!" Roxana is tall, slim, and presents herself well; she's not like the others—not at all. Long black hair. Very beautiful. "If you made more of an effort you could find yourself a husband," Ksenia once told her. "After all, the way to a man's heart is through his stomach." Ksenia had laughed, but then immediately stifled it, such was the look this Roxana had given her. For a moment her eyes had flashed with fire, then instantly cooled.

Ksenia had later come to understand just what this fire meant: one evening, a young man from the gas station—another Central Asian—was drinking beer out on the terrace. Roxana was serving him. He reached out to try to touch her, *hey sweetie*. She jerked away, but that fire had already ignited—and what a fire it was. She uttered something—fast, guttural, no more than a few sounds. The man slumped and left, his beer only half-drunk. Ksenia, standing by the door, had seen everything and decided on the spot: Roxana can stay, and she can get paid. And so Roxana has been here since August, living in the utility room behind the kitchen, where it's warm. It's a space of only about four square meters, but she has almost no belongings.

Ksenia hands Roxana some see-through plastic folders: the menus are all dirty, they need to be changed.

"These pages need replacing, can you handle it?"

Roxana looks up, her eyelashes flicker slightly. Silence.

Roxana does everything in silence. Back in August, a man had come looking for her. One of the Muscovites. Said that she's been teaching his children Russian. Clearly couldn't think of anything more convincing. Roxana had refused to speak to him, and quite right too.

As for the dirty menus, she'll handle them; she always gets things done. She deserves a raise. Yes, Ksenia feels drawn to Roxana. It's a shame she doesn't speak.

"Happy Women's Day, Roxanochka!" Ksenia exclaims.

Roxana shows no surprise, no acknowledgment, simply doesn't respond at all.

The hospital—the council—the courthouse. All are close, within walking distance.

Zhidkov, Ksenia's ex, is in the hospital. Has been for the past six months. His house has no heat, and there's no one to check in on him. What other choice was there—a nursing home? It's not like he's got much time left... He can go back home in summer, if he lasts that long.

Zhidkov has been behaving strangely again: last night he got into the nurses' station and phoned for an ambulance, "I'm in pain, I can't breathe!" But the ER is in the same building, a few floors down.

The chief physician steps out, wiping his mouth—their Women's Day celebrations have already started.

"Ksenia Nikolayevna, would you like to have a listen? We record all calls made to the emergency services."

What would she want to hear that for? "Let's just get to Zhidkov," she says. "And look at how run-down everything is. When are we going to get any repairs done, eh?"

The chief physician hangs back: "I'll be in my office if you need me."

Zhidkov is sitting in the corridor, yellow, shrunken. It's been a long time since she last saw him.

"So you're alive, then?" she asks. "But look at you—how much do you weigh now?"

Can't be more than fifty kilos. She has brought him something to eat.

"And how about you, Ksiusha—still eighty kilos?"

Of course not. Seventy-five to seventy-seven. Nothing's changed.

Zhidkov looks at her pleadingly; he's got some idea in his head. She feels sorry for him, of course, but everyone has to die at some point.

"Are you going to take me home?"

No, not till summer—as he well knows.

"By summer...by summer I'll already be reunited with our Verochka. Though I doubt communists like me are allowed to believe such things..."

Of course he is. Everyone's allowed to believe such things nowadays. A communist! What a country they had flushed down the drain... But no more about Verochka, not today, not again—enough. Verochka was the one who used to visit Zhidkov, you see; she would read him books. Good books, according to Zhidkov, although he can't remember which ones.

"They aren't treating me here, Ksiusha. Other patients get put on a drip..."

A nurse is walking down the corridor. Ksenia signals at her with a jerk of the head: "Call the consultant, please."

The consultant is young, newish, and neat; he's not from around these parts.

"I have already explained everything to your husband. Excuse me—ex-husband," he says. "No, surgery is the only way. Yes, he'll have to go to Moscow; we don't do heart surgery here. Nor anywhere else in this province. Guarantees? What sort of guarantees are you expecting? There is a risk, of course. Let's say...10 percent. But without surgery, the risk is one hundred. Understand?"

Ugh, what a whiner. Calmly, she says, "The specialists I've spoken to in the city beg to differ. Anyway, why would you operate on him—at his age?" To Zhidkov: "Bring me your discharge notes from the city."

Zhidkov clearly can't walk at all; two steps and he's gasping for breath. Ksenia overtakes him and walks into the ward. There are two beds. In the second one lies an old man, festering. Couldn't they have given Zhidkov his own room? After all, he was once assistant secretary of the District Party Committee, not some rough *kolkhoz* farmhand. One must respect the past. Ksenia rummages around in Zhidkov's bedside table and catches a whiff of a strange smell—one not coming from the old man: the remains of some pelmeni she had sent Zhidkov. By now he has finally dragged himself over to the bed.

"Hey, Ksiusha, why don't you buy my beehive?"

"Piss off with your bees! Look, here it is," then she reads: "Treatment at the site of permanent residence."

The doctor grimaces. "Who wrote that nonsense? They don't know what they're talking about..."

And you do? she thinks. The consultant starts explaining again. She isn't participating, isn't listening. Then suddenly she hears him say: "...if he has the operation he could live to a good age. We've persuaded him, almost. So you should stop being part of the problem, and start being part of the solution."

This is going too far. She pays a visit to the chief physician: *He* will give Zhidkov a drip twice a day, every day. *He* is responsible for it. It will be done under *his* personal supervision. And that asshole consultant is not to be let anywhere near Zhidkov. Happy Women's Day to the women on his team.

"And to you, Ksenia Nikolayevna, happy International Women's Day! All the best!"

"Is Pavel Andreyevich in?"

"Oh yes—for you, Ksenia Nikolayevna, he's always in," his secretary replies.

What's that stupid smile about? Oh. The secretary knows.

Five years earlier Ksenia had come to visit Pasha, who had just been elected, largely thanks to her: he was a normal guy and—crucially—a local (a local, plus his grandfather had fought in the war—those were all his trump cards). She had come to his office to congratulate him and wish him many years' good service to the town. After a bit of small talk, Pasha suddenly started maneuvering Ksenia into his back room: "Come on, Ksenia Nikolayevna, let me show you a movie about me."

"What are you talking about?"

"You'll see; it's a good one," he replied.

There was a couch in the room, the curtains were drawn. Pasha jumped on Ksenia from behind, just as his comrades had taught him: women like strength in a man.

"Pasha, what the hell?"

"Seducing you."

"Mad with power, eh? I'm practically a grandmother. Are there no young women in this town?"

Pasha stepped back for a moment, turned his head: "It's status that I need now." Then he threw himself on her again.

"Fine, have your status, you flying falcon. Just give me a minute—turn around."

Pasha: an air-force academy graduate, undersized, no neck to speak of. Despite his big head, everything else is teeny tiny. You're not sure whether to laugh or cry. Their "love" lasted forty seconds and has not been repeated since, but as far as the town is concerned, Pasha and Ksenia are lovers.

Pasha is signing his Women's Day cards. Why does he bother? He has a photocopier. No, he's decided to do it himself—he's a "workaholic."

"You're not looking after yourself, Pavel Andreyevich."

"Ksenia Nikolayevna! And to what do I owe this visit?"

"I have a sensitive matter to discuss."

Pasha assumes a statesmanlike countenance. "Do go on, Ksenia Nikolayevna. Let's see to it that it's resolved."

She lays everything out: they have the plans for the chapel, but there's a small problem—the land. Everything has been agreed upon with the church authorities: the chapel is very much needed. Meanwhile, her neighbor is living in luxury on a fifteen-hundred-square-meter plot of land virtually in the center of town.

"He's doing nothing of the sort," says Pasha. "My Kristinka is his student. She says he lives like ... like a little bird."

Ah yes, like a little bird. A heavenly little bird. And he *feels good.* Pasha suddenly becomes very tense.

"How's that ... program of yours coming along—spiritual regeneration, the Slavonic script ..."

"Since when have we been interested in scripts, Pavel? Let's give this little bird of yours a council house—we'll need all the more space if we're to have this program you're asking about. Come on Pasha, get your head out of the clouds, what are you—a giraffe?" What she wants to shout is: "For God's sake, houses 'burn down' all the time; you of all people should know—you were a fireman!" but that's something she wouldn't dare say, not even to him.

"I thought you were a man, Pavel. You promised me last week!"

"I'm sorry, Ksenia Nikolayevna, but last week was *last* week, and this week is *this* week."

"Where'd you get that one from?"

Pasha had heard a regional governor use the phrase. Oh yes, he is often in the city on public affairs. They have reached a dead end, an impasse. Does Pasha even know what a chapel is?

"I don't see the . . . logistics," he grumbles.

Pasha thinks a bowling alley would be better. Bowling would be more popular.

"Bowling? What are you talking about? Come on, Pasha, you can't really think that. You're an official—you're a man of the state!"

"State, Ksenia Nikolayevna, is a relative term."

He's sulking. Was it the giraffe comment? A man like him should take it as a compliment. Suddenly Ksenia has a light-bulb moment.

"Do you have any idea what that teacher's up to?" she asks, inspired. He may be a heavenly little bird, but that bird shits too. And behind her very house that little bird has built a nest of depravity. "Aren't you afraid for your daughter?" She pushes and pushes, bringing out her handkerchief, dabbing at her eyes. "Do you want her to . . . do you want it to happen to her too?"

Pasha thinks for a while.

"All right. We'll sort this scumbag out." About time. "We'll take care of this. There shall be a chapel—prepare the resolution! Now, let's have a drop to celebrate: happy International Women's Day— here's to health, strength, and love! Bottoms up!"

Oh God, he's had quite enough already.

Visiting the courthouse is more a matter of pleasure than business. The judge, Yegor Savvich Rukosuyev, is a cheerful man who loves singing and does his job well, with a touch of musicality, presiding over trials smoothly and without interruption. His pace has started to slow a little lately; he's lost his hair and has been traveling into the city for medical tests. *Atrophic cerebral changes*—he showed Ksenia the results of his latest consultation. "Don't tell anyone," she laughed in response, "especially not the lawyers."

If there's something Ksenia regrets in life, it's that she never became a judge. She gets goose bumps at every sentencing: everyone stands, the judge announces the sentence . . . it's a powerful thing. They simply type something out, and then—swish: three, five, ten years.

Today two of her former Tajiks are on trial. She fired them in September, and since then they have been up to no good—or, rather, had been. Theirs is a nation of criminals; the exceptions only prove the rule.

It had been an overcast morning, but now the sun is shining. While walking to the courthouse, Ksenia's mood had been buoyant; Pasha's brandy had done the trick. And lo and behold, here they are: the handsome young Tajiks are standing at the back door. It can't be easy, holding a cigarette in handcuffs. "My, you certainly have lost weight without me," Ksenia thinks, "just look at those hollow cheeks! Oh well, that prison food'll fill you out in no time."

Yegor steps outside, priest-like in his robes.

"Let's get started," he says. They keep things simple here. "Come on guys, *eins-zwei*, into the courtroom." Yegor calls everyone *guys*. But these ones, it would appear, don't speak Russian. "You too, Ksenia Nikolayevna, please step inside."

As usual, Ksenia makes for the back room; the door into the courtroom is left ajar so that she can see and hear everything. The defense attorneys (both assigned to their defendants through article 51 of the Criminal Procedure Code); the public prosecutor; the clerk: it appears that everyone has gathered.

"All rise for the judge," says the clerk, and then, before anyone has even managed to move, "Please be seated!" from Yegor. This man could teach Father Alexander a thing or two; that priest'll drag out any old service for two hours. The case number, article, and the defendants' names—both impossible to pronounce—are read; a junior judicial counselor leads the state prosecution; there are no objections, no requests. The defendants' right not to give evidence against themselves is made clear to them. Then it's time to read the indictment. The prosecutor is told he can do it sitting down.

These two men had stolen a phone from a boy—a local—at the bus station. As far as it is known, several boys had been robbed (and several phones taken), but only one boy had reported it to the police. There had also been three Tajiks, not two: one had gotten away. Nothing in life is as it appears in court; it's less streamlined. That's why Ksenia likes it here—there's no need for any superfluous Tajiks, nor superfluous phones, nor victims, for that matter; the latter couldn't even be talked into taking part in the proceedings.

Yegor nods gently, as though to the beat of some internal music. All Ksenia hears from the lawyers is the odd "Stand," or, "Answer the judge's question." The first Tajik pleads guilty to all charges, the second only to some. The first admits: Yes, he struck the victim; it was also he who went through his pockets.

"With your hands?" asks the prosecutor.

What else could it have been? Does the defendant even understand these questions? Ksenia tries to guess how old he is, whether he would have known life in the Soviet Union. If so, he shouldn't have skipped school; he'd at least know some Russian. What a country they had all shared!

The second Tajik is more confident with his Russian.

"Vitalik and I were sitting, eating some Rolltons—"

"Rollton instant soups," Yegor interrupts. "A message from our advertisers, eh?" He turns towards the open door, behind which he knows Ksenia is sitting.

"That's not what you're on trial for," the man's lawyer steps in. "Did you hit the victim? Threaten him? Who took the phone?"

"I can't say anything about the phone," the defendant states. "I was in an intoxicated state." The lawyer just waves his hand: a *screw this* and a *just do your time* in one.

The interrogation of the witness lasts all of one and a half minutes, the closing statements—two. The court adjourns for deliberation. Now let's try and guess: "One year and three?" asks Ksenia, "That is—three years and one?"

Yegor nods: spot-on; she always gets it right.

Ksenia enters the courtroom. It's the climax of the trial.

"I hereby sentence you to..." *Boom* goes the gavel, and it's done! "Remove the convicted!"

Yegor is a good judge: his sentences are never overturned. Back in his office, he puts his robe into the cupboard, from which he brings out a guitar, glasses, and some brandy.

"Don't dry up, Ksenia! Here, slice yourself some lemon, and then we have pickles, olives, salted fish..."

It's the second day of Lent, but hey, it gives Ksenia something to say at confession.

"Happy Women's Day, Ksenia! Chin chin!"

Yegor has tears in his eyes: alcohol goes straight to his head now. In the good old Soviet days Ksenia and Yegor had been *involved*. Ksenia would hurry here after work, they would lock the door, and Yegor would take her in his arms and whisper sweet nothings in her ear, such as: "Guess who they've got over the barrel now, Ksiusha." Oh, those were the days... He tries to take Ksenia in his arms now; she gently extricates herself.

"And what if I have a... sexual surge?"

A *surge*? Yeah, right. His whole life the judge has only truly loved one woman: Alla Pugacheva, the singer. "For that woman," he has often said, "I could kill an innocent man." What he particularly cherishes in Ksenia is her voice.

"Shall we sing something?"

"What's the hurry?" Ksenia asks. "Later."

Yegor leans back in the sofa, narrows his eyes: "In that case, let's discuss your godly matters.... I get a real kick out of it.... What's all this I hear about bar codes supposedly being the number of the beast?"

News takes a while to reach this town. She starts to explain: Each bar code has three sixes embedded in it, 666. "Here, take this bottle," she says, "see? It's there on every product."

"But why do they need these three sixes—if we can call them that? I'm missing something." Yegor picks up the bottle, starts refilling his glass.

She couldn't say exactly.

"Must be some sort of synchronization..."

"Ha!" the judge chuckles. "But *we* have three sevens to get synchronized! Get it? Our good old Soviet 777 port—that's our synchronization!"

Yegor is a cheerful man; with him the world feels warmer, brighter. And why shouldn't he be cheerful? He has money, and the work he does is interesting, important. Ksenia should have become a lawyer too—it was a mistake to give it up. And she had wanted to give Verochka the right start in life... She remembers the morning she has just had; her spirits darken. She needs to tell Yegor about the teacher: yes, there is an outsider in this, *their* town.

"Yegor, do you remember my Verochka? Someone led her astray—did you know about that?"

Yegor's still in a cheery mood—he's pleased with his port joke.

"The teacher, you mean? Come on, how did he lead her astray? You said it yourself—nothing happened between them."

"Yes, the teacher. Some teaching for you. And what about those Literary Thursdays—that poetry, that prose?"

"Ksiusha, what's all this about? I mean, it's not as though Verochka... Look, sorry, but she was never quite all there. It'd be fine if it was only that wreck of a dad she took pity on—but all the lame ducks of this world? Remember when she brought in that bum off the street?"

"What on earth made you think of that? Verochka was only a child then."

"Drop it with the teacher. It's bad for you—look, you're in pain. Take it easy, Ksiusha. It'll pass; time's a healer."

"No, Yegor—now, you listen to me: We've got an outsider in this town. An enemy—well, maybe not an *enemy*, but he might as well be. Or someone else is taking advantage of the situation: Did you know that teacher of yours is writing something? Would you like to have a read?"

Yegor waves it off: Doesn't he have enough to read?

"Your land has certainly piqued their interest," says Ksenia, as though in passing, by the by; it's quite an art.

Yegor knows how to be serious, if need be.

"What land? Who?"

"Does it matter? There are outsiders in our home, Yegor. Outsiders!"

"Anyone—*anyone*—who threatens our . . . this . . . you know, this . . . sovereignty we have, well, they've got it coming!" He slams his fist on the coffee table. Bang! "You and I, we'll show them how our fathers and grandfathers defended this land. From the Germans! And the French!" And, after a moment's thought, "And the Poles!"

He's gone all red, his bald head especially.

"Yegorushka, will you back me up?"

She needn't have asked.

And breathe. Ksenia has said what she needed to say, and she feels all the better for it. She gestures to Yegor: get the guitar, let's sing. She lifts her hand and undoes her bun. Her hair is long, chestnut brown. One more drink.

"Let's sing some Pugacheva," Yegor says, "that 'What's Become of Them' song . . ."

Ksenia smiles: she knows how hopeless Yegor is with song titles. He plays the opening, and then, "Oh, how many have we lost, lost to that distant abyss?" Her voice is high-pitched, clear—how well she sings!

At the end of the song, the judge caresses the guitar strings with his thumb, forlorn. He has also started to reflect upon death. He is confused: two little yellow birds had flown into his house that morning. A bad omen: death. Ksenia comforts him.

"Yellow birds? Oh, that's nothing to worry about; that means money."

Ksenia is a believer; these things are easier for her. Yet the church doesn't appeal to Yegor, no.

"What were we brought up to believe?" he asks. "That after death, that's it. Nothing. But now...now even our leaders are...holding candles, crossing themselves. Mind you, they still don't bow when they pray—nothing'll bring those guys to their knees...but anyway, you: What is it that you ask God for?"

These are not the conversations to be had with brandy. Ksenia asks for whatever she is supposed to ask for. Whatever those high-ranking saints asked for.

"But say we knew God existed," Yegor persists, "what would you ask him for?"

She reflects. "Well, there's no bringing Verochka back, nor our country.... So I'd probably just ask him to knock twenty, thirty years off my age." She smiles. "Oh, go on, another toast: to all the good things."

They have been sitting here a long time. Outside it's probably dark by now.

"Here, look," Yegor rifles through his briefcase for a sheet of paper. "I found a poem. A knockout: 'No man is born immortal, but there's no solace in this truth / the one most feared of all—death nears me with its noose...' Just gets to the heart of it all." He can't be bothered to find his glasses, tries to do the rest from memory, "'Life is but an instant, nothingness is lasting / Something something something, people keep on passing.' It's as though our man saw what was coming."

Ksenia is confused. Whose poem was that—Yegor's?

"No, you'll never guess. Yuri Andropov. Yes, former general secretary Yuri Andropov—can you believe it? Writes better than any of those so-called...'The living born in darkness walk unwavering to dawn / Future generations will carry our torch on.'"

Future generations—isn't that just great.

"But Yegor, you have children, grandchildren, you've done everything right..." Ksenia is weeping; the alcohol is getting the better of her. The tears flow freely. That's what happens when you drink during Lent.

A knock. Ksenia wipes away her tears. What in God's name is *he* doing here? Isaikin! He's dripping in sweat, panting:

"So you've heard?"

"What—heard what? Who let you in here anyway? Well?"

A disaster: a murder. Pasha Tsytsyn is dead. Happened just now. But there's more. It happened in her pelmennaya.

Terrorists! Why wasn't she told immediately? Isaikin himself had only just heard.

"The idiot! What was Pasha doing *there*? But Isaikin, you're not drunk, are you? Fine, you run on ahead, we'll catch up—no wait, hold on!"

Yegor is phoning someone. Come on, come on! It's a long way, and Yegor couldn't possibly run there; he can hardly manage a brisk walk.

"And you said those birds meant money," he mutters to Ksenia.

They had seen the scenes of terrorism before on TV—bombs, body parts—yet around the pelmennaya it is, one could say, very calm. Theirs is a quiet community; in the evenings everyone stays in. The ambulance has already left. The police officers and the public prosecutor are inside the pelmennaya; none of them looks at Ksenia. Where did it happen? In the kitchen? What was Pasha doing in the kitchen? Oh, there's the blood. Dear God, how awful. And how? Oh yes, a knife. But all this cigarette smoke, it's everywhere!

"Gentlemen, please smoke outside." Ksenia has to get the situation under control.

And Roxana? Where's Roxana?

"Who?" asks the police chief, a tubby colonel. "Ibragimova? In our holding cell, of course. She'll be sent into the city tomorrow."

"What? It was *her*? Oh God!" Ksenia is about to scream, but suddenly stops. Now it all makes sense. Pasha had tried to *seduce* the girl. And *Roxana*! What action—talk about taking the bull by the horns!

"Yegorushka, my dear, what do they mean, what's all this talk about the city? Surely this is an article 105.1. She should be put on trial here, by you."

"Those fucking Tajiks of yours have certainly been hard at it today," the judge muses. "Look, this is the head of local government we're talking about, not some damned rabbit. There'll be press—more besides. Want a bit of excitement in your life? Fine. Me? No."

"Yawn at me one more time, and I'll..." That's what Ksenia wants to say.

"We're going to say this was an article 105.2," Yegor continues, reciting the code, *"Murder, committed with especial cruelty,* for one, and—you never know—*committed by reason of national, racial, or religious hatred*...there's two. They come down hard on that nowadays."

"Next you'll be telling me it was in connection with Pasha *discharging his public duties,*" says Ksenia, icily.

"It's a 105.2. She's going into the city. She'll get between eight and twenty...well, twenty isn't really twenty; she could get out after ten."

Ksenia Nikolayevna's nerves aren't made of steel.

"Excuse me, Yegorushka, but are we talking about the same Pasha here? I'm sorry, but is she really going to get ten years for killing Pasha Tsytsyn, that nothing of a man? Have you no shame, Yegorushka? I could find you a hundred other Pashas by tomorrow. I know you were Pasha's friend, of course you were, but come on, the man's only conscience was his dick!" And then, to the police officer, "Show me what you've got written there, you Sherlock fucking Holmes! Stay out of this, Yegor!" And then, reading aloud, "What? *An altercation*—ugh, learn to spell!—*caused by sudden hostilities*? Bullshit. Here's what it should say: an attempted rape." She rubs her hand, now pulsating so intensely that it feels as though the skin is about to give way, burst. "And where's Roxana's signature? Nowhere! None of this will hold up in court! You need to take this all, and go shove it where—"

"Excuse me, Ksenia Nikolayevna," the police officer interrupts, clearly offended, "you are, one might say, a respected figure..."

Her hysterics bring Yegor back to his senses. He reaches for his phone again.

"We have a situation here!" he shouts down the line, "No, why did...just send us back...more...your—damn—medicine!"

It's unpleasant, of course, stressful. Everything around them is covered in Pasha's blood. Ksenia almost faints. So she's weaker than these men after all—at least in one respect. They drag her to the door, throw water over her, give her something to sniff. She hears Yegor's voice nearby.

"In our experience," he declares, "for it to be someone's first time and—with a knife, that's rare. With an ax, maybe, but a knife . . . it's hard to stab someone to death. There's a certain amount of . . . Have you ever cut a pig's throat?"

More voices.

"But was the girl pretty?"

"What do you mean, pretty? They all look the fucking same."

"Pasha must've thought he had a hold on God's own balls—he was heading for the big city."

"That's still where he's heading—only feet first . . ."

"Well, I guess. Pasha sure got himself into one fucker of a mess." Yegor concludes. "Has anyone told his family?"

It's fine, Ksenia's fine. The investigators have taken everything they need from the pelmennaya, now she can clean. Her old ladies will do it. Yegor walks her to her door:

"Another few shots, in memory of Pasha?"

"Yes, but right now leave me alone. You too, Isaikin—stop fussing."

Ksenia doesn't fall asleep, but she goes under, somehow. Around forty minutes later she suddenly comes back to her senses, leaps up, grabs a giant bag, and throws some apples, yogurts, and cooked sausage into it from the fridge. She opens the door to Verochka's bedroom, a room she rarely sets foot in, throws open the cupboard, and dumps some clothes and boots into the bag, even underwear: they're close enough in size. God, what's happening? Just when you start to feel close to someone . . .

Ksenia reaches the police station. Is the colonel in his office?

"Where else would he be, Ksenia Nikolayevna, after such events?" The guard lets her in, of course—how could he turn away a woman like her?

"Just let me check in on our little offender first," he says, looking through the peephole into Roxana's cell. He lets Ksenia look, too. "Sleeping like a log," he tells her. "Unbelievable."

Roxana is alone in the cell. And it's true—she's asleep. She's lying on her back, her breath calm and even, and in sleep she looks even lovelier than usual.

Once *that creature* had thudded to the floor and finally gone quiet, she had waited for her rage to subside and her breathing to return to normal before washing everything off at the hand basin in the restroom—the place she always washed. It was, perhaps, inadvisable to destroy all evidence of contact with the rapist—she realized this herself—but she simply couldn't suppress her desire to be clean. She put her ripped tights and smock into a paper bag and slipped the knife inside too, sheathed in the pages of a magazine. She then put on her only dress and coat, tied her scarf around her neck, gathered some books—her only possessions—from the storeroom, locked the door, and set off towards the police station. And yes, before leaving she also turned off the lights. Her sangfroid would later be used against her, as evidence that she had either invented the signs of the victim's attention to her or exaggerated their seriousness.

At the station she tells the desk sergeant that approximately one hour earlier she killed a middle-aged man during an attempted rape. She produces the contents of the package and hands over the keys to the pelmennaya.

She watches as the commotion spreads through the station, sees the police officers run downstairs and their car drive off towards the scene. They lead her up to the first floor and tell her to sit down at a table. A young officer sits down opposite her. He is in an amiable mood:

"You may call your lawyer."

She doesn't have one yet.

"That was a joke." He had been joking: How could someone like her afford a lawyer?

Ibragimova, Ruhshona Ibragimovna, born 1971, a citizen of Tajikistan. Place of birth: Leninabad, now Khujand. Education: university degree.

The officer breaks away from the protocol. Yes, she's a graduate. Literature, Moscow State University. The officer is clearly amazed; he himself has probably only scraped through two years of correspondence courses in law.

She knows article 51 of the Constitution: "no one shall be obliged to give incriminating evidence," etc.

"Have you been detained before?"

"No, this is the first time."

So how does she know that? She shrugs: she read it.

"The Constitution?" Well, well, well.

He asks her to take him through what happened. His tone is compassionate; if the facts all tally with her statement, he'll take her evidence and release her on bail.

Had she seen the man before? Yes, she had; he would pop by the house to see her boss. She doesn't know his name. Today he arrived at the pelmennaya at about six p.m. and asked for Ksenia Nikolayevna. When he heard she wasn't in, he bought a large beer. Besides them, there was no one there. After draining his beer, he proposed . . . physical intimacy; she rejected him. Yes, the rejection was firm, but it wasn't offensive—she hardly said a thing.

"'Cause there are these types of rejections," the officer explains, "that seem like a rejection, but then . . . you know . . . Women like strength in a man."

She looks at him fixedly. Yes, she likes strength, but *that*—that was not strength. The officer, it seems, doesn't quite understand.

"Anyway, that's beside the point. Let's go on."

When the man stood up and walked towards her, she went into the kitchen. Why? It was her instinct—she hadn't planned it. Where the knife had been—yes, that she remembers, but as for how many times she stabbed him, or where—nothing. Had she wanted to kill him? She had wanted him gone—one way or another.

One more question: With an education like hers, why does she work as a waitress? Ruhshona doesn't see what that has to do with anything. Fine. In the past has she had any jobs more in line with her qualifications? Yes, she taught Russian literature at a university in Khujand, but only for a while.

"But who needs Russian literature there?" the officer asks, puzzled, "They're all..." He had wanted to say *Asiatics*.

No one needs it—Ruhshona couldn't agree more. Totally useless.

Where else? In Moscow, teaching the children of the rich: Russian language, literature, and English. If that could be considered more in line with her qualifications. Why had she gone into unskilled work? She had had her reasons.

"Did you want to feel closer to your people—your *sisters by blood*?" he asks.

"Exactly," Ruhshona replies. "Closer to my sisters. And my brethren."

"*Brothers*. My sisters and *brothers*," the officer corrects her. Hah. A lit graduate—as if.

The desk sergeant hurries into the room, asks the officer to step outside. He returns a minute later. Things are not as simple as they had first appeared. Had she known the deceased was Pavel Andreyevich Tsytsyn, head of local government? No, but she doesn't see why that should change anything—he was still a common rapist. This wasn't murder; it was self-defense.

"A very effective self-defense," the officer smirks. Six knife wounds: to the stomach, the face, the groin. As for her? Not a scratch.

Does she regret her deed? Stupid question—she had had no choice. In the kitchen things had escalated by themselves.

"And you couldn't find a more amicable solution?" The officer's tone has suddenly changed. He fixes his eyes upon hers. This, he has seen, is what his superiors do in their interrogations.

Ruhshona's eyes are black—like the rest of her people's—and if she looks inwardly with them, you won't catch anything. But then the shutters in her eyes click open, and her eyes blaze for a moment, like a cigarette lighter, then close again, the flame extinguished. For a moment, the young officer feels uneasy. "Come on. Just stay calm.

Fill out the report, then get down to the pelmennaya," he thinks. This whole thing is making his head spin—best leave it to the police in the city to deal with. *An al-ter-ca-tion caused by sud-den hos-til-it-ies*, he concludes, his tongue stuck out in concentration as he writes. He speeds through the final declaration like a tongue twister: "*I hereby attest that this statement is a full, truthful, and accurate account of my testimony*. Sign."

No, she isn't going to sign that.

"Want me to correct your spelling mistakes?" Now she's the one joking.

They take her into the cell and lock the door. She looks around, figures out which way Mecca is, and waits for the silence to take root within her. Then she prays, soundlessly.

"*Allahu Akbar. Subhaanak-Allaahumma, wa bihamdik...*"

What do today's events mean? She must delve deep within herself and wait; the answer will come, as it always does, complete. Or not; her internal silences can last years. In which case: humble acceptance of all that He has willed, and thanks. For now, she's just exhausted, bewildered: Why had it fallen to *her* to put an end to that odiousness? And proud, too: proud that she rose to the challenge; that she has overcome.

The Most High had given Ruhshona endurance, freedom of thought, and an unusually good memory. One more virtue: the ability to face danger head-on. This has been clear to everyone since Ruhshona's childhood; if you ever tried to scare her, she wouldn't flinch—quite the opposite—she would lunge forwards, right at you. She staunchly protected her personal space, and when anyone invaded it, she could do serious damage. And for that reason, everyone—children and adults alike—gave her a wide berth. The Most High had also endowed her with the beauty of the woman she was named after—Ruhshona/Roxana, wife of Alexander the Great. Tajik women are often considered elderly at thirty-five, but Ruhshona is still very beautiful.

As a teenager, Ruhshona studies at a Russian school. It is here that she writes such wonderful pieces of work that she is awarded a gold medal of excellence. "Dostoyevsky's Nikolai Stavrogin is a Russian Hamlet, with the same rage, ennui, and masses of pent-up energy." This essay impresses; she is offered a place at Moscow State University. Here, she also lives at a distance from others, and she discovers the works of Andrei Platonov: dreams of a fierce and beautiful world; being overwhelmed with joy at the sight of a locomotive; overcoming death itself through machines. She writes her dissertation on Platonov, on his castles in the air. It's this very thing that Ruhshona values above all else in Russians and in the Russian language, her mother tongue: the ability to erect constructs out of nothing.

And then great change: her Leninabad returns to its former name of Khujand; every other change is for the worse. Her father is killed, a chance victim of fighting in the region: he had gone to Dushanbe on business and never returned; Ruhshona can't get home for his funeral; her brother calls her in Moscow to tell her about other deaths. It's as though the sheer number of victims helps him come to terms with his father's loss. "Stay in Moscow!" he shouts over the line—the connection with Tajikistan is awful. What can she do in Moscow? There's no need for specialists in literature here either. "I lost my father in the process of life," Ruhshona thinks to herself, and in contemplating that phrase—so typically Platonov—she decides that she no longer loves his work; that overcoming death through locomotives and other machinery is simply a philological pursuit: death's omnipresence is no accident, no unhappy mistake. Everyone fears death, just as they fear misfortune, yet death is inescapable, which means it is real. And that we did not invent it. At this very moment Ruhshona begins to see death as the most important thing that can exist within a person. She views those who don't carry death within themselves—who don't live by it—as empty, like wrapping paper, like candy wrappers. Hollow, soulless people. She can pick them out at a glance.

The short-lived enthusiasm brought on by the changes passes Ruhshona by: she can see that these changes are spiritually unsustainable, and that everyone is now ruled by hollow men, by candy wrappers. A giant chocolate bar has appeared on the facade of the capital's most important library: *a sweet treat a day helps you work, rest, and play*. These chocolate bars and their giant posters are the main by-product of these hollow men and the way they run the country. "We all want something sweet and tasty," as Anna Karenina says. "Well, Mother Russia, you'll get your fill of sweets, but it'll make flunkies of your children," thinks Ruhshona, and leaves Moscow.

Her road eventually leads her back to Khujand, with a knowledge of Russian literature apparently unsurpassed by any of her compatriots. She could have applied to the Institute of Education—now a *university*—but they don't pay; they don't pay anywhere, and there is no demand for her private lessons. It isn't the time for literature; there's a war going on; one hundred thousand dead in 1992—the previous year—alone. The opposing sides are known as the Vovchiki and the Yurchiki, "The Yurchiki are the communists," her mother explains, "named after Yuri Andropov, would you believe? Their support comes from the Kulob region, from here in the North, and from the Uzbeks and the Russians. The Vovchiki are from the Pamir Mountains and the Gharm Valley, led by democrat reformists."

"But why such a Russian name—isn't it the communists who should be the Vovchiki?" Ruhshona asks.

"No, it's not Vovchik as in Vladimir. They're Wahhabites—some-how they got Vovchiki from that." Her mother is clearly confused. "And we still haven't found a husband for you," she adds. So that's what she's really worried about: Ruhshona is already twenty-two.

The task of finding a suitor would normally have fallen to her father or her brother, but her father is dead, and her brother will be moving to China any day now. He has his own family to think of. Besides, how could he find her an Alexander with no one around but Vovchiki-Yurchiki?

And soon enough there won't even be any Vovchiki left—at least that's how it seems. Ruhshona's sympathies, if she had to choose, would lie with the Vovchiki: partly because they are Pushkin's *blessed, fallen in battle*—virtually decimated during a false cease-fire—and partly because there aren't any of them in Khujand anyway. Ruhshona begins searching for something, and she searches for it in religion, something she seems to have been born with, but had not previously given much thought. She travels to Gharm, to Samarkand. She picks up Arabic easily, but her encounters with those who describe themselves as Muslims disappoint: with them, the tribal takes precedence over the spiritual; they give their *Adat*—their traditional customs, the laws of man—precedence over the laws of God, Sharia. She wants to tell people that life should be lived as prescribed, in accordance with the laws laid out by the Most High, not with tradition; sin and crime are one and the same thing. However, jihad has freed the Vovchiki from their laws. And besides, who wants to listen to a woman?

Her brother sends what he can to her and her mother, but they still go hungry. Ruhshona despises the idea of economic migration, but when your mother has nothing to eat, migration is no longer a question of economics. So to Moscow again, this time without excitement, nor any great hope. There she hardens, tires, for ten years—well-fed ones, admittedly. She is placed with families, works with their simpleminded children for two, three, four years at a time, and then moves on to the next, neither bad nor good, normal, nondescript. The only time she has to herself is when the children are in school, and even then their mothers, who don't work, fuss about day in, day out, keeping their Roxanochka busy. She even stops learning Arabic. These are apathetic, listless years, but they must have been necessary, somehow.

Her most recent employers are a small, stocky, smiley man and his endlessly panic-stricken wife, who has no tolerance for hearing about illness, death, or other unpleasantness, as though they are contagious. The TV is constantly on: *For strong, healthy-looking hair and nails.* "Insomnia. Homer. Taut white sails[6]...," Ruhshona wants to retort, but she knows that she won't find a kindred spirit here—no one will know the poem. Ruhshona's memory still retains hundreds of Russian poems—but for what? The poets who wrote them now seem to her like distant relatives, ones she had ceased to love long before their deaths. "Poor poets," she thinks, "life didn't go your way."

The child she is looking after is told lies—constant lies—by his parents, even though he no longer asks any questions. "The meaning of life," his father teaches him, "lies in life itself," citing one of those much-revered Frenchies as proof. He's proud he stopped being self-conscious about his small stature. When was that? When he got rich. "So you never actually came to terms with it," Ruhshona thinks, without pity. "You spend your life giving orders like a little lord, but you have no real power over your own life: you're a freeloader. A couple of quotes; that's all your universe is built on."

And then, the summer before these events, this family brings her to their dacha, one not on the outskirts of Moscow—like her other families' were—but in the very depths of Russia. It is here that Ruhshona learns that her mother has moved in with her brother; her mother's apartment has been sold, and Ruhshona now has nowhere to return to, and no reason to return. Day in, day out, she sees the cool sky, the river, the sunset, and suddenly she understands: life is such a simple and austere thing. And all of these little decorations, this tinsel we wrap our lives in—music, philosophy, literature—are completely unnecessary. There is some form of truth to them, in parts, but they themselves are not the truth. The truth can be put very simply.

On the one hand, there is the Most High: the First, the Everlasting, the All-Merciful, Giver of Life and Bringer of Death—Ruhshona knows all ninety-nine of His names. He is supreme, unknowable, master of all thoughts. And on the other hand there we are: insignificant. There are many of us, and we are capable almost exclusively of ill. The gulf between Him and us is boundless: we are, by far, closer to ashes, to the dust underfoot, for we are mere creations. *He* is *One. He* is *Allah, the Eternal Refuge. He neither begets nor is begotten. And no one is equal to Him.*

Ruhshona speaks to her boss, gathers her things, and moves to the pelmennaya. Her *brothers by blood*, the other Tajiks, waste no time in stealing all the money she has saved, but she discovers this only much later—money no longer means anything to her. Physical work awaits her here, as does silence—and the daily, hourly attempts to divine His will. The name of Ruhshona's faith, translated from Arabic, means *submission.*

She is woken by the door. "Hello, Ksenia Nikolayevna." She knew it—knew that Ksenia would come. Ksenia is not like the others: unlike the dacha owners, those guys from the gas station, that lowlife that got himself cut down today, she isn't empty inside. She is a flawed creature, yes, and strange, but . . . here she is.

And so their meeting begins: Ksenia falls to her knees and, arms outstretched, she tries to hug Ruhshona.

"We can do without the Dostoyevskian dramatics. Stand up please, Ksenia Nikolayevna. Here, get up—wait, are you sloshed?"

Lord, what a miracle—the girl has spoken! Must be the shock.

"Don't stop, keep talking," Ksenia encourages her. "Look, I've brought you something to eat. And your Russian—you actually talk well!"

"Thank you. Russian's my native language." Ruhshona scans the contents of the bag. "Thank you for the clothes, too. I don't eat sausages."

"So what should I do with it?"

"I don't know, give it to your husband."

"Did Isaikin also try to *seduce* you?" Ksenia suddenly thinks to herself, "That man also deserves a . . ."

"But it's Lent," she says to Ruhshona.

Ruhshona shrugs: So what? Ksenia can give it to her workers.

"I don't reckon they'd eat it either."

"I reckon they would. What do fools know about laws? They . . . they'd eat anything, Ksenia Nikolayevna."

What sort of law is that anyway?

"Roxana, dear Roxanochka, please, let's drop all these formalities—just call me Ksenia. We aren't such strangers now, are we?"

Ksenia wants to be like Roxana, to be on the same level as her. But is such a thing possible? She feels stupid and old next to this Roxana, this child so suddenly all grown up: Roxana's *act* has raised her so impossibly high, taken her so close to the secrets of the world! Ksenia had always been cunning and quick thinking, had always sought out little opportunities here and there, taking baby steps, bit by bit, negotiating with these ... but Roxana: one act—done. And all on her own. Justice and punishment—all taken into her own hands.

"I was only the weapon," Ruhshona protests, "just the sword. The justice is His doing."

Ksenia somehow hadn't noticed *Him*—a glance to the ceiling—ever getting involved in anything, taking even the slightest interest in human affairs.

"But enough of that—everyone has his own beliefs. Let's discuss practical matters."

"Oh? So what are *your* beliefs?"

Ksenia tries to explain, but can't quite unravel her thoughts—in reality, she's still slightly drunk. "Orthodox Christianity, our national beliefs ... We honor holy men, the saints ... observe different holy days ..."

Ruhshona's eyes are suddenly ablaze. Oh yes, their national beliefs! But what does *Ksenia* believe in? Saint Nicholas the Wonderworker? The Tsar Redeemer? International Women's Day? Or everything—all at once?

"It's all idolatry, *shirk*!"

The look she gives Ksenia is impossible to bear. There's no need to look at her *like that*. It's not as though Ksenia invented all of this—she asks for the church's blessings for everything.

"Oh yes," Ruhshona waves her off: *we know this system*. "And do your priests ever refuse you their blessings? It's all idolatry, *shirk*! *All things are lawful unto me, but all things are not expedient.* How can you act under precepts like that? I once saw a man chase his mother through the streets with an ax. Wearing nothing—nothing but a crucifix dangling from his neck."

Ksenia pictures the scene, smiles involuntarily.

"It's true," she acknowledges with sadness, "such things do happen."

Ruhshona shifts forwards to the edge of her bunk. "*And the truth will set you free.* But free from what? Freedom—what is freedom? Self-will? Lawlessness? Or is it your freedom to self-govern? No, we don't have freedom. But we do have a mission, a purpose. And it's our job to discover that purpose."

"And what, you've done that?"

"Yes," Ruhshona replies. "I know why I was put on this earth and what awaits me after death. None of that in *my Father's house are many mansions*. There are two: heaven and hell."

This isn't like anything you'll get from a priest, from Alexander the Third; Roxana has answers—and what answers! But this is all still abstract, all philosophy; answers are a dime a dozen. Ksenia must gather her strength, ask for more.

She tells her about her daughter, Verochka. She was a good girl. She had felt for Ksenia's workers—pitied them.

"We aren't dogs or little pussycats to be pitied," Ruhshona retorts. "Workers just need to be paid. So, this Verochka of yours? I suppose she loved books?"

"She loved books. Never listened to her mother. She was a beautiful girl. And she finished high school. I wanted to give her a real profession, but she read too much, and listened too much to . . . men who thought they knew better, and she left me. Decided to become a writer, or, I don't know, a scholar, a literary expert . . . and she left, and then she died. She never did anyone any harm. So why . . . why did He . . . take her?"

These last words are pronounced in almost a whisper, but Ksenia sheds no tears. She is watching Ruhshona intently. Ruhshona looks away, then turns her eyes back on Ksenia.

"For her willfulness. Any sin can be forgiven—any sin—but the punishment for rebelliousness, for willfulness, is death. And hell."

That was the first and last truth said about Verochka. Ksenia remembers her own words, "there is such a thing as *having to*, Verochka," and Verochka's reply, "But is there such a thing as *unwanting*?" And that laugh. Ksenia can hear Verochka's laughter right now. Still, she pities Verochka; just thinking about her wrenches her apart.

"It's a pity, in human terms—yes," Ruhshona says, "but for God, disobedience must lead to retribution. And—like a finger in a socket— the outcome is death. And there's no praying someone else out of hell, because everyone must answer for his own actions—on his own." Ruhshona speaks confidently and to the point; it's how people speak when they know the truth. "The punishment for willfulness is death. Weep about it if you like, but the message is clear as day."

The women are sitting on opposite bunks, food spread out between them, as though on a train, as though they were setting off on a journey.

"And the USSR?"

The USSR is a big topic; Ruhshona has stories to tell. Oh yes, recent history has taken its shots at her: Moscow, Tajikistan, war.

"So dangerous," Ksenia gasps.

"I wasn't afraid. No, never."

Ksenia has never trusted anyone as she trusts Ruhshona now. "How could such a country as ours fall apart?"

"We looked to the West. The *sly West*. We betrayed our true purpose."

How to put it—how to explain it to Ksenia? "Did you ever read Blok's *Retribution*? 'But the one who moved, governing / The puppets of every state / Worked knowingly, sending forth / A humanitarian haze . . .'"[7] Surely she doesn't want her to recite the whole thing?

"Why not? We're not in any hurry."

Ruhshona shakes her head. "No. It's not about time. It's that the truth can't be found in poetry."

"Well, that goes without saying. But does it even exist—is there such a thing as truth?"

"Yes," Ruhshona replies, "there is. It exists, and its name is short and simple."

"So say it!"

Ruhshona tilts her head slightly and looks Ksenia straight in the eyes, the sort of look you can't turn away from. She whispers, almost inaudibly: "Islam."

"Islam . . ." Ksenia repeats, enthralled. "But is it hard . . . to be . . . ?"

"Muslim?" Ruhshona stands up, walks around the cell. "It's hard, but doable. Not impossible. You pray five times a day, short prayers; you fast one month a year; you give to charity—not so much, a fortieth of your income; and at least once in your life, if you can, you make the pilgrimage—hajj. Those are the pillars of the faith. Nothing more is demanded of us, except, as the Prophet says, what is *voluntary*. You don't have to give away any property, nor offer up your cheek. Just submit to the Most High."

"And love your neighbor?"

"Sure, why not—if you love him. Voluntarily."

"And if your neighbor is your enemy?"

"There is absolutely no reason to love your enemies. To love your enemies goes against nature. Islam forbids everything that goes against nature. Who loves their enemies? No one."

"How does someone become Muslim?" Ksenia asks—almost playfully, as though out of general curiosity. But she is scratching away at the mole on her hand.

There can be no flirting with the Most High. Only honesty: complete honesty.

"You have to declare in front of two witnesses, 'there is no god but God. Muhammad is the messenger of God.' That's it. It's called the *Shahada*—a symbol of our faith."

Ksenia has heard the word before, somewhere—on TV.

"*Laa ilaaha illaa-llaah . . .*" Ruhshona recites with a lilt. It's unusual, beautiful. "Don't believe what you hear on TV, Ksenia. Especially when it comes to Muslims."

Ksenia turns towards the door—surely not for a second witness? Ruhshona hadn't expected such speed—these people are so impulsive!

"Stop," she commands, "you need to sober up first. And from now on, no more alcohol. Nor pork—it's an abomination."

"Of course," Ksenia nods, "I won't eat it, and I'll take it off the menu."

"And pay your workers."

"Yes, of course, I'm ashamed of myself. What else?"

What else indeed? The thing is, Ksenia has power over people—that doesn't just happen by chance. The issue of power is a key one—one with great spiritual significance. Politics, life, faith—all should be as one.

"Whoever takes power and retains it has been selected by Him; that person has been chosen," Ruhshona advises. "You must take action—yourself, not through those husks of men, those candy wrappers. Take the power—take it all."

"I had already had the same thought," Ksenia admits, "but how can I? It's a matter of who people choose..."

Are they to have more local self-government, more Yurchiki? What place can He have in any of that? No, that can't happen. *He* must govern them all—and He must do it through her, through Ksenia.

This clearly cheers Ksenia up: oh yes, she will do much good for the people. There isn't even a mosque in town...

"A mosque isn't the be-all and end-all," Ruhshona interrupts. "That isn't where I would start."

Why on earth not?

"Trust me, Roxanochka, I know these things better. We'll build a mosque," Ksenia asserts, "right in the center of town. And people will flock to it—we get so many of those Asiatics coming here..."

There is a plot of land; there is a plan. Discussing building projects feels normal, easy. They may not have any designs yet, but they'll get it done. There *will* be a mosque. There will be somewhere for Roxana to pray when she gets out. Ksenia suddenly stops short—as though throughout all of these conversations she had forgotten their current situation.

"But will you come back?" Her whole life hangs on the answer to this question. "Live with me—on equal terms this time. I'm getting old, why should I have a house like that all to myself?"

Ruhshona shrugs: How could she ever come back here, after what happened today? No matter how the investigation and the trial end, she'll still be thrown out, deported.

No, no, Ksenia will adopt her. Roxana will be her little girl, her daughter.

"Me? An adult? Nonsense. Besides, my mother's still alive."

All they need is a competent lawyer. Ksenia repeats: If Roxana just comes back to her, she'll give her everything. And she'll get her a lawyer—the very best. Just come back!

Does Ruhshona really need Ksenia's everything? For what seems like the first time in this conversation, Ruhshona takes a moment to think. Perhaps her purpose in life is to help unhappy middle-aged women discover the true faith, the one God—and to do it there, where she will soon be sent. That's it—that's why today's events had to happen! Ruhshona can already see the columns of women—sinful, lost women, Russian and otherwise—she can see their identical dark blue quilted jackets, their grey prison headscarves... She, Ruhshona, will bring them the truth. She will show them the way.

"I don't need the very best," she says. "Let's keep things simple. Or go without. Don't waste your money on a lawyer, Ksenia."

"But why not?"

"It's not for me to decide. One day you'll understand. But I'm tired now. Please go."

Ksenia looks at her watch: oh yes, the time... it has been a tough day. "Let Roxana rest," she thinks: tomorrow she'll be heading for the city. Perhaps by morning she will have changed her mind—about the lawyer, that is. Ksenia tries to glean something—anything—more from Ruhshona's facial expressions. But there is nothing to be read there, only utter exhaustion. Yes, it's time. But if only she could know when they would next...

They say their goodbyes.

"Allah is merciful," says Ruhshona, guessing Ksenia's thoughts. "We will meet again."

Ksenia clasps Ruhshona in her arms, though she only comes up to her chest. She presses her head against Ruhshona, hugs her, holds her tightly, not wanting to let go.

"Say something."

"Allah is merciful," Ruhshona repeats, then knocks on the door to call the officer. "Please go."

"Happy International Women's Day, Ksenia Nikolayevna," the officer says with a nod before locking the door behind her. Ksenia looks at him in bewilderment, as though she didn't understand.

She steps out into the fresh air, breathes it in deeply, then takes a walk through this dark town, *her* town. The people are sleeping and she's awake, but that's fine, these people have been entrusted to her. Now she knows—knows Who has entrusted them to her, and why. She sees her house, and can clearly picture a big, beautiful minaret behind it, the tallest tower for many kilometers around.

Through the dead of night Ksenia sits in the clean, empty pelmennaya, smiling to herself and eating cold cuts. Her mind is occupied with the burning issues: finding a lawyer and contacts in the city, organizing the building project, consolidating her own power in the town. She is calm. She can handle this; she can handle everything.

Her drunkenness has passed, as has her tiredness, although this has all been rather a lot for her, at her age, to absorb in one day.

"You aren't getting kicked out of anywhere," she whispers to herself, "my girl, my daughter. You'll stay with me. The officials in the city are only human, after all, it'll all work out. We'll get rid of our local monsters, and then we'll take things in hand here in town. We'll live by the law, by Truth. We'll work; we'll do it all together. We'll get everyone working, from sixteen—no—thirteen years of age. To hell with all those intellectuals and priests, those wimps and weaklings—to hell with them! I'll drink to that!" Ksenia stops short, realizing what she has said. It seems absurd: "Am I to give up drinking straightaway?" she thinks. "No, I'll drink," she decides, "but only on holidays. The big, real, important holidays."

She dwells in these thoughts for a long time: until the cock crows—a herald, one might say, of her new, all-encompassing knowledge. Then she goes to bed.

The day's events had passed the schoolteacher by. He had taught four classes—one of which was a double—and then had some tea and cake in the staff room to celebrate Women's Day, a meaningless event, but a good-hearted one, generally speaking. And then he had set off towards the river, to see whether the ice had melted yet.

By the river he runs into Father Alexander, who has come for the same reason; both gaze, smiling, at the sun. No, the river is still covered in ice. The teacher doesn't know Father Alexander very well, and it is only now that he notices the priest's beaten, pained look. He has probably been unfair to the man.

"Say," the priest suddenly asks, "I wonder why the river doesn't freeze through completely?"

The teacher explains: Unlike other substances, water is at its most dense not at the point of freezing—zero degrees—but at plus four, so the water that does reach the freezing point will always be on top. That forms ice, but what's below remains liquid. It really is a wonder—if not for this, the rivers would freeze through, killing all the life they hold.

The priest gently nods his head, "Yes, a wonder indeed—more proof of God's existence." The river, the sky, the sun: these will remain, but all the rest will pass, ground down in the millstones of time—this is what the priest seems to be thinking.

When it's so sunny outside it's a shame to sit indoors, so the teacher decides to linger for a while in town. He is standing outside the new hairdresser's, and he sees one of his former pupils through the window. She waves to him. Well, why not? He hasn't had a haircut in a long time. She washes his hair; the warm touch of her fingers feels pleasant against his skin. My goodness, two children! She gave up on her studies, of course—they never really taught them anything there anyway. She's not a beautiful woman, but she is kind—best not to ask about a husband unless she mentions him herself. How deft she is with a pair of scissors! And does he remember Dmitry Chubkin? No? Dmitry was her former classmate; now she's Mrs. Chubkina—how could he have forgotten?

"You know, Sergey Sergeyevich, your literary evenings, those were the best things we ever had," she says. "*When you are unwell and browbeaten . . .* how does it go?"

"Worn down," the teacher corrects her, "*When you are worn down and browbeaten,*" filling in a few more lines, then internally reciting the entire epilogue of Blok's *Retribution* to himself. She sweeps up all the hair on the floor, and he looks at it, and at her, and thinks:

Blok had thought it impossible that an educated person could go through life without reading Ibsen's *Brand*; and here he is—a teacher of literature—and he hasn't read it. What does he even know of Ibsen's work? Only what Blok quoted elsewhere: "Youth is retribution." Retribution? Against whom? The parents? Or even: ourselves?

He goes home and eats, so ridiculously absorbed in Ibsen that half an hour later he couldn't remember whether he had eaten at all. It has been a happy day, one without the hint of a shadow, almost dull. In the evening he hears noises outside, but he pays them no attention. He lies down in bed and starts formulating the end of his confession.

It's time for me to figure out what I believe, and why, despite everything, I remain improbably, wildly happy. Why do I sometimes wake up with that special feeling, like in my childhood, that this is heaven, right here? There is ground beneath me, and sky above me, and there, within reach, there is the river, the trees, the little carvings on window frames, the muddy roads of spring, the cry of domestic fowl, and then, even closer—Lermontov, Blok. Do I, finally, believe in God?

The main barrier between Him and me is Verochka. Verochka's death was unnecessary; death shouldn't exist at all. Viewing death as some sort of meeting place, awaiting it like a lover—no, that doesn't work. So must I then make peace with it, pretend I'm used to the idea? The conditions of this peace are too much for me to bear: go on, sign the surrender. Some say that God didn't create death—man did: the forbidden fruit, all of that. And others say that it's part of a logical process; that it would be terrifying to imagine the lives we would live without the prospect of death. So, what, was Verochka just a sacrifice for world order—is that what she died for? Questions, questions . . .

But there are answers too. I believe that a well-placed comma will open many doors for my kids: don't ask me how, exactly—I couldn't say. But from these details—comma placement, geometry, continents and channels, the dates of Suvorov's campaigns, love for Chopin and Blok—sprouts an active, harmonious life.

And, finally, I am free. "Rejoice in the simplicity of the heart, trusting and wise," that's what I say to the children, and to myself. I can't claim to have been the first to say this, but I repeat it so often that I've made the words my own. Just as much my own as the sleepy children in my classes, as Russian literature, as all of God's world.

2009, 2012, 2015
Translated by Alex Fleming

RENAISSANCE MAN

BRICK

POLITE, smartly dressed, with friendly gray eyes, he asks me to tell him about myself.

What's to tell? I don't drink, don't smoke. I have a driver's license.

A personal assistant, he says, needs to be quick-witted.

"May I ask you to solve a puzzle?"

You're the boss. Though I'm a little too old for puzzles, I think.

"A brick weighs two kilograms more than half a brick. How much does it weigh? You understand the premise?"

What's to understand?

"Four kilos."

Apparently, no other applicant had managed to solve it. Well, construction is my sideline.

"And your primary occupation?"

I'm a pensioner. In our field, we tend to retire early.

Victor, something like the junior boss (I haven't got it all sorted out yet), asks: "Pension too small?"

Not as small as some, but it's still not enough. The senior boss straightens things out: "Anatoly Mikhailovich, you don't have to explain why you need money."

The name is Anatoly Maksimovich, actually, but beggars can't be choosers. He's the only one around here who addresses me by name and patronymic. Victor and the rest call me Brick. Well, so be it. The main thing is, I have the job.

*

We're high up. It's quiet. The office takes up the whole of the sixteenth floor. He lives on the seventeenth. That's the top, nothing above that. He's got a private office up there, bedroom, dining room, living room, and—what do they call gyms these days?—ah, yes, a fitness room.

I heard Victor say: "The boss understands how money works better than anyone. I've got a long way to go before I catch up."

Victor's a pint-size fellow, neat, muscular. I was like that myself, way back when. He comes by almost every day, but never sits down. He works the land, as they say—fertilizes the soil. Fixes things. What sorts of things? That I don't know. My own thing is to make sure there's plenty of coffee, to replace burned-out bulbs, and to keep track of who's in, who's out. The boss appreciates cleanliness: nothing lying around, no papers, no dust, no smells. Cleanliness. And when it comes to people, a clean nose.

"Our office," says Victor, "is one big family. Anyone who fails to understand that will be fired. Isn't that right, brother Brick?"

I don't need to be told twice.

I've been here—how long now?—since August. Big workroom, two meeting rooms, kitchenette, set of stairs to the seventeenth floor. Dead quiet, like a graveyard. Global financial crisis.

Most of the time I just sit and wait. That's no trouble—I'm an old hand at waiting. Watching, listening, waiting.

The rich, as they say, have their quirks: the boss, for instance, plays the piano. Nothing wrong with that. In America, people take lessons at seventy, but here—well, we're not used to it. He had a piano brought up, one of those big numbers; they had to move the walls. So what? If they had to, they had to. Like I said, the rich have their quirks.

We get visits from Yevgeny Lvovich, a decent fellow, and Rafael, an Armenian who teaches music. Victor calls them *intels*. Intelligentsia, he means. Only, I feel Yevgeny Lvovich really is a cultured person, while Rafael—well, I'm sorry, he just isn't. That first day he came out of the bathroom, waving his pink little wrists, and went straight to Yevgeny Lvovich. Didn't even look at me—zero attention, as if I wasn't there.

"Have you seen the john? Makes a strong impression." Would a cultured person talk like that? Especially on first meeting someone. "May I ask what you're doing for the patron?"

"I'm a historian...History lessons." Yevgeny Lvovich glances around, as if he feels guilty of something. He looks—well, can't say he looks very healthy; his glasses are patched up with tape. And he's got this tic—he'll fall silent for a while, then say, "It's all very sad."

They've taken to calling the boss *patron*. Fine with me.

"Have you known the patron long, Yevgeny Lvovich?"

How's it any of your business? You've just met Yevgeny Lvovich yourself. Your lesson's over—get moving.

"At the end of October. On Lubyanka Square, by the Stone. Do you know the Solovetsky Stone?"

"Sure," says Rafael. "And what was he doing there?"

Aren't we curious? Sticking our nose where it don't belong...Not my kind of guy, this Rafael. Although, in general, I've got no biases— I treat everyone the same. We had all sorts in the service.

"Well, he was walking past, saw the crowd, and came up..." answers Yevgeny Lvovich.

Then the patron drove him home, to Butovo. Butovo, I think: that means we're neighbors.

"You know, I've never traveled in such comfort."

What's so sad about that? There's a first time for everything.

"We spoke the whole way, if you can imagine, about patriotism."

Rafael immediately loses interest; you can see it in his face.

"But it was a beautiful conversation, most useful. It helped me clear some things up. You know, when you speak only to people from your circle...Well, a lot goes without saying..."

I think to myself, Why's he apologizing?

Yevgeny Lvovich starts telling Rafael about some woman: "Imagine, her husband is executed. Both daughters die. Another child is stillborn, in prison. And through it all, such unbending, intractable patriotism. What explains it, in your opinion?"

Rafael shrugs his shoulders: "I don't know. Fear. Collective psychosis."

"Yes... Our patron, as you call him, was of the same mind. But if you ask me, no, it isn't fear. Do you remember the book of Job?"

Rafael nods. Sure, they remember, but how? These intels turn everything upside down, make it suit their needs.

"Job faces a dilemma: 'yes' or 'no'? Should he tell the whole world, tell all of creation, 'yes,' or, as his wife advises..."

"Curse God, and die."

"Exactly. And the Soviet Union, for those who lived in it then, represented just that—the whole world. So..."

"That's a stretch, Yevgeny Lvovich. Many people still remembered Europe."

"Some remembered, yes—as one remembers childhood. But they knew their childhood had passed. What's left is what's left. The Soviet Union was the present, it was what was. Now we can travel abroad. But then, it was either 'yes' or 'no'—'curse it, and die.'"

Rafael cocks his head to one side.

"There's something to that. You could write an essay."

Yevgeny Lvovich no longer looks so guilty.

"What a practical mind you have, Rafael!"

"If only..." Rafael looks around the office. "Ten years of living out of a suitcase... What kind of history do you teach him, anyway? Soviet? Communist Party? The patron ought to have covered that in school. I mean, how old is he? About forty?"

"No." Lvovich smiles. Look at that, he can smile! "We had to start deep in the past. We've started with, let's call it, sacred history. *In the beginning God created the heaven and the earth...*"

Why did he lower his voice?

"Yes..." Rafael slowly shakes his head, and there's a little smirk in his eyes. "It's wonderful, isn't it? It means the country stands a chance, so to speak. Think of it: with you, our pupil studies history 'from Romulus until this day,'[8] and with me, music. And then he plays sports—some nontrivial sport, to be sure—and works in finance. That's a field in which we—in which I, at any rate, am very much behind, if you know what I mean." It's impossible to tell whether Rafael is serious or not. "Where there's finance, there's mathematics. Just today he was trying to tell me something about the chromatic scale, about the root of some degree or other…What range! What scope! I mean, he's a real Renaissance man!"

Lvovich mumbles something to the effect of: Yes, in a certain way…

"You know," he suddenly says, "what he told me after that first meeting? At parting? 'Our conversation made a favorable impression on me.' Just like that."

Rafael breaks out laughing again, then his eyes take on a wild look: "Excuse me, Yevgeny Lvovich, are you saying he's never read the Old Testament?"

"Neither the Old nor, I'll tell you frankly—"

"Wait, listen, but they all go to church now! They all, I don't know, go to confession, take Communion."

Lvovich looks deflated. He had said too much, gotten carried away. I understand that feeling. But it isn't his fault; it's Rafael's.

"I don't know, I don't know…Yes, they take Communion…" He removes his glasses, wipes them. "Like little children." And then he adds quietly, but I hear it, "I don't know about you, Rafael, but this work has great value for me. In every sense." And, with a sigh: "It's all very sad."

Then the phone rings. Rafael jumps up: "Your turn. It was a pleasure to meet you. You're also here Mondays and Thursdays? Perhaps we can continue this at my place someday? But only if," and he winks, the little bastard, "the conversation made a favorable impression on you. We're close by, on Kutuzovsky. Although, my wife is renovating…"

Well, well, well. On Kutuzovsky. Expensive tastes, eh? So that's why you're giving private lessons. Or are you lying? Maybe you haven't got a place on Kutuzovsky?

Rafael always shows up first, then Lvovich—after lunch. We don't get lunch; it's just a manner of speaking. In other words, around three.

As for Kutuzovsky, Rafael told the truth. I ran a search. Seven people registered at the address: his own sister, his wife's sister, kids... Yevgeny Lvovich, on the other hand, has no wife, no kids. Just him and his mother. She was born in 1924, he in 1957.

Looks like today it's Rafael's turn.

"He found me all by himself, if you can imagine," he says, blushing with pleasure. He's half-gray, but still blushes like a little boy. "An amazing story—I tell it to everyone. The patron likes to survey his surroundings through a pair of binoculars. In his free time, when he's not occupied with the construction of capitalism. And so he sees, and sometimes hears, that, day after day, year after year, certain people—some young, some not so young—are practicing instruments from morning till night. Girls and boys lug around cases larger than they are. Then our patron inquires as to how much a professor at the conservatory earns, how much musicians are paid for philharmonic concerts, how much of their own money they spend to make a record. And he discovers that all this activity has almost no financial component, you understand? As a person with a lively mind, accustomed to operating with economic categories, he develops an interest. And so he invites me... The thing is, back in the spring," he blushes again, "a *New Musical Encyclopedia* was published, edited by, er... your humble servant..."

In short, the patron went to a bookstore, to find out who knows a thing or two about music. And they recommended this guy, this Rafael.

"I wasn't hard to find. I teach the history of music and..." now he's beet red, "sometimes check in to see how the encyclopedia is selling."

"Extraordinary," says Yevgeny Lvovich. "You too—'from Romulus until this day'?"

"So far, it's 'Chopsticks,' 'The Flea Waltz.' We do a lot of listening. Today, for instance, it's the Russian Trio..."

The historian nods: "Katz, Goldstein, Berkovich. KGB. The Russian Trio. That's what we used to call it when I was young."

Even when Yevgeny Lvovich laughs, it's only with his mouth. His eyes don't change. But Rafael, he guffaws like a clown, his whole head shaking. It's a circus. Then he looks at me. What's he looking at? Is he nuts or something? Come on, out with it. Finally, he moves his head towards Yevgeny Lvovich:

"You know, we're participating in a grand experiment. I don't know about you, but I'm not even doing this for the you-know-what . . . I just wonder what will happen. Imagine, our patron wants to do away with the bass clef. I'm afraid even to mention the alto! And yet, these people," his points his finger at the ceiling, "are our only hope. You and I, Yevgeny Lvovich, are a dying breed, don't you think? Has he asked you about the brick yet? No? Oh, he will. Anyway, it's time to go."

I'm getting used to Rafael. But that's a fool thing to say, that he doesn't need money. Who doesn't need money?

He leaves. I say to Yevgeny Lvovich: "The brick weighs four kilograms."

"What are you talking about?" he asks.

And I think to myself, You'll soon find out, Yevgeny Lvovich.

"Would you like some coffee?" I ask.

He looks at me so pitifully.

"Yes," he says, "thank you. I wouldn't refuse."

Good. Now I can ask.

"I have a book here," I say. "My neighbor gave it to me. The diaries of Nicholas II."

He looks to be near tears.

"I wouldn't recommend it," he says. "Very upsetting. Rode a bicycle, killed two crows, killed a cat, liturgy, prayers, handed out medals to officers, ate breakfast, took a walk. Lunch, *maman*, killed another two crows . . ."

"Crows," I say, "are scavengers. No sense in feeling sorry for them."

"All the same," he says, "a nobleman, even just a normal person, shouldn't spend all his time shooting crows. Especially at such a historic moment."

All right. Just don't go mourning for crows *up there*, Yevgeny Lvovich . . . He looks at me for a long time. What's the matter with him? A normal person wouldn't get so upset about crows . . . Rafael must have worn him down.

"Don't worry," I say. "He's not even Russian. He's," we still have an acceptable word for it, "an immigrant."

Yevgeny Lvovich goes over to the window, puts his cup on the sill. In principle, that's no good: it'll leave a stain. But fine. I'll wipe it off afterwards.

"What does that have to do with it?" he says, "Immigrants. If you want to know the truth, we're all immigrants. You, me, even our patron. Everyone who's thirty or older. A different country, a different people. Yes, and a different language. Now, the younger one—what's his name? Yes, Victor. He's a native. I saw him take part in a religious procession, or rather, saw him circling the Golden Ring in helicopters with priests—with governors, holy banners, all the trimmings. There were photos in the newspaper," he says. "As for us...We ought to leave the city, go somewhere far away, deep into the provinces. Our foreignness isn't so noticeable there."

I just don't get it. Have I said something inappropriate? Whatever I said, I didn't mean anything by it. Why's he acting like this? But it happens. Sometimes you just can't tell. Maybe his mother's dying. When mine died, I was down in the dumps for weeks.

That's our routine. I've gotten used to Rafael and, from time to time, I have a chat with Yevgeny Lvovich. Our patron probably bought ten lessons from each. But the last time they came, or rather, the next-to-last time, our chat, unfortunately, didn't turn out so good.

It started the usual way. Rafael comes down from the seventeenth floor, stretching like a cat. Feels right at home now. He smiles at Yevgeny Lvovich: "A grand piano he has up there—*really* grand! But just between you and me, I'm casting pearls before swine. He'll never get a decent sound out of it."

It's your job to teach him, I think, so do your job.

"Our lessons are unproductive," he says. "I don't know how you're getting on, Zhenya," they no longer use patronymics, "but I'd give up, if it weren't for...the you-know-what..."

"Don't lose heart," answers Yevgeny Lvovich. "Playing the piano isn't so easy. I myself never managed to learn, although my mother taught the instrument professionally. By the way, she thanks you for the encyclopedia. And I wasn't forty when she tried to teach me."

"Yes, he's no spring chicken," Rafael says. "But it isn't a matter of age. For instance, today we were listening to . . ." and he comes out with some long name. "A good friend of mine, by the way. And you know what he tells me? 'People can't possibly get any pleasure out of that!'"

"Muddle Instead of Music,"[9] Yevgeny Lvovich says, nodding his head. "Frankly speaking, I myself haven't yet come to appreciate her art."

"Yes, muddle, muddle . . ." Rafael repeats. Why's he so pleased with himself?

They talk a little while longer about all sorts of music, then Rafael says: "Do you know what conclusion I've come to? Our patron is a man of above-average abilities, right? But the highest form of aesthetic pleasure he can appreciate is, alas, order."

Yes, we maintain order. What's wrong with that? But this guy just won't let it go: "Everything's smooth, clean, polished—the toilet is unrealistically white. My women must dream of a toilet like that." He looks at his watch. "Late again. By the way, speaking of order," this seems awfully rude to me, "I'm holding you up."

"I'm in no hurry, Rafael."

The little Armo's awful brazen, I think. Get going, already. We welcomed you in on time, didn't we? All right, let's teach him a lesson—though I've gone pretty soft since leaving the service.

"Young man," I say.

"Don't you call me *young man*! I'm a professor at the Moscow Conservatory!"

My, aren't we worked up! Eyes bulging and everything. The first time he's paid any attention to me. I must be furniture to him. Don't you worry, professor, we've broken harder men than you. I say to them, calmly and correctly: "Yevgeny Lvovich will be invited in as soon as the videoconference is over." And add, to give it some weight: "With the chairman of MosTourBank."

Did I say it wrong? Even Yevgeny Lvovich turns his face away. And the other one's laughing so hard, he's doubled over: "Masturbank!" he says, slapping his knees. "Zhenya, did you hear that? Masturbank!"

Lvovich turns to me and says: "No, that can't be right. Must be a joke."

How should I know? To hell with you both ... There's something strange going on. It's half past three. I make them coffee. Rafael has also taken to drinking coffee. Looks like we've made up. Can't figure them out for the life of me. I thought you were running late! He's sitting there on the windowsill, this professor, his feet dangling.

"Hey," he says suddenly. "What's going on? A crow just fell off that roof over there. Look, another one. Are you seeing this? Another one, look—just flew up and *bam*! Down."

Yevgeny Lvovich isn't looking out the window. He's looking at me.

"Are you seeing this?" Rafael squeals like a little boy. "See that one limping, jumping down to the edge of the roof, like there's something wrong with it? *Bam*! What's going on? It's not that cold out. Maybe it's a virus? Avian flu?" He struggles to open the window. Unskilled hands. Just leave it alone, professor.

Call from above. Today's lesson is canceled. You'll be fully compensated for the wasted time, Yevgeny Lvovich. No, he doesn't wish to speak to you.

A total mess. Even the Armenian, who only has eyes for himself, seems to catch on: "Although you have to admit," he says, "the patron is a striking character, isn't he?"

"Yes," Yevgeny Lvovich answers. "A Renaissance man." And after a pause, he adds his go-to phrase: "It's all very sad."

LORA

Women appeared in his life like targets on a shooting range, immediately taking up all his attention—for a short while, but all of it. After hitting the target, so to speak, he would keep up the relationship, very briefly, then break it off. So it went, as it should go. He had once read in some American book that love is a "power game." He knew enough English to read books on psychology: the secret of success, how to win friends and influence people. When he was starting his business, these books proved useful to him; now there are Russian translations. In his memory, his girlfriends turned out to be more pleasant and enticing than they had been in reality. Their most valuable features were curves, surfaces, lines—and, of course, the overcoming of initial resistance, of mutual fear; all this remained in his memory, while the disorder these women had introduced into his life eventually faded away.

With Lora, however, things turned out differently. But instead of admitting that he had lost the game, or deciding that the "power" model is not universal and, in Lora's case, simply broke down, and then moving on to make more money, work at self-improvement, and, in due course, meet new women—instead of that, he's sitting at an open window and shooting crows.

It isn't cold, though it's already December. The thermometer shows five degrees. Rifle, telescopic sight—he's sitting on the windowsill and knocking dirty black birds off the neighboring roof, one after the other. Shooting crows isn't as easy an activity as it might seem: not only does one have to hit them, one also has to avoid making noise, not to mention avoid dinging people. He's high up, above a quiet street leading to Bolshaya Nikitskaya; in the distance he can see the sidewalk in front of the conservatory, a sliver of the monument to Tchaikovsky. A good rifle he's got, quiet. Shooting doesn't make him feel good, exactly, but it does make him feel better.

Rafael had left forty minutes earlier. Once again, they had spent more time listening to music than playing; for the last two weeks, he's had neither the time nor the desire to practice. First, humming, swaying, Rafael had played something old, rather pretty. That was all well and good, but then—he himself had asked to be introduced to some contemporary work—they put on a recording, and he developed the strong sense that he was being taken for a fool. Two and a half months—which was how long he'd been taking lessons—certainly isn't a very long time, but look how much he had managed to learn and experience: he had heard all the Viennese Classics, as well as

Shostakovich, and now he knew, for example, that there were two Strausses, and that it's in poor taste to like Johann Strauss, whereas Tchaikovsky can go either way, and one must decide for oneself. He had also learned—Rafael loves to gossip—that Poulenc was gay, that Shostakovich wasn't a Jew, and that 3/4 is triple meter, while 6/8, despite all evidence to the contrary, is duple. But the recording he had heard today—what was the woman's name?—could such a thing bring anyone pleasure, delight, joy, as music ought to do? No, never.

Things were going no better with sacred history, with his study of the most popular book in the world, that distillation of human wisdom. A welter of unmotivated violence—and he's supposed to feel bad about shooting crows? Brother killing brother; father commanded to sacrifice his son, without any explanation; whole peoples wiped out—what had they done to deserve it? And why was Seoul—Yevgeny Lvovich always corrects him—Saul, why was he punished? For the humane treatment of prisoners? Mankind has come a long way since antiquity. "For thou wilt save the afflicted people." Really? Then explain the flood, please. No, he's a polite person, he wouldn't bring this up with believers; in fact, he's even going to study the book all the way to the end, very carefully, though it's hard going—the thing is crammed with details and totally devoid of humor. He did complain about this the last time, and Yevgeny Lvovich promised to tell him something about sacred humor today, but it wasn't meant to be. And besides, what did this sad, soft man—clearly a heavy drinker—know about humor? Today, in any case, wasn't the day for jokes. Lora had called.

As for crows, to close the subject once and for all, they are nasty, filthy scavengers that carry infectious diseases. They attack children, pecking at their heads. There's a crow near the conservatory that smokes. It grabs lit cigarettes out of people's mouths and smokes. This is no urban legend—he has seen it with his own eyes, on the day he first met Lora. In fact, that crow had brought them together.

He remembers: it was a warm Saturday evening; he comes out of a café and sees a group of youngsters laughing near the monument—they're watching a crow with a cigarette in its beak. He finds himself walking in the direction of what he would later learn is Rachmaninov Hall, following the crow, but his attention is diverted by a skinny young woman with long legs and long hair. The girl is a brunette. Brunettes are his type.

"Would you care to hear some music, young man?" the brunette asks. She's standing by the glass doors, legs crosswise, also smoking.

He would, but only if she would accompany him. That's his condition. What are they... playing? Performing? What's the right word? He can't very well admit he's never been to the conservatory before. The girl nods at the poster, which reads, in large letters: FRANCIS POULENC, *THE HUMAN VOICE*. And in even larger letters: LORA SHER, SOPRANO. So will she accompany him? The girl examines him rather boldly.

"Of course." She tosses her cigarette butt and leads the way.

He has to leave his jacket at the coat-check counter. The brunette walks up the marble staircase, giving him a chance to see her from the back. Not bad. A minute later he's already in the hall. Where's his companion? Nowhere to be seen, though the audience is small and sparsely distributed. On the stage is a pretty young woman in a burgundy dress—a redhead with very white skin. That's Lora.

A burgundy dress and a black telephone handset with a long cord. *Hello, hello, madame...* "A lyrical tragedy," he would learn from Rafael's encyclopedia. "A work of profound humanism and dramatic power." The piece was written for a soprano and orchestra, but Lora is backed by a single grand piano. *O Lord, I hope he calls me...* There are also theatrical elements: Lora moves deftly about the stage, interacts with a chair, a music stand. She wraps the cord around her neck. *Hello, my dear, is that you? You are so kind to call.* The black chair, the red music stand, white Lora with her red hair. It makes an impression. A strong one.

Forgive my weakness! Lora sometimes addresses the pianist, sometimes the handset, but, most of all, the audience. She tells him that she has poisoned herself. *Oh yes, I know I must seem silly!* She begs him never to spend the night in the hotel where they usually stayed when visiting Marseille together.

I love you, I love you, I love you . . . Lora almost whispers the last "I love you," looking directly at him. Or is he imagining it?

He hurries home, picks up the first vase he sees, along with the cloth on which it's standing, and heads to the corner flower shop: "White, red, doesn't matter—just not yellow. That's bad luck."

Where can he find the performer? "In the dressing room. Down there and up the stairs." He doesn't know how it is with them—artists, musicians—but it's probably like any other business: If you need something, go and take it. Before the others snap it up.

He might have overdone it with the flowers. Lora, now dressed casually (sweater and jeans), seems more surprised than pleased.

"Merci." Lora's speaking voice is not at all like her singing voice. It's somewhat low, almost hoarse. And her mouth, it seems to him, is too small for a singer.

"Do I get a thank you, Lora?" the smoking brunette crows from the corner of the dressing room. "Haven't I snagged you a nice little oligarch?"

In his circle, people don't make light of material wealth; but in their circle, things must be different.

"You're tired, aren't you?" he sympathizes with Lora. Her face, despite her youth, already shows signs of aging. Wrinkles around the eyes, little lines. A person's true age is determined by minor indications of this sort. How old is she? Twenty-eight, maybe thirty.

The brunette examines the vase and shouts, as if he weren't there: "Lora, it's Hermès!"

"Only the cloth. The Hermès company specializes in textiles. They don't produce vases," he explains. "And it's pronounced *Ermé*. The company is French."

"Well, well, well—live and learn . . ." The brunette feigns amazement. And what's *his* company called? What do *they* specialize in? She wants to know the status of the man to whom she has entrusted Lora's care.

They certainly get straight to the point! His firm is called Trinity.

"Trinity!" the brunette exclaims. "You hear that, Lora? Trinity!"

"See, there were three of us in the beginning. And we specialize in . . ."

"Contract killings?" The brunette.

Lora: he must forgive her friend, she's had some wine. He can simply ignore her.

An older fellow pops in with kisses and congratulations.

"You're alive? No? Then may I venerate your relics?" He hugs Lora—a bit too tightly, it seems.

A gangly young guy shuffles in and tells her, in a very lively manner, about his latest messy breakup. Then the others leave, one by one, all of them. He and Lora are finally alone. An interesting bunch, generally speaking—he's never come across their kind before. Would she allow him to accompany her home? By car. He's parked just around the corner. "Yes, thank you, *you're so kind.*" She hasn't quite emerged from her role.

She sits with her eyes closed, her hair flowing down the sides of the beige leather headrest. The car doesn't impress Lora—she doesn't say a word about it.

"Tired?" he asks again.

Yes, of course—the stage, nerves. Graduate students hardly ever get a solo evening.

"Are performers always nervous before concerts?"

"Of course. What a question!" Lora is genuinely taken aback.

"Why be nervous? Pilots, surgeons—they don't get *that* anxious before doing their work. And in their cases, it's a matter of life and death, while in yours . . ." He feels he's figured it out: "In yours—it's a matter of fame. Is that why?"

Lora laughs: "No."

No, answers Lora—if she had sung poorly tonight, no one would have died . . . But it would have meant that she wasn't really a singer. Does that make sense? Yes, in the other cases, it's life and death, but in hers, it concerns the *meaning* of life, its content. Does he understand?

"To be honest, not really . . ."

"Right there, thank you."

She lives here? What is it?

"The conservatory's dormitory."

So Lora isn't married?

"As they say: it's complicated."

He would love to continue their conversation . . .

"About how complicated it is?"

"No, about the content, the meaning." He's confused, embarrassed.

"How was I tonight?" He hasn't said a word about the concert.

To be honest, it's hard for him to judge. This being his first concert.

"An honest confession," says Lora, "has never lightened anyone's sentence."

How can she be so confident?

Lora's skin is exceptionally white. As he understood it, she shouldn't spend too much time in the sun. So he doesn't whisk her off to the Promised Land, or to Greece, or to Italy. How about Norway?

"That would be nice," she says, somewhat evasively.

A little Georgian restaurant, a walk by the Novodevichy Convent. He brings her something expensive each time, something Hermèsian, prompted by the brunette. A pure gesture—he expects nothing in return. What's wrong with simple kindness? They talk: What, exactly, is so complicated? She won't tell him the details. But basically, the complication is a pianist, conductor, composer, author of philosophical books—a creative type. The one who accompanied her as she sang Poulenc—does he remember? It's better that he doesn't. "Philosophical . . . Imagine that . . ." Yes, philosophical, musicological, and, in the deepest sense, erotic—does he understand? The creative type is writing an opera about the tsar's family. Lora will be the ballet dancer Matilda Kshesinskaya, Nicholas's mistress. He's already completed two acts. "And does the creative type have a family of his own, by any chance?" More than one. That's where things get really complicated. Why ask? It's not her secret—not hers alone. He'll have to get a sense of this guy, he thinks without hatred. Jealousy is a foolish emotion. Foolish and insulting. We always want to possess someone else. It's like Yevgeny Lvovich says, every human being is an end in itself.

"Let's talk about something else," Lora pleads. "What do you do at your 'Trinity'?" Whatever it is, she knows, isn't holy.

Why isn't it holy? They tread the line, like everyone else, but lean strongly to the "right" side. It's an investment firm. They look for weak spots. The market decides everything, of course—it's all about the market—but the market can always use a hand, in part through their search for weak spots. He hopes he's made himself clear, that she's aware of the primacy of economic relations. It's shameful to be poor: If you're poor, then you're either lazy or no one needs your talent—and everyone has a talent. On the contrary, if you earn well, you improve the lives of hundreds, of thousands of people all around you. He's been learning a lot from her, but he would like for her to see a few matters from his perspective.

"Oh," says Lora, "no problem."

He wants to tell her about Robert: "When they put Robert away..." Her face shows sympathy. "We didn't share enough with the Russian Trio, as the musicians say." Rafael had taught him that. She doesn't laugh, doesn't understand. She wasn't even listening. Rather, she wasn't listening to his words—she has little interest in the content of speech.

Lora's purring something softly.

"Is it nice, having music in your head all the time?"

Hard to say. She doesn't know what it would feel like not to have music in her head. It turns out she loves folk songs.

"What's there to like?" Miserable stuff, he thinks.

"It's like when you were a kid, and you'd dream you were falling, falling and falling, plummeting down, and you'd be so scared you couldn't breathe, and you'd never reach the bottom," Lora explains, gracefully moving her hand through the air. That may have been the last time she really spoke to him, giving as much as he gave.

He's got a piano now, and he's got Rafael. Will he manage to learn to play?

"I can't really say no," Lora tells him.

Easily, rather too easily, she winds up in his bed—but why shouldn't these things happen easily between young, liberated, physically attractive people? Oh, is it important to him? Well, then, let's go. And what about her? Yes, sure, it's important to her too. No need to go into motives. In some respects, women are more complicated than men; he knows that from experience, not books on psychology.

"May I take you to Norway?"

"Perhaps..." She slowly runs her finger from his chin down—all the way down to his solar plexus. "Perhaps not..." Her mind is elsewhere.

Lora rises from the bed, wraps a sheet around herself, and goes into the living room, to the piano. She touches the keys and tries her voice. An empty office below, nothing but the sky above: You can play all you want. Play and sing.

"Why do you have a piano?"

He's been studying music. Doesn't she remember?

"Not a word, my dear friend, not a si-i-gh, we're together in silence..."[10]

"Why such a sad song, Lorochka? Lora?"

Now her singing is intended for him alone. She stops. "Not a si-i-gh," she sings, a bit differently, and then a third time, with another variation. A fine time to practice.

Why don't they go to Norway?

"Fjords, the water's so still, so smooth..." He strokes the piano. Maybe a white one would have been nicer. White, like Lora's skin. Or maybe red, like her hair? He strokes the piano, strokes Lora. He loves smooth surfaces.

It's a fine piano, says Lora, a very fine piano. The creative type is forced to settle for a less luxurious instrument. What's there to say? All he can do is shrug. Lora, apparently, considers it unfair that the creative type lacks something he possesses. The piano is just an object—one shouldn't personify objects. Fortunately, she needs no instrument. She herself is a marvelous instrument.

So, Norway...What else does he want?

"Oh, lots of things. To learn to play the piano as quickly as possible, and to bone up on the Old Testament. Every cultured person should know a thing or two about that."

Now it's her turn. He expects the usual, elegantly evasive answer, but she puts it plainly: She needs to master the art of singing.

"That I know."

And also...Also a sense of fullness...

"Fullness? I don't understand."

The fullness of relations, of everything...She wants to build a real life. She can't explain it any more clearly. What does his life consist of?

"Same as everyone's," he says. "Work and leisure." He works a great deal, a very great deal.

But he understands, of course—she needs a husband, children... Well, he might as well warn her: He has no interest in children. That may change down the road, but for now...

When talking about children, fear flashes through his eyes, and he sees that this flash doesn't escape Lora's attention. Oh, but he's got nothing to worry about, not now, not at this moment—there won't be any irreparable damage. Why so squeamish? They're liberated people.

In the morning, almost fully dressed, Lora watches him make the bed. Neatly, very neatly, leaving no wrinkles. Where did he learn to do that, in the army?

"Why the army?" He's always liked it this way.

He's in the shower: it would be nice to step out to an empty apartment. Lora does take a lot out of him. He knows just what he'd do: fall back onto the freshly made bed and recall the events of the night. Much to his surprise, this desire passes; when he steps out of the shower, Lora is gone. *Not a word, my dear friend*...Not to worry, she'll be back. He's an excellent lover, objectively speaking. She'll be back. And yet, as it turns out, that night remains unique in the course of their relationship.

And now, in early December, he's standing at the window, contemplating his failures. There are no more crows.

Once he simply asked her if her small mouth interfered with her singing. He had always assumed that singers needed to have big mouths, like pianists needed big hands. So what was wrong with that? He just wanted to know.

Another time he'd asked her about the brick.

"Do you think all singers are morons?" was all he got out of her.

But how much does the brick weigh? Even his assistant, a former flatfoot, had solved it.

"So make out with your assistant!" She never did tell him how much the brick weighed.

Sad state of affairs. He kept pestering her with questions about the creative type, about whether the man was a good lover or not, and one time Lora lost it and said: "He suits me."

Since the end of November, he had been trying to break the habit of Lora, like people quit smoking. Apart from a few setbacks—of the "I hope he calls me" variety, only in reverse—the process was going smoothly; they hadn't spoken in two weeks. The wound was now covered by soft, delicate tissue, but today, after Rafael had gone downstairs and he had almost managed to reach an agreement with the bank—Victor had nicknamed the intransigent bastards "Masturbank"—just then, when he was about to summon Yevgeny Lvovich, Lora called, and everything grew complicated again.

She needs to see him. Khaki-colored tone. An actress. And instead of saying that he *never* wants to see her again, nor speak to her, he says, as calmly as possible: "Saturday at eleven, at our spot, near Novodevichy?"

And still he comes off as pitiful, ingratiating. Should he pick her up?

"What? No."

Will she be coming from the dormitory? *Not a word, my dear friend...* Retreat.

Half an hour later, he remembers about the teacher. Not good. Yevgeny Lvovich will be compensated for the wasted time. He summons Brick.

"Was he offended?"

"Why should he be offended? Yevgeny Lvovich respects you."

Where did Brick get that? He himself isn't sure about anyone any longer.

"You know what they call you?"

"What do they call me?" he tries to sound casual, uninterested.

"Renaissance man. And also—patron."

Nothing so bad about that, it seems. And yet—it doesn't feel right. It means they talk about him down there.

He recalls: when Rafael first laid eyes on the piano, the look on his face said, "That enema ain't going up that ass." Or maybe Rafael doesn't know the expression? He knows it. He knows everything—he's a man of learning, an encyclopedist.

"What else do they say?"

"The music business is over my head," Brick tells him, "but Yevgeny Lvovich says a lot of interesting things."

What sorts of things? Brick can't lie. Out with it, construction man! "About Nicholas II, about the fact that he also..." Ah, yes. He also—shot crows? Well, the emperor shot not only crows, but cats and roosters too. He's afraid to look at Brick. As for the teachers, he had thought more of them. After all, he was paying them.

Saturday morning. The snow that had fallen throughout the night was now dirty slush. It was still late autumn in Moscow. How carelessly people drive... Why can't they stay in their lanes? Why can't they sit still at traffic lights?

Why did she call him? She must need something. To rent a hall, maybe. She's hopeless with money. One can't have a calm, measured attitude towards money; one can be profligate, greedy, or, like

Lora, excessively contemptuous. He'll find out why she called soon enough.

He drives up to the Novodevichy Convent. It's eleven. Lora has never shown up early, or even on time. He walks down to the pond and looks around.

The convent's wall is covered with inscriptions. He had seen them before, but had never bothered to read them. What do people ask for? Nothing original, in most cases. They ask a certain Sophia, or sometimes—simply, intimately—Sofushka.

"Saint Sophia, help me get back on my feet and give me strength to overcome these trials." It would be good to find out who this Sophia is. He certainly doesn't believe in such nonsense. But then he thinks: it's worth a try. No, absolutely not.

Lora hasn't shown up. A few more inscriptions of the same type: restore my vision and health, grant me happiness in life. "Sofushka, dear mother, help me find a cheap apartment, already renovated. With all the proper paperwork."

If he were a believer, he'd be a Protestant. Life in Protestant countries is both more orderly and more humane. And they don't have any of these saints, either, as far as he knows.

He seems to be standing in some woman's way. He snaps a few quick photos with his phone. Now he'll take a seat on the bench—their bench—and read.

"Help me find my son Sergey," some woman has written. Poor lady. But then a funny one: "Let my income afford me the car of my dreams. Rostik." Lora will appreciate that. When she gets here.

He scrolls through the photos he's taken. "Restore Anna's health and bring her back to me." Of course, she's no use to you if she's sick. What about him? Would he have any use for Lora should she fall ill? He feels he would. Depending on the illness, of course.

It's been a half hour now. He should give her a call. Come on, answer...

"Saint Sophia, grant me wisdom and peace." Finally, a change of pace. Not another plea for children. As if children were born by request.

"Saint Sophia, I wish to become a highly paid professional in the field of design and photography." Very specific. And below: "I want to be happy. Help me forget Vlad." If only: A snap of the fingers, and Lora's forgotten. No more Lora.

He keeps an eye on the convent's wall. One after another, women come up and leave new inscriptions. He runs through the countries he's visited and ranks them according to quality of life: Protestant, Catholic, and, in last place, here. Lora, incidentally, is Orthodox—despite the name Sher. She wears a cross around her neck—of a slightly lighter color than her hair.

It's ten to noon. She isn't picking up the phone—which he had given her—and hasn't called him herself. There's nothing to worry about; he's sure she's fine. But he's not fine. He rises from the bench and sees that there's a dirty pink piece of gum stuck to his pant leg. Why hadn't he noticed the gum when he was about to sit down? He'd gotten carried away with all this drivel . . . Disgusting—someone else's saliva, someone else's filth—and he'll never get it off . . . Makes him sick.

Now he'll get back in his car—after waiting for over an hour—and drive away, as fast as he can.

When he regains the ability to think—already some twenty kilometers outside of Moscow—he comes to understand the following.

Lora needed help—to rent a hall or an orchestra, to assist the creative type. He would have helped. But she changed her mind. Perhaps she found help elsewhere. Then suddenly he remembered all of the Mashas, Olyas, Katyas on the convent's wall, and the blood rushed to his face: What if Lora was pregnant? The chances were next to nil. So why had she called? Maybe she wanted him to knock her up. What was she ever going to get out of the creative type? Whereas with him, both she and the baby would be set for life.

He sees the situation from the outside: look what she's done to him! He'd been close to tears at Novodevichy. Now he feels better, almost his old self again.

BOYS

Why did he leave the city? Where is he going? Wouldn't it have been better to have a driver for such trips to the country? Probably so—life outside of Moscow is frightening and unpredictable—but he prefers to be behind the wheel. He's a superb driver. And besides, any servant is a witness to the life he or she was hired to serve—a witness who hopes to become part of that life. Our people's experience with modern economic relations is relatively limited, and we learn too slowly.

He thinks of Rafael, of Yevgeny Lvovich. He doesn't think ill of them—he's just puzzled. There was nothing offensive in what they had said, exactly: the emperor, the crows... And he should probably take *Renaissance man*—he says it aloud, in English—as more of a compliment than anything else. But the overall tone, the sense of superiority—what right did they have? What value have those two created; whose lives have they improved? He suddenly realizes that he's had enough of his teachers—enough of Rafael's swagger, of Yevgeny Lvovich's alcohol-soaked melancholy, and of their all-knowingness, their relentless, unassailable correctness.

Whereas Lora had simply forgotten about their meeting. And she's spending her nights at a friend's place, so to speak; otherwise she would have let him pick her up. She had needed something—money, obviously—but then she scrounged it up someplace else and got out of the jam she was in. She had arranged to meet him, then forgot all about him. That's exactly what will happen after he dies. Everyone will forget. Rafael, that eternal survivor, will sound off in his usual condescending manner: he'll mourn a charming man, a seeker, then give a speech about art, our era, and, first and foremost, himself. Lora will praise his straightforwardness, recalling the flowers with the vase and the cloth—one shouldn't laugh at a memorial service, of course—and then she'll sing, with feeling: *Not a word, my dear friend*... making that graceful gesture with her hand. And Rafael, swaying back and forth, will accompany her on the piano. Victor will gnash his teeth in grief; he'll shell out for an archimandrite or—what do they call him?—an archbishop to conduct the service, for a plot at Novodevichy Cemetery, for deluxe wreaths and banners. Yevgeny Lvovich will complain, secretly, that the whole thing is in poor taste; Rafael will complain openly. Too bad Robert won't be there.

Strange thoughts come to mind at the wheel. Best not to die quite yet. And why would he? He's got plenty of life left to live.

He's driving out to Robert's dacha. After Robert was arrested and his wife and children moved to England, where they were eventually joined by Robert himself—the Russian Trio had driven a hard bargain over that—the dacha was entrusted to him for safekeeping. Robert didn't want to sell it; he still had hopes of returning. And in the meantime, he requested that everything be left as it was, including Alexandra Grigorievna, Old Sasha—the woman who made sure, as Robert put it, that there was life in the house. She comes by once a week, on Sundays.

This Old Sasha—again, in Robert's words—is a woman close to sainthood. She supports her niece, her dead sister's daughter, who drinks like a fish, along with a whole pack of grandnephews. Of course, if she stopped supporting them, maybe the niece would drink less, find a job. So it's unclear whether Old Sasha's feat is actually doing anyone any good. Say the grandnephews—as many as five of them, by now—grow up to be parasites? She also feeds birds—takes the bus to some special market where the grain is cheaper; Robert always found that touching. In any case, she's here at Robert's request. A fresher face might be nicer.

Outside of Moscow, it's already winter. He finds winter to be the best time of the year in these parts—because of the snow, the smooth white surface that conceals the ugliness and uncleanliness of it all. To the left is a field covered with snow, while to the right and slightly ahead the snow has been partially swept away by the wind, exposing dirty, withered vegetation. In the Baltic countries, they call that kind of unworked field *rus*. Some rusted-out piece of machinery. Reckless-ness, rudeness. To be frank, it's a country of fools. Yevgeny Lvovich would add: "And saints." That's a tough proposition. We don't often run across saints. That is, if you don't count Old Sasha, who, by the way, curses like a sailor and smokes like a chimney. In any case, people like him, like Robert, and even like Victor, for all his faults—people who work—are in awfully short supply.

There are two routes to the dacha. There's the short one, through the village where the locals live, including Old Sasha; that route is ill-advised—the road is bad. Then there's the long one, around the rus fields: a few extra kilometers, but no sign of human presence. He wants to test the car on a slippery, bumpy road, so he chooses the shorter route. The car handles it beautifully.

At the entrance to the village is a gas station. Beside it huddle a bunch of boys, not even in their teens yet. He gets out of the car, stretches his legs, arms, and back. His malaise has all but dissipated: the sun, the snow—soon he'll be straddling a snowmobile . . . And the joy of liberation, of recovery—he's adopted that stupid word from the intels, among whose number he now counts Lora (she gives off that vibe). He's only gone a little ways out of town, and it's already a whole new world, other experiences.

Fuel delivery. He has to wait ten minutes. Daylight is short, so he'd better hurry, but ten minutes won't change anything in his life.

Yes, the sense of liberation is a pleasant thing. Once, at a party, Robert had told them about the happiest day of his life. He was a young PhD back then, with a head full of ideas, and he had wanted to talk about these ideas with a certain world-class mathematician. And one day in Pärnu, on the beach, Robert sees this very mathematician, stripped down to his shorts. He agrees to talk: "But first you need to take a few lessons. My student will see to it. In exchange, he'll eat at your expense." Robert is more than willing. The student knows his stuff—they eat and talk, day after day. But then, one time, the student finishes his main course, sticks a toothpick in his mouth, and asks: So, what're we gonna talk about today?

"And you know what I told him?" Robert lets it hang there a minute, scanning the others' faces with his big eyes. "Get the hell out of my sight! And the student scrammed. That was the happiest day of my life." Robert would never see the student or the great mathematician again, and soon he was on to other things—the stock market, shares. In those early days, Robert, with his math skills, seemed like the perfect man for the job—but later it turned out that the most reliable strategy was "go and take it."

"Hey mister, want your windows washed?" one of the boys shouts, and he immediately begins smearing dirt across the windshield. Another is already busy with the headlights.

Good boys, he thinks—already working. It pleases him to think well of them. He fills up his tank—hands off, he'll do that himself— and gives the little fellows some change. Then he walks around the car and sees another boy standing behind it. A bit older than the others, but still small.

"And why aren't you working?"

The boy doesn't look up: he's mesmerized by the rear window. He follows the boy's gaze: iridescent oily patterns and colored spots left by the cleaning chemicals, interspersed with reflections of the sky, sun, and clouds. It really is beautiful—diffraction, refraction, interference—wow, he's forgotten so much.

The boy has reddish hair, not exactly like Lora's, but he suddenly thinks: If Lora and I . . .

"How old are you?"

"Eleven."

The boy's name is Kostya.

"Would you like to go for a ride, Konstantin?"

Would he!

Incidentally, the only inscriptions that had truly moved him at Novodevichy had been left by children. "I want to be good at school, then people will be nice to me." And another one: "Make sure nothing bad ever happens to my mom, ever." What's Kostya's mom's name? He shouldn't have asked. Looks like the boy doesn't have a mother.

"Kostya, do crows peck at you?" So many birds by the roadside. If only he had his rifle!

"No," answers Kostya. "They ate the neighbors' grain, and they give chicklets a bad time."

See, what did he say.

The neighbors had to get a scarecrow. Kostya does an impression of the scarecrow. They've arrived. A shame.

People walking along the street. Glum and surly. It's the same in Moscow. Of course, in Moscow, it's that everyone's in each other's way—but what's the matter here? The economy. He's been to the Italian countryside, to the Netherlands... Is there any comparison? Hard to be a patriot, Yevgeny Lvovich, almost impossible.

For some reason, he follows the boy into his house. A single-story dump—half a house, actually. The stench of rot, soot, and urine hits him in the nose. On a bed, in the semidarkness, sits a man covered in rags. The boy's father? His bare feet are monstrously thick, his nails twisted, his face unshaven, puffy. This, he thinks, is what Yevgeny Lvovich will look like ten years from now, if he doesn't stop drinking.

The man rasps: "Kostya, that the doctor?"

No, not a doctor. But he can call the doctor... One moment... He needs to step out and get some air. The man will be taken away, to the hospital; they'll do everything in their power. The negotiations take a rather long time. Why is he doing this? Because he has the money. And not just the money, but the responsibility. If you're a person of wealth, then the lives of hundreds, of thousands of people all around you must improve.

How will the boy get along without the man on the bed? How did he get along *with* him? How does Kostya feed himself—who does the washing, the ironing? He returns to the house: the doctor is coming. And he and Kostya will take the snowmobile for a spin. The boy will have a chance... The man makes a vague gesture.

Robert's empty house, which has known far better days. But never mind, thanks to Old Sasha, it's in relatively good shape. Tomorrow's her day, by the way.

They walk through the house: You see, Kostya, this is the house. His friend's house. Here's a black-and-white photo of Robert, with beard and glasses; he looks like Freud, but in a sweater. We'll see the rest later.

"The snow isn't soft at all," he explains to the boy. "See, feel it."

Kostya, with an intelligent look on his face, squats down and touches the snow, as if for the first time.

"Snow is as bad as asphalt. Keep this in mind: a snowmobile can be especially dangerous. It's not like a motorcycle. A motorcycle falls into the turn..."

Kostya, he sees, is really trying to understand.

"Look," he draws lines in the snow with his shoe. "When a snowmobile loses equilibrium, it falls along with you. You fall, the snowmobile somersaults—and lands on you. Especially on a slope. All right, let's go."

He remembers what it was like to be eleven. It's a wonder that boys survive into adulthood. Most of them, at least.

"Kostya, this is the main thing: in case of danger—jump."

It's nice that Kostya listens to him. Not like Lora: not just to his voice, his intonation, but to his words.

"Last year, two people fell through the ice," Kostya tells him, his eyes getting wide. "Drowned."

But apparently, Kostya isn't the slightest bit scared. He lies down on his back, swinging his arms up and down, then stands up and shows him the imprint: Look like an angel?

"Absolutely. Time to ride?"

He sits Kostya in front of him, holds the steering wheel, but tells the boy to hold the wheel tight too. The boy's cap is so threadbare... A little string of hair, and a skinny little neck. He'd really like to see the boy's face right now. He adjusts the mirror so he can see it.

"You've got the controls—this is the brake and this is the gas."

Kostya focuses. And it looks like he's happy. It's so easy to make kids happy.

They ride up to the little river—a stream, really. How did anyone manage to drown in that? Then they turn left, to ride along the field. They need the headlight to find their way back. A wonderful outing.

Kostya's things need drying. They find him something to wear—all huge, adult size. The sleeves dangle, like on a straitjacket.

"Let me help you roll them up. Kostya, you like pizza?"

Silly question: Kostya likes everything. Everything and everyone. They find the phone. A bar crawls across the computer screen: it's loading. In the meantime, he calls Brick: He needs clothes for a boy of eleven, a whole set, from head to toe. Buy it, bring it, and you're free.

"Can't make it today," Brick huffs. "I'm sorry, but there's no way."

Brick will try for tomorrow morning. All right, fine.

The boy lies down on the banister and slowly slides down from the second floor to the first.

"What are you doing, Kostya?" This isn't your house.

"I'm loading," the boy tells him. Loading, like an app.

Amazing, he thinks. A talented kid. Phenomenal. If Kostya were to get a proper education...

Food delivery. A thick, pallid woman in a compact car. Pizza, meat casseroles, soup.

"Eat up, boys."

It feels good to hear that: "boys."

Kostya eats carefully. He's obviously trying.

"Listen, a brick weighs half a kilo more than half a brick..."

The boy, apparently, is unfamiliar with this type of puzzle.

"The bricks—are different..."

"No, it's the same brick. Two halves of the same brick: One weighs half a kilo, so the other must weigh the same. Put them together, and you get a kilo. Do you understand?"

Aha. Then Kostya says something terribly sweet and irrelevant, and it's clear that he didn't understand at all. The boy's been neglected. They'll have to make up for lost time.

He had picked up the brick puzzle from Robert, who used to pose it to everyone who applied to work at their firm. Robert called those who answered incorrectly—and there were many of those, more and more over the years—aliens. They weren't hired.

What next? he thinks, putting the dishes in the dishwasher. In the next five minutes, and in general. And what is, so to speak, the status of his relationship with Kostya? He can't just take the boy back to that empty dump. But who are they to each other?

The immediate future takes care of itself. By the time he returns to the living room, Kostya's asleep. He carries the boy to the bed, covers him up, and even allows himself an intimate gesture—he pets Kostya's head. Boys sleep very soundly. What a good lad! Noble, simple. A proper little gentleman.

It's completely dark outside. He'll call Lora again. Better yet, he'll write: "I've found us a wonderful redheaded boy, a young gentleman." Or maybe he should wait, give it some thought?

He calls Victor, who apologizes for the bad connection. He's out hunting boar with Oleg Khrisanfovich. They'll talk in the evening. But it's already evening. Who's Victor out hunting with? He couldn't make out the name. With the gov—the governor. Oh, the gov, well, that's important.

He himself has abstained from these gubernatorial hunts lately. Maybe Victor's right—maybe his abstaining is harmful to their business. But, first of all, the howling has begun to turn his stomach: They sing prayers in unison before each hunt. And then everyone stares at him: Why doesn't he want to make the sign of the cross over his forehead? And finally, he's always been against humiliating the prey. The last time he and Victor spent hours chasing a fox; she was exhausted and couldn't run any longer. Victor hoisted her up by the tail, as a joke, and she swung around and bit his arm; Victor had to get rabies shots. He remembers how the fox looked at them. He didn't feel too sorry for Victor. Yes, he thought, about time they parted ways.

The boy sleeps and sleeps. He calls Victor back late at night.

"Well," he asks, "how goes it for the favorite of the gods and govs?" And then he tells Victor what needs to be done. Fast. Deprive one wino of parental rights. That's step one. He tries to make it sound as if it were an everyday trifle. He can't make it sound like a favor; Victor is attuned to every sign of weakness.

"Let's just whack the wino," Victor suggests. "Cheaper, and a service to society."

What is he, drunk?

"Come on, I'm just kidding. Wino, step one—what's step two?"

Step two, he sighs, is that he wants to adopt the wino's kid. He and his girlfriend. Well, she isn't fully decided yet—in regard to her, this is a preliminary conversation.

And in regard to him, asks Victor—is the conversation final?

"Yes," he sighs again. "Yes, it's final."

"The kid's name? Age?"

He tells him.

"Great idea, boss!" Victor exclaims. "I've been doing all the dirty work. I mean, the menial work. And now we'll have Kostya..."

It's worth discussing, Victor suggests. Thoroughly. Of course, everyone decides for himself in regard to his personal life, but you have to take your partners' interests into account—in this case, Victor's interests. After all, they're one big family, aren't they? Kostya's not so little, he can take part in the business. Potentially. So it's best to consider this from all angles. Just in case. No sense bringing up past troubles, but does he remember—and if not, Victor can remind him—the mess they got into with Robert's family?

It looks like Victor isn't drunk.

"Of course, you're the patron, everything's up to you..."

But it needs thought. Wouldn't it be better to become—what's it called?—a guardian? Victor will look into the laws. Guardianship is closer to the mark. But not quite, not quite. It's just as irreversible. What if—here's an idea—what if he just gives Kostya a big wad of dough?

Has Victor lost his mind? Kostya's a little boy, eleven years old—what would he do with "a big wad of dough"?

"Whaddaya mean, what?" Victor says. "When I was eleven, I knew just how to spend my dough. I'd saved up a neat little sum, by today's standards. If you care to know, at thirteen, I even bought myself a whore."

It's morning. Everyone's up. Kostya's in his own clothes, sitting on the banister again. Hmm. Same joke again...The banister's strong, it can take it.

Old Sasha's taken charge of the room where the boy had slept. She's dragged the mattress out into the snow, and the bedding's piled up on the floor.

"Good morning, Alexandra Grigorievna. What happened?"

"The little fella pissed himself... My eldest, Galka," Old Sasha mutters, "she found herself a husband, and on the first night he goes and pisses himself. How you gonna live with such a pisser, I ask her?"

Quiet, quiet, the boy might hear. It's involuntary; the child's not to blame. And can she at least not smoke inside the house?

Total disarray. It was so nice yesterday... Before the young gentleman wet the bed. He ruffles the boy's hair.

"It's okay, it happens. Been a long time since you washed your hair?"

Now he wants to do something entirely for himself. That's it, he's taking a shower.

If he smoked a pipe, say, then maybe he wouldn't need to stand under the running water for half an hour each day. But as things stand... It's long past time to turn off the water, dry off, dress, and talk to Kostya—he knows what he has to do. But the water keeps running and running. And all sorts of thoughts swim through his head, thoughts he ought to banish. After all, it's decided—guardianship is the perfect compromise.

"The little fella rode off on that there snow thing..." Old Sasha informs him.

Without permission. Took the snowmobile and went. That's a fine turn of events.

"Hope you had a good soak!"

Thank you, thank you, Alexandra Grigorievna... Rode off on the snowmobile—what the hell!

Brick ought to be here by now. He'll wait another hour or so, then he'll go out and look for the boy.

The ground is covered in fresh snow. Isn't that the track they left yesterday? No, it looks new. It took them ten minutes to reach the stream on the snowmobile; the walk is a long one. The track breaks off. He remembers the two drowning victims. He walks along the stream, to the left—no, Kostya couldn't have crossed here. He calls the house: the boy's still gone. He calls Brick: on his way. Hell of a morning. He's wearing the wrong shoes. The snow's nasty, though not very deep, and it isn't cold. Actually, he's hot, sweating.

"There's that bridge there," Old Sasha tells him.

Apparently, he ought to have turned right at the stream. He finds the bridge. The metal ropes are rusty, and some of the wooden slats are rotted through. Kostya probably made his way across it. Had he known, he would have driven straight to the village and waited for the boy to show up. No point in regretting it now...

It takes him about four hours to drag himself to the village. The day's almost gone—already dusk.

Kostya's street, the snowmobile, the house. The boy's lying on the bed, facing the wall. There's a note, in capital letters: I WAS TAKEN TO THE HOSPITAL. WE WILL SEE EACH OTHER AGAIN, SON. He meets the boy's eyes. He didn't know Kostya was capable of such a look. Don't... Don't... He remembers the fox. Though really, Kostya isn't the injured party here—he is.

The reeking man had been evacuated, but the stench remained. He should have told the boy about his father's hospitalization. His mistake.

He has a sudden, painful desire to go back to Moscow—if not to the realm of reason, exactly, then at least to the realm of common sense. And what about his assistant? Here at last, drinking tea with Alexandra Grigorievna.

"And why so late, if you don't mind my asking?"

"Family circumstances. By the time I found a car..." He can tell Brick's sweating bullets on the other end of the line.

He ought to look for a more effective assistant, without any of these circumstances.

He gives Brick the address and tells him to get in the car and make his way to the village. Brick can't drive. "What about your license? Did you lie on your application?" He has the license, but he hasn't driven in a long time.

Let Brick figure out how to get him out of the village; he's tired of figuring things out. That's it. On Monday he starts looking for a new man.

At long last, they're all in one place: he, the car, Brick, and the bags of things. They leave the bags in the dark entryway. Clothing, shoes, a little money. What about the snowmobile? Leaving the snowmobile is almost as risky as giving the boy "a big wad of dough," in Victor's words. The snowmobile is tied to the porch with a dog chain. To hell with it: if the boy has a conscience, he'll return it himself. He's had enough of this—time to go home.

They're driving back to Moscow, back to late autumn.

"Take off your hat and coat, Anatoly Mikhailovich. It's warm in the car. Here are some napkins, wipe your hands."

What's Brick going on about? That he also has a son ... What does he mean, *also*? Let him think what he wants to think.

"He's twelve years old, my boy, but can't talk. Devil knows what's the matter. We've taken him to all sorts of professors, healers, psychics."

It takes superhuman strength to listen to this drivel. He thinks to himself: God damn it! I'm supposed to feel sorry for you, too? But he keeps his cool, endures it. By the time he drops Brick off in Butovo, it's already quite late: Nonsense, how else would you get home? It's the dead of night.

He tries to read before falling asleep: "Abraham begat Isaac, and Isaac begat Jacob." What sense does it make? What's it all for?

BLACK MONDAY

He stands at the window, shooting crows. His aim is sure: the crows burst into clouds of feathers. Each game bird calls for a specific weapon and ammunition; today's choice corresponds to the target perfectly. It isn't enough that you can't take a step in Moscow without bumping into a car or a person, but now the streets are teeming with these tenacious winged bastards.

Soon the unsuspecting Rafael will show up. He has to respond to Victor's message: more negotiations with the bank. Today should do it, Victor believes. And he has to call the agency, start looking for Brick's replacement.

He could have let the teachers go over the phone, but he prefers to say goodbye on good terms. Two envelopes—for Rafael and for the historian: fees for ten unfinished lessons. For each. Very generous.

He rarely spies on the office, but today he is driven by natural human curiosity. He turns on the camera. He wants to see the look on the encyclopedist's face as he takes the money. There he is. Brick announces the boss's decision, extends the envelope. Look at that: he won't take it! Sure, but he's looking at the envelope—if he knew how much was in it, he'd take it. Too proud. The swagger's worth more than money, as Victor says in these cases. Now he'll go bragging to everyone he knows. Damn it.

He'll have to wait till three to see whether Yevgeny Lvovich accepts his compensation. Rafael's gone; he can turn off the camera. Wait a minute. What's Brick doing? Putting all the money in one envelope. Wants to be generous at someone else's expense. No sense in retraining him now.

While he was watching the events below, more crows descended on the neighboring roof. Now he'll take care of them. A new box of ammunition. One, two, three, no more crows. He looks up the street, towards the conservatory.

Red hair, a familiar coat. Lora? He raises his rifle, looks into the sight. Yes, Lora. Lora with the brunette. That crow of a brunette, that devil. He would love to split her head wide open. Dangerous thoughts for a man holding a weapon. That's fine, that's fine; he can control himself.

Binoculars would be more appropriate and safer, but his pair is in the bedroom—Lora would be gone. His phone's right here, though. Come on, pick up. Lora pulls her phone from her purse. She looks at it—sadly, it seems to him—and shakes her head. She puts it back in her purse and turns to the brunette. The brunette laughs. He takes aim at Lora again. He can't bear it. Lora is gone. The danger has passed. Both for him and for Lora.

Put down the rifle. No, he can't tear himself away from the sight of this life—festive, idle, parasitic. All of them—the conservatory brotherhood, the little Kostyas, their drunken dads, the women scribbling on the convent's wall—they're all parasites, feeding off the working minority.

And down below, the feast of the parasite continues. Where the brunette had been, he sees another girl, thicker and younger, also dark haired. Brunette 2.0. She's with a guy—shaggy, like Rafael. He's put his cello case down on the sidewalk and is waving his hands, telling some funny story. The girl is bent double with laughter; then she straightens up and pushes the cellist in the chest. What are they all so damned happy about? Can anything be that funny? Kids hanging out. Show them a good time. A good time and easy money. Play your cello, play your piano, sing—do whatever; it doesn't matter.

It's time to pry himself away from this meaningless scene and make the necessary call—to the bank. But something terrible is happening. A pale pink bubble emerges from the brunette's mouth. The cellist tries to poke it with his finger, but she turns away. The bubble grows and grows. What's so funny? It's disgusting. Chewing gum, like the crap that stuck to his pant leg at Novodevichy. Soon the bubble will take up the whole of his gun sight. Come on, burst! And without wishing to do anyone any harm, he pulls the trigger.

He's far from the scene and can't hear anything that's happening down there. Instead of running away—who knows what's in the shooter's mind?—the fools have huddled together, over the victim, blocking her from view, so it's impossible to tell if she's alive or dead.

They're waving their arms, running out into the roadway, pointing in the direction of his building. Sheep. A herd of sheep.

Gradually, the reality of the situation dawns on him. The safety was off. And there was a cartridge in the chamber. What key cancels the preceding action? There is no such key. Undo isn't a feature. Soon they'll come for him.

The road is blocked by policemen. Let the ambulance through! It seems the whole conservatory has crawled out onto the street. What's the use in crowding around? Make way, disperse, get rid of the cars. How stupid and clumsy this whole thing is!

Nevertheless, they'll soon be coming, no doubt. He doesn't even think to hide.

Someone else's hands all over him. Strangers addressing him without respect. He'll have no choice but to respond. No, he won't allow it. Something shameful has happened—irreversible, fatal. Bad luck. Now he'll have to eliminate himself.

The heart? Where's the heart? Not in the chest, higher, almost in the throat. He takes off his shoe, his sock. Some famous writer did it this way—with his big toe. His rifle's fairly short; he can reach the trigger with his hand. Or maybe he can run a loop around it.

It is time, or should he wait? Nobody comes. He slips his foot back into his shoe. The window's open. He's trembling now.

Paper, pen. COMPENSATION FOR THE VICTIM. He doesn't know her name or surname. He doesn't even know whether he's killed her. ENORMOUS COMPENSATION. Victor will take over the firm. He'll take good care of it. What else? He writes: IT WAS AN AC-CIDENT.

Nobody comes. He's tired of waiting. Time to decide. He's tired of everything. Now? Now: one shot and he's gone. The phone rings. Who is it? Don't check. Now.

He never wanted to hurt anyone.

Funny that one can think up until the last second.

BRICK

Now Victor runs the show, up there and down here. He's easier to deal with.

"So, brother, now I'm your patron." Real casual, none of these hang-ups and headaches. "You know what my name means?"

How should I know? Turns out it means *winner*.

"All right, let's test your mental faculties. A brick weighs one kilogram plus half a brick. How much does it weigh?"

"A normal solid brick?" I ask.

"As normal as they come."

"Four kilos."

Victor laughs—he laughs a lot lately: "Why?"

What does he take me for? Solid bricks weigh four kilos. I should know, I work in construction.

January 2011
Translated by Boris Dralyuk

THE WAVES OF THE SEA

THE PRIEST had a dog. An obedient, patient dog with a reddish coat. A bitch. Applied to their own dog, the word *bitch* struck the priest's wife, the *matushka*, as unsuitably vulgar. She would say: *girl, our girl*, although the priest didn't care for this boy-girl business—he was against anthropomorphizing animals, and didn't really get them anyway. The dog, incidentally, didn't belong to him, Father Sergius, so much as to Marina, his wife. At least in the beginning.

Years ago (he knew exactly how many: fourteen), in despair of ever getting pregnant, Marina went to the monastery to see the elder—an astonishingly young elder—to ask whether she ought to adopt a child, and the elder said no. This wasn't what she had been expecting, but the elder said his no very firmly, and Marina decided that they didn't in fact need a child. She got a dog instead, and for the dog they didn't seek the church's blessing.

It was strange that the elder had said no back then. The nineties had given rise to many children who didn't have families, and the procedure for adopting wasn't all that complicated—although why turn to the elders for advice if you're not going to heed it? This is what her husband thought. But don't children give meaning to married life? asked Marina. For his part, Father Sergius had nothing against adopting—at the time, incidentally, he wasn't yet a priest. Just Sergey, Seryozha, the Lord's servant Sergius, as you like. They called the dog Mona. A ridiculous name from some Hollywood movie. They couldn't just call her Kashtanka, like the red dog in Chekhov's story; everyone does that.

Once a uniform carrot color with a reddish tinge (a color women sometimes dye their hair), Mona had now lost her looks and was stippled with gray. Her face especially had gone almost white. Although the dog had grayed and grown sadder with age, she remained thin. Marina's friends praised her. "You're feeding her right!" they said. Although it wasn't Marina who fed her; Sergey had taken on this responsibility. In his own way the priest had become attached to the dog. All of his attachments he formed with difficulty and in his own way. Sometimes it seemed the only link between him and Marina was the dog. Other than the fact that, should they divorce, Father Sergius might wind up defrocked. He had seen what happened after these divorces.

It was also his wife who led him to the church some twenty years before. They had all begun going to church back then, their entire crowd, but no one could have imagined that Seryozha, the laid-back geologist, dependable (a quality they particularly prized) and soft-spoken, would suddenly—just like that—turn into a priest. He didn't even have a decent beard. A geologist without a beard is unheard of, a priest even more so. The beard wasn't an issue, of course: back then people often became men of God just like that, even without a seminary background. Still, it was strange, to just up and get ordained. Many of their friends disapproved of this move. They disapproved silently, to themselves, which made it even more unpleasant.

They were a mixed crowd, mainly hiking friends from their university days. What sort of priest would Seryozha make? He couldn't sing for his life. And a priest had to sing well, and be somewhat theatrically inclined. Unfortunately, Marina shared this opinion. But once Father Sergius started doing something, he wouldn't stop. For instance, they had all gone on a special diet where you had to chew your food at length. They followed the diet for a while, then they stopped. But Father Sergius kept on chewing and chewing. This was the price for their youthful diversion—sitting and waiting for him to finish his food. Then Marina got tired of waiting, so when they sat down at the table together, Father Sergius frequently ended up chewing alone.

The women in this group of theirs weren't very pretty; they were overly masculine. Marina stood out in a good way. She was a theater critic. She wasn't all that crazy about theater but for some reason it just came to her naturally. In her younger days she took an interest in the most varied things, an interest that would flare up and then go out, but now, as they approached fifty, the range of her oscillations had contracted. She spent her days in her bed—or, more accurately, on it. She and Father Sergius had long slept in separate beds. She'd be on the computer, searching for this and that, and even when the computer wasn't at hand she managed to read all manner of stuff on her phone. She sent messages, laughed, looked at pictures. Her relationship with the church had all but ended. Or been reduced to something Father Sergius couldn't see.

He, however, got off to a bad start with theater. Marina had taken him to a production where the actors fell to the floor and rolled around while talking, and then to another production where everyone shouted except for one actor who, by contrast, performed his role wonderfully. Clearly he was ignoring the director and performing the way he liked, the way he was accustomed. But even then Father Sergius had to go out and wait for Marina in the foyer.

Such is the backstory. Not happy.

The story itself begins this way. Father Sergius is sitting in the kitchen reading a book. The events take place late in the spring, in Moscow. He reads a lot—philosophy, theology, art, everything: old and new. Reading is his greatest pleasure and interest. He's stuck to the habits of his youth. And so Father Sergius is sitting there with a book when suddenly it occurs to him, in a roundabout way, that it's quite probable that Mona is about to die. To speak of her as passing on seems too solemn for a dog.

"What does it matter what word we use? She hasn't eaten in three days."

Father Sergius brings Marina into the kitchen. Mona is lying beside the food and water bowls, head on front paws, looking up.

The priest goes to the window, undoes a button on his sleeve, and his watch throws a spot of light onto the wall. Mona used to get all excited by these spots—she would jump up, growl, and snap at them—but now she just watches without moving her head, then looks at her masters. She doesn't even attempt to get up.

"Leave the dog alone!"

Why so bad-tempered? It's not Father Sergius that's killing her.

Telephone conversations follow and a vet turns up. One of Marina's friends has recommended this person as "the Vet from God." Father Sergius can't remember the vet's name, insofar as he radiates nothing but indifference. And greed. Even Marina had to admit as much. Nonetheless, he inserted an IV: now at least Mona won't die of dehydration.

They try to do more for Mona's health, hurriedly and without coordinating. They have analyses done—there are leukocytes and protein in her urine. Now what? The Vet from God asks: "What do you think?" Then says: "It's age." They need to take Mona to the dacha: there they can bury her decently.

On occasion Father Sergius and his wife still act as one: they don't even say the word *bury*. Over many years of married life, however inharmonious, an understanding evolves. Marriage—as his neighbor in the hospital, a writer, will tell him later—requires two of three conditions, in any combination: a passport stamp, cohabitation, and a shared bed. They have the first two.

In the taxi there's a radio—Mona lies there quietly, but she used to react, especially to female voices. She would howl, striking various high notes. The disappearance of Mona's musicality affects Marina more than the knowledge of the protein in her urine; all the way to the dacha she sobs and strokes Mona's head.

"It's just a dog," says Father Sergius. He's sitting in front.

This statement offers little comfort, however true it may be. It would be better if he hadn't said anything.

Oh dear, such heartache. Somehow they manage to unload the things, and Mona, from the car. They put her on the floor, cover her, and try to feed her. They are beginning to accept that the dog is near the end.

"In a way, animals are luckier than we are. They're unaware of death's existence."

Rather than hold forth, Marina says, you could go to the pharmacy and buy some medicine. We need to put in the drip. So of course he goes to the pharmacy and puts in the drip, and the house takes on a particular smell—the apartments where Father Sergius administered the sacraments smelled like this.

At one point Mona manages to get up and even walks around the room a little. Then her hind legs give way and she falls, making a loud noise as she collapses onto the wooden planks. Father Sergius looks at his wife: she too is probably thinking "the sooner, the better."

Whatever they do, the dog should not be made to suffer long. But then another vet turns up—a local, around thirty, with a soft voice. He palpates Mona's stomach, making her hiccup almost like a person, and says he needs to do an X-ray, an ultrasound, more tests. So in the morning Father Sergius orders a car and it takes him and Mona to the veterinary clinic. Marina stays at home: she doesn't have the strength.

Mona lies on the glittering table. The sun is in the window and there are sun spots everywhere, but she's no longer interested.

"Here," says the vet, indicating her X-rays. "Here and here."

Round white spots—cancerous metastases.

"And here's another," says the vet relentlessly.

It's his view that the dog should be put to sleep, to spare her from suffering.

"But she doesn't really seem to be in pain."

"Dogs are awfully tough," the vet explains. "And she feels bad because she can't serve you."

"Euthanize her" is what he says. And—yes—he's ready to do it. Here and now.

"Just a moment," says the priest.

Euthanize isn't the word—they're about to kill off the dog.

He has to make a phone call. To talk it over with his wife.

"Of course." The vet understands. "But be quick, please. Other people are waiting with their dogs."

Father Sergius looks at Mona: "I'll be back soon."

He had often said this to her, but then he would go away for the day, and Mona probably thought "I'll be back soon" meant "I won't be back soon." It would hardly cross her mind that her master would lie to her.

"Do what you think best." Marina is weeping.

And now Mona is in a cardboard box, dead. This dog hospital has special boxes. Simple, without any writing on them. White boxes.

"Dogs are buried in boxes?" asks the priest.

The vet shrugs.

"You can leave the dog here. There's a collection service."

No, thank you, he needs no more of their services.

It all happens quickly, and twenty minutes later Father Sergius is digging a hole in the garden. As a former geologist he knows how to dig quickly. He doesn't feel anything. Mona was a dog who had a good life. She never had puppies, but then—what can you do?—they hadn't found her a mate. Marina is watching him from the window. Of course he didn't bury Mona in some box. While covering her with earth, he automatically hummed "Beneath the Waves of the Sea": the hymn that led him to leave geology and be ordained into the priesthood.

In the mid nineties the future Father Sergius was going to church so often he'd all but given up his real job, all the more so as they weren't being sent on expeditions and basically weren't being paid anymore: no one seemed to need their geology—at least not his type of geology.

Going to church with Marina, the future Father Sergius set himself the task of observing the cycle of divine services for an entire liturgical year, which he did for one year, then two, and he struck up a friendship with the father superior, Father Lev, the sick and widowed archpriest who lived there in the little clergy house. He began sitting with him late into the night—Marina was spending her evenings at the theater; they didn't have Mona yet—and he rejoiced in the spontaneous religiosity of those around him, a quality he lacked. He had envied people their spontaneity, their ability to act on impulse, ever since he was a child.

Father Lev was frequently visited by family—sons and nephews, young priests and deacons (dea*cones*, they said), some of them living just outside Moscow, others in Ryazan and Tambov provinces—and at these times the future Father Sergius observed not only spontaneous faith but also a spontaneous drunkenness for which he had not been prepared. Several priests had been prohibited from administering church services because of their drinking—some for several years—and, surreptitiously, so that their higher-ups wouldn't find out, they served in other parishes. Sergey liked their company. He liked the gentleness and humor of these people, and it flattered him that they let him hang around, although he realized he wasn't of any particular interest to them.

"God and a broad," repeated Father Lev, watching his kinsmen drinking. "God and a broad are life itself. But as for vodka..." He shook his head. That he had actually said *broad* seemed impossibly daring.

On one of those evenings Father Lev related how he had gone to administer Communion to an elderly man, a man with a nasty streak. He had once been important, almost a general, but now he was dying on the outskirts of Moscow. After making the long journey on several minibuses, he confessed the man at length, but when he began to give him Communion, he realized he'd left the sacraments behind. At which point the archpriest had the courage, as he put it, to use bread and wine to give Communion to the general: he deceived him, dunking a piece of altar bread in Cahors wine and giving it to the old man. And he told the general to take Communion for three days. Then the next day and the day after that he did the same thing all over again, this time with the real sacraments. For a misdeed like this he could have been not just banned from administering services but defrocked altogether.

"If they ban me, all right," said Father Lev, "so long as they sing 'Beneath the Waves of the Sea' at my burial." What he had in mind is that "Beneath the Waves of the Sea" is sung when priests, but not laypeople, are being buried. "He who in ancient times hid the pursuing tyrant beneath the waves of the sea-a-a-a," Father Lev began to sing in a low voice, and it was this, astonishingly, that settled the matter for Sergey—the matter of whether or not to become a priest. "Sometimes unexpected things strike through to the soul," he explained to Marina. She looked doubtful: he didn't use to express himself so solemnly. As for herself, she couldn't even learn the Credo.

The future Father Sergius knew he could only handle so much, that he had to limit himself, and during this period he lost interest in non–church people. This may have included Marina, for the time being.

"Still, it's strange that we trusted that butcher." She's talking about the local vet.

"He seemed like he knew what he was doing. And the X-rays looked convincing."

Marina splutters.

"X-rays! My God!"

Of course it's not his fault, she says, and by this she means it is his fault. Mona's death, and much else besides.

Right now, more than anything else, he wants to bathe, go to his room, and lie down. Still, he tries to reach out and touch Marina's shoulder.

"Just a dog, you say. But what does that matter?" She won't let up. "We cry over Madame Bovary and she never even existed!"

Who's crying over Madame Bovary?

Evidently he's no longer capable of feelings, Marina suggests, any feelings whatsoever.

But no, he feels bad about Mona.

And there are all sorts of feelings—what's the point of talking about them?

Father Sergius is used to failure, this is what he thinks. Although why should he consider himself a failure? He wanted to become a priest, and he succeeded. Is there really anything loftier than the priesthood? His wife... The things he could say to no one but her had become fewer and fewer, there was hardly anything left. It was odd that she had begun to do without... how to put it?... physical intimacy with him. From his experience of receiving confession he knew that towards his and Marina's age physical intimacy becomes increasingly important for women, while men become indifferent towards it. Although for Marina it had always been important. It was awful to think of her having... a friend. In that case there certainly wouldn't be any "Beneath the Waves of the Sea." Although people do change. Deep in his heart, however, Father Sergius knew that they don't change. People forgive themselves, God forgives them, but they don't change.

He's lying in his room and thinking: he lacks spontaneity. He always has. Like now. He could go to Marina, console her, do whatever seems right—even shed a few tears with her. His reaction to any misfortune occurs after a certain delay—to another person's misfortune, yes, but also to his own. Yet it's not something you can explain to someone else.

Suddenly he recalls when he was in year nine or so at school and they were all driven somewhere to shoot a machine gun. The shooting he can't remember. What he remembers is this: on the way back, along an empty suburban Moscow street, his classmates began chucking snowballs at a glass phone booth—no one was inside—and for some reason he too grabbed a chunk of ice, chucked it at the booth, and hit it, breaking the glass. The others all ran on ahead but he lingered, and a passerby, an elderly man, stopped and looked at him, slowly and reproachfully. He can't remember how old the man was, maybe fifty, maybe seventy, and he's not even sure it was a man. But the look he does remember. On the other hand, he thinks, he never joined the Komsomol. The others joined, the whole class did, despite no longer believing in any of it, of course. The memory of the Komsomol briefly raises his spirits. But he's feeling unwell nonetheless, physically unwell.

Of course he was a failure. Take his first parish: a church known throughout Moscow where they had sent him to replace a priest who was infamous for his daring views. Here you found women who said to each other: "Move back, you're keeping me from the proscenium." They did not accept Father Sergius. He remembers his first and only Christmas at that church: three priests standing with chalices, he of course being one of the three, only there were queues of communicants before the other two priests, while before him—no one. The regular parishioners preferred the other fathers to him. The choir there was very good indeed. This is where it became apparent that Father Sergius could not sing. So, out of kindness, some of the parishioners began confessing to him. "I used the icon as a mirror," said a lady one time, the one who referred to the soleas as the proscenium.

On the other hand, there were lots of children in that parish. Father Sergius liked talking with them. He discovered, for instance, that they would often take money and tear it, burn it, destroy it, testing the limits of what they could do. He told one small girl the story of the phone booth. He gave her quite a scare, it seemed.

One time, upon entering the refectory, he overheard: "Think of him as someone who hasn't fully overcome his autism." One of his priestly brothers was talking about him. "One mustn't just dismiss someone as an outsider," replied another. "And the last shall be the first." Father Sergius, faltering, tried to smile. "We're discussing the new president," said one of the brothers adroitly, also trying to smile. This was in 2000.

Then there had been another church, absolutely new, the church where he first became father superior. There were scarcely any parishioners, but the church prospered thanks to its proximity to the district court. It had lots of casual visitors, not regular churchgoers. Different people every day. In anticipation of the court's judgment of their cases, civil and criminal, they gave generously to the church, and Father Sergius took substantial sums to the bishop. He always found it uncomfortable looking at him, but there was no one he could go to for advice—his beloved Father Lev had died. At the funeral, together with the council of priests, many of them kinsmen of the deceased, Father Sergius had read the Gospels and sung "Beneath the Waves of the Sea," glancing over at Marina and regretting that he couldn't grieve with her at his side.

At the time these monetary matters greatly disturbed Marina; they confounded her belief. The bishop wasn't a bad man, he was just too taken up with building works—and then, bishops faced a greater variety of temptation than did simple priests and the laity. It wasn't because of them, the bishops, that Father Sergius hadn't become a good priest—it was his own fault. Twice a year Father Sergius shared his doubts with his official confessor—was he equal to the burden of the cross? He said nothing about Marina, although it didn't even occur to him that his confessor might let something slip about his troubled home life.

Now he was serving in a small church in the center of Moscow, a parish, as they put it, consisting of "one and a half old women." It was just him and a dodgy choir—made up of amateurs, that is—and from here there was nowhere for him to go. People asked, of course: What's the matter with the matushka? Meaning: Why don't we ever see your wife at church? "She's indisposed." After a while they stopped asking, and for some reason there wasn't any gossip. Over the course of ten years the parish didn't grow, but the "one and a half old women" evidently respected Father Sergius. If only his relationship with Marina had not gotten into such a state ... He knew what she was doing at that very moment: looking at photographs of Mona on her phone.

He hadn't eaten a thing all day—there wasn't any food in the house anyway—but he didn't feel hungry. He had a pain inside, deep inside—not exactly in the chest or abdomen, but somewhere in between, in the pit of his stomach. Somewhere Father Sergius had learned that the first sign of a heart attack is fear. But fear wasn't what he was feeling.

Father Sergius constantly confronted death, the deaths of other people, but he rarely thought about his own death insofar as he hardly ever thought about himself. When he did think about death, he did so in quite positive terms—never as the end to his worldly travails, but rather as an opportunity to dispel his fear and ignorance of the afterlife.

The pain, though, was getting worse and worse. Telling himself that the pain was something apart from himself, apart from Father Sergius, was not getting him anywhere. He drank a cup of tea without anything in it, by himself. It was already dusk. The pain didn't go away. And now he was feeling nauseous too.

Father Sergius, like all priests, was afraid of vomit. This is why he decided it was time to take action. He dialed the emergency services, explained where the pain was, listened to their advice. Finally he found out that there was just one ambulance and it was out on a call. He ordered a taxi. Father Sergius hoped to leave quietly—he was embarrassed by his indisposition—but Marina had heard. She shot out of her room and began getting his things together in a frenzy.

No, he didn't need a cassock, he didn't want to make an impression.

Somehow Father Sergius knew what was going to happen: Marina would take him to the hospital and they would say their goodbyes. It was a bit soon for this; he wasn't even fifty yet . . . Of course, part of him was afraid. A feeling like you're about to go under in a cold river. He had to hope he would acquire a new body after the soul parted from the one he had. The Lord would give him another form of existence. He might even give it to him today.

The hospital. They had arrived. Only the upstairs windows were lit, on the third floor; without their light the empty forecourt would have been in complete darkness. Around the door stood a number of grim-looking men.

Inside, he was put in a wheelchair, as if he hadn't just arrived on his own two feet, and without any warning a heavy woman began wheeling him in the semidarkness from one room to another. Father Sergius no longer belonged entirely to himself.

He had only ever stayed in a hospital once before—when he was seventeen, on the instructions of the military commissariat. He was there with two men who told him he was a deserter and kept sending for vodka. At night the men snored so loudly they seemed not to snore but to roar, like a couple of saber-toothed tigers. He couldn't remember anything of a medical nature from that hospitalization.

Everything must follow its course. Marina calls a friend who knows about everything here: The main thing, the friend says, is to get up to the third floor as soon as you can—that's where everything medical happens. Soon Maya Pavlovna will be down. Maya Pavlovna is the department head, she's on duty today; the friend says they're in luck.

Back to waiting: Maya Pavlovna is engaged, go up to her yourselves. On the way up, to the kingdom of light, there's a small incident.

"Go on! What are you waiting for?" Marina yells at some middle-aged women.

The elevator isn't working. How can that be? It was working just a moment ago!

Marina has an effect on people. The nurses, aides, and—what are they called?—the paramedics, they're scared: some fellows will be along shortly. They'll help out, pick him up. He can't go up there on his own: Maya Pavlovna would kill them. Any pain above the navel requires a cardiogram.

"Then do it!"

Marina ought to keep quiet, thinks Father Sergius. It would be better if she went home. Of course she's worried, in her fashion, but it's obvious: nothing works in this place.

He says: "I'm quite capable of going up the stairs. I'm not as bad off as that."

"But you are, you are." Marina won't let him get a word in. "He's never complained about anything before." This is directed at the people around them.

What's the matter with the damned elevator? It turns out there's a dead woman in it. The dead aren't to be sent to the morgue until two hours after death, which is why they are put in the elevator.

Dead bodies don't frighten Father Sergius. He gets up, takes the bag from Marina, and opens the steel door a little. "You stay here." He doesn't even kiss her goodbye.

He bangs the door shut and presses button three. There is indeed a body, wrapped in a sheet.

Father Sergius will learn the deceased's story later. The ninety-nine-year-old woman had been frozen to death by her children and grandchildren, their husbands and wives: they didn't attach any significance to a round number, didn't wait for their relative to reach one hundred. They laid her out on an oil cloth and undressed her—in recent years the old woman had been utterly helpless—then opened up the window—the May nights are cold—and waited for her to stop breathing. Then they called for an ambulance. "Come confirm she's dead," they said.

"What are the windows open for?"

"To air the room. Is that a problem?"

The radiators in the room had been switched off. Anyhow, they came and confirmed not that she was dead but that she had acute hypothermia. Down to twenty-eight degrees. She still had a pulse. The police were informed, and now the old woman's relatives were awaiting investigation and trial. She lived a couple of hours longer thanks to the intervention of humane medicine, Father Sergius will be told by his writer neighbor—what *didn't* Maya Pavlovna do to try to warm her up.

These details he has yet to hear. For now he's standing in the corridor by the elevator door, across from the intensive-care unit (a small one, with two beds), waiting for the aide to change the sheets. Although you can't see anything because of the screen, there is someone moving in the bed on the other side.

A few steps from where Father Sergius stands is the staff room, and beyond that is Maya Pavlovna, cornered by three men—the ones they had seen when they were getting out of the taxi. Maya Pavlovna is a dark-haired woman, on the short side, and about the same age as him.

"Convey your thoughts," Maya Pavlovna is saying, "to the investigator. As for the cause of hypothermia we have no comment. We can only confirm that this is what caused your relative's death."

Maya Pavlovna goes to the stairwell and pushes the door. The door is locked.

"How did you get up here?"

One of the men indicates the other end of the corridor: they had come in through the kitchen. He's the oldest and has a hangdog look. A son or a son-in-law. When he raises his arm, you can see a tattoo on the inside that reads: "Life is hell and then you die." Father Sergius thinks: The stairs are locked. Marina can't get up here. Let's hope she's already on her way home.

"She was ninety-nine!" exclaims the youngest, turning his back to the doctor and gesturing grotesquely. "What did they bother bringing her here for?"

"In normal countries they have this thing called euthanasia," utters the third—in the middle, agewise, and obviously the most articulate of the three.

Maya Pavlovna gives him a hopeless look.

"The investigators will look into all of your concerns."

"Now you listen here, Madam Doctor!" The young man smacks his side for some reason. "Ninety-nine! You got that? Ninety-nine!"

This is no longer speech but the howl of a beast. And he'll likely howl this way throughout his term in the prison camp for murdering his own grandmother.

"Leave right now. I'm calling the police." Maya Pavlovna closes the staff-room door and locks it behind her.

Why, Father Sergius wonders, can't he speak so firmly with people who are in a state of clear, grievous, recurrent sin?

"Lie down now, my dear," an older woman is saying to him, a woman affectionately referred to here as Miss Masha, the angel aide.

They're doing his cardiogram. While observing what the nurse is up to, Father Sergius looks at his own bare chest and its sparse fair hair as if it belonged to somebody else. The way you look at your home when you have visitors whom you don't know very well. Make your body a temple of the Holy Spirit... The nurse dribbles cold gel on his chest, attaches rubber bulbs. Everything around him is alien; even his body seems not to be his own. Bright and clean, the dark blue bulbs, the rhythmic beep of the monitors: you can't tell which is for your neighbor's heart and which is for your own—there's a coldness on your chest and inside it. The pain is gone, there's nothing but emptiness, and even that only if you listen very carefully. In a state like this he wouldn't have sought any help.

"Is it a heart attack?"

He knows what she's going to say: Maya Pavlovna must examine him.

What's the nurse giving him now? No, not giving, taking—she's taking his blood.

There's a noise from behind the screen.

"Oh Lord, oh Lord," moans his neighbor.

Something overturns and a yellow liquid spreads across the floor.

"Miss Masha, see to him!" the nurse shouts.

"What have you done now, eh?" the angel aide asks as she tucks the man back into bed.

"My legs are atremble," he replies.

Atremble? Oh my!

"I'll show you how to cause a stir," says Miss Masha, although there's no menace in her voice.

Somehow or other everything settles down behind the screen. The floor has been wiped and both of their monitors are beeping again. The nurse and Miss Masha have gone. Father Sergius realizes he's forgotten to bring a book. All he has is a notebook that he carries around and writes all manner of things in. He'll just lie there and think. But then a sigh comes from behind the screen.

"Oh Lord, oh Lord!"

"Are you unwell?" asks Father Sergius.

"Better now," the neighbor replies. "Reality is so empty, so meaningless and superficial!"

So that's why he's sighing. Clearly he's someone out of the ordinary: he belongs to the intelligentsia.

"Have you been here long?"

Since yesterday evening, his neighbor believes. He's not quite sure. He was in a very bad state, he nearly died, almost spoiled their statistics—not a bad euphemism for dying, eh? They say he's got pulmonary edema. Twaddle! What do they know? He has weak bronchial tubes—they diagnosed him in Moscow, at the LitFund clinic.

Does he have a dacha here too?

No, it's just an occasional visit. That is, on occasion of his daughter living here. With her mother. And young man. She's grown up already, twenty-two. And now his wife's come rushing into town. Younger than his daughter. She was enrolled in his seminar. If he loses her he can't live. To someone who hasn't been in his position . . .

"Has anything like that ever happened to you?" his neighbor asks.

No, answers Father Sergius, he's only had one love in his life—and realizes that he isn't lying exactly, but also is not being entirely forthright about his situation.

What kind of seminar was his neighbor teaching?

It turns out he's a writer.

"And what do you do?"

Father Sergius wants to say, "I'm a bad priest," but instead he says, "I'm a geologist."

"I see," the neighbor replies, not at all interested.

So, he's a writer.

"But my last name won't mean anything to you. It's Puryzhensky." He pauses.

If they ever get out of here, the neighbor promises, he'll give him a copy of his book, the latest one. He has to find it. He's run out of author's copies.

"Do you know how hard it is asking for your own work in a bookshop? 'Have you got anything by . . . Puryzhensky?' It's like buying condoms. Remember? When you were young?" The man has cheered up a little. "'Item number two,' remember?"

Father Sergius would prefer not to reply.

Once again despair takes hold of Puryzhensky. He can't even sign a book, his handwriting has gotten so bad, so wretched. It's a few years since he's written anything new anyway; he's just looked after his earlier works: second editions, dramatizations, screenplays...

"You know what they said about my last novel? That it bore the stamp of a losing battle between author and alcohol. Can you imagine?"

The best—or most flattering, rather—estimate he ever received from the critics was: Puryzhensky is a minor yet nonetheless enjoyable writer.

All right then, but Father Sergius still doesn't want to form an opinion about his neighbor's work before he's read it.

Last winter some crackpot started coming regularly to Father Sergius at the church: he maintained that he could resurrect the dead. On one occasion, while turning him out onto the street, Father Sergius thought: If it were true that this madman could resurrect the dead, then by depriving him of the opportunity, he was committing blasphemy against the Holy Ghost. In that case the risk had obviously been nonexistent, and in this case it was minimal, yet he still couldn't deny Puryzhensky his talent without first reading his work.

The writer had gone back to his complicated life situation. Olya was pregnant. Olya? His daughter? No, his wife. That is, he and his first wife hadn't yet divorced, but that's nothing but a stamp in your passport. If Olya were to leave him . . .

"Why would she do that?"

What would she stay for? To have on her hands both a child and a physical wreck like himself? He can't offer her health or wealth. And Olya herself is little more than a child. The writer sighs.

"What's the matter? They'll take care of your bronchial tubes."

The light is getting brighter. Maya Pavlovna comes into the ward. She addresses Father Sergius.

"Let me put your mind at rest right away—you haven't had a heart attack, Sergey..."

"Petrovich," prompts the priest.

"Can you tell me when the pain began?"

Suddenly he feels warm. They always ask: When did it begin? *How long is it ago that this came unto him?* After all that has happened today, now, Maya Pavlovna, a very pleasant person, has brought him the news that he is going to live, that it wasn't a heart attack. Everything is becoming simple and good.

"Why are you upset?" She has misread his mood. "And please, when did the pain begin?"

"Today, in the afternoon. My wife and I had words." He's trying to remember: What was the time? "I'm . . . I'm afraid I was in the wrong."

"Sergey Petrovich, is this something I should know as your doctor?" True, he wasn't at confession. "What is your job?"

He doesn't want to deceive her, but what can he do?

"I'm a geologist."

She's examines him, listens. Nothing unusual. His right hand is trembling. This is common among priests; they hold the chalice with their right hand. How is he going to explain this now?

"Sergey Petrovich, are you with me?" Her eyes are smiling at him ever so slightly.

Here's the plan: he'll remain until morning, have a few things checked, and then they'll decide. For now they'll keep him hooked up, and if nature calls, the nurse can unhook him. He'll need to take a few pills. And get a shot in the abdomen.

"No," she laughs, "not for rabies!"

For now they'll regard his condition as unstable, although most likely there's nothing wrong. A healthy person can feel rotten too.

She's crossed over to his neighbor. He can hear every word: there are no secrets in an intensive-care ward.

"You mustn't remove that from your nose!"

"Nothing's coming out of it!"

"There's oxygen coming out of it. And please drop that complaining tone of voice."

The conversation goes on along the lines that if he, Puryzhensky, stops receiving treatment, his situation will be bad, and even if he doesn't, it's still not good. That the tube delivering the medicine is working, and if the writer can't see the piston moving, that doesn't mean the piston is still: We don't notice the hands of a clock moving, do we?

As for what Puryzhensky has to say about the LitFund clinic, Maya Pavlovna states that she doesn't know of a Susanna Yurevna—or a Zhanna Yurevna either—and that it was very good of Zhanna/Susanna to listen to his lungs, but if she had also occasionally listened to his heart, she might not have missed the problem there, which is why he's here. Tomorrow she'll try to make arrangements with the surgeons—no, Moscow surgeons—but Puryzhensky won't make it to the operating table unless he lets them treat him.

At first she seems to have broken through his resistance, but then he says, well, the hospital isn't a prison, and he, Puryzhensky, demands to be discharged and released immediately. And, despite it being three in the morning, Maya Pavlovna repeats all of her arguments in support of continuing his treatment, and they agree that Puryzhensky will think it over, but as soon as she leaves the ward, he says he's leaving.

"Forgive me for interfering," Father Sergius says. "You're making a mistake."

"That's easy for you to say," Puryzhensky replies. "Your situation is different."

What he wants to say is, you haven't had a heart attack. And it's true, we're all different from one other. He especially. As a priest, he's different from everyone, always.

"A man has to have a full range of emotions," continues Puryzhensky. "I can't live in a world where there's just one sorry necessity."

Father Sergius has finally gathered his thoughts: "It's obvious that Maya Pavlovna is an absolutely exceptional physician."

"I don't think so. She's too pretty."

Puryzhensky presses the button. The nurse was clearly sleeping but she responds quickly to the call and sets to the matter with alacrity: they're very weary of this patient.

Puryzhensky's monitor goes silent, the writer's tubes are removed and dropped to the floor—Miss Masha, take these! We can't keep you against your will. Write that you refuse treatment and that's it, goodbye—to be treated at your place of residence.

"What should I write? Oh dear me, the pen's run out of ink!" Puryzhensky is in complete despair.

Father Sergius gets up from his bed to hand the writer his own pen. Pushing the screen aside, he sees him.

He's half-naked and prematurely aged, his neck short and thick, his hair long and matted; fat lips, chest, and abdomen; an abundance of gray hair on his body. Bandages on both arms. Stubble. Tongue protruding from exertion.

"I, so and so," the nurse dictates, "refuse inpatient treatment. I have been warned of the possible consequences. I have no claims on the staff. If you do, indicate what kind of claims these are. Your signature and the date."

Puryzhensky can barely keep up.

"What claims could I have?" He waves his free arm.

The priest watches this unattractive, confused person and suddenly thinks: But that's me. Not my brother or my fellow human being, not the "other I" of philosophers and writers, but simply me. Our circumstances and stories are different, but it's still me. Me. Barefoot, almost naked, sitting on a cot and waiting for something. Staring into space with unfocused eyes.

"Get dressed," the nurse says, "and out the door with you. As for your sick-leave certificate and the sick list, we'll deal with all that tomorrow. Well, what are you waiting for?"

"But where am I going to go?" Puryzhensky asks suddenly, still not looking at anyone.

"You're not going. Stay here." Father Sergius doesn't notice the nurse signaling at him. "Stay. Maya Pavlovna will forgive you."

Again the dim light, the monitors beeping out of sync: for every two beats of the priest's heart the writer's heart beats three or four times. Both listen to the beeps, noticing the moments when they coincide.

"I should write about this, all of it." Puryzhensky's breathing really isn't good.

"And you will."

"It's too late. Don't you think I know?" He falls silent. Breathes. "If only you'd seen her trying to warm up the old woman!"

He's in a bad way, he says. Hopeless. He won't be writing anything.

"And what isn't written doesn't exist. Like it never happened. Can't you see?"

Father Sergius can see very clearly: he prefers reading above all else.

"Is that so," the writer says indifferently. "I'd imagined something different, a hiking group, songs . . . Do you write any poetry?"

"With a last name like mine you can't write anything but poetry."

"What is it?"

"Tyutchev."[11]

For the first time that night they both laugh, quietly.

"You know, a long time ago I wrote something along the lines of a poem . . . When I parted company with a certain group. Which just so happened to be a group of hikers. Or, more accurately, they parted company with me." Father Sergius reaches into the bedside table for his notebook, waits for Puryzhensky to ask him to read. "I've never shown this to anyone." He's still waiting. "Why aren't you saying anything?"

"I'm waiting."

There's nothing to do. He must read.

> We went barefoot around the house
> For we were the children of our time,
> We were sentimental,
> Loved simple poems, meaningless and sweet,
> Gave sympathy one-sidedly,
> We were good in misfortune, we were bad at joy,
> We were adept at practical matters,
> We knew AC from DC, we could assemble

A canoe, a tent, solidly, surely.
At first we did not believe in God,
There was plenty to disturb us:
About Isaac and Abraham,
The gilding in the church.
Then suddenly we believed,
Began living almost righteously,
Or else our emotions receded.

What am I talking about all this for?
Rucksacks were still made of aluminum,
Or duralumin, or I don't know, titanium,
Lightweight and very convenient
For moving house, for moving heavy loads.
We knew how to carry things, boxes, heavy loads,
How to help out when moving house, and at funerals,
To go after passes, hold a place in a line,
We helped more or less, after a fashion,
To the extent that we felt this to be right.

Their kindness was a priori,
Of course it went without saying,
But the way they spoke of people was vile,
They were the children of their time,
They loved Alexander Grin,
The film *Stalker*, songs by Vysotsky,
Children of the Arbat, watching *Dolls* on TV,
Conversations with Joseph Brodsky,
These days there's nothing they really like.

What conclusions can be drawn from this?
Not to fall captive to objective qualities,
Not to fear sentimentality,
Not to be taken in by a first impression.

"Is that all?" asks Puryzhensky after a pause. "Something's missing at the end."

The priest picks up his pen and adds:

> Remember: nobody has the right
> To a neighbor's love.

The last two lines he doesn't read out loud.

He slept. Not for long, but he had obviously slept soundly because when he awakes and realizes where he is, he notices big changes in both his surroundings and the light. It's morning, and the overhead light has gone out. Besides that, the dividing screen has been pushed right up to his bed, and the ventilation unit is shining through it as it noisily pumps air. Worst of all, tubes are sticking out of his neighbor's mouth and he's unconscious.

Maya Pavlovna enters.

"Has the pain come back? No? Then get your things and go to examination room number two."

"Maya Pavlovna..." He wants to ask about Puryzhensky.

"It can wait until later."

In the examination room she takes a lead with adhesive strips at one end and attaches them to Father Sergius's chest, then presses the buttons on an enormous machine that occupies the middle of the room—a treadmill he's supposed to walk on. They're short of nurses, she says, and adds something else that requires no answer. Towards morning Maya Pavlovna looks more like the lady docs, those worn-out female doctors Father Sergius has come across before.

They begin. At first it will be easy, then get harder and harder.

His neighbor isn't doing well, says Maya Pavlovna. Sergey Petrovich should concentrate on his walking and not get distracted, otherwise it will throw his breathing off.

The conveyor beneath his feet is going a little faster. He carries on walking. For now he's just fine.

"Maya Pavlovna to ICU! It's urgent!"

She rushes off. Either she's expecting to come right back or she's forgotten to stop the treadmill. Father Sergius now carries on by himself. The incline is getting steeper, and the treadmill is going faster. Every few minutes the cuff on his arm inflates, then deflates, and a cardiogram pops out of the machine. He carries on walking.

Father Sergius has begun to sweat, especially his head. It's no longer enough to walk, he must run. His legs are aching—it's all right, they'll get a break—and he's trying to catch his breath, his heart's pounding hard and fast, his sweat dripping onto the conveyor—it's hot like a fiery furnace, but—he must keep on going, keep on going, go even further! There must be a cable he can pull and bring it all to a stop, but while he can, he'll carry on. He must. For some reason he must.

"That's enough! Stop!" She's back.

His pulse is 170.

"That's more than enough," says Maya Pavlovna.

Excellent news: Sergey Petrovich is fine, in perfect health. He can go wash and freshen up. He's a star: he hung in there for eighteen minutes. Almost an office record.

And Puryzhensky? Not good at all. Better not go there.

She holds out her hand in farewell. He's always liked it when women hold out their hand in greeting and farewell—it's uncommon these days.

Outside he's once again left to his own devices.

He should let Marina know he's all in one piece, but she's probably still asleep. He wants to move, doesn't want to stop, so he decides to go home on foot. It's good when the surface beneath you is stationary and it's up to you whether to go slow or fast.

He often has to rise early, and he loves the feeling of responsibility for the whole world that comes when you're walking through a somnolent city. Although right now his thoughts are back there, at the hospital, and he doesn't even notice how he has ended up at his house. There's the fence in front of him. It's old, and beginning to rot here and there, but it doesn't break up, doesn't mar the surroundings, and lets you see all around. The gate is fastened with a rope: Marina makes sure it's closed in some fashion.

Spring has come late this year, and the flowers on the trees, many of which should not have flowered at the same time, have unfurled all at once. The names of most of them he doesn't know. The one with the little white blooms—what's that? A tree or a shrub? This one's a cherry tree, and that's an apple tree—it's grown wild, and every August it bears tiny green apples that are unfit to eat. In front of the porch there's a lilac—a shame it's almost finished flowering. And even on the spruce that he buried Mona under yesterday he can detect something flowerlike. Yellow on green, he's only just noticed. Spruce trees also flower.

He looks around a little bit longer, then opens the door. On the table there's an open bottle of wine and an ashtray full of cigarette ends—Marina hardly ever smokes now, but yesterday was not an ordinary day.

Quietly, so as not to awaken her, he goes through to Marina's room, sits on her bed, touches her shoulder with his beard.

"Heavens!" Marina looks at him in astonishment. She seems happy to see him. "Wait a second, I'll get dressed."

"No," he says. "What for?"

"Are you all right? Are you sure they haven't made a mistake?" asks Marina when he makes a sound that could have been a laugh or a moan.

No, no, there's no mistake, he's in perfect health.

"Then why are you shaking?"

Now he really is laughing, there's no mistaking it: "I'm all atremble."

It's amazing, says Marina, he doesn't smell of the hospital at all. Perhaps it's a good idea for him to get some sleep now?

And so he goes to his room, looks around, and thinks: It would be good if it could always be this way, well into old age. These books on the crowded shelves, this dark orange plaid, in places already threadbare, which he uses as a bedspread. The Greek icon by the headboard, also in shades of red and yellow. To live this way until he gets old. There's still time left. "God and a broad"—he remembers Father Lev. It's good to be alive. He closes his eyes, thinks about his neighbor the writer: what isn't written doesn't exist.

Where should he begin? The priest had a dog...

October 2012
Translated by Anne Marie Jackson

POLISH FRIEND

THE STORY doesn't start with a joke; the joke butchers it, crushes it. *The past, present, and future walk into a bar. It was tense!* And that's all, folks. Laughter. No, a story demands expansion, movement.

Here: a girl has just landed in a major Western European city. She holds a suitcase in one hand, a violin case in the other. The young border guard asks her the purpose of her trip. It's a long story: she has to play for a few people, test out a new violin... Her knowledge of the language is poor, so she keeps her answer short: "My friend, he lives here."

The border guard looks long and hard at her passport: whoa, they're almost the same age—he'd taken her for about fifteen. So why is she traveling on a Polish visa? He has to let her through—the EU, Schengen Area and all—but she ought to explain.

Polish visas are the easiest ones to get. After a brief pause, she says: "I have a friend in Poland, too."

The border guard gives her a sleazy grin. But that's okay. The main thing is that he lets her through.

And that is where the story starts.

Like all of her peers, this girl has studied music since she was about six—late kindergarten. She is now in her fourth and penultimate year at the conservatory. Her professor, well into her ninth decade, has devoted her entire life to ensuring the violin is played clearly and expressively. In the whole world there's not a pedagogue more renowned.

"Listen to yourself," the professor says. In essence that's all she says. "What am I to do with you, eh? You love music? So what—go listen to a CD. Well, what are you just standing there for? Play."

Not everyone can stick it out, but most of them do. They'll be made to repeat a particular move, year after year, until suddenly she'll say, "If only you weren't so dim..." which means they've finally got it, and now they'll never lose it.

The girl and the professor have finished for the day. The girl is packing up her violin.

"Say," the professor catches her off guard, "what instrument did you want to play as a child?"

What an odd question. The violin, of course.

The professor looks surprised.

"And how did that come about?"

And so the girl explains: in an old apartment she had found a violin, a one-eighth size, without any strings, but she had held it, twirled around with it in front of the mirror, and...

The professor mutters pensively: "So your dream's come true?"

Was that a question or a statement? And in that very moment, who is it that the professor sees—perhaps this student of hers, but sixty years down the line? Or is it just a memory?

We examine photographs from 1934, when the professor was ten years old. Those same regular features, that same detachment, that same calm. And here, a short concert program, a children's concert: Leva, Yasha, her. If the photos were of a higher quality, you'd be able to make out the little mark on the left side of each child's neck, the mark that gives away a violinist.

There's more—from the years of evacuation: Leva and Yasha again, by now with grown-up concert programs. And another: Katya and Dodik, or that's what it says on the back. *So your dream's come true...* There's a story there too, of course, but that one can't be unwrapped without losing something important, something that can't be put in words.

"To love alone does music yield," wrote Pushkin. But does it?

Let's get back to that Polish friend: once again, he's about to come in handy.

The girl returns from Europe with a beaded necklace of singular beauty. When questioned by one of her classmates (yes, a classmate— she has no real friends) she replies, not quite knowing why: "My Polish friend gave it to me."

This classmate is a violinist too. She's gabby, impetuous—excessively so—although, it must be said, she does have an occasional flair for striking imagery: "It's like opening a window, and whoosh—a soldier!" was how she described the feelings evoked by a particularly joyful modulation.

She was already engaged by this point—much to the professor's dismay: "Married? But she hasn't even played the Sibelius! There are those who are my students," she had continued, "and those who are just instructees."

In the end, the classmate had to study under another professor.

"Oh, friend, I'm so happy for you!" she says of the girl's necklace. "And there I was, thinking you'd end up like one of those arctic aardvarks."

And just like that, the Polish friend takes on some sort of existence. But it won't be long before he comes through for her big time.

Finding a violin, one that speaks in your voice, is always an event. And this violin—which, despite its sudden arrival in her life, she already knows will never leave her side—has a rich and noble sound. There isn't a hint of screechiness, not even on the highest of notes. An Italian model—half-Italian, at least: violins, too, can be crossbreeds; the body of one, the scroll of another. It's fairly young—a hundred and some years. A good man, himself rather long in the tooth, has given it to her. Certain peculiarities in the circumstances linger in the air, but neither the girl, nor indeed we, will ever learn the details.

He is a good man, comfortably off, and troubled by his conscience—
yet which good people aren't troubled by their conscience? He gave
her the violin with a single condition: that she wouldn't tell a soul.

Her classmate also takes a liking to the violin.

"How much did it set you back? Go on, say—just for a laugh."

The girl shrugs: Why is that something to laugh about?

"That Polish friend of yours again? If you ask me, I'd be terrified
carrying a thing like that around."

"But not your child?" her classmate is already a mother by this
point.

"Never much liked Poles, myself... But maybe I'm missing something?"

Apparently so.

"I mean, they're so proud, so arrogant..."

The girl isn't about to let her friend be insulted like this: "That's
not arrogance—it's integrity."

"Is he even coming to visit?"

"What's it to you?"

Her classmate shares absolutely everything—whether about her
now ex-husband, or the man or men she's currently seeing. What
secrets could they possibly have? Come on, it's no big deal!

"Can I at least ask what his name is?" her classmate asks. Clearly
she's hurt. "Seriously—not even that? Fine, have it your way."

Soon enough, everyone at the conservatory knows all about her
Polish friend. He's generous, has good taste—that's enough to stir
up some jealousy. "Still waters run deep," that's what the more experienced of her contemporaries say about her. But they're wrong: her
placid surface concealed no roiling depths.

Graduating from the conservatory is no piece of cake. For the ensemble exams, the girl wants to take on something more obscure. She
listens to music for different ensemble types. A horn trio—maybe
that could work? She finds the horn player who's considered the best
in her year: "Do you know the piece?"

"No."

"Well, would you like to play it?"

The horn player goes with his gut. "No."

For the state exams she has to do without a horn.

Now, with the conservatory behind us, it is time for the girl—and us—to move on into the future. To do more than listen, watch, and take note; to conjecture, imagine. For example, could we have foreseen the futures of the children in that photograph from 1934? Probably, yes. First, there is no such thing as chance, and second, fate is but an aspect of personality—or so it appears to us.

Of course, certain external circumstances are impossible to predict. And, where there is no such thing as chance, there is such a thing as uncertainty, and a rather broad one at that. For instance: Will our country last? Its predecessor, with all its might, was more short-lived than your average violin, for which seventy years is nothing, a piffling age: seventy-year-old violins look virtually brand-new; they have no cracks to speak of; sometimes luthiers have to imitate wear and tear. As it currently stands, it doesn't appear that this country, successor to the one in which Leva and Yasha and Katya and Dodik grew up, has a long life in store: it'll fall apart, disintegrate, too many cracks to count. But then again, that may not come to pass. We shouldn't look to contrive an outcome—let that story run its own course.

Another example: the latest technology. Why fixate on objects that evolve so rapidly? Leva and Yasha lived their entire lives without knowing a thing about computers, and, quite frankly, wouldn't have cared in the slightest. All of these gadgets are so far from perfection—is there any point in going into the nitty-gritty of how they work? How will people get around thirty-odd years from now, when our story reaches its end? What devices will they use to speak to one another, to listen to music? We are disinclined to fantasize—after all, does that really make any difference?

However, there is one thing of which we are certain. Bows will still be wound in silver wire or whalebone; ebony frogs will still be inlaid with mother-of-pearl eyes; and children's violins—one-quarter size, one-eighth size—will still bear delicate trails of salt, the salt of tears from children, who cry as they play, not stopping, not ending their music.

As for serious matters such as politics or economics—music isn't about to develop an influence on these overnight; if it does, it will be tangential, by implication. It was recently discovered that, while our Yashas and Levas were under evacuation, the Steinway & Sons piano company came to an understanding with American HQ, whose forces bombed Bechstein, Steinway's rivals, down to the ground, to the very last keyboard. It would be naive to imagine world history as a contest between two rival piano factions, especially as neither Yamaha nor Red October was involved in anything of the sort. And yet, it is also around those times that a certain pockmarked, mustachioed creature would quip facetiously of his former German ally: "He has his Goebbels, but I have my Gilels."[12] The disgust that this little witticism evokes in us convinces us of its authenticity—of the fact that the man himself truly did say it.

However, all of this politics has distracted us from our main subject—the girl's relationship with her Polish friend. With jerks, with roundabouts, our story progresses.

Travels, travels, more travels—festivals, competitions, less a life, more the continuous howl of a turbine, the nonstop clatter of wheels (it's highly doubtful any new forms of transport will emerge in the next ten to fifteen years). Once you're over thirty-two, playing in competitions is all but ruled out, so that's when your first students start arriving. Naturally, as in any business, there are the usual human elements to navigate—intrigues, scandals, backstage agreements—but these determine little. What is the difference between the violinist who, standing, plays Sibelius's violin concerto, and those who, seated, accompany her? They too could play the solo. So does the difference lie in their level of ambition, their personality? People will say the difference is fate, but that's as good as saying nothing at all.

Although in age our heroine is no longer a girl, there is still a certain preserved, fixed childishness to her persona. Every artist needs an affectation—a term the profession finds unflattering, but an apt one nonetheless. Just as surgeons, teachers, and even soldiers need particular attributes—a certain swagger, an individualistic approach, perhaps—an artist can't do without an affectation. And it's a great boon if your figure—slight, somewhat angular—and your childish facial expression reflect the music you make, when within you playing inspires joy, freshness, and wonder.

And so, she is a musician, with a first-class training and one small secret: the existence of her Polish friend, it seems, is common knowledge. And even should a husband and children appear on her horizon (what would her life be without them? And yet, with such an intense focus on music, on bowing and intonation, it would be entirely possible for her to remain alone), not even to them would she reveal her secret. She would smile, keep mum. To be fair, no one would be likely to ask.

A dacha, a house on the Oka River. For about one month a year the river is big. In the mornings our heroine walks out to look at the floodwaters: that yellowy flow, those protruding sticks. It's surprising how persistently this pitiful beauty repeats itself each year.

"How was your walk?" her former classmate asks, herself just out of bed. She's recently had a bit of a setback: they're making her reaudition for her seat in the orchestra, so she's come out here to practice. Shall we have a go at the Sibelius, just for a laugh?

Her form has dipped considerably since graduation. She puts down her instrument, turns to our heroine: "Hey, how about we message Roma and Vitalik? We could go for some shashlik, shoot the breeze . . . You can put me with Roma, and you can have Vitalik—which one do you like more?"

Sadly, tempting as that is . . . she's expecting someone else.

"Your Polish friend? Things are getting serious, I see."

To be sure. Never more so.

"Well, then, I guess I'd best be off. I wouldn't want to get in the way of your happiness."

"You've got a good heart," our heroine says to the classmate as she leaves.

"Sadly, no brains to match," the latter laughs in reply.

After her old classmate has left, our heroine will spend the evening taking in the spring sky and the trees. She'll play—not much, but well: skills learned young are never unlearned. Nor is the ability to listen to oneself.

Similar invitations, with other shashlik, other Romas and Vitaliks, often crop up on her travels, where ties are easily made, less easily untangled. But it isn't for practical matters alone that her Polish friend comes into use. And it isn't that she forgets he's just an imaginary figure, a cover story for classmates and border guards, or, say, that she develops any particular interest in Polish culture or takes up the language: the Poles she has met do actually seem rather proud. Besides, her Polish visa has long since expired—and who knows what will have become of the EU, the Schengen Agreement, by then?

No rational person believes in fantasies, but anything that has been said for decades—especially when said in whispers—acquires a most important quality: substance. It is the same way that myths—familial and national alike—can come, if not to heal, then at least to console. After forty, our heroine's Polish friend will make the occasional appearance in her dreams, dreams that stay with her in her waking hours. He has neither name, nor voice, nor face; he's just an undefined pleasantness. He'll appear in the morning, just before she wakes up. If he makes an appearance the night before an important concert, it's a sign that it will go well.

As the years go by, these important concerts shrink in number, but her number of students grows. Her pedagogical power isn't what her professor's was; she prefers praising children to anything else. And while there is a significant level of nuance to her praise, in her classroom the tears flow less freely than in Katya and Dodik's times. But some degree of waterworks is inescapable—essential, even.

It is highly unlikely that the world of music will have widened by the point at which our story ends. With the adult world, that world of *productive forces* and of *relations of production*, music will still hold but a parallel existence. Now middle-aged, our heroine will once again fly to a Western European city—the same city where it all began. A chamber-music festival, a very attractive form of music making—for performers and audiences alike. The auditorium is comfortable and always full; their program is excellent: it's a joy to be invited to such venues.

Will sheet music still exist thirty years from now? Even if not, there will still be plenty to carry: a violin, bow, rosin, strings, concert attire. It has now been a long time since her Polish friend last made an appearance; she hasn't had time to think of him—she is onstage every day. Everything is performed after just one rehearsal, two at most, but this comes at no detriment to the quality, such is the musicians' level. They rehearse in the morning, rest in the afternoon, and in the evening look at their fellow player or players, nod—*here goes*—wipe their hands on a hankie, walk out onto the stage . . . and play.

Our story is reaching its denouement, the final day. The horn trio—yes, that very same one—finally she has the chance to play it, and as the closing number, to boot. The horn player is wonderful, or so they all say—she herself has never heard him play.

However, he is running rather late to the rehearsal. She and the pianist, an aging, red-haired man-child whom she has known for many years, dip in and out of the piece as they wait. Eventually the door opens and a violist steps in: Hasn't anyone told them? The times have all had to be changed. And the horn player? Yesterday he ate something iffy, but he'll be right as rain by the concert. Horn players love food; they need it for inspiration.

The violist smiles. He was only called in this morning, but he knows the music, has always dreamed of playing alongside them, and hopes not to disappoint. Besides, he'll only be there for the rehearsal. He's a tall man, with salt-and-pepper hair—but no, this isn't the time to study him, they're already an hour behind.

They begin to play. It very soon becomes clear that the music is exactly how she had imagined it. And from the end of the first movement she feels a burgeoning sense of joy, extraordinary, from some unknown part of her being, a joy she has never felt before. She must heed the music, not her joy; listen to herself, to the others. But that joy is there, and it's swelling.

Music deals in barely discernible note values. The rhythm, no, not the rhythm—the meter, the pulse: the biggest challenge here is ensuring that everyone maintains the same pulse. The rest—crescendos, diminuendos, bowing—can all be easily fixed, but as it happens, nothing here needs to be fixed: it all comes together well—frighteningly well, for that matter.

The viola's sound has a passion and warmth to it, a desire to impart something important, something crucial; to find out about her; to reveal itself. The violin responds: "Look at the trees and the sky, and think less about the important things," or something along those lines.

And then it's over. Breathe. The pianist breaks the silence, reminding the others of his presence: "In that section with the trills, I didn't come in too strong, did I?"

No, not in the slightest.

"Oh. Well, that is my solo, after all. Shall we run through it again?"

They exchange looks. She and the violist: you can, but we won't—that run couldn't be bettered.

The violist is a German of Polish descent. He has lived in this city his whole life, and he saw her all those years ago, when she was a girl auditioning at the conservatory—back then, he too was a violinist. He didn't dare approach her then. He never really found his way until he switched to the viola. Now he plays in the local orchestra, a respectable orchestra. But she had played wonderfully, clearly and expressively; he can still remember those pieces.

His hands are large, beautiful and round, and, like hers, the skin around the nails is picked to the point of bleeding—even their neuroses are the same. He accompanies her back to her hotel, talking all the way. He'll come to watch her that evening, and after the concert ... after the concert, perhaps he might have the honor of ...

And now, for the first time in her life, she realizes where the heart is. The throat. It's in the throat.

He escorts her, pays his respects, and goes. And so ... so that's the sort of fellow he is. Ineffectual, rambling thoughts run through her mind. *That evening, and after the concert* ... Where's that joy now? It's gone.

She sits on her bed, aimlessly flipping the lock on her case. Polish friend, Polish friend. So her dream's come true? For some reason her heart won't settle down.

And then: Where's her bow? It's a disaster—her bow's gone! Flushed and sweating, she races back to the auditorium where they had rehearsed, desperately hoping not to bump into you-know-who. At first she can't find the right door. Everything is scattering around her, somehow.

She has lost minor things in her time—keys, jewelry, that very passport—and even certain larger things—suitcases, for example, had gone missing more than once. But her bow? That had never happened. Oh, thank God, there it is—it's on the piano.

It appears that everything is as it should be. Without knowing why, she calls the organizers. What has gotten into her? It's fear—she is afraid.

"Well, hello!" The organizers are pleased she has called. "We were just about to touch base. The horn player has rallied—could you spare him an hour to look at the music?"

"No!" she can barely hold back her tears, "That's not possible, I can't!"

Yes, she is aware that she herself selected this piece, but for some reason now it's the last thing she wants to play. She reels out a few contradictory excuses: something's happened at home, her shoulder is hurting. Why are they going on about contractual obligations? It's not like they've ever had to cancel a performance because of her before, is it? She asks them to call her a car, let her go quietly—they can come up with something.

It's only when she's on the way to the airport that her heart begins to settle down. *To love alone does music yield*—the words circle around in her head. But who has yielded what here, and to whom?

On the plane she sits by the window: the trees aren't visible, of course, but there's more than enough sky. She lands back in her home country—God knows what name it will go by, by then. But we've already mentioned that.

A day or two later she will walk into the classroom, look at the girl—her student—and say: "Well, what are you just standing there for? Play."

June 2013
Translated by Alex Fleming

THE MILL

WE HAD it worse during the war. And the years that followed weren't exactly a bed of roses, either. No, we've never had it as good as we do now.

The town's name is Liebknechtsk, but by force of habit many still know it as the Mill, even though the mill itself was shut down some years back; now it's overrun with grasses and maples. Japan Sashka's house is run-down, too: its owner, Sashka Oberemok, was a local who ran off to Japan. Or maybe it wasn't Japan—either way, we're splitting hairs: of those of us still in town, Uncle Zhenya's the only one who's ever been abroad. He served in Poland in the eighties.

"Uncle Zhenya, tell us about your time abroad!"

After all, you have to find something to talk about. You can't just sit there.

"Well, they started kicking up a fuss..."

"Who're *they*?"

"Whaddaya mean, who? The Poles. So we went in, set up a few missiles..."

"And the Poles?"

"The Poles, God knows! You think they'd give us a report? Look, our job was to hold a position—we had four military districts there. So we showed up, spread out..."

Events here are infrequent and poorly remembered. It's been almost three years since the Liebknechtsk Integrated Paper Mill, a so-called city-forming enterprise, closed down. Condenser paper, cable-insulation paper, filter paperboard, corrugated-cardboard boxes... the mill had dozens of different product types. Of course, there had been some problems with the market, but they kept on working; the cylinders turned; the fabric conveyors looped; the pulp was dried. This was peerless equipment, made back in the GDR.

As to who owned the mill, no one had ever given that much thought. After all, everything had been state owned. And then it belonged to the labor collective, to the workers. And what do workers need? To pocket their wages on time, or at least without too much delay—very few can actually wrap their minds around all these different forms of property ownership. Anyway, directors came and went, and life, of a kind, carried on; they kept on working. They built new homes—and not only for themselves, but for the local teachers, and the doctors, too.

And then, after some time away, Sashka Oberemok came back to town and made it clear just who the boss of this mill was now. Sashka could quite happily knock your teeth out, then follow it up with a broken or dislocated arm—which is, by the way, exactly what he did to a certain Tatar; for some reason Sashka had never liked Tatars. But not just them. Not long before that run-in, Sashka had also dealt a heavy blow to a young waitress, a girl he'd studied with; she had, perhaps understandably, not been too thrilled about serving a former classmate. They said he broke her nose. And let's put it this way: she wasn't about to go complaining about it to anyone.

Sashka built himself a big house—redbrick, with towers—so that everyone would see just how high he had risen. Almost a million rubles in debt to the electricians alone—that's the sort of house we're talking about. People said his family would move here too, though no one ever caught a glimpse of them. Be that as it may, Sashka well and truly had risen: he was a deputy now, a local deputy—not a federal one yet, but the man was still shy of forty.

To begin with, things went well for him at the mill: he took out a loan, gave the boys a bit of a bonus. He spared a bit for himself, too:

new businesses appeared in town, all of which belonged to him, Sashka. But then things took a turn for the worse, and the mill stopped earning. The boys started kicking up a fuss, just like those Poles. Though truth be told, they never did stop working.

A city executive came to town, listened attentively to what the workers had to say.

"I understand you," he said, "and this situation you're in. But it's not only you—timber-processing businesses everywhere are struggling at the moment."

So what was the point of all this fuss, if it was happening everywhere? As we say, we had it worse during the war.

Then one of the women piped up: "But Mr. Oberemok wasted millions just on beautifying his house!"

The executive sighed.

"Was that beautifying—or *beatifying*—his house?" and with that he promptly closed the meeting. Before leaving, he made one enigmatic remark: "You all have rights; you just don't know how to use them."

The above-average level of phenol in the local water was an issue that, the executive said, the workers had raised correctly—it would be discussed in Parliament. He was already in his car as he said this, sitting sideways, shaking off his boots: the winter had been long, snowy. And he promised, by the by, to help out with the fuel oil—the entire town's heat depended on the mill. And one final thing: as he drove past the church, he was seen crossing himself.

At that point Sashka, too, was on the executive committee. He chewed his way through the assembly. He was always chewing gum, or at least had been for the past few months: he'd quit smoking, they said, that was why. And, once the trial was over (percentages, loans, in short—complete bankruptcy, so much so that people started to pity Sashka: despite everything, he was still one of us), a man showed up in a pinstriped jacket, his hair slicked back into a ponytail. A crisis manager. He brought Sashka money—just under a million dollars—to,

you know, *go quietly*—and transferred the mill over to its new owners, along with the affiliate businesses. But Sashka—apparently enraged
by this man's presence—took the chewing gum straight out of his
mouth, and pressed it into the man's chest pocket. This happened in
his waiting room; his secretary saw it all. He didn't take the money.
Instead, over the May holidays he gave some cash to a few of his boys,
and they shredded all of the fabric in the paper machines. None of
it could be glued or sewn back together, nor in any way replaced. He
only gave them about five hundred rubles each for the job, but his
boys were glad even of that. And that was that. The machines, ruined,
still stand there to this day.

"But how could you, Uncle Zhenya?"

Uncle Zhenya was one of the guys who shredded the fabric. What
else was he going to do? It was boss's orders.

After that, an entirely different group of men arrived—no pony-
tails—and Sashka made off to "Japan."

What else is there to remember? Sashka would shoot at his neighbors' goats from an upstairs window if they ever strayed onto his
property, but he never hit them; he probably just shot to scare them.
His portrait remained—enormous, about three meters tall: Alexander Yurievich Oberemok in an ermine robe. And his date of birth.
Everyone knew the year Sashka was born anyway: he had a tattoo of
his name across one set of knuckles, across the other set, the year of
his birth. But the portrait is a poor likeness. You can see for yourself—they say there are still photos of Sashka online.

Almost three years have passed. The town lives. It's nothing to
rave about, but still, we've never had it so good. The state supplies our
fuel oil, the boiler house works, and homes have heat—hot water,
even. Some of the boys from the mill have found jobs in security,
some in taxis. Uncle Zhenya's registered at the job center. And so the
mill, Sashka Oberemok—that's all in the past. And the present? In
the present, a young woman, Alya Ovsiannikova, lies hooked up to
a ventilator in the intensive-care unit of Liebknechtsk's hospital.
Every day her husband comes to the hospital, but he isn't allowed

inside, and he doesn't ask the doctors for anything, either. Alya's husband's name is Tamerlan; her doctor is Viktor Mikhailovich.

———

Viktor Mikhailovich is held in good regard. First, he doesn't drink, and second, he is a man of advanced years, experienced. He is careful behind the wheel and keeps his car in good condition: always clean and in working order, as it has been for the eight years that Viktor Mikhailovich has lived in this town.

"Today's cars are no less complex in their composition than human beings."

When Viktor Mikhailovich talks about his car, his face lights up: "This car holds seven different types of liquid alone: brake fluid, cooling fluid..." He knows what all of these seven liquids are, and he refills and changes them precisely when he should.

He had initially been recruited to Liebknechtsk because of his certification in intensive care and anesthesiology, at a time when the town could still offer him an apartment. Had he not moved here, they might as well have closed the hospital: it wouldn't have met its licensing requirements, and the entire mill complex would have had to go God knows where for treatment. They do hardly any operations here, and anesthesia is administered by an anesthesiology nurse, but naturally nothing is possible without that license.

"If it's necessary, it's necessary; quite correct. The men who made these laws must surely know better than us."

Viktor Mikhailovich is paid a part-time wage as an intensive-care physician in addition to a full-time wage as a therapeutist. The latter is his primary occupation, although over the course of his life Viktor Mikhailovich has tried his hand at a number of different disciplines. He holds certificates in many specializations, including public health management. His indicators are some of the best in the entire province: the health plan is being implemented—exactly the right number of patients, staying exactly the right length of time; the mass health examinations have been carried out; and his department is even in good working order. He himself is never absent during working hours, and he is always sober, even on public holidays. Visiting hours are normally between six and eight p.m. Naturally, no visitors are allowed into the intensive-care unit.

His preferred treatment method is anything that can be administered through an IV drip: this is both easier on the grannies—they feel they're getting the treatment they deserve—and adaptable to the needs of the health plan. Simply lie back, take in the medicine for a while, and then you can get back home to your TV. In six months' time, come in for some more repairs. He once heard someone call them *dripairs*. They're good for any illness. The grannies he treats here have the full gamut.

"What else do you want? As far as I can tell, a diagnosis of 'old age' has never been reversed."

Yes, the grannies come to him—who else do they have? There are two other district therapeutists, both women, but they're never at work past lunchtime. They'll say they're being called out, but no one is fooled by these calls of theirs. Both are of retirement age: the hospital is starved for staff, but that's the case everywhere nowadays.

"Doctors used to have to come here on placements," Viktor Mikhailovich explains, although he prefers not to elaborate on general topics of conversation.

In the past, Viktor Mikhailovich had notions of what was bad and what was good, but over the years he's gotten used to it all—to life, to himself. Like anyone else, he tries to avoid unpleasantness. If he is asked to prescribe one medication or another, to run a particular test, or to send a patient into the city, he will ask: "So *that*'s what you need, eh?" But as a rule he always complies: if you don't, they might dash off a complaint. And while complaints in themselves are nothing terrible, the smooth road is always preferable to the one with potholes.

His working day runs from eight a.m. to four p.m. After that, any questions go to the duty doctors. Viktor Mikhailovich dislikes being pestered with questions: So-and-so and such-and-such—how can we treat it?

"Look on the Internet. There is a lot of information there."

Viktor Mikhailovich doesn't use computers himself. And the new ventilator the hospital received—the one sent to all hospitals as part of a recent presidential modernization program—remained unassembled until just last week. "You can't teach an old dog new tricks" is his favorite saying. Another favorite: "Get your head out of the clouds."

Ovsiannikova is critically ill. Critically ill patients—especially young ones—are sent to the city, if they can make it that far. If not, they are sent across the road instead, to a red building behind the garages. Every *unfavorable outcome* causes some level of distress, particularly if it involves a person of working age. Of course, with the elderly, it isn't so complicated: at seventy, eighty, why bother resuscitating?

Whenever a nurse informs him that you-know-what has happened, Viktor Mikhailovich will resort to the same stock phrase: "That's the patient's right." He will fish out the records and set about filling them out. But he won't go to look at the body—hasn't he seen enough dead people?

Ovsiannikova, however, is a special case. Viktor Mikhailovich has calculated that she will live just over one more month. Five weeks, to be precise. Although her brain has been damaged irreversibly, her heart still beats, and the ventilator keeps her breathing. Her condition, as they say, is critical.

"Critical, but stable," Viktor Mikhailovich tells Tamerlan, Ovsiannikova's husband—if he can't get the nurse to speak to him instead. No one likes to have to deal with the relatives.

Ovsiannikova was brought to the hospital to give birth last Friday. It was urgent; there wasn't enough time to get her to the city. Births are a rarity in this hospital, and thus not particularly well coordinated. Viktor Mikhailovich didn't oversee the birth: there's always someone else capable of running around and barking out orders. He only saw

Ovsiannikova towards the end of the working day, after she had given birth. The child had already been taken into the city, but Ovsiannikova had been moved upstairs. He hadn't wanted to give her a bed: *Call the city hospital, get them to send their emergency-response unit—all I have is a therapeutics department.* But in the end he took her in: If she hadn't held out until their ambulance arrived, whom might he have had to answer to? After all, Viktor Mikhailovich was a certified intensive-care physician, and here was a young woman whose blood pressure was up to three hundred, whose body was in convulsions—as soon as one seizure ended, another would begin.

As he walked up and down the stairs between the two floors, Viktor Mikhailovich started to feel a pain in the nape of his neck. Ovsiannikova was given one drip, and then another, and Viktor Mikhailovich administered a number of different treatments while waiting for the city's medics to arrive. Initially, Ovsiannikova's blood pressure would not drop, but then, after she vomited, it dropped completely. This happened just as the emergency-response unit's yellow Volkswagen pulled up, these new mobile ICUs another result of the government's modernization program.

He should, admittedly, have called them sooner. But Viktor Mikhailovich calls for backup in only the most serious of cases: in they drive, casting their aspersions, trying to teach him medicine. And that would be fine, if it were only his authority that took the hit, but you can never leave while they're still in the department, and on top of that you have to host them, put out a spread, as they say. And Viktor Mikhailovich almost never drinks, no: he has hypertension.

Some newbie stepped out of the ambulance—a redhead, about thirty by the looks of things. Viktor Mikhailovich had never seen him before. He was wearing a down jacket and a short doctor's coat, a set of keys dangling from his neck.

"Right, hit me," he called out to Viktor Mikhailovich from the doorway.

Hit me? Is that any way to address a colleague?

"Well, high blood pressure, convulsions," he replied.

"I see. Eclampsia then. And your treatment?"

Viktor Mikhailovich was finding it hard to keep his composure. "Did we bring down the blood pressure? Yes, we did," he thought to himself. "So why are you looking at her records? Next you'll be wanting me to get out the used ampoules too!"

"How could it be eclampsia if she's already given birth?" he asks—aloud, this time.

"It happens. In the first forty-eight hours. Hold on—she's not breathing!"

Viktor Mikhailovich doesn't quite recall what happened next: his legs turned to jelly, his eyes clouded over. But he *did* help; he participated. The youngster inserted the tube, fitted the ventilator, and initiated artificial respiration. Watching the young man's hands flit deftly over the flashing buttons of the ventilator screen, Viktor Mikhailovich couldn't help but mutter: "You youngsters have it easy," he said. "You know foreign languages. In my day we had to figure it all out for ourselves."

What was so funny about that?

They finished up, took off their gloves and went into the staff room. It had been a hard day; time to relax. Edik or Erik—Viktor Mikhailovich didn't catch the young man's name. He filled the man's shot glass to the brim, but gave himself only a few drops.

"So what now?" Viktor Mikhailovich asked. What he actually meant was: Can you take her? It was clear the youngster wouldn't. "And if she wakes up? We should probably immobilize her arms, no?"

The youngster shrugged. "That's hardly likely. Her brain's probably already gone."

That was that then. Nothing to be done.

"So who is she? Looks like a well-raised young lady to me."

Who knows? By the looks of things, yes. Best not to give such matters much thought.

"And what's your normal demographic? Grannies mainly, I'll bet?"

Who else?

"Grannies, yes. And the working class."

The youngster laughed again.

"The working class. I thought they only existed in books nowadays."

They sat for a while, chatting about this and that, nothing work-related. Things like when they would actually get some proper roads. Oh, yes, on that note, there was something Viktor Mikhailovich had been wanting to find out for some time: "Is it true that those Volks-wagens of yours have a boxer engine?"

The young man looked at him, his expression unreadable.

"Online," he advised, "look it up online, I'm sure it's all there. As for her," he said, nodding in the direction of intensive care, "call me." He gave Viktor Mikhailovich his phone number.

How can anyone drive a car and not have the slightest interest in its cylinder configuration? Although tired, Viktor Mikhailovich stayed even later, filling out the records. Best to do it straightaway; by Monday it would have slipped his mind. So, eclampsia. Why not. He looked up its code: O15. No other extraneous thoughts. Otherwise you'll drive yourself mad. Burn out emotionally.

At the start of this week *he* called—the youngster from the city.

"How is she—I don't suppose she woke up? Oh. So that's it, then?"

Of course not. Viktor Mikhailovich is going to try to keep her going. For forty-two days.

"Forty-two? Why forty-two?"

Oh, young academician, is it possible that you could be ignorant of something so simple? Forty-two days is six weeks. Death in the six weeks after childbirth is considered a maternal mortality; after that, it isn't. That's the system. What, don't they write about that in your Internets? Get your head out of the clouds. And done.

———

Alya Ovsiannikova was born in 1991. Her mother died in childbirth; no one knows what happened to her father. Uncle Zhenya is her only relation, so it's his name that she bears as her patronymic: Yevgenievna. But asking him about her parents is a pointless pursuit—Uncle Zhenya doesn't even remember his time in Poland, where he served. It's not that he drinks so very much—only as much as anyone else—but something has changed in him lately. Tamerlan thinks it's because he broke the machines at the mill that time. But he also says that Uncle Zhenya is a truly good man for not sending Alya to an orphanage when she was little—the nineties were tough on everyone. It had never even occurred to Alya that she might have ended up in a home.

What's her first memory? Oh yes: Uncle Zhenya bathing her in a basin in front of a hot wood-burning stove. They used to have to stoke the stove regularly; Alya's job was to tear the bark off the firewood. Of course you can also pack the stove full of newspaper, but bark's much more fun to burn. What else? Alya used to have a knack for finding mushrooms; she had a special book about them—she learned to read in kindergarten—and she still knows all of their names.

How did she get by without a mother? Another one of Tamerlan's questions. She hasn't known anything else. Tamerlan often asks her questions she doesn't quite know how to answer. Alya isn't used to talking about herself. And all the people around her—her neighbors, teachers, classmates—also speak rarely, as though they find it difficult. For the most part, people aren't rude, they're shy—at least that's how she sees it. Alya isn't rude either; she's soft-spoken, although towards the ends of sentences she does sometimes raise her voice unexpectedly. She also holds her head high, as though in some act of defiance, but then again, that's just appearances.

At school she was neither a good nor a bad student, nor particularly interested in her grades—especially after a run-in with a math problem about a caterpillar in a well: "If the caterpillar climbs three meters during the day, but slides down two meters at night, when will it get out of the well, if the well is five meters deep?"

Alya ponders this caterpillar's movements as she sits in her darkened room. Uncle Zhenya is already back from his shift; she can hear the sound of onions frying from the other side of the net curtain. This means it'll be buckwheat kasha with onion for dinner. Uncle Zhenya calls her.

"Coming!"

She pictures that little caterpillar: one meter at the end of the first night, two at the end of the second, two plus three is five ... So it'll get out of the well on the third day.

The teacher is checking the class's workbooks. Alya shows hers. Five, five; everyone except Alya has come to the same conclusion. To Alya's surprise, the teacher says: "Excellent, top marks for everyone, except you, Ovsiannikova—you get a three."

"But Olga Yurievna, if it's wrong then why not a two?" Alya asks chirpily.

Olga Yurievna doesn't want to mar her grade book with twos—the mark of failure. The school has an inspection coming; they now make regular checks of grade books. She checks the back of the textbook in case; it also gives the answer as three. Oh dear, must be a typo. Ovsiannikova should have thought for herself, not simply copied from the book. She doesn't actually believe that the rest of the students are idiots and that she's the only one with brains, does she?

Alya almost never cries—she doesn't really have much to cry about—but when she does, her forehead breaks out in red blotches. And even so she is beautiful, with her slender figure and long fingers, everything about her—her mouth, her eyes—elongated. Her hair is light, golden; her friends envy her her hair. Tamerlan says it's a shame there isn't a single photo of her as a child in the house; all they have are school photos, official ones, and in those, no one looks like themselves.

Their home (or half home—it has only two rooms), her school, the snatches of countryside that form the backdrop to the local tarmac and chimney stacks: as a schoolgirl Alya has never seen any other landscape. Not far from her school, there is a lone, abandoned monument: Karl Liebknecht, Knight of the World Revolution. His statue is stooping, with round glasses and a small head, and Alya finds it appealing, somehow. She sometimes comes out here just to stand beside it for a while. But then she discovers that *Knecht* doesn't mean knight, but slave, servant—and not even one of the revolution. She tells her friends about her discovery; they laugh: *God, what rubbish her head is filled with*! They already have admirers, suitors—boys, in a word—whereas Alya goes straight home after school, or, if she takes a detour along the way, she does it alone: she has no close friends. The girls tease her, tell her to wait for her Karl. So be it: she's bored of her peers. All they know is drinking beer and swearing.

How did she end up in the police force? A vacancy came up, and Uncle Zhenya had stopped earning by then—they were both living solely off the benefits Alya received as an orphan, and even those were to end when she turned eighteen. Besides, the uniform—a dark blue skirt and a light blue blouse—had caught Alya's eye. The police clerk's tasks are limited: just sit and type out some columns of figures, then you can carry on reading. Her desk is by the window, the sun is shining, a hair falls down onto the page; she picks it up, pulls at it . . .

Why didn't she leave town after finishing school, Tamerlan asks—was it the money? No—how could she have left Uncle Zhenya? Besides, she had never been anywhere else, other than into the city, and there everything's just the same as it is in their town, only bigger, with lots of cars. Plus: If she'd left, how would she have met Tamerlan? Alya knows this is why he asked the question.

Tall, thin, and stooping, he had appeared at the police station during the May holidays, his arm wrapped in a bandage. It was clearly causing him a lot of pain: he kept wincing, touching his bandage, wiping the sweat from his forehead. He said that he wanted to file a complaint; he had a hospital certificate to support his case.

"Who did that?"

"Oberemok," Tamerlan replied, "Alexander Yurievich Oberemok."

By this point he was no longer speaking to just the officer on duty: the others had overheard and sidled over, and Alya had snapped her book shut. Everyone knew who Alexander Yurievich was.

"But why?"

It emerged that Tamerlan had refused to take Oberemok's cash and destroy the mill's machines—not only that; he had tried to prevent others from doing so too. He asked the officers to initiate proceedings, on whichever article they saw most fit.

The police were not aware of the particulars of the vandalism at the mill, but a complaint against Alexander Yurievich? That, of course, was something quite out of the ordinary. The young man had, presumably, been drinking over the holidays? There was normally a spike in accidents then. No, Tamerlan didn't drink. He had expected such questions, so he had had the doctors test him for that, too. Another certificate. His trousers were torn, grubby. He was a pitiful sight.

"Are you sure you don't want to rethink this? This is the director of the mill—your boss. After something like this . . ."

"Just take my statement—it's your job."

"Fine, if that's what you want. Go on, write."

But Tamerlan couldn't write: his arm was either dislocated or broken. He was left-handed.

"Come here," Alya said, "I'll write for you."

And that's how they met. Then Alya took him home and mended his trousers. Uncle Zhenya came home late that night, and he was in no state to be asking questions. By the end of the May holidays, they had given notice at the local registry office; Alya did the writing this time too. As they waited for the wedding, Tamerlan's arm healed, and, for reasons already explained, no one was able to pursue the first complaint Alya had made on his behalf. Their wedding was a modest one, quiet; Tamerlan had no relatives in town. Everyone shouted "*Gorko!*" and Tamerlan kissed the bride.

What surprised Alya the most: Tamerlan had no tattoos. Alya had seen very few men undressed, but Uncle Zhenya, for example, had an eagle on his chest, his blood type, various other things.

"What, did you think we're born with tattoos?" Tamerlan mocks her.

Also: he doesn't drink vodka—no vodka, no wine, no nothing. Not that he's a particularly religious man; that's just how he was raised. He confesses: there was one time when he did drink—a lot—but the morning after was terrible. His neighbor had been selling his car, a Volga Universal, a pickup (Alya doesn't know about cars). The car had caught Tamerlan's eye, but he had no money, so the neighbor made a proposal: "Have a drink with me, and I'll give it to you half price." He was desperate to get a Tatar drunk. But he also kept his word. Having the car has been a big help to them, especially now that there's no work at the mill. Tamerlan uses it as a taxi, and to transport various goods to shops. He transports whatever he's given; he never turns down a thing.

They live with Uncle Zhenya, have done so for the past year and a half. He has started getting money from the job center—more, even, than what he was earning towards the end of his time at the mill. Every evening Tamerlan meets Alya at the police station. They have plans: to build something; buy soft furnishings; go away somewhere. Neither of them has ever seen the sea, and they want things—all sorts of things, things Alya hadn't even thought to dream of. But neither soft furnishings nor the Black Sea preoccupy her a great deal: everything will come in its own time. After all, she's met her Liebknecht, without even having to seek him out, or wait so very long. And then she gets pregnant.

Alya, strangely, never gave this possibility much thought, while for his part Tamerlan had probably started to want children—he was already thirty. In any case, this isn't something they had discussed. But watching Alya's stomach transform, touching it—that turns out to be even more exciting than dreaming of any old sea. The same goes for choosing names. They haven't sought any advice from the hospital; Alya went there once, for an ultrasound, but they told her something she didn't understand. So she asked them not to say whether it was a girl or a boy—she didn't want to find out yet. Pregnant women often have their own little quirks. And so time passes, right up until around the sixth month, when Alya's arms, legs, and face start to swell, and Tamerlan takes her into the city to see a doctor, and she is hospitalized to protect the pregnancy. Alya speaks of it as the worst experience of her life.

First of all, they riddled her arms with needles—to insert the drip—which is fine, Alya would have been able to bear that, but for some reason they took her clothes and, more importantly, her phone: the chief physician was against pregnant women using mobile phones— something to do with signals, some sort of waves—whatever it was, Alya didn't understand. And no visitors were allowed, either: they were all concerned about infections. Alya sat on her bed and cried; she had never cried so much in all her life, and then she decided to speak to the chief physician. The old man was sitting in his office, scary, bald, tanned…

As Alya tells him her story, Tamerlan hugs her, kisses her forehead and her eyes.

…tanned, like completely brown. And all around her, his whole office was plastered in huge religious icons, red and gold—she had never seen so many in one place before. Not to mention certificates, gold and silver as well. She speaks to the guy in a normal voice, so that he can see she's not crazy, that she just wants to go home, that she needs her things and her phone. And he tells her she won't get anything; she'll have to lie there for twelve to fourteen days. That's their system. And when she does eventually cry, he laughs and tells her to take it up with the police. But then she remembers that she is the police, and then they give her her things and her phone, and they promise to send her her medical certificate and discharge notes, and she takes the bus home because she doesn't want to wait the hour and a half that it'll take for Tamerlan to come and collect her. Besides, he probably has his own things to do.

There are many other things that she doesn't tell Tamerlan, things that happened to her when he wasn't there. Life goes on for another five or six weeks, and these aren't bad times, but she has already started to feel quite unwell. And then she suddenly goes into labor, which is also unexpected; they thought she still had one month to go.

And so an ambulance takes Alya on ahead, and Tamerlan follows behind in the Volga, and when they wheel her out of the vehicle he's able to catch a glimpse of her. She is looking at him—the look of a shortsighted person who has suddenly dropped her glasses. But Alya has never been shortsighted.

———

We already know what follows. A girl is born. Alya Ovsiannikova's condition is critical, but stable. Viktor Mikhailovich has calculated that this is how she will remain for five more weeks, although he himself has his doubts: it's difficult to keep a person alive on a ventilator, and it's also impossible for over a month to go by without a single power cut hitting the hospital.

So life, for the moment, goes on. Uncle Zhenya wanders around, pestering his boys: "Buddy, got smokes?"

They never refuse him.

"Uncle Zhenya, tell us about those missiles you set up in Poland..." But most of them know the situation he's in, and simply hand over the cigarettes.

In the evenings Tamerlan cooks food for himself and for Zhenya, and every morning he sets off on his one-and-a-half-hour journey into the city, to the children's ward (they don't take inquiries over the phone). By three or four p.m. he heads back to Alya, or, more precisely, to the doctor: Doesn't she need any medicine? How's she doing?

Viktor Mikhailovich is hurt by Tamerlan's constant questions. Hasn't he already explained it all? Nothing is needed. And even if it were, there are directives: relatives cannot buy medicines or care products for patients. Her condition is stable.

Today is a short day, a Friday. When Viktor Mikhailovich heads home at the end of the working day, Tamerlan is waiting for him in the street.

"How's Alya? Is there any hope?"

Viktor Mikhailovich gets into his car, sits sideways, shakes the snow off his boots, and then turns to face forwards in the seat: "There's always hope," he says. "As long as one's living, there's always hope."

September 2013
Translated by Alex Fleming

AFTER ETERNITY

The Notes of a Literary Director

MY RECALL for faces is dreadful, and I have a difficult time committing my patients to memory. I can hardly remember anyone after their first visit, especially if they just came in for a checkup or, worse, to get my name on some paperwork: a referral to a health resort, say, or a letter to the Medical-Labor Expert Commission recommending disability benefits. The latter I refuse ruthlessly: show any sign of yielding and you'll get a stack of requests under the door. Medicine is serious work; we aren't in the hospitality trade, thank you very much. As for all your Expert Commissions, they're rotten to the core. Don't you know how to pay a bribe? And anyway, that's none of my business.

That said, I didn't chase away Alexander Ivanovich Ivlev, the author of the notes you'll soon be reading. He made an impression on me from the start. He approached me in the corridor and addressed me either as "Doctor" or by my first name and patronymic, but there was so much dignity in his tone, and so little insolence—an exceedingly rare combination in our neck of the woods. I asked him into my office.

There was something out of the ordinary in the old man's appearance, in his frame, his bearing, the way he walked—something birdlike. A straight back, fine, long fingers, light eyes—almost colorless, not watery but transparent—and a large, pointed nose. But no, there wasn't anything remotely demonic about Alexander Ivanovich. On the contrary, he seemed boyish and cheerful, quick to smile, capable of having a pleasant conversation that didn't devolve into hysterics, as so often happens in hospitals—my colleagues will know what I mean. And he was dressed well, better than the average patient, with, as it turned out, artistic taste. But I won't go into who was wearing what; that's well beyond my powers of recall.

I sat him down in front of me and leafed through his paperwork.

"How are you holding up, Alexander Ivanovich?"

"In keeping with my age and social status." Quite a response.

He had once been the literary director of a theater. Our town had no theater ("thank God," he said), besides which, Alexander Ivanovich had retired long ago. He was compelled to turn to me for a sad reason: to fill out an application to a home for the elderly and disabled.

"For veterans. We call ourselves veterans—I'm not sure of what, exactly. Do forgive my distracting you."

What kind of counterindications can there be for what is really a poorhouse, however you choose to call it? Just sign the paper, stamp it, and send him on his way. But I decided to examine him first. I wanted to do something nice for this charming man, and what's the nicest thing a doctor can do?

The nurse helped him onto the examination table. It was only then that I noticed that physical exertion was difficult for Alexander Ivanovich.

I'll let you in on a secret: we experience a thrill, almost a pleasure, upon encountering a serious, rare illness, especially if we're the first to diagnose it, if it's curable, or if it's not directly related to our speciality. This affords us a chance to demonstrate our powers of observation, the breadth of our knowledge. In the case of poor Alexander Ivanovich, however, I experienced no thrill. It's not that he was in perfect health (he wasn't, not at all), but that, during our brief acquaintance, I had come to like the old man. And to diagnose someone you know and like with an illness, even a curable one—no, that's no source of pleasure. And how was a lonely, elderly pensioner to cope with our system of so-called high-tech care? After all, it wasn't a happy family life and prosperity that had inspired him to move into a home for the elderly, whom he so kindly calls veterans.

Needless to say, I'll skip over the medical particulars of the story.

"An operation. Well, if that's what the doctor orders . . ." Alexander

Ivanovich took the news of his diagnosis with unusual equanimity. "How long do you think I've got left without it?"

A year, I told him. A year. And not a good year. We need air more than we need food and water.

I know how to persuade people. Some even consider me a tyrant. That's putting it a bit strongly—it all depends on one's motives, doesn't it? But Alexander Ivanovich wasn't hard to persuade. And so: it's off to Moscow (here's the address), having phoned ahead of time (I'll give him the number), to obtain an opinion from the professor who'll perform the operation, then back to the regional office for a fee waiver, and if they don't give it straightaway, call me immediately—the number is right here, on the paperwork. "You'll find the word *prosecutor* is very helpful at the regional office. Will you remember?" A hesitant nod. Then, in a month or a month and a half, two at most, he'll receive a summons. When the surgery's done, come back and I'll take care of you.

To be frank, this process doesn't always work, especially for the elderly, but we've also had some success. We have to try. We bid each other a rushed, awkward farewell. I don't believe I even held out my hand: there was another patient waiting.

In the evening, as I was tidying up, I found a notebook wrapped in plastic. It had Alexander Ivanovich's name on it. Appeared to be something personal. Should I call? The nurse says he doesn't have a phone, neither a landline nor a cell. Oh, well—he's bound to remember, and when he does, he'll come for it. I slipped it into the desk drawer where I keep all sorts of odds and ends.

It may well be that I'm now investing my impressions of Alexander Ivanovich's manners and appearance with what I learned from his—whatever you want to call it—narrative, notes. I may be filling things in, fleshing them out, but back then, he was a patient like any other. Pleasant enough. Our business is to cure illnesses, earn a living, worry about our families. Let's not idealize the profession: yes, it's a good one, possibly the best, but it's still a profession—it has its boundaries.

We must play as small a role as possible in the lives of our patients. Still, some weeks later I remembered: How's Alexander Ivanovich getting on? Was he admitted? Operated on? I telephoned Moscow: How's our old man doing? Apparently he never showed up. Or maybe he had, but they simply didn't notice, maybe neither the seriousness of his condition nor his personality had made an impression.

"A shabby old fellow?"

No, neat, well preserved. And not all that old, either.

"We had someone come up from your parts. A woman."

They seem to keep no records, no notes. It's true, I had sent a woman up. I might as well find out how she's doing.

"All right then," they say, "send us your old man."

Calling the regional office is pointless, not to mention unpleasant. I asked the nurse to do it. "We can't be of help"—QED Alexander Ivanovich wasn't at the home for the elderly. No one had called him an ambulance. He hadn't passed through our morgue.

All right, he didn't have a phone, but we had his address. Ours is a small town. It may seem a bit extravagant to turn up at a patient's door unbidden, but I drove out to see him anyway.

He didn't have the house to himself; he shared it. There's a man in the doorway. A typical local fellow, unmemorable. I say something quickly, not very distinctly, but with force, confidence. No one listens to the words you say. What matters is the tone.

"Hold on. I'll ask ma."

By now I'm well versed in the local lingo: *ma* means *wife*.

I push Alexander Ivanovich's door half open. Strange. It's unlocked. Looks like the neighbors have encroached on his territory. To say that he lives (lived) modestly is as good as not saying anything at all. Times are hard for lots of people these days. But here you can still get by: the standard of living's low—it's the provinces.

The wife comes in, so now there are two of them, and you can sense the aggression building. Both are heavyset, disheveled, and the smell is bad. I explain why I've come—no, they can't help me.

"What are those jars for? Are they his? Alexander Ivanovich's?"

"They're ours," the wife replies. "We'll take them."

Their neighbor's gone. He left.

"When? Where'd he go?"

"What, he's got to tell us everything?"

Typical: though they have no qualms about barging into his home, the pair take offense at the very suggestion that they might have paid the least bit of attention to their neighbor. The bedrock of the regime. I'm just saying, as an aside.

In the evening I had a thought: What if they'd killed my Alexander Ivanovich? And why not? The fat man and his ma had that look about them: practical. And the last name fit too: the Krutovs—hard-boiled. They killed him, hid the body or buried it somewhere, and now they've got the use of his room. There are fewer and fewer odd folks around, fewer and fewer eccentrics—not just in Moscow, but here too. When I was young, they were every place you looked. So where had they all gone? I tell you where: they succumbed in the struggle for existence.

I shared my thoughts with the chief of the local police.

"The Krutovs? No," he says, "I don't think so. It's not the nineties any more."

Strange logic.

"But if it's gotta be done," he said, "we'll look into it." He added: "Put the screws on . . ."

"So long as it's all by the book."

He took offense: "When have we ever done otherwise?"

Well, you know best.

At that point I remembered the notebook. Read it. And if you were to read it, you'd probably understand the persistence of my inquiries.

I didn't turn to Makeyev directly (you'll learn about Vladilen Makeyev, a local author, in Alexander Ivanovich's notes). I asked my neighbor to do it—a female artist of unquestionably Russian stock. Makeyev was also, naturally, no help.

Several more months passed in anticipation and unsystematic searches, with telephone calls to all sorts of unpleasant institutions—regional, Moscow, federal . . . I left no stone unturned, no number undialed. It became ever clearer: Alexander Ivanovich was not among the living.

Before you read the notes, I'd like to say a few words about the bombardment of the city, which was—what do they say: executed, carried out?—by the commander in chief. I haven't managed to discover any direct confirmation of the aerial attack on Eternity—that is, of the event Alexander Ivanovich describes. But I did come across an item reporting on the bombing of the House of Culture in a similar town. It was called Dead River, or the Dead River Valley, in translation from Nenets, and it too was situated in the Far North.

A couple of quotations: "The news agencies report that the abandoned settlement's House of Culture was subjected to bombing by strategic aviation. A group of bombers conducted a test of new long-range cruise missiles on the settlement target. On board one of the planes was the commander in chief," and so on.

It isn't difficult to track down the details: "The mayor was at the test site when the missiles were launched. According to him, the first missile flew slightly above the target, but those that followed went straight through the building. 'The president gave us twenty minutes' warning,' our witness says with a smile. 'We found bits of missiles that were still hot. Amazing technology, and an amazing strike,' the mayor states."

There's a clip on the Internet chronicling these events: the takeoff from the airport, the aerial refueling, the missile launch, the return. "Judging by the expression on the commander in chief's face, he's satisfied," an offscreen voice declares.

"They talk about him like he's some sort of animal," my nurse said when I showed her the clip, as if she were personally offended.

Let me repeat: I've found no direct confirmation of what Alexander Ivanovich describes. But cruise missiles have been tested, and they'll continue to be tested. And there are a number of settlements named Eternity on the map. Not just Eternity, either, but also Happiness, Loyalty, Bravery.

The reader is sure to have questions. Can a murderer really become mayor? Or: Where did the line about the Pont Mirabeau and the Oka come from? I'll reply: I'm no expert in the contemporary practices of appointing leadership, or in contemporary poetry, but it's unlikely that Alexander Ivanovich would get things wrong or invent them.

I have lingering questions of my own. Should I have admitted him here? But if one begins hospitalizing patients not for medical reasons but on humanitarian grounds, on the grounds of personal sympathy, what would that lead to? We don't perform major cardiac surgery, and there was nothing else we could do for him here. And also: Why did he want me, of all people, to have his notebook? Did he simply forget it? Judging by the myriad insertions and corrections, Alexander Ivanovich took great care with his notes. What did he know about me? What was he trying to warn me of? The danger of getting swept up in the theater? I keep my distance from the theater as it is.

A year has passed since the author's disappearance. I gave him about a year to live, at most, and could not have been mistaken in my diagnosis. As I understand the law, Alexander Ivanovich can already be declared a missing person, which means it's time to publish his story. And if, against all likelihood, he is alive, he probably wouldn't be too upset: men rarely keep notes "for themselves," and Alexander Ivanovich's narrative style assumes a reader. All I've done is add chapter titles; there weren't any in the manuscript.

Here's my fantasy: let's say Alexander Ivanovich had the operation and is alive and well in Germany, say, or even in America. Well, this publication might get his attention. That would be wonderful in and of itself, and would give him a chance at fame (or as Makeyev put it, repugnantly, "to make a noise"). I'd gladly transfer the fee to his name.

After all, there'd be no more need for all my forewords and afterwords.

I haven't bothered changing any names.

June 2015, Tarusa

THE GRAPE

"'I must have been born for some lofty destiny...'[13] Men always have notions, dreams. So, Alexander Ivanovich—did you always dream of becoming a literary director?" Lyubochka asks me.

Lyubochka Schwalbe is one of the people I'll miss for the rest of my life. Schwalbe is the German word for *swallow*—a little swallow. She takes a large green apple from a tray and pokes it with her index finger: "The real thing," she says, and takes a bite.

"Lyuba, what are you doing?" cries the props mistress. "You'll gobble all my props! Next time you'll get plastic instead."

"Forgive me for speaking with my mouth full, Valentina Genrikhovna. For your information, apples are an excellent source of vitamin E."

Valentina Genrikhovna waves her arm: "You've already got plenty of E in you..."

Valentina Genrikhovna has worked at the theater almost as long as I have. An amazing person: not only does she manage stage properties, she also handles the catering. Without her, all of us—actors and lighting technicians and so on, including the administration—would have starved to death. And she's right, apples like those aren't easy to find around here.

"You see, Alexander Ivanovich, they begrudge me perishable props," Lyuba says plaintively when we're alone again. "So, you were going to tell me..."

I love when she's in a talkative mood. What did I dream of becoming? No, not a literary director, of course. I'd had a different dream. But no regrets.

Lyuba leaps up: "Oh, Slava's calling me! Alexander Ivanovich, why don't you do any writing? Please, write something! Promise?" She's already flying up the stairs.

A memory—a timeworn memory.

And something more recent. My friend here, Vladilen Nilovich Makeyev, a member of the Union of Writers of many years' standing: "Come on," he suggests, "let's write something about your life. Great material. We'll place it in the newspaper, in *October*. Write whatever comes into your head, and I'll do my part, polish it up. I've got a title for you, ready-made: 'I Come from Eternity.'"

Makeyev isn't a bad fellow, although he has his issues, you might say. He's admitted to me that his name isn't really Vladilen. His passport gives it as Vladlen.

"It's on the plain side, don't you think? Vladilen is more interesting."

I go out for a walk with Makeyev nearly every day. What else am I to do? I'm retired, sitting on my hands, but Vladilen Nilovich amazes me: Where on earth does he find the time to prepare those tomes of his? Last month he brought me a manuscript: *No Hand in the Matter*—one thousand, two hundred pages, a novel. It bothers him that I haven't yet read it.

"Well, if you aren't going to read my work, you can at least write your own. Let's do it, one step at a time. When you're done, we'll go over it, tidy it up. If you ask me, there's nothing like the memoirs of ordinary folks. If you don't want to give it to *October*, we'll shop it around to the Moscow papers. You can make a noise at the national level. I'm telling you, it's a good title: 'I Come from Eternity.'"

I happen to come from greater Chelyabinsk. Still, why not have a go at it? I'd been given a glimpse of a little slice of the world. There must be some reason for that. It was a very brief glimpse of a very little slice—but I saw it. I did.

A small town outside of Chelyabinsk. Not even a town, really— just a factory, practically in the open countryside. And beyond it—

concrete cubes, caravans, little houses. A school over here, an infirmary over there, a women's dormitory, and the smaller cube is the men's. People from Leningrad, Minsk, Kiev had been sent here, across the Urals. They'd evacuated entire institutes: If you don't bring production round by autumn, then it's on your head, they said. No one complained; they did what they had to do—there was a war on. Nor did they consider whether what they were manufacturing was dangerous.

I hardly even remember it, the war, and it was soon over, anyway. Only we were in no hurry to leave the Urals: there was no place to go, really. A person could make a life anywhere, my mother said. Home is where you lay your head; in that sense, I've taken after her. My mother and I lived in the dormitory, with her two sisters. The other women weren't self-conscious around me—nor have they been especially self-conscious around me since; I don't know why.

School. Not much to say about that. Besides, I promised an episodic account of my life, not a full one. My mother asked me to learn more poems by heart: you can take poems wherever you go; they don't weigh you down. She always was on the move.

I was about eleven years old and there was one thing I desired with all my heart—a microscope. I felt this pull, a terrible pull, to see the invisible. I probably wouldn't have turned down a telescope, either, but I was pining for a microscope.

One time Mother took me along to Chelyabinsk. A consignment shop. Mother's rummaging through odds and ends, and suddenly, there it is. I can't believe my eyes: under the glass on the counter—there it is! Mother, Mother, come quick! I remember it like it was yesterday: a little microscope with a cardboard tag that read, in black ink, "four hundred." Mother gazes at it sadly: we've been promised a bonus... But she sounds so uncertain. She takes me by the hand, we leave the shop, and I don't ask her for a thing. Which means she doesn't refuse me. We walk on, tending to her affairs, but evidently I looked so disappointed that she decided to take me to the theater.

It's hard to say who was sorrier for whom—Mother for me, or the other way around? Word of honor, I don't remember what the theater was called or what they were staging. Some fairy tale. We sit in the dark, me thinking about the microscope, and then... Nothing special, really: the actor places a grape in his mouth. Couldn't have been real—where would they get such grapes in the Urals? And the actor looks straight at me, and his face assumes an expression of bliss, an absolutely natural expression of bliss. And I begin to taste the sweetness in my mouth. It seems to me I've never tasted anything more delicious in all my life. And the actor wipes his hands on his trousers. Mother always told me not to do that. The grape juice had made his hands sticky—and even when he comes out to take a bow, he keeps wiping them. He isn't acting any longer; he's not pretending. Mama, do you see that? And that was that: I was going to be an actor. I didn't need any microscopes.

Mother laughs: remember how stubborn you were—didn't want to learn how to pronounce *r*? We laugh about that the whole way home: "Great grapes do grow on Ararat." And the next day she brings me a book: *Boris Godunov and Other Dramatic Works*.

The first pages are torn out, so *Boris Godunov* begins straight off with: "How shameful, prince."[14] Boy, do I like that opening! I run around the dormitory, weaving between lines hung with linens, shouting, "How shameful, prince! Prince, shameful!" giving the women a fright.

"Have you ever gazed into the abyss, Alexander Ivanovich?" asks Lyubochka, raising her big eyes to my face.

Why do you ask such things, dear, and with that expression? I nearly said: Like a provincial actress. She might take offense. Of all people, Lyubochka is the last I'd want to offend. No, most of what I know about the quagmire of passions comes from literary sources. Even though I'd been married, and barely escaped with my life. It was thanks to my marriage that I wound up in Eternity.

"Oh, tell me, tell me—pretty please!"

It was like some sort of dream, my family life. Is there any point in describing dreams?

"You're a cheerful person," Lyubochka says with a sigh. "And I bet you've done everything right, since you were a boy."

Since I was a boy... No, all I've done since I was a boy was try to enroll in acting schools.

"So it wasn't meant to be." This is our Slava speaking, Slavochka Vorobyev, the audience's darling, whom all the actresses love. Our Hamlet, Oedipus, Don Juan.

You shouldn't eavesdrop, Slavochka. But yes, you're right.

After the morning's rehearsal, the actors go their separate ways, and Lyuba and I are again on our own. She stares at the door Slavochka has just gone through: "Alexander Ivanovich, tell me, what should I do?"

At the time I didn't understand what she meant.

But let's get back to it, one step at a time, as Makeyev instructed. A degree from the teacher's college, with a specialization in Russian language and literature. An assignment to a labor youth school, LYS. The army didn't want me: a heart murmur. Eight times I tried to enroll in an acting school. Didn't manage to get in. But I did manage to get married. Then I buried my aunties, and after them, Mother— she went quickly, without warning.

By that point I'm thirty-three, teaching Russian to the "lice" (as they referred to themselves). I'm married. My wife had an uncommon name: Aglaya. I called her Glashenka. A German teacher. The school had allocated us a room, with quiet neighbors. Summer, holiday time. I'm sitting in the kitchen, looking through the paper—Party members subscribed to *Pravda*, but we got *Izvestiya*. In the main room, Glashenka is getting dressed, prettying herself. She isn't trying too hard to hide the fact that she, as they say, has someone else. Nor do I want to meddle in her affairs, create scenes, dramatic confessions. They were right to reject me from acting school: I lack the proper temperament. Now I understand that about myself, but back then...

Back then I sat with the paper over cooling tea, and the paper said that in the Far North there is a mining town named Eternity where they extract rare types of coal. And that it featured all the amenities— a bathhouse, a hospital, and even—beyond the Arctic Circle!—a little park. And recently, *Izvestiya* reported, culture had arrived. A library had opened its doors, a theater had been built—a truly unusual facility for such a small territorial entity as Eternity. The theater was described in detail: fly system, revolving stage, side stage . . . Evidently the correspondent had also been rejected from acting school.

My wife left for her date; I took out a piece of paper and wrote: I would like to work for you. Are you in need of a literary director? I have the relevant education, a degree in literature. I'm married, with a clean record, able to obtain a character reference. Address: Severogorsky District, Eternity, Theater.

To my surprise, and to Glashenka's even greater surprise, I received a response, by telegram: Come, we're waiting. It went without saying that I'd be making my way to Eternity alone. My wife would take her time, think things over . . . A few months later she—actually, the notary—sent me divorce papers. She could have sent them herself, of course, but she never much liked writing letters. I took no offense.

To this day I can close my eyes and see: two-, three-story buildings, everything flat, symmetrical, if not for the river. The river added a bit of variety, even though it was iced over from September through May. A post office, a savings bank, a tiny market, a single track, the station. Now I bet only the ties are left, without rails, but back then we had trains coming and going: freighting coal, carrying passengers. What else? Carousels, a shooting range. A Lenin statue, not too tall, surrounded by skinny trees: the park *Izvestiya* had mentioned. The fact that the sun never sank below the horizon in the summer—that was, of course, surprising. But eventually you get used to it. Just as you get used to the fact that it doesn't appear at all from the end of November to February.

I moved into the theater right away, into the attic above and a little behind the stage. A corner room, with windows on two sides. Accommodations for visitors. No one had lived there before I came along. A table, two chairs, a bed. Even a pitcher. What good fortune! My office and bedroom, all in one. Just for the time being, they said, until permanent housing could be arranged. Time passed, and it never even occurred to me to remind them of their promises.

Mir Savvich—that was my first director's name—took me up the stairs and showed me around.

"We beg your pardon, but water will be a problem for the time being."

Don't worry, I'll get along.

He was a good man, Mir Savvich. Even tempered, thoughtful. We worked together for a long time. Then he retired and went back home, I don't remember where—Pyatigorsk, Kislovodsk. They say it's hard to adjust to a new climate at an advanced age, dangerous. Yes, he was a good man.

I never did keep a diary, unfortunately, and the days of my past flow into each other. What am I saying, days? Years and entire decades flow together and fuse in my mind. But my first evening at the theater I remember in all its detail. I unpacked my suitcase and put my books and photographs on the shelves, jittery with joy. I went downstairs after midnight, into the auditorium: the doors were shut, the darkness impenetrable. I waited for my eyes to adjust, got up onto the stage, and strutted around. I took a few deep breaths, wanting to cry out: "How shameful, prince!" Or at least: "My carriage, quick, my carriage!"[15] But all I managed was a quiet laugh. Then I stood there in the dark, for a long, long time.

THE GIVEN CIRCUMSTANCES

To the right of the stage is the actors' canteen. I ask Valentina Genrikhovna to give me an egg with peas and soup.

"It's yesterday's soup, Alexander Ivanovich. Have the fish. It's good."

Valentina Genrikhovna writes what we owe into a notebook. What does she do with these notes? In the course of thirty years, I've never seen her refuse food to anyone—and I don't mean just employees, but also theatergoers. I always settle up, but not everyone is in a position to do so. As Pushkin wrote, "We aren't playing for the money."[16] Am I right, Lyubochka?

Lyubochka is out of sorts today. I make my way into the auditorium. There's going to be a rehearsal of Pushkin's *The Stone Guest* in ten minutes. Should be interesting. A young director has come to us from Saint Petersburg.

"While far away—in Paris to the north..."[17]

Laughter all around: Don Juan appears in the gallery, naked to the waist, a guitar hanging around his neck.

The director gives the cue: "Shouldn't you get dressed, Slava?"

He himself is in a coat with the collar raised. It's forty below outside. The theater has heat, but not enough. Our Laura is treading the stage in a quilted jacket. A redhead, all in ringlets—they call her Hairspring.

Lyuba didn't get a role, but her husband, Zakhar Gubaryev, an Honored Artist of the Republic, was cast on the spot. Like Slavochka, he needs no makeup: Gubaryev is the Commander incarnate.

The director removes his glasses, breathes on them, wipes them with his handkerchief. Then he addresses Slavochka again: "You have a handsome body," he says thoughtfully. "But let's put something on it."

No, Slavochka has prepared some kind of acrobatic feat. He used to be a circus man. Dona Anna takes a swig from a thermos—everyone knows that the "tea" in her thermos is warming. The director from Petersburg doesn't know, but perhaps he too can guess: not all city folk are dense.

"What's the holdup? I don't understand!" screeches Dona Anna. "Come on, get to it, block the scene!"

The director stops the rehearsal, gathers the actors into a circle.

"We'll search for the scene together, try things."

Gubaryev comments: "In other words, he doesn't know what the hell he's about to stage—you see?"

Everyone smiles but the director and me. It hurt me to see it, and it hurts to remember it now.

The director turns to Dona Anna: "I'm afraid I'm going to have to let you go. Why? You can't venture a guess? Do you want me to say it in front of everyone? And I'll have to lodge a complaint with the management..."

"Oh no you don't!" shouts the actress. (I'll omit her surname. For all I know, she's still working today.) "I'll tell them how you cursed. I 'bungled it,' eh? 'Bungled it'? That sort of language has no place in the theater..."

The director laughs. His teeth are a brilliant white. No one in Eternity has such teeth. They say there's something wrong with our water.

Why do I remember this scene in particular? A lot had happened before then, and a lot would happen afterwards. Did it just happen to come to me? No, there's a reason for it: *The Stone Guest* was the first in our stagings of classics, our little stagings.

The director came in February, that's for certain. Lyubochka was born in February, she's an Aquarius; this meant something to her. But what year it was I can't be sure. 2005, I think. Or 2006.

"Did you hear, Alexander Ivanovich? Your Petersburg protégé has left us. He tore up his contract."

Yes, Lyubochka, he came round to say goodbye.

Gubaryev is smiling broadly: "He couldn't take the pressure." Is that any cause for celebration? "Now he can flash his teeth on Nevsky Prospect."

"At all the bronze horses!" jokes Slavochka, with whom it's impossible to be seriously annoyed.

"You've got to be able to take it on the chin." Gubaryev won't relent. "Strength of character, that's what you need in this profession. Take it from an Honored Artist of the Republic."

Technically, Gubaryev hasn't yet received the title. The documents had only just been submitted.

"Alexander Ivanovich, why didn't they let me play Dona Anna?"

I shrug my shoulders: artistic whim.

It's hard to tell things in order when you've lived a simple, peaceful life, the same routine every day. The seventies, the eighties—a quiet life, very quiet. Obviously the literary director isn't the main figure in any theater. There's the art director, the troupe manager, the stage manager (I won't say anything about each play's director—our directors were all by invitation), but if you work long enough, you acquire clout, whether you want to or not: you recommend staging something, comment on the distribution of roles, and they listen to you. My relationships with the actors were stable, problem free. They had their misunderstandings: an actress wants to rehearse a role, reaches for her notebook, but it won't open—someone has dripped jam in between the pages. Where do they run? Upstairs, to me. I'm not bragging, just stating facts.

The country was starting to change—someone would go to the capital and report back—but the news had a long way to travel to Eternity, and to the theater in particular. This is what life was like: rehearsal first thing in the morning; rest during the day, while the actors went over their parts; and in the evening—the performance. Our troupe wasn't large; everyone had things to do. The actors loved their work: we'd put on two performances a day on Saturdays and Sundays, and children's matinees on top of that. How did we do it? How did we cope? No time for television; in all those years I never even had a television set. Plays were my window onto that other world. The job had me reading a lot—the themes of the plays did change, that's true.

Here's some of our repertoire from the nineties, just off the top of my head: *Dmitry and the Drum*, about the beautiful life, a comedy. The language wasn't particularly interesting, but it had lots of action, lots of roles for women. The audience liked it. People would come to see it several times. Another comedy, a translation from English—*Never Smile at a Crocodile*—a solid piece about life in an American prison. And in complete contrast, *Better Off Being a Jew*, a melodrama about a special relationship between men. The audience didn't get it—a very short run. I was surprised myself at opening night: Why had I suggested it? Something must have grabbed me, and it did cause a stir in Moscow and Petersburg. And another comedy, *Who the Hell Knows*, which I don't need to describe—a famous piece. Such was our repertoire.

The *Severogorsk Messenger* wrote us up frequently. "His Majesty Art reigns on the stage." Always the same viewer, but she used all sorts of pseudonyms—Muse Vasilyevna, Melpomene Sidorovna, and even sillier combinations. "Your correspondent hearkened and gazed with eyes wide open and heart aflutter. Her ears rang from the ovations." Slightly exaggerated, one might say—but our troupe ate it up: they'd cut the articles out and paste them to the dressing-room walls, especially if the paper had included their photos. Actors need attention, and when Melpomene was silent (although, to give her her due, she wrote about everyone), one still needed to put something up, if only a thank you letter, a certificate from the theater on the occasion of an anniversary, in recognition of many years of conscientious labor.

Once we even made it into a Moscow paper. The article was titled "The Vale of Tears."

"Against the background of rather amateurish performances, several catastrophes occurred. First, during the intermission, the female lead seemed to come down with some sort of illness: she emerged swollen and puffy, and although she had been all squeaks in the first act, she now spoke in a deep contralto. Her fifteen-year-old daughter, at the appearance of the object of her ardor, began smacking and licking her lips. And the village priest paced the stage in a metropolitan's garb and crossed himself without cease. Was he driving off an evil spirit? Or was he simply desperate to keep his hands busy? To complete the picture, his pronunciation suggested he had been summoned from the Ivanovo region. The audience, however, took it all in stride. Eternity is a small town: beggars can't be choosers. The theater didn't manage to print the poster and programs in time for the premiere. People were selling synthetic fur coats in the foyer. The vale of tears."

"During the intermission! All squeaks!" they say behind Anna Arkadyevna's back. She's our leading lady. Actors aren't hard to amuse.

"Alexander Ivanovich, let's think about avoiding living authors," is all Mir Savvich had to say after he read the article.

I agreed: it wasn't written by a critic. Critics give you a hard time if you're well-known, successful—who were we for them to give us a hard time? I won't name the author: he traveled to the premiere at his own expense—and he paid Valentina Genrikhovna three and a half thousand rubles to arrange the reception afterwards, but then didn't show up.

You know, I say to Mir Savvich, there's a Petersburg director who's long dreamed of putting on *The Little Tragedies* at our theater.

"Well, well, well," sighs Mir Savvich.

In other words, do whatever you like, my dears. He's already taking his leave, going home to Pyatigorsk.

And so, in February of 2005 or 2006, there's a change in management. Our new director is Gennady Prokopyevich. Small, energetic, he all but flew around the theater—although, incidentally, he too was born in the forties. Eternity was on the small side for him, of course. He had been in charge of the Krasnoyarsk Regional Philharmonic Society. There were all sorts of rumors, which I won't repeat.

Gennady Prokopyevich gathered us together and examined us with his right eye—his left eye was made of glass, only good for winking: "Had your fill of art yet? Let's make some money."

That's how we first learned of grants. We'd never even heard the word before. Grants, said Gennady Prokopyevich, are most readily allocated for classic material.

"We'll put on a lot of work, quickly, using our own resources. A month of this, then a month of that. Alexander Ivanovich, you're responsible for the artistic angle." A wink in my direction: "You can't lose your shirt on the classics. Tried and true."

Everyone threw their support behind Prokopyevich: down with visiting directors—all they do is get in the way, make a mess of things. And contemporary plays are worthless. Nothing but dull, bleak stuff, or dumb comedies. It's time to get serious. The stockrooms are overflowing with old costumes and props—we can mix and match. We aren't an academic theater; we needn't get everything right, to the letter. "That's the global trend these days, anyway." What, exactly, is the global trend? "Never mind. Theater is a contingent art, it implies experimentation."

It seemed like just another conversation. Mir Savvich had also grumbled about our lengthy rehearsal process, our constant delays. But who could have guessed that the wind arising from that meeting would sweep away not only us and the theater, but the entire town. I call it up in my mind—some of it clearly, some of it not so clearly—and try to make sense of the motives of all involved. And I think: How reckless we were, how oblivious, toying with providence, with fate. The classics! Plays that theaters in the big cities would rehearse for several years and still decide not to stage . . . We'd take—what was on our list? I hesitate to utter the great titles—put it through its paces for a month or so, fetch some costumes and props from the storeroom, blow off the dust, and let it fly. Open, close, then go after another grant. We didn't need to get our hands dirty, didn't need all that money. Wasn't Valentina Genrikhovna feeding us well enough? We all got along, staging our comedies—everyone was happy, always hugging: Wonderful dress rehearsal, Anna Arkadyevna! Brilliant premiere, Alexander Ivanovich! And things could have gone on that way forever.

The accountant informed us that strangers had appeared on the payroll—stage managers, costumers, set designers, even composers, and, it's hard to believe, a teacher in elocution for the stage, an Armenian!

I kept silent at that February meeting, asking just one empty question: What if there's an inspection?

"There's no need to fear an inspection"—and that was the end of it.

Later on many people laid the blame squarely at Prokopyevich's feet—but they shouldn't have. The man acted in accordance with the given circumstances. Incidentally, theater jargon came to him very naturally indeed: "Our people have long lived in accordance with the given circumstances. It's you up here in Eternity who have your heads in the clouds."

It wasn't long after this meeting that the fellow from Petersburg, the visiting director, came knocking at my door. He had had a talk with Prokopyevich. They didn't see eye to eye. The contract was terminated.

"I missed the mark with Dona Anna...Your—what's her name? Schwalbe. She's far too pretty; anyone would have eyes for her. But that..." He says her name. "They warned me she was a boozer. Well, I thought to myself, that's just what I need—a tippling widow. Don Juan doesn't pass up a single woman. Like old man Karamazov—'No such thing as an ugly woman, that's my motto...' Staging the classics is no easy undertaking, Alexander Ivanovich."

I had to look away.

The new director ushered in a new generation of actors: Zakhar Gubaryev and his wife, Lyubochka Schwalbe. And soon we took on Slavochka Vorobyev. Don Juan was his first big role.

Zakhar and Slavochka struck up their friendship just when the actors had acquired an unprecedented degree of independence. Gennady Prokopyevich was seldom present, and I—well, how could I manage them myself? Especially when the actors were so exceptional, especially these three.

Lyubochka, that little swallow: past thirty, but how pretty! Not a single line on her face; long, long lashes; and that voice...And that hair!

"Zakhar and I were the most beautiful couple in our class!"

"I can imagine what sort of class that was!" laughs Slavochka.

Gubaryev is older than Lyubochka. He didn't go into theater right away: first the army, and even a course at the artillery academy.

"Artillery is the god of war." Gubaryev loves weaponry.

He used his share of the grant to buy a revolver. He'd take it out to the shooting range. What did you need it for, Zakhar?

"So there wouldn't be any questions."

A round, shaved head, a broad nose—an expressive face. Many people recognize Gubaryev from his roles in film. He was lured to us with bonuses for working in the Far North, an apartment that was all his own, and the prospect of an honorary title. Lyubochka followed along: "Zakhar used to be a totally different man. He lo-o-oved me." Lyubochka drawls the *o*, tilts back her head. A beautiful throat—so white. "He used to kiss each one of my fingers, wrote me poems."

Slavochka and I exchange glances: Gubaryev writing poems! Lyuba, give us a dramatic reading.

"I wanted children so badly, Alexander Ivanovich!"

I marvel at her dizzying leaps from one subject to another.

"But Gubaryev couldn't care less. He's a Sagittarius, you know. Sagittarriuses couldn't care less about women, children. Especially children. Alexander Ivanovich, what do you think, is Fedyunin gay? He's always hanging around Zakhar."

The questions you ask, Lyubochka . . . I doubt it. But I'd rather not talk about Fedyunin—not now, not ever.

It's far more enjoyable to think of Slava. Slavochka Vorobyev, my neighbor and friend. Slavochka came to Eternity on the run from somebody's husband. He got onto a train and kept going until he arrived—he liked the name of the place. He didn't have an apartment either, and moved into the theater, on the same floor as me. He called me Uncle Sasha.

Glorious biography: he'd been a circus man, an aerialist—walked the tightrope, turned somersaults under the big top. He'd climb a drainpipe to the fourth floor.

"You'll break your neck!"

He'd shrug: been taking tumbles all his life, ever since he was a kid.

"What on earth were your parents thinking?" That gets a laugh.

"How should I know? Left home at fourteen." A woman had fallen for him, an animal tamer.

How could anyone not fall for Slavochka? All the actresses adored him. You ask:

Out late again? He smiles: "You know I can't do without hot water." You'll get used to it.

"Easy for you to say, Uncle Sasha. You're past your prime."

It wasn't only the actresses but all the single women—costumers, makeup artists, bookkeepers—who were glad to lend Slavochka a helping hand. Some days he'd take two or three warm baths. And no one kicked up a fuss, no one quarreled—marvelous people like Slavochka don't come around very often. I'd never met anyone like him before. And I never would have, were it not for the theater. I sometimes reflect on how lucky I was, how fortunate . . . As for the shadows that fell on my life, the dark patches I went through—I'd brought them on myself.

He knew how to do all kinds of things, juggling, eating fire. He could learn a text without the help of a notebook: he would take one look at a page and have it by heart. And how he played guitar! And sang! Even our Valentina Genrikhovna, a person of great restraint, would save the tastiest morsels for Slavochka.

"Our communal treasure," that's what she called him.

Out of the hundred—more than that—actors who'd worked with us over the years, fate chose three, and placed them on a collision course. Of course, we ourselves helped fate along. We thought that we could move mountains, cycle through practically the whole of the world's classics. One mistake, followed by another, and a crime—then fate takes over. In our case, the result was plain to see: no more theater, no more town. I myself am partly to blame: we could have left the Greeks alone; if not for me, no one would have thought of *Oedipus*.

It's foolish to brag about my intuition—where had it been earlier?—but I do remember that when we dared to put on *Hamlet*, I was already expecting some sort of punishment, was even wishing for it. The inspectors came, and I felt: here it comes. No, fate was just letting us swallow the bait, nice and deep—the inspection went fine.

Where are they coming from? Audit Chamber? Cultural Commission? Everyone's panicking. We'd never had inspectors before. "From the ministry! How many are there?" Four! Can you believe it?

I run into Valentina Genrikhovna: she doesn't know whether she's coming or going. What first? Hurry to props department? Burn the credit notebook? Ready a table for the inspectors? I stop by the wardrobe department, to get my jacket pressed—they're in a tizzy too.

Gennady Prokopyevich alone is as cool as a cucumber. He summons Gubaryev, me, a few other men.

"Fellas," he says, "don't you worry. What's on today? *Measure for Measure*? Who's that, I forget—Shakespeare? Well, go get to work. Send the suckers straight over to me. Oh, and don't you bother feeding those spongers. Waste of money."

A man of remarkable equanimity.

Late in the evening—the theater is empty, dark—the inspectors notice a light under my door, come in. They'd never come across anything like what they experienced in Eternity. Gennady Prokopyevich had sat them down in reception, didn't even offer them tea, put on his coat, and left.

I went down to the lobby, where there's a telephone.

"Alexander Ivanovich, I'm on leave. So is the accountant. I signed off on it last week."

I give them tea and biscuits. They look round and see *Hamlet* on my desk.

"Putting this on?" They leaf through it. "But where's the stamp of the Ministry of Culture?"

No one had asked me that before.

"Have you heard? They're going to shut you down soon. The entire town is being liquidated. No sense in keeping the mines going. Not cost-effective."

These people from the ministry had a sad look about them: What did they really know? And still I ask: How can an entire town be liquidated?

They shrug.

"Just like that."

OEDIPUS

"Am I always going to play his mother from now on?"

Lyubochka asked me that when we had finished with *Hamlet* and, to our misfortune, set to work on *Oedipus*.

Not that *Hamlet* was uneventful. Hairspring—our Ophelia—comes running up to me: "Come quick, Lyuba's lost her living mind."

Lyuba is playing Gertrude, and Gubaryev is the ghost. Slavochka, naturally, is the prince. It's rehearsal time, and Lyuba—either she's forgotten her lines or she is just in one of her moods—keeps going on about how her aged husband had made her get rid of her children.

"Bawling her eyes out, Alexander Ivanovich, and saying straight-out—if she should get knocked up, under any circumstances..."

How awful! What could I say to Hairspring—that it's a new translation? I run downstairs. Lyuba is standing there, face turned to the curtain, and over her looms the Commander: stilts, armor—nothing goes to waste around here. There's a fire in Slavochka's eyes: "You're a jealous one, my dear Zakhar. You oughta play, what's his name, Othello."

Gubaryev's face and neck are flushed.

"Look, Gubaryev's learned to turn red!" Slavochka laughs. "Like Signor Pomodoro."

Then Zakhar tried to hook him with a crutch. I myself didn't understand what was going on between the actors. I thought they were just joking around. It seems they themselves wanted to believe that. The rehearsal broke off.

But *Hamlet* still opened. Lyuba didn't lose her mind; she remembered all her lines. Everyone performed to the best of their abilities. Melpomene Sidorovna was satisfied.

"And whom is she playing next, your precious Lyubochka? Cleopatra? Mary Stuart? Perhaps Juliet? She *has* turned fourteen by now, hasn't she?"

I offer explanations: Anna Arkadyevna, you know that what we're doing is not, alas, very serious. We're trying things, experimenting with new concepts, but always in a rush—we've got a grant to account for—and just look how much we've bitten off this season. But we'll find you a role to play right away, don't you worry—it's just that you learn your lines so slowly; you take time to enter into your role.

Anna Arkadyevna draws on her cigarette, releases the smoke.

"Alexander Ivanovich, we weren't taught to *play* roles, to say nothing of making money with our body and voice. No, we were taught to live and die onstage. I don't *learn* a role, I *live* it. Do you understand the difference?"

I promise, both myself and Anna Arkadyevna, to discuss the situation with Prokopyevich. Incidentally, he never did watch our performances. People with one eye, he said, couldn't perceive depth.

Tanned, trim, Gennady Prokopyevich is feeding his fish—not little goldfish, but real sea creatures. The huge aquarium takes up the whole wall, and in it splash all sorts of colorful monsters. I notice a new writing set on his desk. I inform him that, from my point of view, our method of staging the classics has outlived its usefulness. Plays that ought to stimulate our development are instead causing fatigue and irritation. The problem isn't the actors, and it certainly isn't the great works we've had the opportunity to put on. No. I am the problem. I'm nothing more than a literary director, and an old man at that—an old man without theatrical training.

I had prepared a whole monologue: what it had cost us to start making money, how everything had gone to pieces. Who were we now? *Poor, bare, forked animals* (we had staged that, too). But Prokopyevich interrupts me: "Do you want the medallion or the ride?" That's his favorite expression of late. I can't work up the courage to ask what it means, fearing it might be indecent. "You're tired, Alexander Ivanovich. When did you last take time off? Never? Well, it's high time! Off you go."

Go where? Prokopyevich had caught me off guard. Where am I to go?

"What do you mean, where?" He points to the aquarium, as if calling the fish as witnesses. "There's Sharm El Sheikh. There's Greece."

I lose my bearings altogether, go weak. In the end I ask his permission to stage *Oedipus*, tell him it's long been a dream of mine. I'm astonished at my own words. Prokopyevich shrugs: he doesn't meddle in artistic matters. You want *Oedipus*? *Oedipus* it is.

"Strophe, epeisodion, antistrophe. It's all Greek to me. What's it actually about?"

About the truth, Slavochka: about the fact that the truth is, for some reason, necessary. Even though it can sometimes bring us pain.

"You're like the Sphinx, Uncle Sasha. You talk in riddles."

All right, then: it's about fate. The play's about fate. You know the expression, Slavochka: no flying from fate.

A sigh: "So it seems."

Suddenly Moscow remembers Gubaryev—he's offered a role in a miniseries. He also wants to find out what happened with those documents for the honorary title. Five, six years have passed since they were submitted. Looks like we'll have to make do without Zakhar, which is a pity. He would have made a good Creon. Or, better yet,

Tiresias, the blind prophet: Gubaryev knew how to throw a scare into people. Although foresight clearly wasn't his strength. We've all got excellent hindsight, but what happened between Lyuba and Slavochka came as no surprise to Valentina Genrikhovna: "The sparks were flying between them even before Zakhar left. Every time you went near them, it was like you were in their way."

I had the opposite impression. It seemed to me they were always looking for company.

"No contradiction in that. You don't understand the first thing about the sins of man, Alexander Ivanovich. Not a thing."

That may well be. Dear Valentina Genrikhovna! I remember what she was like twenty, thirty years ago. Stern, focused, always hurrying somewhere in that apron of hers. So much time has passed, so much has changed . . .

We erected an altar, arranged the choir around it in a U. The choir was mixed, which isn't by the book, but each member was given an olive branch to hold. They wave their branches, dance around, sing strange songs, and they have fun doing it: "Alexander Ivanovich, it's just like rap!"

Slavochka stopped spending nights in the theater. Now they came to rehearsals together, holding hands. Many thought they looked crazed; I only noticed that they'd lost weight. The young actresses feel for Slavochka, but express surprise: What, was Lyuba smeared in honey or something?

"I've got no idea what he's doing to her, but your Lyuba has gone insane." That's how Anna Arkadyevna sees it. What concerns her most is the fate of the show. "Of course, it makes sense that Jocasta should be slightly deranged, but within reason."

But the state of the leads suits me just fine: they're worn-out, but tuned-in, focused. I may not have any theatrical training, but I do have eyes and ears.

And we'd thought up a nice role for Anna Arkadyevna too, without any lines. She was to play the governess to Ismene and Antigone,

Oedipus's daughters. They were also Oedipus's sisters, Jocasta's grand-daughters, and their own aunts and nieces.

"Quite a family," sighs Anna Arkadyevna.

"Ah! My poor children, known, ah, known too well..."[18] Slavochka is a true king, although he's younger than everyone else.

"Can you imagine Slavochka as an old man?" Valentina Genrik-hovna once asked me. "Neither can I."

I went through a great deal of literature at that time, entered into correspondence with specialists in Moscow. "My dears," I address the actors, "this is Greek tragedy. Here you mustn't live and die onstage. What we need isn't an expression of tragedy, but its depiction. Do you understand the difference?" Not really, Alexander Ivanovich, but we'll try. "Forget what you were taught in school—don't live onstage, just show us." For the first time in many years, we might have a serious production on our hands.

Lyubochka handles her new situation well, with dignity. But, to be honest, several scenes make me nervous: this isn't the first time Lyuba has played a queen, and I still haven't forgotten our adventures with *Hamlet*. But no, she doesn't work herself up into a state when the talk turns to how remorselessly Laius, her former spouse, had treated their child: "Its ankles pierced and pinned together, gave it to be cast away by others on the trackless mountainside." And even when the other actresses try to hinder her—use Lyubochka's props or intentionally say her lines—she remains the same: fine and aloof. Where could this composure have possibly come from? It is astonishing.

And now, with the same queenliness, she moves into Slavochka's room. Zakhar would soon return—so why should they hide? Sure, they'd have to work together, the three of them, but they're all adults. Civilized. "Then thou mayest ease thy conscience on that score." No, our Lyubochka was not to be deterred. Later, we'll deal with it later—right now we have *Oedipus* to perform. Even the other women laid the matter to rest: now Slava was a married man, and Lyubochka had a new husband.

"A lovely couple," Valentina Genrikhovna says.

"Like Yesenin and Isadora Duncan."

"Fedyunin, curse that tongue of yours! Finish your meal and get out."

Valentina Genrikhovna is especially stern with Fedyunin. She once confessed: "Ugly people frighten me."

Well, now even Fedyunin has had his say. The fellow was in our company, though I don't even know what he did, officially. One time Prokopyevich asked: Do we actually need him? Can't we do away with our annoying friend? We took pity on him: he'd been around so long... And how would he ever find another job, with that red rash covering half his face? Have you taken a look at his hands?

And in general, one feels sorry for weak people. He even wrote plays. Not a single theatrical journal would print Fedyunin's efforts; they were utterly hopeless. I'd hedge, sidestep—so as not to insult him too badly, but also not to give him too much encouragement. Again, I'd say, with the beaver collars, the fainting spells, the hussar uniforms, the spurs... And he'd respond: the genre of historical reenactment demands it. All right then, if that's the way it is—but you'd better not bother Gennady Prokopyevich; just bring the script directly to me.

Fedyunin had recently been showing up at the theater quite often, more often than usual. No one attached significance to this.

All the same, what about Gubaryev? Gone, all but forgotten. Theatrical memory is short: old man Laius, the former husband, has departed—to Thebes, Corinth, Elysium—and turned into a ghost.

We probably began rehearsals in October, with the premiere scheduled for February. Gubaryev didn't return for New Year's—or did he leave later? At any rate, Slavochka stopped spending nights at the theater in January, and I don't think Zakhar was with us for the Sun Festival at the end of that month—we always celebrated the return of the sun in January. Strange. Yes, those were rich days, the best in all my years in Eternity... I couldn't possibly keep them straight. A premonition of triumph and, at the same time, disaster. I wasn't alone in feeling that. Many others felt it too.

We had a dress rehearsal before the opening. A success, without major losses. Was it possible? Could we actually bring it off?

No rehearsals on the day of the premiere. I go down to breakfast. Slavochka is in the canteen, alone. Nothing on the table in front of him but a shot glass and an ashtray.

"That's his fourth," Valentina Genrikhovna whispers to me. "I made him a casserole, but he refused to touch it."

A clear case of nerves. I, on the other hand, am perfectly calm: there's plenty of time for Slavochka to sober up before the performance, and he's never shown himself to be an alcoholic. I ask him anyway: Why drink in the morning?

He gives me a guilty, helpless smile: "So as not to smoke on an empty stomach."

SAGITTARIUS

"Slavochka, do you want coffee?"

Does he hear the question? No. He gets up, smiles again, and walks away with his cheerful circus gait, a little unsteady. White turtleneck, black trousers, black shoes. I should be worried—why's he dressed up?—but I'm too busy with my own concerns. Concerns that are now entirely irrelevant.

Could I have known that a terrible act would play out on our stage that morning—the most repellent, meaningless act one can imagine? Could I have interfered with fate? At first, looking back from a close distance, I had believed: Yes, of course, I should have known, interceded. I blamed myself. But then Slavochka's misfortune took its rightful place in a series of other catastrophes, and my, frankly speaking, insane belief that we hold any sway over events simply evaporated. It's all written down somewhere, preordained. We must accept the inevitable, and help others accept it too.

I remember it clearly: Valentina Genrikhovna removes the shot glass and ashtray from the table, I ask her for a casserole and tea, and suddenly we hear a loud clap, followed by what sounds like a window shattering. What was that? The stage is set; the stagehands shouldn't be fooling around back there. We exchange glances—and hurry off to see what happened.

The door to the stage is closed. Why? We never lock it. We pound on it with our fists, kick it, pull at the lock. Later Valentina Genrik-hovna will weep, saying that it was then, in those moments, that she first learned where her heart was located. We'll run around looking for her medication. But in that instant she understood right away: "Gubaryev. He's going to kill him."

She hardly had time to say it before we heard another clap. Never before had I heard the sound of a revolver, a real one, up close: a dull, loathsome sound. We freeze in horror. The stamp of feet, the door swings open, Zakhar emerges. In one hand he holds the mop that had been blocking the door, in the other, the revolver.

"*Finita*. Our aerial gymnast has taken his last tumble. Bring Lyubka. I want her to take a good look at her beau. You shoot a squirrel in the eye." He pushes us aside and limps away.

Slavochka's face is one huge wound. Blood—not the cranberry juice he would have smeared around his eyes in the evening. Valentina Genrikhovna covers him with her apron.

The rest I recall piecemeal. Fedyunin races across the back row and slips into the foyer. "The rat," Valentina Genrikhovna pronounces distinctly. Gubaryev sits on the floor, not far from the door, his bald head drooping. The fight has gone out of him: hiding his face, knees crouched up, trembling. He's tucked the revolver under his legs. Someone has draped a jacket over Gubaryev's shoulders and placed a glass of water beside him. People approach, but not too closely, talk quietly—when will they take him away, already? Due to the fact that Gubaryev has developed a limp, some speculate that Slavochka had managed to wound him. Not true. Slavochka had shot into the air, shattered the projector. Gubaryev had tripped over the weight holding down one of the scenery flats; we'd all stubbed our toes against those weights over the years. Nothing to cry over. He'd walk it off.

I go to tell Lyubochka what happened. She waves me away, turns around. The tears come only in the evening. Fortunately, I manage to keep her upstairs.

"Fourteen meters, eighty centimeters." I help Irina Vadimovna measure the distance between the flats.

Irina Vadimovna, a lieutenant of the Investigative Committee, is anywhere between thirty and fifty years of age. Judging by her appearance, she's closer to fifty; but in her manner of speech, she seems much younger. She asks: "Why not go plug each other out in the street?" And supplies her own answer: "'Course, in this weather you'll freeze your balls off before you can say, 'Shoot!'"

Yes, Eternity isn't Pyatigorsk, where poor Lermontov met his end, but it isn't a question of weather. Fedyunin, historical reenactments. I never saw that man again. He had come to the wake, expounded on an officer's honor, the code duello: it's against the rules, of course, to duel with a single revolver, taking turns, but then again, the men had shared more than just a gun. And the shot into the air was the second mortal insult that Gubaryev had been made to suffer. Prokopyevich took Fedyunin aside, told him something, and after that the fellow disappeared for good.

"You're kidding me." Irina Vadimovna is shocked when we tell her where the idea for the duel had come from. "An officer's honor, in the twenty-first century. That's a laugh."

Gubaryev and Slavochka were taken away towards evening. I barely remember the next few days—time suddenly sped up. Lyuba couldn't talk at all. I would bring her food, which she sometimes ate and sometimes left untouched. Prokopyevich ordered us to post an announcement: "The theater is moving to a new facility and all performances are canceled." We had always respected Prokopyevich, but only now did we give him his full due. He went up to Severogorsk, made the official rounds, and on the ninth day returned with Slavochka's ashes. We take the urn up to Lyuba's room together and place it on the windowsill. Lyuba cries for some time; we stand beside her. And we agree to make arrangements for Slavochka's burial when the weather turns warmer. His relatives might turn up by then; we'd sent a telegram to his hometown.

Prokopyevich says something to the effect that we ourselves don't know where we'll be when the weather turns warmer: strange, he usually avoids platitudes. We invite Lyuba to come down to the canteen, for a wake. No, she doesn't want to be seen in her present condition. In that case I too will probably come down later. I follow Prokopyevich into the corridor. He nods at the door: "Actress. Thinking about appearances. She'll be fine."

God willing, Gennady Prokopyevich. I want to thank him for what he's done. He stops me.

"I'll be taking off. You're in charge now."

But what do we do? What can we stage without Slavochka and the others? The old repertoire—*Who the Hell Knows*, the thing about the crocodile? Everything seems to take on a new, inappropriate meaning.

"Alexander Ivanovich, relax, will you? The real question is what can I do with all those fish . . . Never mind, just a joke. I mean, you know the news."

I nod. I really did think I knew the news.

"Telling the truth is easy and pleasant, so let's be frank." Irina Vadimovna had managed to get statements from many others before she met with me.

She takes measurements, writes them down; I help by holding

down the tape measure. It's interesting to watch Irina Vadimovna move, putting pressure on the whole foot with each step, involuntarily raising her arms: very different from how actresses walk onstage. Just an observation. It's hard for me to be here, even though the set is gone and everything's been cleaned up. You know, I say to Irina Vadimovna, you've been on your feet all day. Let's go get some supper.

We feed her. There was a lot left over after the wake.

"How about a drink? After talking to your Schwalbe, my head feels like a lead balloon. First she tries to sell me a bill of goods, claims her two boyfriends were rehearsing something. Oh, sure, with live ammunition. An occupational injury, right? And if that's true, where's the second heater? Doesn't add up. Then she tells me it's all her doing. So I ask, Ms. Schwalbe, did you knock off Vorobyev? Are you prepared to take the blame?"

Poor Lyuba. She must really feel that way. She has to tell the whole story.

"We don't need the whole story. Have a talk with her. The fact that Gubaryev used to kiss each one of her fingers hasn't the slightest bearing on the investigation."

Other women never accorded much respect to Lyubochka. We ask what awaits Gubaryev.

"Murder without aggravating circumstances: six to fifteen years. What did you think, he'd be exiled to the Caucasus, like some dueling aristocrat? Now, if the victim had also shot at him, he might have gotten less than the minimum. Does he have small children? Don't worry—men like your Gubaryev get on pretty well in prison: he's famous, they've seen him on TV. Let's just hope he doesn't get too used to the criminal life—he's a fine shot. And you'll see, when the press gets wind of it, they'll make a hero out of him. All right, I've wasted enough time blabbing with you. Time to get back to the station."

I hand Irina Vadimovna her coat and lead her to the exit, where there's a large portrait of Slavochka. We pause.

"A shame." She sighs. "But at least he managed to live a little. My son's twenty-five. What's he doing with his life? Nothing. Dodging the service. Spends all day in front of the PlayStation. Never had a girlfriend. Hard to say which one's better off, am I right?"

I come back to the canteen, sit down. It's all too much for me. Valentina Genrikhovna sits down beside me: "Alexander Ivanovich, I'm leaving." She laughs: "I'm going abroad." She has a brother in Mariupol. "Well, it is another country, isn't it?"

Yes, of course, we have to go on living, don't we? I suddenly sense just how tired I am. But I still have to check on Lyubochka.

"What about you, Alexander Ivanovich? Have you thought of anything?"

In what respect? I feel I can't go on talking. My head is spinning.

"The town is being evicted." She clasps her hands: "You mean you didn't know? People are packing up their things, sending them off—the post office is a madhouse! Haven't you noticed the crowds at the station?"

I find it hard to think today. Is it possible to evict a whole town? I suppose it is, if Valentina Genrikhovna says so. Why would she want to lie to me? I never received any instructions. I'll think it through tomorrow—now I'd better lie down.

"Alexander Ivanovich, do you ever get the feeling that we've lived someone else's life? That this whole theater isn't our true story?"

I don't know. What would I have done instead? Taught literature? Everything happens for a reason. I rise, ask her forgiveness. I must have reeled.

"Oh dear, let me give you a hand," she offers. "I'll take you to your room."

No need, no need. I can manage.

"You're a good man, Alexander Ivanovich. The best I've ever had the fortune to meet."

That was Valentina Genrikhovna's goodbye. And I couldn't even thank her, didn't even ask for her new address.

*

Everyone has been sent home. Only Lyubochka and I are left. How do we keep ourselves busy? We don't, really. We've tried cards, chess. In the evenings we sit in the canteen, laugh about this and that. We make no plans, don't talk about the past, and sleep both night and day. No, we aren't busy. Just wasting electricity.

In earlier years, I used to like it when the actors went on vacation. I'd manage to do so much: read books and magazines, discover new plays, receive guests from out of town—we'd have visits from folk ensembles, amateur competitions. And now it's as if we ourselves have gone on tour. For how long?

Forty days since Slavochka's death. We sit together for a while, drink a little wine, then go down to the auditorium for some reason.

"Alexander Ivanovich, it looks like it's over. We won't be coming back here. Time to pack things up."

Hold on, Lyubochka, what if it gets sorted out somehow? We shouldn't have come here. She allows me to lead her out, but I notice the look of pity in her eyes.

I lie in the dark and think. One shot! What if the gun had misfired? What if Gubaryev hadn't hurt himself on the weight? Maybe he would have spared Slavochka and also fired into the air. And he wouldn't be behind bars now. The "duel" would have been hushed up and we'd have put on *Oedipus* in the evening. And then, who knows, we might have taken it on the road. It had shaped up into a fine staging.

Nonsense, I tell myself—historical reenactment. It's impossible, downright insulting to think that things happen by chance, that human life is determined by a series of trifles. Slavochka couldn't help but fall for Lyuba, Gubaryev couldn't help but shoot to kill, and it wasn't by chance that I'd suggested *Oedipus* to Prokopyevich: it wasn't just because he had mentioned Greece.

And so I fall asleep, thinking these thoughts, and in the morning I receive the notice: By decree of this or that, Eternity is to be liquidated. Optimization, resource management, development of new lands—the letters dance before my eyes. I try to arrange them into some meaningful order, and hear a voice, clear as day:

> What expiation means he? What's amiss?
> Banishment, or the shedding blood for blood.
> This stain of blood makes shipwreck of our state.[19]

Slavochka's voice. Unmistakable.

AFTER ETERNITY

Music played on the platform, then we moved off. I remember the flakes of snow in the beam of a searchlight, and a communal sigh when the town suddenly sank back into the darkness. "Mother asks you not to chop down the cherry orchard until she's gone," recited Hairspring. "They've switched off the transformer substation," someone who knew such things responded. There were tears, of course. I went to fetch some boiling water for tea and bumped into Anna Arkadyevna. She was standing in the vestibule, in almost total darkness, and didn't see me. Around her shoulders was her favorite wrap, which she called, for some reason, "a wrap with a reputation." She was standing there, smoking and singing some quiet song, punctuated by sobs.

In those days people were being sent off to Severogorsk by the trainload—no other way to do it. They were put up in hotels, hostels, even in schools and institutes. The first available apartments went to those with children; more would be built for the rest of us, just as soon as possible. According to rumors, some people had to be dragged to the train by force. What's the alternative? You can't abandon people without light, water, heat. By the time they caught on to the plot, it would be too late. I myself only tumbled to the truth quite late in the day. Eternity is no more, gone. How? Just gone.

The theater people were evacuated at the last moment. We were given two carriages, with compartments—another stroke of luck. I sit opposite Lyuba, moving backwards. We're alone in the compartment, with our things—mainly Lyuba's—in the overhead racks.

"Alexander Ivanovich, you have a wonderful gift for avoiding clutter," Valentina Genrikhovna used to say.

I prefer, I would tell her, to work only with props that fit neatly into my suitcase. There it is, in the overhead rack—metal corners, wooden ribs—still in great shape. I remember how easy it was, all those years ago, to race up the stairs with that suitcase in my hand . . . And now I've managed to drag it to the station, hoist it up into the rack.

The train is moving slowly. Snow and gloom outside the window. Yes, the chain of events has linked up. It began with greed, the exploitation of the classics, then—forbidden passion, and then a crime. The heroes have been punished with death and penal servitude, while we, the extras and the chorus, have been sent into exile. Can anyone of sound mind insist that life lacks a plot?

I rise, glance at the luggage. The urn—where's the urn? Lyubochka's eyes, which are already unusually large, open wide in horror: she forgot it on the windowsill! It would be indecent to blame her; she herself is in despair. We rationalize: now no one will disturb Slavochka's peace. He lived a good life in his room, didn't he?

I sit back down and close my eyes. Another event to be inserted in the chain. It couldn't have been by chance that we left Slavochka's remains in the theater . . .

"Alexander Ivanovich!" Lyuba pauses for a long time. "I think I'm pregnant." Another pause. "Don't you have anything to say?"

What does *I think* mean? I'm afraid to ask. That would be good, wouldn't it?

"You think it would?"

The train stops, not for the first time: a blizzard, the rails are covered with snow. I pace along the corridor, thinking. The conductor comes up to me: "What's the matter, Grandpa, can't sleep?"

I rather like it: Grandpa. I return to the compartment, look at Lyubochka, cover her with a blanket. This time we stop for an especially long time, waiting for the snow-clearing equipment. From then on, it's stop-and-go. We arrive towards morning.

Severogorsk: tall houses, apartment blocks, a huge administrative building, pipes sending up smoke. A proper city: a sports arena, a detention facility—where, incidentally, Gubaryev, Lyubochka's lawful husband, is still being held. "Well, time to go, then?" The actors pull their bags down from the racks, take them out of their compartment. Now we'll probably be issued our new addresses and head for our new homes. We'll pay each other visits, reminisce. "It would be nice if they put us all in the same neighborhood." "Are the apartments furnished? Modern appliances?" "Where have you ever seen such an apartment?" I don't participate in these conversations, nor does anyone really try to involve me in them any longer. "Take it easy"—is that what Gennady Prokopyevich advised? Everything happens quickly in the theater. Retired, Grandpa.

My thoughts are elsewhere. I didn't shut my eyes for a second all night—spent it looking at Lyuba as she slept, adjusting her blanket. What will she name the baby: Maybe Sasha? It's a good name, universal. I'll teach it a tongue twister: "Shy Sasha sashays in her sashes." Or mother's, about Ararat.

The new arrivals are asked to gather in the station building. Lyubochka takes a long time getting ready—she's very slow these days. By the time we enter the building, there's so much noise you can't make anything out: some are threatening to call the police, others the press, and yet others to sort things out their own way. The woman official begs everyone to quiet down, to put themselves in her position.

"Ladies and gentlemen, you are being called on to act humanely!" Anna Arkadyevna's tragic laughter first gives way to a coughing fit, then to sobbing.

The news is this: we are to stay on the train—they have nowhere else to put us. "Consider this an agitprop train, as in the war. Agitprop brigades didn't leave their trains for years." But the war's over, isn't it? An evasive answer: "For some."

From my point of view, and I'm even afraid to admit it—this isn't so terrible: the carriage is warm, well lit, there's plenty of room. We'll be attached to the station dining room, given coupons for three meals a day. There's a working shower in the hall for passengers with children, and you can at least use it at night. Don't cry, Lyubochka, please. In the little carriage in which I began my life, there was no such comfort in sight. Did you hear that? If the power is cut off, they'll issue us coal briquettes. Coal briquettes! We couldn't even have dreamed of that back then. And the first-aid post at the station is open around the clock.

Lyubochka's forehead breaks out in red blotches—no time to waste. I make my way through the crowd and, without considering the volume of my voice, tell everyone that Lyuba is expecting. For some reason, this provokes laughter. Actors are like children—they can be cruel.

The woman in uniform shrugs: "I'm sorry, I can't birth her an apartment."

A solution will soon be found: Lyuba will be sent to the hospital, to save the pregnancy. She'll lie there a while, calm down, undergo analysis, no hurry. I escort her back to the car. She gives me her forehead to kiss, smiles in parting.

It turns out I was right: life in a modern train carriage isn't that bad. Quiet, warm, plenty of food. At first the constant stream of announcements was a distraction: train so-and-so, coming in from so-and-so. But you soon get used to it, stop noticing. The station is in the center of town, everything is near at hand: shops, laundry, even a swimming pool. For those who hadn't left Eternity in years, there is much that is new to explore. Some make the rounds of all the government offices, make scenes, seek compensation for lost property; others look for work, call acquaintances. I find myself doing less and less, but reading more and more—aimlessly, disinterestedly—and even memorizing poems again. I'll walk over to the station, have breakfast, exchange a few words with familiar faces, find out the news, and then back to the bunk, to read.

Of course, there are fewer and fewer familiar faces. Hairspring vanished straightaway: word was that she went off to Petersburg, to the white-toothed director. They had developed a liking for each other when she was rehearsing Laura with him. Anna Arkadyevna was invited to work at a children's theater in Syktyvkar.

I went to the hospital once, to obstetrics—I got lost, it took me a long time to find it, and they still didn't let me see Lyubochka. Maybe there was a quarantine, or maybe they never allow visitors, or maybe just not men; everyone offered a different explanation. I had brought her books, fruit, water. They told me they'd pass them along: Schwalbe's fine, temperature is normal. That calmed me down, so I went back to the carriage—to read, to dream.

"Well, well, well," as Mir Savvich, our unforgettable director, used to say. My dreams were sweet, and although I now know how they ended, I still don't think I dreamed in vain. At night, when they'd turn off the upper light, I'd lie in the dark, remembering the little songs my mother used to sing to me, going over the funny phrases and rhymes I'd learned in childhood. How little I know myself: here, it turns out, is what I needed all along! I had singed my fingers on Glashenka and decided not to risk it again. No, in truth, I didn't decide any such thing—just lived the life I was born to live.

"So, what, I'm Medea to you?" She's screaming, attracting attention: I couldn't resist telling Lyubochka about "the life I was born to live."

Hush, hush—the partitions are paper-thin. Then again, what does it matter? Cry, scream, it makes no difference now.

Lyubochka was in the same department with women who were planning to get rid of their pregnancies.

"Abortion, Alexander Ivanovich. It's called 'having an abortion.' What's so cruel about that? Besides, you were the one who shoved me in there."

To be brief, one day a priest came to visit the women. Everyone went to see him, and she did too. He was a young man. How did he manage to get in there?

"Priests are probably immune to infection, Alexander Ivanovich. Anyway, he spoke well, he'd prepared. Fire and brimstone...All the girls cried. I didn't: What do I care? I just came for the company. So I'm sitting there, listening, watching him. Tall. Neat, trimmed beard. And I notice he's also looking at me a lot, more than at the other girls. He sees I'm not taken in, not dissolving in tears. Asks me who I am. An Aquarius, I say. He smirks: 'I mean, what do you do?' A dramatic actress. He shakes his head: 'You wanted the easy life. Well, look at how these other girls live.' What are you talking about? 'About the fact that hypocrites will not be saved. That's what actors are: hypocrites. Woe unto you, hypocrites! You know what they called the theater in the old days? "The spectacle." Shameful spectacle. It's not for nothing that they bury actors behind a fence, next to the suicides.' I ask: Isn't it a little too early to bury me, Holy Father? 'I am not your Holy Father,' he says. All the more so! He turns away: 'Forgive me, dear sisters, for steering the conversation away from the matter at hand,' and goes on with the eternal agony and the gnashing of teeth. He doesn't look at me anymore. The girls are so-o-obbing. I think to myself: Effective lecture—they'll be in labor before you know it. He wraps it up—and they start! 'I've got no apartment!' 'I got laid off!' 'Have you seen the waiting lists for kindergarten?' 'You don't know what my mother-in-law's like!' One's unemployed, another has no roof over her head, the third's husband is a drunk. The priest hears them out: 'You should have thought about that earlier.' And leaves."

All the girls went through with it, had their abortions. Every single one. Including Lyubochka.

"Alexander Ivanovich," smiling and crying. "The priest, he sounded like he was summoned from the Ivanovo region. Remember?"

Do I ever. "The Vale of Tears."

You wanted to spite the priest, is that it?

"No! Why can't you understand? He was right! I should have thought about it earlier..."

About what? Look at my mother: she gave birth to me, raised me all by herself. Her circumstances weren't exactly favorable either.

"And what was the point? Look at us now: no one cares whether we live or die. No family, no home, no work."

I was going to say that she was my family, but why force myself on her? You, I say, are an actress. Think of how many roles you've played! Any theater would be glad to have you. While I have a pension. And I've even saved up a little—just a little, of course, but I have. I could always work as a teacher, too.

The poor girl is crying, thrashing about: "Alexander Ivanovich, dear Alexander Ivanovich, forgive me, forgive me."

I don't even know how much time has passed. A week, two? I see Lyubochka only sporadically. One day I'm coming back to the carriage after breakfast and there she is, on the platform. I ask: Where are you heading?

"Now I'll always have to give you a report, right?"

Lyubochka has a kind heart: she notices that her answer has upset me, so she takes me with her to the pool. That's where she was heading.

I don't swim, never learned, but I stand there and watch. Of course, you can't make out too much: it's May, the sun's out day and night, while the air temperature is below zero, so there's a cloud of steam over the water. So how did the Gemini fish her out of that soup?

A few days later Lyuba comes to me: "Congratulate me, Alexander Ivanovich. I met a man. And I'm moving in with him. I have a feeling this time it'll work out."

Well, who is he? What does he do?

"Nothing interesting—an engineer. He's a Gemini. You understand? I've never been with a Gemini before. Nothing but Aries and Sagittariuses. We're going to get married, move to America."

I congratulated her, of course, wished her happiness. Lyuba's her cheerful self again, that's what matters. And she has a new hat, I notice.

We also talk business: "Please don't forget, Alexander Ivanovich, you and I have an appointment the day after tomorrow. The social-welfare agencies just can't wait to see us."

Yet another round of visits to the agencies, all seemingly pointless.

"Take what you can get..." Lyubochka was given compensation instead of an apartment: determined by the cadastral value. I can't wrap my head around what that means.

"As for you, my dear fellow," they say (that is, as for me), "we cannot offer compensation. Our records tell us you were only a temporary resident of Eternity. And besides, we only compensate those who have lost personal accommodations, not those who had them provided by their place of work."

Lyubochka gets angry, starts to shout: "And you told me to have the child, Alexander Ivanovich!" She turns to the audience, mocks them: "'My dear fellow.' This man," she points to me, "has more dignity in his little finger than all of you taken together."

I hide my hands in the pockets of my coat. Lyubochka will remind me of that. The audience—a line of applicants and the workers—is taken aback: she's on a real tear.

"Are you in greater need than the rest of us, lady?"

Another question: Schwalbe—what kind of name is that? Doesn't sound very Russian.

Oh, Lyubochka swung around and gave them a look to end all looks: Jocasta, Gertrude, Elizabeth of England! She doesn't need much to get her going. Calm down, whisper, let's get out of here.

The chorus chimes in: "Wait, isn't she the one that actor went to jail for? Remember, he played that bald major on TV?"

I grab Lyubochka by the hand, drag her to the exit, pleading: Don't raise a fuss, I don't need these scenes, I don't need anything. Have we any right to complain? As if we're blameless.

We go out into the street:

"What do you mean, as if we're blameless? Wake up, Alexander

Ivanovich! Eternity wasn't shut down because of some play we put on, or because I slept with my husband and Slavochka at the same time—by the way, it was never at the same time—or because Gubaryev shot him. You yourself said it: the truth is necessary. Well, here's the truth for you. It's politics!"

The Gemini had probably explained politics to her.

"It isn't just towns, whole countries are folded up and thrown away. But not in America—there it's different. There, if they want to run the road through your house, you're in luck."

Really? Why is that? Lyubochka and I look at each other and start to laugh! Don't they determine things by the cadastral value? We're in stitches, repeating the same words with every possible inflection. The people who walk by must think us mad. Lyubochka quiets down before I do: "You go back to your carriage. I've got to visit the prison and divorce a certain convict, before the public turns on me for abandoning a hero."

It's summertime. Everyone has found something by now, except me. They'd forgotten all about me, then suddenly remember: "Let's get you into a nursing home, old fella."

Lyubochka snorts when I tell her about this: "Not a chance! Let's go to the real-estate broker, find a house. Where would you like to live?"

We spent a long time looking at the options. Lyubochka was such a help. She even pitched in with a little money: "Take it, take it—don't force me to persuade you."

What have I done to earn such a reward? I take it, thank her.

"Alexander Ivanovich, is fate a part of one's personality?"

What a question! Lyubochka posed it last autumn, before we parted. Why didn't you ask me earlier?

"Would you have had the answer back then?"

OF THE PONT MIRABEAU…

In the end I settled on Tarussa, near Moscow. There was another good option, Abkhazian Gudauta, but at my age, it's hard to adjust to a new climate, dangerous. Although, to tell the truth, it isn't a matter of climate: "Of the Pont Mirabeau, where the Oka doesn't flow…"[20] It's true, there's no Pont Mirabeau over the Oka, in fact, there's no bridge at all. Still, there's a lot to like about Tarussa.

I do a lot of walking. The natural landscape is marvelous. And I've struck up a friendship with a local author, Vladilen Nilovich Makeyev, whom I've already mentioned.

"Alexander Ivanovich, don't you ever *choose* your friends?" Lyubochka once asked me.

I don't know, my dear—it seems you're right: I feel you ought to make peace with the friends fate has brought you. And it turns out Makeyev and I have a great deal in common. We're almost exactly the same age; both our fathers were sent away to the camps when we were children. Of course, Vladilen Nilovich's father was an important figure, a bigwig, while mine was only a tram conductor.

There's only one thing: Makeyev loves to complain. Not that it bothers me much when people get things off their chest, if it makes them feel better—as long as they don't work themselves up into a lather.

"Another award season has flown by, leaving me empty-handed. A bunch of Yids took all the prizes. Yids giving prizes to Yids. That's the whole literary process for you."

Look, I try to tell him, look all round us, Vladilen Nilovich. Such beauty. I feel the lilacs are about to bloom. Do you know how many years I've gone without seeing lilacs?

"'Russian Spring,' they're calling this. Sure, the spring may be Russian, but who gets all the prizes?"

I'm certainly glad I didn't become a writer. I had, at some point, entertained the thought. I point to a tree: Look, is that an alder? Grows all by itself—no need to plant it, no need to tend it. I rejoice at these trifles, can never get used to them after the north. I mean, it really is a miracle!

"A miracle, certainly... I love our nation's landscape. And yet it wouldn't hurt to make a noise, just once more."

When the weather permits, I go for a walk, either alone or with Makeyev. The rest of the time I'm in the library. It opens early in the morning, closes at seven. I've managed to catch up a bit, but there's so much more to read.

I've found a good place to stay again, but I try to be home as little as possible: I don't like to bother Antonina Feodorovna. She and Mikhail Stepanovich are my neighbors; we share a wall, a yard. And half the garden is also mine, but I told them they could use it—I'm no gardener. They used to share the house with their relatives, but there was some sort of falling-out; I do not know the details. I get along better with Mikhail Stepanovich. For example, he once gave me a hand when it was my turn to clear the ice from the yard: I hit the ice this way and that, but couldn't break it up. Mikhail Stepanovich saw me struggling, and came out and taught me how to hold the scraper properly, get it under the ice.

"I'd do it for you, if not for..." He nodded at the window.

He calls his wife, Antonina Feodorovna, *ma*. I confess, at first I thought she was actually his mother. That would have been something... All those Greek tragedies must have really sunk their teeth into me! It was pure luck that I didn't say anything. The situation is fairly bleak as it is, frankly speaking: for the first time in my life, I have my own home, and I just can't get the hang of it—the theater has spoiled me completely. You take your shirt or jacket to the costume department: they'll press it, sew on a new button, or let you swap it for something else. Need a haircut? No trouble there either. Anyuta in makeup—we called her Nyuta—always spat on her fingers before arranging anyone's hair. We'd laugh at her for that. To say nothing of food, scrubbing the floor, throwing out garbage, paying for electricity... I never had to concern myself with any of that. I lived without a care in the world, didn't leave the theater for weeks.

All right, I can learn to wash my clothes and cook for myself—but the fact that Lyubochka doesn't write to me is harder to deal with. I stop by the post office every few days, to see whether they have anything for me in general delivery.

But everyone has worries of his own. Makeyev and I talk about his work quite often.

"Since my novel is in the historical-patriotic genre, it might be wise to rename it. In light of recent events. What do you think of *Korsun* for a title?"[21]

I was fond of *No Hand in the Matter*. Although, in all honesty...

"In all honesty, dear Alexander Ivanovich, you still haven't found the opportunity to acquaint yourself with my writings. Artists are easily offended. I'm joking, of course."

Oh, yes, I know. I begin to explain to Makeyev about my cursed glasses. I wasn't planning on telling him, these things happen, but he's rushing me.

An unfortunate incident: my glasses vanished. I rummaged through all my things—nowhere to be found. I can't read or write without them. Even food doesn't taste as good if you can't see what you're eating. And you know, I'm not so well off that I can order a new pair of glasses just like that. Suddenly my neighbor Mikhail Stepanovich comes in and brings me my glasses. I run up to thank him—where on earth did you find them?—and he tells me he found them in my room. Imagine that. He came and took them when I was out.

"I thought they'd work for me," he says. "But no, too strong."

Makeyev hears me out: "I don't know how things are done up north, but in Central Russia it's common practice to lock one's doors.

At any rate, now nothing prevents you from reading my novel, am I right?"

Yes, I'll read it, I promise.

And I would have read it, without delay, if Eternity hadn't reminded me of itself again. I didn't expect news from that direction! And to think: if it weren't for Makeyev, I would probably never have known how the story of my theater ended.

It was like this. We meet at our usual place: in the garden in front of city hall, near the river. Vladilen Nilovich, as a rule, is a bit late, but on this day he comes early. And the expression on his face is unusual, cunning:

"My dear Alexander Ivanovich, have I got a surprise for you." He pulls a newspaper out of the inside pocket of his raincoat, but holds it in his hand, doesn't give it to me. "This morning I pick up the newspaper and start to read it. On the front page there's a lot of material about the wonders of our military technology. And about the fact that the commander in chief has personally—personally!—taken part in testing it. A supersonic, variable-sweep wing, heavy strategic bomber. Do those words mean anything to you? Our pilots call it the White Swan."

Vladilen Nilovich is standing in the middle of the garden, enthusiastically describing all manner of objects that fly through the air. I'm afraid to mix them up—I myself have never flown, only traveled by train and bus.

"Aerial refueling...Four missiles!" Makeyev exclaims. "Hit the target every time! And then...Pay attention, please. And then, Alexander Ivanovich, I look at the caption beneath the photograph. Hold on just a moment, I tell myself: Is that not our Alexander Ivanovich's native soil? Indeed: Eternity! Here," he holds out the newspaper, "see for yourself!"

I don't remember taking the paper from him or sitting back down on the bench. My thanks to Makeyev: he caught me before I keeled over. My theater—there it was. The women's dressing rooms—a hole, a huge ragged hole. That's where one of the missiles had entered. To the right, one floor up, my window. No glass, blackness. There's the cornice Slavochka would use to climb up to his room, so as not to wake the watchwomen. Did the urn survive? How could it have . . . I burst out in tears. Never mind reading it—I can't even look at the pictures.

Lord, who's that standing there, holding up pieces of metal? Isn't that Zakhar? Smiling ear to ear. He was never exactly skinny, but . . . No, it really is him: Head of the Severogorsk district, Zakhar Gubaryev. They sprang him loose quickly! There he is, in all his glory—our Sagittarius, the Commander.

Poor Makeyev is shoving napkins into my hands. I mumble: Forgive me, Vladilen Nilovich.

"Alexander Ivanovich, no one was hurt . . ."

Of course, of course. Don't pay any attention . . .

We sit for a while; I calm down a bit, only the tears keep coming. Makeyev moves closer to me, puts his hand on my shoulder: "Do you know who our commander in chief is?"

Well, yes, of course. I haven't fallen that far behind . . .

"But do you know his real name?" He glances around: "Silverstein. It's Silverstein."

The shock dries my tears. Where, I ask, did you get that from?

"Everyone's saying it."

I didn't go for a walk that day. After apologizing to Makeyev, I went down closer to the water and read the whole newspaper, front to back: a lot of things I hadn't known. Yes, serious matters—and here we are, with our little heartbreaks.

For a long time I didn't dare look at the photos again, turning and folding the paper so as to hide them. Finally I looked again—this time without tears. It was as if a weight had been lifted off my shoulders: the story was over; there was nothing to worry about. Fate had delivered four final blows, killing no one—you could even say it had smiled down on us, waved to us with its wing. Nothing left to be afraid of. And Slavochka would have liked this finale: *bang*! Cast to the wind. Lyubochka too would be fine, I was sure of it.

And—impossible to believe!—the next day I received a letter. Yet again, providence. How could I not think that my life was already written down somewhere? Not a letter, exactly—a postcard: "Alexander Ivanovich, we went to the ocean today, to watch the whales. I fell asleep in the car on the way back, and I saw you in my dream —not you, but some man who said you were gone. I cried so hard I woke up."

Now I have Lyubochka's address. I sent her a telegram: "Alive." They laughed at the post office: no one sends telegrams anymore, and if they do, the content is usually exactly the opposite. I'll write to her later, tell her everything.

At that point I stopped dreaming of it. I had no more dreams about the theater, or about Eternity, for that matter. As to commanders in chief, we'd never really given them much thought. Just once, after a long performance. We sat around talking, late into the night. Lyubochka suddenly says, so plaintively: "If only someone turned their attention to us. How hard we work, how we suffer."

Gubaryev, across the table: "Whose attention do you want? The president's?"

"Yes, the president, and why not? I'd gladly"—and she had only had one little glass—"give him an heir."

Gubaryev bangs his fist on the table: "Who needs your heir, you idiot? NATO's already at the gate!"

Gubaryev wasn't like the rest of us. He followed the news.

Makeyev follows it too. Another month has passed. We're out on our walk. I stop from time to time, as if to look around or touch a twig, but, in truth, in order to catch my breath. I've had trouble with that lately.

"Have you heard the news?" Makeyev laughs: "No surprises this time, Alexander Ivanovich."

Vladilen Nilovich, I answer, you know I don't read the papers, don't watch television. Sometimes I hear the Krutovs' radio through the wall, but that doesn't count. You're my radio and television.

He nods: "We've made serious progress in recent days. Reinforced our position. Stirred a fine cauldron! Gave 'em hell!" His words were stronger: "Shoved it where the sun don't shine!"

Makeyev looks fresher, rosier, his eyes are burning—you can't help but admire it! Events of this sort have a rejuvenating effect on certain older men. "If God should send us war, then I'd remain prepared to mount, if groaningly, my horse once more..."[22] And so, Vladilen Nilovich:

"I'm raring to go. When I served my compulsory stint, they called me a machine gunner from heaven. Sergeant Makeyev, a top-notch student of the arms. Remind me to show you the photos. I was one with the instrument. Did you serve, Alexander Ivanovich?"

No, I wasn't accepted. Vladilen Nilovich, you and I are old men. But Seryozha, your grandson—aren't you worried he'll be called up?

"No, Seryozha's in Germany, with his mother. Studying."

He pauses, then says: "You know what I've decided? If my novel is passed over again, I'll push off for Germany myself. At least they have a normal medical system, unlike ours—you can't get anything out of our doctors. I'll sell everything I've got, the whole kit and caboodle, before the economy goes to ... Ah, yes, I forgot: you don't like me to use real Russian words!"

Oh, I don't mind. If you're in a mood to use them.

"I understand what you're thinking, Alexander Ivanovich. But the idea of dying ... I hate it. It's as if you're a guest in someone's house. The hosts have plans: tomorrow they'll go to the movies, the day after—somewhere else. And you—well, time to leave, you know what I mean?"

Are you unwell, I ask?

"No," he replies, "nothing like that. Not yet, touch wood."

We reach our destination—the crossing over the stream. We usually say our goodbyes here. And he suddenly asks: "What will become of us? What do you think, Alexander Ivanovich?"

I don't know what to say. You have to trust ...

"Trust what? You don't read the papers, don't listen to the news."

No, I had something else in mind. I can't express it. Somewhere someone knows what's best for me. Yes, that's probably all I can say.

The lilac has long since faded; the days are warm, but I can no longer go on walks with Makeyev: I stop at every turn, take every hillock with difficulty. But I visit the cemetery, the old one, more and more often. It's right around the corner, quiet, green. I wander through the rows, read the inscriptions, look for my mother's family name or at least a similar one. It's an ancient town, many people are buried here—it's easy to find any kind of name. Or maybe I find a plate with the letters worn off—reminisce, read a poem.

A home for the elderly is an unhappy place, but it's time to take a closer look. They have one here in town. That's good.

"For veterans," the director corrects me. Quite a young man, not yet forty. "We call ourselves veterans. No one knows of what!"

He's easily amused: "In our line of work, if you don't laugh, you'll go crazy."

I race after him up the stairs, which isn't easy for me, but I don't stumble, I make it.

"The rooms are on this floor. Are you coming alone, Alexander Ivanovich, or with your wife? Ah, then we'll find you an interesting neighbor. Perhaps an eligible bachelorette?" He winks. "Let's pop in here."

But there are people in there.

"We don't stand on ceremony around here." He opens the door to someone's room.

No need, I've seen enough. And on the first floor?

"'The Feebler.' For the ill and enfeebled. We won't go down there.

And we also have a certain…Problematic population. They steal people's teeth—hell, entire jaws! We have to call the cops every other day. And I'll tell you one other thing: the hazing is as bad as in the army. You'll have to prove yourself right away."

We go to the kitchen together, sample the food, which I like a great deal: it's been a long time since I've had anything hot. Then we walk to the director's office. Suddenly he takes me by the elbow.

"I have an offer you can't refuse." He hugs me around the shoulders— I don't remember the last time someone hugged me like that. "Let's establish a theater at our facility."

A theater? I even coughed. How does he know of my theatrical past?

"Espionage. I'm kidding."

He shows an issue of the local paper, *October*. A short note, quarter of a page: "I Come from Eternity," by V. N. Makeyev.

"The higher-ups want us to do something artistic. We'll go around the region, and then—who the hell knows?—maybe secure a governor's grant. Let's get you signed up quick. We'll put you in a luxury suite."

I start laughing and can't force myself to stop. The director might take me for an epileptic. What kind of plays could we put on? Shadow plays? Or are we not shadows yet? Do we still cast shadows? Or no?

"Why shadow plays?" Now he's surprised. "A normal theater. Normal plays, comedies. Positive material. Old age is no picnic, Alexander Ivanovich."

I can't stifle my laughter. The director's goodbye is far less friendly than his greeting. It figures, considering how much time he'd wasted on me.

I leave his office with all the admission papers, and I think I'll take the long way home. There's more to see along that route, while the light lasts, and besides, the short way runs through the ravine. And I don't believe I can take the ravine today. I don't want to start out in the Feebler. I can get used to any place, of course, but that wouldn't be very pleasant. Not to worry—I'm not so far gone, I'll bounce back. I'll just sit down on the bench for a minute, catch my breath.

I see people wending their way to the door—veterans: six p.m., time for supper. I watch through the glass as those who will soon be my companions file into the dining room, sit down in their places. I should go too. It looks like it's about to rain, and I don't want the papers to get soaked. I'll risk it—through the ravine. Not such a long climb. What will become of us? We were born in wartime and we'll die in wartime. Isn't it obvious?

I notice something: all my life, while death was far away, it wasn't exactly always on my mind, but I did think of it. But now I seem to have completely forgotten about death. It's only from time to time that I'll take stock—not of what was, but of what is, what's all around me—and think: How I'll miss it, all of it! Those vast, those endless fields on the other side of the Oka. Past the woods there are towers, lights, a real town, but on the other side of the Oka—no, I don't want to. In the evenings I wait for the buoys to light up; I take deep breaths, gaze up at the dark sky. I didn't manage to see very much, to learn very much, but I'll miss many, many things. Not only trees and rivers. Flakes of snow in the beam of a searchlight. Poems—first and foremost. Is there no way to take them with me, just a handful? It all comes back to me: the Urals, Lyubochka, Eternity.

"While far away—in Paris to the north..." I never did see Paris. But really, there's no cause for disappointment. No one held me back by force. I had, after all, been given a glimpse of a little slice of the world, a slice all my own—and for a fairly long time, when all is said and done. And the things I witnessed in that time!

And so I stand there, thinking, until it grows too cold, too dark. Time to head home.

Great grapes do grow on Ararat.

Translated by Anne Marie Jackson and Boris Dralyuk

ON THE BANKS OF THE SPREE

SELF-CONFIDENCE is born of constant, lasting victories.

Liza, Elizaveta, a natural blonde, what some would call a steely blonde, is on a flight from Moscow to Berlin. Liza she is to her father alone—to everyone else she is Betty. And spirited, witty...yes, Betty suits her to a tee.

That maxim on self-confidence was supposedly coined by chess champion José Raúl Capablanca, although, if faced with our Betty, even a Capablanca would struggle to hold his ground: her hair is short, impeccably styled; her figure is sculpted, with long, strong legs and arms; she wears an elegant black blouse and light, close-fitting trousers that show off her flat stomach; and on her neck she has a subtle, abstract tattoo. Were it not for the single crease across her forehead, one might describe Betty as a thoroughbred, but Betty is no horse, no Arabian mare to probe for flaws. In any company—even as motley a crew as the passengers on a plane—Betty always commands attention. Beautiful, mature, sober, and erudite, she is also a project manager, second in command at a very famous corporation. Self-absorbed, but that goes without saying—who in Betty's position wouldn't be?

During the flight, Betty reads a magazine—cerebral, yet glossy. She reads every issue from cover to cover, the analytical pieces and the literature alike. Right now she's reading a short story, by turns sad and funny, about the wedding of two mathematicians. In it, the bride is meeting her father for the first time: her parents' was a whirlwind romance, a one-night stand; her father had, until recently, no idea she existed. Fast-forward to the wedding, the parents renew their, ahem, acquaintance, and the plot thickens, and there are also funny portraits of the artsy guests—many of whom are given wittily appropriate names, like something from a Mozart opera. Betty, as it happens, knows a lot about the opera. As a matter of fact, she'll be going to the opera today—but not on her own, oh, no. Berlin always has something good on: be it concerts or operas; the fall of the Wall doubled the city's cultural activity. There's plenty of choice, and, from what the reviews say, the East has just as much to offer as the West. She doesn't quite make it to the end of her story, but she finds it both funny and timely, almost as though it were written for her.

"What is the purpose of your trip?"

The border guard asks her in English, but she replies in German: She is here to see her sister.

"Good for you girls."

That's putting it lightly—he doesn't know the beginning of how good it is. He gives Betty a long look all the same. Not her passport or face, mind you: he looks at her neck, then her chest. What's her sister's name, he asks, and has it been a while since they last saw each other? Her sister's name is Elsa, and, yes, it's been a while. Betty's cheerful, the officer's in a good mood, *bam, bam* go the stamps—welcome to Germany.

"Friedrich-von-Schiller-Allee, number 14," Betty says to the taxi driver in German, relishing the words. "Kremer & Kremer. It's a riding shop."

She smiles as she remembers the advice her father gave her on the way to the airport: "Horse is *Pferd*, *Roß* is steed, nouns are capitalized. But the Central Committee has handled more difficult issues than that," the latter being a phrase he often pulls out in tricky situations. As they said goodbye, he gave her a long, tight hug.

To be young, single, strong, and beautiful: Could there be a happier state? Men make their appearances in Betty's life—how could she go without?—but she never keeps them around for more than a few months. They tend to end up being too sporty, somehow. Not that

Betty has anything against sport—it teaches hard work, and the ability to jump hurdles—but for a serious, long-term relationship she's looking for something more: fun, flair—brains, ultimately. This is no fixed principle, no misandrist (misandronist?) philosophy of hers. No, Betty isn't one for such philosophies: just live and let live.

"We're not in any hurry, okay?" says Betty, after a somewhat coltish maneuver on the driver's part. She needs to be at Schiller-Allee at six—closing time—no earlier.

The taxi driver is a dull, poorly shaven, bloated man the wrong side of fifty. She asks his name, but immediately forgets it: Günter, something like that. From East Germany. Betty was under the impression that only Turks or Russians drove taxis in Berlin. She quickly slips in that she's Russian, just in case. He'd taken her for a Dutch woman, maybe even Swiss. That's kind, she thinks. Maybe this Günter can enlighten her, show her something of the city: Betty very much wants to love Berlin. She is full of goodwill.

Berlin is currently warmer and more humid than Moscow, but it's also darker, somehow. The sky is gray, no rain. To the right is the new Brandenburg Airport: they keep building and building, and yet not much happens. It's still nothing to look at.

Anyway, back to sport: Betty's father had taught her to swim. She knows swimming as well as she knows herself; it comes as naturally as reading or talking. She had also taken lessons in fencing, running, horseback riding, even shooting: the modern pentathlon—a most harmonious sport. What she took most pleasure in, naturally, was the horses. But, as it happens, they were also why Betty had had to drop the sport: her eyes would water uncontrollably in the stables, an allergic reaction to the hay. So she had dived into synchronized swimming instead, kicking those legs up out of the water, much to her parents'—especially her father's—delight. As a child, Betty had always associated her father's past, before his marriage to her mother and her own arrival (which came relatively late in his life), with water, lots of it: he had a degree in geography from Moscow State University, he spoke many languages—German, English, Serbian, Arabic (the latter only with a dictionary)—and he was a superb swimmer. Even at seventy, he swims in the Moskva River from mid-May to September, and in a pool the rest of the year.

As for now, outside the window everything still feels somewhat disjointed, stuck together at random. Concrete, steel, glass . . . so much is new. Berlin: a city of unfinished ideas, unfulfilled potential.

"That's Karl-Marx-Allee," says the driver, breaking the silence. He points out the buildings where the GDR leaders once lived. Slightly bigger windows, slightly wider balconies, but somewhat derisory by today's standards. It'll take more than architecture like that to impress Betty: she grew up in a so-called *house of superior design* in Moscow's Strogino district. As a matter of fact, her father still lives there, as did her mother, to her very last days.

Her poor mother: her death was so empty, so out of the blue. She had popped into the hospital for a health check—more for reassurance than anything else—and never left. To this day, Betty and her father treat Russian doctors with suspicion.

But yes, let's not dwell on such sadness. A few years ago, Betty had moved into the city center, to Moscow's Golden Mile. With her father's help (why hide the fact?), she had taken her first steps into the world of business. He had introduced her to the right people, but everything beyond that was all her own doing. With her smarts, knowledge of languages, and looks, why shouldn't Betty, of all people, go far? It's not as though her father had helped her so very much; there's no point exaggerating.

Through these thoughts, Betty doesn't notice them entering the western part of the city. How strange Berlin's layout is: all these great big avenues that lead nowhere; that end not in squares, nor at monumental buildings, but more often than not, in nothing at all. Theaters, concert halls, embassies, government institutions: it's a city of bohemianism and bureaucracy. Ah, there's the opera house, the one she and Elsa will be going to tonight. Her plan is to pick up Elsa from the shop, then take her to the opera, followed by dinner and some frank discussions. Betty would be open to any type of food—Elsa can choose what they eat. Something tells her Elsa doesn't eat meat. And if she's a bit dim? Her English is certainly far from fluent—not a good sign in a youngish German. But she's bound to enjoy the opera: the Germans are a musical people, after all, and even simpletons have to eat. It'll all be fine. Betty has a good feeling about this.

Betty hasn't gone to the trouble of booking a hotel; presumably Elsa will invite her to stay with her. Elsa is forty-two, and appears to live alone. No matter how humble her living situation, Betty will have to make do: you can't choose your family. Never mind. Who knows, her place might even be all right. Besides, having an ally in her sister won't be without its advantages for Betty, what with all of these new laws about overseas bank accounts. But that isn't why Betty's here.

"Let's take a right," she instructs the driver. "I'd like to drive along the Spree."

Stone, tiles, railings: here the Spree bears off straight into the embankment. It's a so-so little river, kind of lousy, really—slightly bigger than Moscow's Yauza, perhaps. Anyone with the slightest swimming ability would find it impossible to drown in there.

Betty takes out her mirror and inspects herself. Her father has exactly the same crease across her brow, although his is considerably deeper. It's particularly visible in that photo of him as a young man, the one she'd finally been able to get ahold of—though not without some difficulty! When asked where he works, her father replies that he lost interest in everything after his wife's death. Yes, he says, he works, the odd job here and there, but then he'll wave off the question and cover his eyes: no one cares about the particulars. He curates projects, noncommercial projects. Publishing, education. The commercial world doesn't sit well with him: little Liza can take care of those things.

The city itself is behind them now. It's not even parks that surround them, but forests: the birds are chirping, the squirrels darting around. Where else would a riding shop be, if not in the sticks? There must be foxes and hares out here, too, and soon, by April or May, the old men will come sauntering out to sunbathe: Germans love baring all for the sun. Must be a sight.

We're almost there. Betty unlocks her phone, turns off the sound, and flicks through the photos again. Then she checks she still has the opera tickets and takes one last look in the mirror before putting everything back in her bag and running her hands over her hips. Her fingers are long, with prominent, deeply carved joints.

"Oh heart, be still on this snow-filled night," she sings, very quietly—almost inwardly, "As the band sets out on its brave patrol..."[23] It's a song that never fails to balance her spirits. As ever, she learned it from her father. He could never hit the high notes, but Betty would sing along, accompanying him on the piano. Oh yes, besides everything else, Betty once studied at the music academy.

Schiller-Allee, number 14. Where are the other 13? Probably somewhere over there, beyond the trees. Kremer & Kremer, half an hour before closing. It would be poor form to arrive late—as it would be to arrive early.

Betty gets out of the cab behind the building and lets it drive off before she takes a good look around. There is no one there—no security guards, no customers. Only a tiny, grayish car with horses' heads painted on the hood and the trunk. No question whose that is. The sight sends new waves of sympathy coursing through Betty.

It's overcast but not cold here; the rain has passed over but the air still hangs heavy. There's a smell of freshly cut bushes: a strong, nondescript smell. Betty wanders around for ten minutes or so in the twilight. The time is now a quarter to six.

The store windows are brightly lit. Bridles, reins, browbands, numnahs, saddle pads in every color, fur-trimmed sleeves for saddles and nosebands: it's all familiar, close to Betty's heart. For a brief moment she forgets why she is here. There's more: riding hats, top hats, and oh! What lovely breeches, with a suede seat—such a shame she wouldn't have anywhere to wear them. Those boots, on the other hand... she'll remember their name. Tiffany. All right, let's go.

When learning to shoot, Betty was always taught to exhale fully, inhale slightly—maybe 25 percent—hold her breath, take aim, listen to her heartbeat, and then, in the interval between two beats, pull the trigger. Betty puts her hand on the door handle, pauses for a moment, then opens the door.

"Hello, Elsa," she says, stepping up to the counter. "I have some good news for you."

This story has a backstory. At the end of February, Betty's father had called her and asked her to come over. His tone was sober, business-like: he had two pieces of news. Start with the bad, as usual?

Cancer.

He'd rather not go into . . . Yes, of the male sort. The prostate. His so-called urologist at the polyclinic had said it was just a bit of cancer, nothing special. But she had recommended—as Betty's father reached this part, he couldn't restrain a yelp—she had recommended *castration*.

"And where's their guarantee that'll help? There isn't one!"

Of course, Betty wouldn't stand for such barbarism. She would find him the right doctor. They would go abroad, to Germany.

"Ah yes, Germany," said her father, suddenly calming down. This was why he had called her.

However, there was one obstacle. They aren't allowed—

"Who's not allowed?" Betty interrupted.

"Do I have to explain everything?"

They—former employees of the First Chief Directorate of the KGB (yes, *that* KGB)—aren't allowed in Europe, anywhere; it's an open ban. Her father said it all quickly, even with a hint of distaste: You're a smart girl, quit feigning surprise.

She'd picked up on the odd thing, of course she had. Once, when she was thirteen, Betty had happened to overhear a neighbor she knew as Uncle Savva in their apartment. He was chuckling about how one of his and her father's colleagues had almost killed a surgeon who'd performed a successful operation on him. Turns out he'd given the surgeon a bottle of top-notch whiskey or brandy in thanks, but the bottle contained huge amounts of a certain poisonous substance (Betty had forgotten the name). A bit of a boo-boo, really: he'd taken the bottle from the wrong safe. Betty's father had quickly shushed him and kicked him out. And then Betty heard that wonderful

English phrase for the first time, as muttered by her father: *Ask me no questions, and I'll tell you no lies.* Plus there was the fact that he never traveled abroad, instead preferring to vacation at home. If she gave it some thought, she'd have been able to remember more.

Anyway, that was the bad news: cancer. Not to mention the prospect of being treated in Moscow, by some old Homo Sovieticus. Betty hates the term Homo Sovieticus herself: though she was barely alive during that period, she's sure many aspects of it get overlooked, including a great deal of good. But when it comes to their health care, she feels her contempt is justified. So what was the good news? There was something her father was in no rush to share.

He smiled, pleading, pained. He was embarrassed—something Betty had never seen in him before. The good news? Betty probably had a sister, in Germany. It was clear why he had kept this under wraps for so long—Betty's mother—and why he was speaking up now: a family reunion was his only chance of treatment in the country.

As for the circumstances: from the start of the seventies until 1982, he had lived in West Berlin under the Serbian name of Milić. Why not Fischer, or Schmidt? What can you do? Maybe his German just wasn't up to scratch. Where did he work? What was he doing? He worked with maps, geographic maps, in a bureau. It fit with his academic background. The only thing is, his maps were all but unnecessary: by the seventies, things in Berlin had settled, an equilibrium had been reached. Which gave him time to make his trips to the river; get married; have a baby girl. His wife's name was Anna. What did she do? Nothing much, she just taught music. She was quite a lot older than him—by now she'd be retired, if not already dead. All in all, he'd lived well enough—had it easy, some might say. They had made plans together, no hidden agendas. They were planning to buy a house, raise their little Elsa. Then suddenly he got his orders to come home. Someone had been compromised; there'd been some sort of leak, not from him. *Ask me no questions*—Betty knows.

So he had his orders. They gave him a good amount of time to prepare—two whole days. He set out early one morning, as he often did, to the Spree, left his clothes on the shore, and then . . . he had his methods. They'd offered to bring over his family, but Anna would hardly have wanted to go along with it: as far as he could tell, she had no great liking for Russians, nor for the socialist camp. Anyway, it never came up.

"But our relationship was fine. You know me, Lizonka, in principle I get on with everyone."

He got up to show her to the door, and then he gave her an unusually big hug: "By the way, I wanted to ask, when you mention things over there…"

"What—where?"

"I never, in any way… see what I'm getting at? I never did Germany any harm."

What had made the biggest, bleakest impression on Betty was not her father's revelation, nor his diagnosis, but the stifling, slightly sweet smell of rotting flesh that she caught on his arms and mouth when he hugged her. She went home, quickly washed him off her, and started looking for her sister. She found her.

There she was: Elsa Milić, born 1973. Luckily she hadn't married, hadn't changed her name. A useful thing, Facebook. Elsa had sixteen friends, a bit subpar, frankly. Someone had been taking photos of her, at least. In all of them, Elsa was alone, not counting the animals. The dogs were shaggy and ancient, and the horses weren't the freshest, either. Travel, food, politics, missing children: she seemed uninterested in it all—horse rations and the health of stray dogs were the extent of her concerns. There was a photo, uploaded the autumn before. She hardly looked like their father at all—her face was quite flat, with a high nose and cheekbones. Reddish hair, flecked with gray. A little makeup would help. Still, this must be one of her better photos, otherwise she wouldn't have put it up. Another one: Elsa standing with some horses, in profile. If Betty were going to be blunt, she'd say her sister was a bit pear-shaped, stumpy. No sign of any mother, but then, there's no obligation for an old lady to be hanging out on social media.

Betty had asked her father to remember something—anything—about Elsa: she had already started to pity her.

"Her successes, you know, they weren't anything special, nothing compared to yours, you're much more capable," he'd said. "Once I told her: 'Some kids you have to tell off or punish so they'll try harder; others you have to praise or spoil. But which one you are, Elsa, I have no idea—with you, none of it works,' and Lizka, can you imagine what she said? She said: 'Dad, just make your own mind up.'" He had thought for a while. "Even so, Lizka, I'd set my sights on the girl, not the mother."

On Facebook it's fine to get straight to the point. So Betty had written to her sister in English (better for negotiations—it's a language foreign to them both): "If you are the daughter of a man by the name of Mirko Milić, please let me know. I have extremely important information to disclose. I'm willing to travel to Berlin." A few days had passed before Elsa read the message (Facebook's symbols told Betty as much), and a few more passed before she replied, in terrible English: Come to the store at closing, any workday.

So here Betty is, at the counter. She holds out her hand and says, in German: "I have some good news for you. You are looking at your sister."

Gestures are more convincing than words. Betty has planned and rehearsed this first scene meticulously: she would shake Elsa's hand for three seconds; place her left hand on Elsa's right; make eye contact.

Elsa's eyes are red and inflamed, her eyelids swollen: allergic conjunctivitis. Elsa works with hay, after all.

"I'd get itchy eyes and a runny nose, too, back when I rode."

A shared allergy, a shared passion. So far, so good. Elsa's better looking in person than on Facebook, despite the conjunctivitis.

"No, that can't be," Elsa says, her voice quiet and husky, like a smoker's. "You're a decade younger than me; you couldn't possibly be my sister."

Twelve years, actually, if they're going to get into that. Anyway. Betty gets out her phone and shows her the photograph of their father when he was young. They had had to turn his apartment upside down to find just one old picture of him. In the end, they had taken a photo of his old Komsomol membership card.

Elsa studies the photo intently. It's not the way you look at a stranger.

"Where did you get this?"

It sounds stupid: *Kommunistische Jugendverband. Der Komsomol.*

"He died when I was eight—I don't know anything about his Yugoslavian past. No photos of him were left."

Jesus, Yugoslavia already. Is now the right time? Even good news can come as a shock, but she's going to have to put it all out there at some point.

"Elsa, that's the thing…" she says. She wants to take her hand again, but Elsa's already moved it out of reach, "you see, our father isn't dead. He's alive."

She almost throws in something about him not being in tip-top shape right now, but decides to save that little nugget for later.

Betty swipes the phone screen to bring up a new photo: "This is what he looks like now," Betty had spent ages trying to get her father to pose for that shot, but Elsa throws it only the most cursory of glances.

Is she stupid? Or just very restrained? Elsa rummages around in a drawer and pulls out a photo wrapped in plastic. She places it in front of Betty.

A lawn; two gravestones. One bears a cross with two crossbars, the inscription MIRKO MILIĆ and the years of his life: 1944–1982. The other: ANNA MILIĆ, with the image of an angel, and beneath it the words *Der Rest ist Schweigen*—the rest is silence.

Though she's ashamed to admit it, the news of the death of Elsa's mother comes as a relief to Betty. She and Elsa, it would seem, have already had their fair share of woes.

What she died from is unclear. Elsa refers to her mother by her first name: *Anna didn't like to visit the doctor.* In her last four years, she never left the house. Elsa still remembers her father's funeral: the candles, the singing. There was a Serbian Orthodox priest, too. That stuck in Elsa's mind.

"Where, where was it?"

"At the cemetery."

Betty smirks—probably a bad move, but that response reminds her of a joke about IT support: technically correct, but absolutely useless.

"I should hope so. But which one?"

Elsa waves her hand, shuts her eyes, and bows her head. It's exactly what their father does when he doesn't want to respond.

"Elsa, my dear, your father isn't under that gravestone."

To Betty's surprise, these words have no effect, either.

"Of course not—he drowned. His body was never found. He was declared dead in absentia. They buried the clothes that were left on the shore."

And why does Elsa suppose they were never able to find his body?

"The Spree flows into the Havel; the Havel flows into the Elbe…"

Betty wants to interrupt: "And the Elbe flows into the World Ocean." Instead she simply asks, sweetly: "Elsa, why all this geography?"

"The Havel and the Elbe went through the GDR. That impeded the search." So that was how it was explained to them.

Can Betty get a quick snap of the headstone? No? Fair enough. But Elsa should listen to what she has to say. Betty lays out the little that she knows about the Berlin period of her father's life. The fact that he could have taken his family with him, however, she neglects to mention.

"Very interesting," Elsa says, pensively, without looking up, but her voice—her voice is shaking, and her hands probably are, too. Why else would she have put them in her pockets? "Very interesting," she repeats. "But why now?"

"Oh, please don't bring up perestroika and all that freedom-of-movement baloney…" Betty thinks.

"Why not before, while Anna was still alive?"

Betty shrugs: Life, eh? What can you do?

"Listen, Elsa, I understand you must be pretty… surprised, shocked, and all that, but that's life; things happen. You have to be able to take it for what it is, right? This was all news to me, too." Betty takes a look at her watch. "Look, I've got tickets to the opera. Do you like opera?"

Elsa looks at her strangely, as though she doesn't understand. Yes, clearly she's a bit dim. Difficult, too.

"I thought you were all music lovers," says Betty. It's like she's constantly having to justify herself. "*The Magic Flute*. It's an opera. By Mozart."

"I'm a music teacher by training," Elsa eventually replies. But she doesn't appear to want to get up.

"Really? Why did you give it up?"

"I didn't give it up. I graduated."

Fine, we'll save that for later, too. Are they really going to have this conversation from opposite sides of the counter?

Elsa shrugs.

"I'm comfortable here."

Something hasn't quite gone according to plan. Betty's going to have to lay all her cards on the table.

"Okay, first things first, let's leave Dad out of this for a while—especially seeing as he's not well right now. He's got a tumor."

Elsa doesn't bat an eye. It's like trying to talk your way out of a speeding ticket: you have to throw all you can at it, hope that something sticks.

Secondly, Betty herself only learned she had a sister a few days ago, and already she's found her and flown here to offer her friendship, from the bottom of her heart. And Elsa should take it from Betty: she's a good person to have as a friend.

Still no reaction. It's really quite impolite.

"And thirdly, as they say: let he without sin . . ." here Betty lowers her voice slightly, not wanting to push it: in this country, guilt is thrust upon kids from kindergarten. "Look, the man never damaged Germany's interests in any way . . ." That much Betty can guarantee—her father would never lie to her. "Let's give him a chance, let him try to iron everything out, build bridges."

Now it seems like Betty's getting somewhere: Elsa looks up from her photo. But she says nothing.

"Needless to say," Betty continues, "it's too late to ask Anna for forgiveness, but . . ." Unsure what this "but" might be, she decides to change tack and pull on the heartstrings, "And fourthly, and fifthly, and one-hundred-and-twenty-fifthly, our father was serving his country. Whatever his orders were, he had to execute them. As for Anna . . ." Yes, that's it, she can say he meant them no harm; it wasn't directed at Elsa or her mother: "you know, as they say, *nothing personal*. It's not like he left you because of another woman."

"Nothing personal," Elsa repeats.

Now Betty's sure she's done it: she's snatched victory from the jaws of defeat, saved every last shot on goal. She checks the time again.

"Look, I'll tell you what: I'll talk to Dad, I'll get him to phone you. Then—if you want to, of course—we can go to Moscow together. We'll cover everything—the visa, the tickets, you name it. I mean, you'll have to visit anyway, now that you're half Russian . . ."

Elsa interrupts her: "No, I'll tell *you* what: leave us alone."

Her gaze is fixed back on that photo. Us? Whom does she mean by *us*? Herself and Anna? All three of them? Her flat face gives Betty little to read. She just needs some time to think, some breathing space: different people react at different speeds. Betty steps away for a moment to go and pick out a pair of boots. Things are getting tight—if they want to catch the opera, they'd better be heading out, on the double.

For some inexplicable reason, her dear old sister chooses that moment to lose it completely: "We don't have any boots in your size." Her voice is clear, almost vicious.

Betty is already at the Tiffany shelf: the boots are right there. Besides, how could Elsa know what size she wears?

"I said no!"

All right, all right, why stress out? How about a hat then? Is Betty allowed to treat herself to a hat?

"Take one, if you must! The till's closed. Take any!" Elsa shouts, slamming the till shut with a crash. She picks up the phone and shouts down the line, "Taxi, please! Right away. Or else one lady," that's what she says, *eine Dame*, "will be late for the opera."

To hell with her, with her hat, with everything. There's nothing Betty can do.

"God grant you health," Betty says. She had wanted to add, "And a sober husband," but she resists; that half-witted big sis of hers wouldn't appreciate the humor.

She couldn't possibly go to the opera alone. What—and have all those fascists leer at her? She'll give the tickets to the taxi driver; what's-his-name—Fritz, Hans, blah—can get some culture for a change.

Betty will get the red-eye back to Moscow. The flight will make her feel herself again, somehow, and she'll finish reading that story about love, although by the end she'll like it much less.

When Betty arrives at Strogino and tells her father about the death of his first wife, and the fact that they are buried beside each other, he becomes unexpectedly uneasy. Then he pulls himself together. As for Elsa, he says: "So the girl ended up with some character. Who'd have guessed." Then he waves his hand in the air. "By and large, I never really understood those Germans," he says.

He starts coughing for no reason; lately he's started coughing quite heavily. The cancer can't have spread to his lungs yet, can it? She gives him a few claps on the back. His cough abates.

When he says goodbye, he tries to console her: "The Central Committee has handled more difficult issues, Lizchen. Israel has decent urologists, too."

March 2016
Translated by Alex Fleming

GOOD PEOPLE

No, there are no children here. They're in a different part of the hospital.

The stout gray-haired woman looks Bella straight in the eye. All Bella remembers is the woman's surname and that she works for Compassion.ru. At the children's hospital named after... Bella can't remember the name. And the ".ru" is a total mystery to her. This Ordzhonikidze woman has the fixed gaze of someone obliged to tell the truth, no matter how difficult that truth may be. And her voice is low: "Reading to children—that's nice. It's a nice thing to do." The *i* of *nice* is drawn out.

Everything they do here, they do for the sake of the children. Does Bella have children of her own, grandchildren? No, no children of her own. Bella seems to recall having answered that question already.

"So you're all by yourself, then?" There's a lingering hiss to Ordzhonikidze's sibilants. "We don't usually take on people undergoing a bereavement reaction, but since Angelina Andreyevna put in a good word for you..." Ordzhonikidze's voice softens on "Angelina" and her upper lip rises in the semblance of a smile.

Some of her words have gone right over Bella's head: What kind of reaction?

Ordzhonikidze gets up—that will do for today.

"You'll remember about the clinic, won't you?"

Bella apologizes: she's been so scatterbrained lately. Yes, the TB screening—she promises to bring the records. And in that same instant she forgets her promise.

*

There's no shortage of good people in this world, even in the world of the theater. The good people haven't abandoned her. Her girl-friends—actresses, makeup artists, set painters—bring her food, cook, set the table.

"Bella—our poor, sweet Bellochka." They keep her informed: everyone's ill, everyone's got troubles. "We knew old age would be tough, but who could have guessed it would be so humiliating?"

Bella listens but doesn't hear them—and if she were to hear them, she wouldn't think the words applied to her. She gazes around, peers at her guests.

"My, my—you're so forgetful these days. High time you got a checkup, Bellochka. Valentina"—doesn't Bella remember her, the dramaturge's assistant?—"well, she lost her husband too, may he rest in peace. We've got a good neurologist at the clinic. The man did wonders for her."

Bella's in the kitchen, washing dishes. She can heat up her own food, doesn't flood her downstairs neighbors, and is careful with the stove, the electricity. She can look after herself just fine, she thinks—she doesn't need any help. Looks like it's time to serve the tea. But Bella takes fright: so many people in the sitting room—people she doesn't recognize.

"What do you mean, Bellochka?" the women ask. "These are your friends—your and Lev's friends. Don't you worry, dear—just have a seat, have a seat."

They'd better order her a little bracelet with her address on it, just to be safe. So it goes . . . Someone can't walk, needs a hip replace-ment—but at their age, the risk . . . Someone else has terrible hyper-tension . . .

"And our Bella Yuryevna, well, her head's gone soft. Like Lenin's." Petya, the lighting technician, must have hit the bottle a little too hard. He wanders into the kitchen. "Who's our theater named after? You remember? Pushkin, Gogol, Stanislavsky?" Bella nods in confu-sion. Petya waves his hand: "It's a lucky thing, I tell ya—she's as good as brain-dead." They cut him off, push him out the door, even threaten to slap him once he sobers up.

The people at the theater like Bella, though at this point she's really just a name on the payroll. She hasn't actually gone onstage in a long time. It would be good to keep her busy, occupy her mind. Otherwise she's a goner. Maybe Lina, dear Angelina, will stop by—she's sure to come up with something. People really are good, Bella thinks. Lev says actors make terrible friends, but she doesn't agree. He says they're always spying on you, looking to steal your emotions, which is why, when something goes wrong, they're always the first on the scene.

Oh, Lina's here—our angel. She can only stay for a minute, but it's so kind of her to drop in.

"We knew she'd come up with something!"

Lina's a wonder. She takes on so much, and manages all of it so beautifully. She's like a child, really—so natural, so direct. She wears almost no makeup. And she dresses so simply: everything's small and elegant—why, her shoes are so tiny, they look like they came from the Children's World department store. And that adorable, touching little backpack. Everything about Lina is touching, everything is good: her gestures, facial expressions, intonation, the look in her eyes—it all goes together perfectly.

"Doing good for others, Bella Yuryevna, is the greatest pleasure of all." Lina lowers her head and presses her right palm to her chest. "What a marvelous picture of Lev Grigorievich!" Lina would love to stay, but they're waiting for her downstairs.

Here's something Bella can do: read to children. The foundation is called Compassion. It's ten minutes away by trolley, and if the weather's good, she could even walk. Fairy tales, stories, novels—Bella Yuryevna has a great reading voice. And she'll be surrounded by all sorts of wonderful people. Lina smiles at Bella, and Bella returns her smile.

A thick notebook of quadrille ruled paper—the kind that used to cost forty-eight kopecks in the old days. The page on the left is blank, and on the right: *Hello, little boy*—a wavy vertical line—*today*—

underlined—*I'm going to tell you a story*—a check mark, for breath. An actor of the old school will never work with printed text; everything has to be copied out into a notebook. *Once upon a time there lived an old man and an old woman . . .* A wavy vertical line indicates a brief pause; double underlining—special emphasis; two vertical lines—a longer pause. The intonation is marked by arrows pointing up or down. The left page is for commentary. Suddenly Bella remembers: the clinic. Was it a TB screening, vaccines? She gets lost in thought—she feels she'd met Ordzhonikidze before, long ago.

At the offices of Compassion, Bella gets to know a bright, cheerful young woman named Natasha—whom everyone calls Tasha—and other girls, but she can't get their names straight. Tasha promises to help her out with the paperwork. She says she can whip up a copy on the computer, make it look better than the real thing. Bella just has to be patient:

"You know we're expecting important guests, Bella Yuryevna."

Bella nods: yes, yes. Still, she'll just go and find out when she can start.

"No, not yet." Tasha will give her a sign.

Until she has the paperwork—TB and hepatitis screenings, drug and HIV tests—she won't be allowed anywhere near the children. We'll get it all sorted out, but today isn't convenient. Ordzhonikidze just came from the Ministry of Public Health, Tasha says, and she's fuming. The employee they assigned to deal with Compassion has just resigned, after promising to take care of everything. So now we've got to start from scratch. It's not the first time the ministry has pulled that trick.

"You think they give a damn about these kids? They could care less, believe me." Tasha wants to lend a dramatic note to her words, but her eyes open wide and sparkle with glee.

So what's Bella planning to read, anyway?

"Please, anything but the Brothers Grimm, with all those witches eating plump little boys and girls! The poor darlings have enough to worry about . . ."

Each of Tasha's nails is painted a different color, and she has little scars above her wrists—the same on both hands—filled in with some kind of brown substance. All the girls talk very quickly, swallowing their vowels; they don't seem to open their mouths wide enough to get the words out.

Tasha is chirping away about the little jackets she bought at Children's World, and how the saleswoman playfully asked where the little boys were going to go, all dressed up, and how Tasha had upset the woman by saying that the jackets were going to be worn only once, on a very sad occasion, so there was no need to worry, the boys would never grow out of them, and how this had stunned all the salespeople. They even forgot to give her a receipt, so Tasha got an earful from Compassion's bookkeeper.

The girls had been crying all day, and Bella was also emotional, though she didn't quite know why. There were more and more gaps in her mind, and the pathways and partitions between them were steadily narrowing, shrinking. She feared that the gaps would soon merge into one, and that there'd be nothing left in her head but... what do you call that whitish liquid that swims up when milk goes sour? Ah, yes, that's it: whey.

So what should she do? Go wash the cups, then find a place to sit. And whom are they expecting, anyway?

"Guests. From high up." Tasha cheered up again. "The guests are 'from high up,' but we were told to corral the shortest doctors we could find for the group photo—no taller than 1.7 meters. I mean, it sounds like the makings of a joke, doesn't it?"

The days go by, the weather changes—it's very warm now—and all Bella can do is listen to the girls chat, wash the cups, and remember. Some of the islands in her mind are safe, solid. One of them is her first meeting with Lev.

It happened in winter, at a resort in the Vladimir region. How did Bella, a young actress, wind up at this far-flung resort? Doesn't matter—she liked it: she'd never seen so much sky in all her days. But it wasn't only the sky she was watching, it was the vacationers too.

And because she was shortsighted and too shy to wear glasses, she watched them at close range, eyes open wide.

Lev—stocky, dark-haired, with thick lips—had come up for a semiofficial mathematics seminar and was now standing in the lobby before the glass-encased "Rules of Conduct at the Kuibyshev Resort." He noticed Bella's reflection in the glass, caught her peering at him with what appeared to be intense, loving interest, and thought: This won't be difficult. He invited her to share the pleasure of examining the rules, but Bella had already been there for several days; she had the rules by heart.

"First," she declaimed, turning her back to the display. "It is prohibited to store suitcases, food, and skis in one's room." She breathed with her diaphragm, as she was taught to do. "Second. Guests are required to keep their beds in order. Third. Moving from room to room without the express permission of the attendant on duty is strictly forbidden. Fourth..."

Suddenly Bella realizes why Ordzhonikidze seems so familiar—she was the attendant on duty. She hasn't changed a bit. But then an opaque fluid again envelops Bella's mind, and she stops without finishing her thought.

Lev knew how to relax the attendant's vigilance, but Bella could only visit him for an hour or two at a time, while his roommates were busy at the seminar, and even then, they had to keep quiet. Bella had almost no romantic experience; she didn't understand that their relationship stood little chance. In the first place, he lived in Leningrad and she in Moscow. In the second place, he expected to be put away for dissident activity. (He was probably exaggerating about that: they never did put him away, or even fire him.) And in the third place, Lev was married. Human beings are polygamous creatures, he explained. He had said as much to his wife, as well as to anyone and everyone who would listen, whatever their gender. And although Bella noticed no such inclinations in herself, she'd nod in agreement: Well, if we're polygamous creatures, so be it.

*

Bella wanders around the empty hospital courtyard. It's hot; she fans herself with her notebook and looks for a shady spot. She's somehow managed to understand a thing or two: here, in this building, Compassion occupies several rooms—there is the office of the director, Ordzhonikidze; the bookkeeper's room; and the big common area, where Tasha and the other girls bide their time. A sign by the door reads: "Patients and relatives are forbidden from entering the office building." And a handwritten postscript: "Thank you for your understanding." Which means there are no children here—they're in another building, across the courtyard.

Several times throughout the day, a plump young man with a small beard appears in the courtyard, dressed all in red—or rather, crimson. A nasty fellow, people say, but a specialist like no other. Then again, where would he be if not for us, if not for the foundation?

"Sasha, you've got to quit smoking," Ordzhonikidze shouts down from her office, then slams the window shut so as to keep out the smoke.

"If you've forgotten my full name, you can call me *doctor*," Sasha snaps back, but Ordzhonikidze can no longer hear him. He turns to Bella: "A powerful dame, am I right? She ought to be minister of public health. Or heavy industry, like her Bolshevik namesake. She may get there yet."

For some reason, Bella trusts him. As for Ordzhonikidze, she looks like the attendant on duty. Bella likes how he laughs: so loudly, so sincerely! It's the first time she's managed to make anyone laugh in this place.

Sasha had seen her onstage once, long ago, and he remembers liking her performance very much, though the role was small. When Sasha was in his teens, his mother and stepfather would take him to the theater almost every evening. His stepfather had taken charge of his sentimental education:

"You were with...which theater?" he snaps his fingers, waiting for Bella to tell him the name, then quickly examines her face. "I'm sorry. It doesn't matter."

*

Nothing much happens. Days are filled with conversations, the meaning of which is never entirely clear to Bella, but it seems that everyone is used to seeing her sitting in the corner with her notebook or moving around the courtyard. They pay almost no attention to her. But their cups are now clean. And Bella has got used to them as well. She asks no questions. The theater teaches you to be patient: you don't achieve success overnight—that's what they say in these cases. To-day—or was it the day before?—she ran into Ordzhonikidze, who looked over her head and simply said: "We're waiting."

"When I first came here to manage the department—well, that was a different era." Sasha's taking another smoke break. "I used to bring bags full of instruments and drugs from abroad. My friends over there would filch a little from their hospitals, collect samples. Then she showed up," he points to Ordzhonikidze's window, "with her foundation. It's not that we aren't grateful—the woman's done a lot—but our own administration is enough of a headache. More than enough."

Bella listens attentively. Sasha has excellent pronunciation: his vowels are large and round.

"And now, on top of that, your Angelina is the face of Compassion," he raises his voice. "Did you catch that jingoist crap about Crimea she wrote the other day? Or signed, at least—not much of a difference. You're lucky you don't read the papers."

Sasha wants to appear strong. She needs to find something to tell him. The other day Lev said: "Bellochka, a person who wants more from life than the bare necessities will step on anyone who gets in his way."

Sasha looks confused: Who's Lev, her husband? He has to go: office hours, children are waiting. She and Lev, on the other hand, left the Kuibyshev resort together, only he went off to Leningrad and she to Moscow. They agreed to meet in three weeks at the Red Gates in Moscow, and they set a definite time, because Bella didn't have a phone yet.

*

That evening—or perhaps a day had passed, or maybe a few days—the girls sit around and talk. They say that more and more people are quitting because they don't want to deal with terminally ill kids, but that this is the case all over, and that soon there won't be enough money to send the kids abroad to get treatment. And then it would be like the old days, with parents weeping, groveling at Ordzhonikidze's feet—not a sight for the faint of heart...Who but the old dame could take it? They'd have to fall back on a lottery again, pulling names out of a hat. So now all hope rests on tomorrow's very important visitor—otherwise it's a Grimm fairy tale, right, Bella Yuryevna? And what bad luck they've had, with people raising such a stink about Angelina's article—or maybe it's a good thing.

Then Angelina herself arrives, and she's in a terrible funk. She greets Tasha and the other girls, but hardly nods to Bella and immediately looks away. While Bella tries to figure out what she might have done to upset Lina, Ordzhonikidze enters the room: "They've never held anything heavier than a phone in their hands, but now they feel they can sit in judgment...Tasha, don't just sit there—go on, ring up oncology. Tell them to send over a good-looking fellow, a minority. No, wait, let's send Lina over there. Tell them to get some scrubs ready. And shoe covers—for her and the photographer."

When she returns from oncology, Lina has coffee with the girls and cries. She presses her palm to her chest and repeats that she'd do anything to save the children, anything at all, even sell her soul to the devil. And all the girls keep saying how wonderful Lina is, and taking photographs, and crying—except Ordzhonikidze, who only frowns. Bella also takes part in the general outpouring of affection for Lina, who has, after all, done so much good for her, but who now, for some reason, won't meet her eyes.

Then Sasha comes in, and Bella notices for the first time that he's a redhead. Sasha's also piqued, but for some other, personal reason. He keeps shooting glances at Lina, and asking Ordzhonikidze to temper her ardor, take it down a notch, and stop spreading all sorts of nonsense about his oncology department—they're no miracle workers: "I'm telling you, it's nothing." He stammers in agitation.

"So we treated a Japanese boy. So we operated on a non-Russian. That's news? I've been fighting off journalists all day..."

Ordzhonikidze shrugs her shoulders: what a delicate flower.

"Colleagues, let's focus on tomorrow." She asks one of the girls to print out copies of the script for the visit and distribute them, so that the participants can learn their roles.

"But will...will he really come?" one of the girls asks.

"We're still on his schedule, for the time being."

"A photo op," Sasha grumbles. "I don't want any part of it."

"It's not about what you want, Alexander Markovich," Ordzhonikidze objects. "It's for the cause, for the sake of the children. And by the way, a photo like that won't do you any harm." She grins. "You've passed the height test, anyway."

Tasha interjects: "Put that photo in your passport and you'll never have any problems at customs or with traffic cops."

"But will you take a picture with me, doctor?" Lina asks suddenly, with absolute innocence. Her tears have dried up. It's the old Lina, sweet and calm.

Sasha's cheeks and forehead turn red: "With you? Yes, of course..."

The conversation moves on to the topic of what, exactly, they should ask for. It's dark outside the window, quite late. Bella leans her head against the wall and closes her eyes. Tasha whispers: "Let me walk you out."

No, she'll sit and listen.

Sasha and Ordzhonikidze go at each other again, and that wakes her up: "Well, well, well—an hour ago you were too good to shake you-know-who's hand, but now look at your list of demands!"

"What do we need a chapel for when we can't pay our nurses?" Sasha shoots back.

"Not by pills alone, Alexander Markovich...The chapel will make an impression. He's a man of faith."

The lanky photographer who showed up with Angelina has grown terribly bored. He cuts in: "He also knows what the Leningrad Symphony is about."

Ordzhonikidze—also sweating and flushed—shakes her head: You see?

"What's that got to do with anything? And how do you know?" Sasha's stammering again.

The photographer shrugs his shoulders: It's a well-known fact that he's a man of culture.

"You'd never say that about a normal person: 'Oh, what a fine fellow—knows what the Leningrad Symphony's about!'"

"Don't start, Sasha." There are always a few steely notes in Ordzhonikidze's voice, but now they aren't just individual notes—they're a thunderous rail.

"You wouldn't give anyone else special credit for that—not me, not my nurse, not even that poor demented old lady!"

A pause. Sasha storms out, while the others sit with their eyes cast down. Ordzhonikidze alone looks at Bella, searchingly: "Do you know what the Leningrad Symphony's about?"

It's Bella's cue. "I'll have to ask Lev," she says. "He knows Shostakovich like the back of his hand."

Lina walks over to Bella and impulsively kisses her on the shoulder. What's the matter? Bella's mind is filled with a sense of confusion. Tasha accompanies her to the trolley, and then ends up taking her all the way home, although Bella would, of course, have managed just fine on her own. Tasha puts her to bed, and Bella cooperates, although it isn't her bed, and the whole apartment looks different, strange.

"Listen, Bella Yuryevna, you just stay home and rest up . . . I'll call you when he's out of our hair." Tasha has white teeth and big eyes: you can see them shining in the dark.

The apartment Bella remembers as her own really isn't the one where Tasha has left her. It's on the same metro line, but closer to the center—in Khamovniki. And it's not an apartment but a room in a communal apartment. Her neighbors are Aunt Shura, a pensioner, and Nina the housepainter, a hopeless drunk. The apartment is located in the basement—that is, on the ground floor—and you can access Bella's room in two ways: the usual, through the main entrance and down the stairs, or, if you remove the bars, through a window near the ceiling.

Of course, she could have given Lev the address, and he would have come straight there, or not come—three weeks is a rather long time to be apart, and many things could have got in the way. For example, Lev could have been arrested, or he could have simply changed his mind (she herself had no doubts, but he had given her an opportunity to decide). And it wasn't entirely clear how his Leningrad wife actually felt about polygamy.

And so she wakes up very early on the day of their meeting, looks around the room—trying to see it as Lev would see it—has breakfast, noting that Nina is already at work (good!) while Aunt Shura is where she always is. There's still enough time to do her hair. It seems she was just at the salon, but now her hair is long again. The girls had warned her not to cut her hair on the new moon: it would grow right back before she knew it. Rainwater, by the way, is great for the hair, but you won't find much of that in March, so she'd have to settle for tap.

Instead of a hair dryer she uses a hand dryer—a most convenient gadget stolen from the public restroom of the Red Army Theater and given to Bella as a present: you just sit under it and pull the lever above your head. There's plenty of time, but Bella's already a bit tired; for an actress, eight in the morning is still nighttime. So she closes her eyes for a bit, but by the time she opens them it's already eleven. Oh, no! This is the worst thing that's ever happened to her! What a screwup—to put it mildly. There's no way he'd wait two and a half hours... She jumps from car to car at every stop: come on, come on—Dzerzhinskaya, Kirovskaya.

The Lermontov Monument—when Lev first told Bella where they'd meet, he'd added: "The sculpture is by Isaac Brodsky." Leningraders are just born knowing that kind of thing... Her Lev is strolling up and down the steps—and he's brought a backpack full of books and two suitcases. Blind as she is, Bella mistakes the suitcases for dogs. "Oh," Lev says. "There you are."

There's a gap after that—but no, Bella remembers how deftly he had slipped into her basement with the suitcases, and asked: "Well, then, shall we make some noise?" And how Aunt Shura accepted Lev's arrival in the apartment with surprising meekness, never asking about his residence permit and, in general, staying out of their way all day.

They talk and talk . . . Most of their talk, of course, concerns Lev's state of affairs: he won't starve—there's always a call for tutors, he could translate, and if push came to shove, he'd write dissertations for idiots. As for his dissident activity, he'd probably stop—not out of fear, mind you, but because he was tired of the responsibility, tired of constantly having to think of himself as a good person. They talk about anything and everything, and go out for a stroll. They pass the Church of Saint Nicholas in Khamovniki, which the government never closed; and the Tolstoy House Museum, which Bella, to tell the truth, had never visited; and walk all the way to the Novodevichy Convent. Bella wants Lev to like Moscow. She's delighted to see that there isn't a trace of that typical Leningrad haughtiness in him. And then, on the way home, Bella suddenly begins to cry. She tries to hide her tears, but it's no use. God forbid he should think she's some typical hysterical actress—and by the way, actresses aren't typically hysterical; men are far worse—but Lev says her tears are perfectly natural, they need no explanation, because this moment isn't just any moment, it's special, and it will never come again.

It rained all night. Bella would wake up, toss and turn for a while, then fall asleep again. She woke up for good when the phone rang. A woman's cheerful, laughing voice gushed from the receiver, swallowing its vowels: "Bella Yuryevna, it's canceled, he isn't coming. What do you mean, who?" Laughter. "The one who knows what the Leningrad Symphony's about." More laughter. "Maybe he's got a cold—or maybe his tummy hurts. Oh, and we've printed up your paperwork.

Bella Yuryevna, it's time to read to the kids. Oh, come on! Don't you recognize me?"

Bella hangs up the phone, thinking hard. Paperwork, symphonies—she can't make heads or tails of it. Should she go? Yes, it's time. Looks like she overslept again, missed something important.

She stands out in the courtyard for a while, with her head thrown back, and watches the clouds. How full of joy they are, full of fun— why, that one there is about to burst with rain! You just watch, it'll come down in buckets, like in Lev's favorite movies—water everywhere. Then the sun appears, and Bella squints, turning her wet hair to it. Rainwater is good for the hair.

For the first time in a long time, Bella's mind is completely clear. And there he is, across the courtyard, the one she's been waiting for. She calls out to him, waves. He must hear her...Why won't he respond? And where did he get that dog? She and Lev never had any dogs. No dogs, no children. Never.

July 2016
Translated by Boris Dralyuk

OBJECTS IN MIRROR

"Hold it, bastard."

Now they'll grab him by the arms and drag him to the Volvo. A terrible force—oppressive, but also attentive, making sure he doesn't howl, isn't hurt. Before they shut his mouth, he'll manage to ask one idiotic question: "But why?" Then darkness, followed by a whole different story—if there's to be any story at all, if it isn't straight into the furnace. He'd had other plans for this day, especially for how it should end, but these things do happen—without warning.

"You," he had planned to say to the eight young people who'd enrolled in his course, "you are the salt of the earth, worth your weight in gold. The screenwriter is the only true auteur. Directors? Directors can sit on their hands: the actors will act, the cameraman will make sure they look good on film, and the editor will splice the film together. That's why everyone wants to be a director." He'd shake his head: "Directors direct nothing... But you," he'd repeat, "are worth your weight in gold."

First he'd intimidate them with his erudition, then he'd tell them a story in which he himself would come to look foolish, silly. He had a vast reserve of such stories and they never failed to charm. He was the master, and they were his pupils. Their business was to learn from the master, his was to elucidate the nature of cinema: what constitutes a film, and what does not. Then they'd watch a movie together.

"Transformation," he'd snap his fingers. "It's all about transformation. If it takes place, then...You understand?"

That would be enough for the first day. Then he'd go see the twins and give them his collected scripts as a present. The food would be good. Then home to Varya, his wife, and Anyuta, his daughter. They'd already be asleep. That was his plan.

The day began with a funny, insignificant incident. While taking the elevator down from the top floor, he glanced into the mirror that had appeared after the last renovation and found himself face-to-face with a ceremonial portrait of the Leader—in his marshal's tunic, studded with medals—which had been pasted firmly to the opposite wall. He was about to scrape it off with a key when he saw an inscription, in blue ink, across the white tunic—HANG-MAN, with a hyphen. There was no mistaking Anyuta's writing. On the one hand, it was rather sad—the Gnessin School focused on music, but shouldn't they at least teach her how to spell? On the other hand, it was touching. He scraped the hyphen off the Generalissimo, along with the marshal's star.

The building was old and solid (a clever thought: it was now Stalinist in every respect), with only twelve apartments, so there could be no doubt as to who had put up the portrait—a tenant with the repellent name Vobly. Who else would bring that trash into the house? Certainly not Vadik, the virtuoso violinist. Not Tamara Maksimovna, the voice coach. No, it had to have been Vobly, the former KGB stooge—who else?

He ducked a bit when stepping out of the entrance. The renovation was done, but the building was still surrounded by all sorts of metal structures and scaffolding. He expected to see Vobly, who spent most of his time outside during the warmer months; Vobly's family didn't let him smoke inside, and, after years in the service, loitering around entrances was probably a matter of habit with him. Though in the past few weeks Vobly had been coming out with a little stool—something wrong with his spine, he said.

"We've all got bad backs, from working on our feet. We didn't have all these surveillance cameras back then. Didn't have all these cell phones, neither."

True enough.

"Off to the salt mines, Andrey Georgievich?" Vobly would ask and look at his watch. He'd nod in response and feel a momentary pang of guilt—it was noon, and he was only now leaving the house. And then he would indeed set off for work, on foot. That summer the sidewalks in their neighborhood had been widened and the roadway had been narrowed, so the streets looked odd to him. He'd make a detour, so as to pass by the French school where he'd studied: a typical five-story building, recently furnished with an extension, a glass cube—not a stylistic match, exactly, but Moscow is an eclectic town. Actually, he hadn't spotted Vobly at the entrance. He hadn't seen him for several days now, but that wasn't unusual; he might be at the hospital again, for his back. Well, let him get some rest. That HANG-MAN must have given him a good laugh.

Yes, he had gone to the French school, the best in town. And he had done well for himself after graduating, too, enrolling at Moscow State's Mechanics and Mathematics Department, though he had no particular aptitude for mathematics. Nor was he especially good at French—nor, he sometimes felt, was he especially good at anything. But to his friends, of whom there were many, he seemed, on the contrary, to be a man of great and varied gifts.

"You love me as a thing, not as a person." Stravinsky, he recalled, had said something similar after Feodor Chaliapin's death. Maybe it hadn't been Stravinsky, but someone had said it.

"No, Andryusha, you've got it wrong—you love yourself as a thing," his friends would respond. "We just love you."

And that would reassure him, for a time. The feelings of friends are conditional; they require periodic updates. The desire to be liked (in his case, an entirely innocent desire) is obviously a character flaw, but, for an artist, it's simply natural. Or common, at any rate. Of course, the worst thing he had ever done, from a civic standpoint, was to join the Communist Youth. Just think, here he was, a boy with a family history of anti-Soviet activity—his parents' apartment had been searched twice ("raided," the grown-ups had said). He still remembered the look of surprise on his teacher's face: Andrey was one of the first in his class to submit an application. Foolishness, utter foolishness, and not even close to mandatory in 1987. On the other hand, he had always been totally honest with women, which is why he was on his third marriage.

He was a screenwriter now, and well known enough, although there's really no such thing as a sufficiently appreciated artist. He used to write plays, too, before getting into film. And then, after Anyuta was born, he had gone over to television. His degree? They say mathematics is the highest achievement of human thought. He had enrolled at the department without any practical goals in mind. Frankly, it had been a concession to his parents. He had other ambitions: to put on plays, to act, to compose. Back in those days, the student theater at Moscow State, where he spent nearly every evening, was going great guns. When exams would roll around, he'd cram and pass. Seems he had some aptitude after all. And of course the university kept him out of the army.

Mathematics is nothing, really—some things are much more difficult to master: remaining sober and alert, not losing heart. Nothing he faced today could compare to what his parents had dealt with, to say nothing of his grandparents. Yes, things had gotten a bit frightening. But more dreary than frightening, no? There was certainly no point in adding to the woes of others, of those one loved not as things. Maybe it wasn't so bad, anyway? Maybe things were better than they appeared? At any rate, one couldn't just sit there and hate the regime. One had to work, write, teach the kid Russian, music (his wife, Varya, taught harmony). But those whom he didn't cherish quite as much, those whose peace of mind meant less to him, got very different advice. He would tell them to flee as soon as they could:

"A lack of imagination. Emigration is a terrible thing: a garret in Paris or, I don't know, some apartment building in Brooklyn . . . But imagine a guard in a watchtower, imagine being dragged out of bed at six every morning—yes, a lack of imagination."

His own imagination was in perfect working order. After lecturing others about watchtowers and guards, he'd find himself tossing and turning all night. He'd promise himself that he'd wake up the next morning full of joy and gratitude to his parents, his daughter, his wife (he believed in God less and less), and even his friends—but now, more and more often, he awoke with his heart pounding, feeling trapped. He was sure he'd get ahold of himself soon enough. In any case, his girls mustn't be allowed to suffer. He had lived under this pressure, had dwelled with these thoughts for the past few months, until the beginning of the school year, September 1.

"Andrey Georgievich, why did you leave your television job?" asks Lydia from Krasnodar. Low forehead, bangs, a typical regional twang.

"Anyone with a shred of decency abandoned television." Hadn't she noticed, down there on the Kuban? And what did it matter where she lived? This Lydia was an active girl. What did she do before coming here?

The screenwriting students were all in their late twenties, thirties. They all had educations, professions.

"Municipal services. Why?"

So why *did* he leave his job, she asks.

"I decided I wasn't going to join the Communist Youth again. You don't get it? Good."

His new class: two Nastyas, two Olyas, a pair of ordinary-looking young men (these two, he knew, would soon fall away, just stop showing up), Lydia, and, finally, the main source of danger—Rachel, a clever, toothy brunette. It was a two-year course, and commercial, so he had to accept all applicants. There were only two kinds of students he feared: the mad and the clever. So here was one such student: big eyes and large crooked teeth. You could see her upper gums when she smiled. She wouldn't be able to write a screenplay for the life of her. Not a lick of imagination. Her head was full of French postmodernists, Derrida and Deleuze. She'd drive him crazy with her endless comments. But still—Rachel, born in 1987: someone had dared to give their daughter that Old Testament name back in '87.

And now it was up to him to teach them the craft of screenwriting. Yes, yes, my dears—the craft. The Romantic era, which had lasted nearly two hundred years, was now over. Gone were the days when artists had sat at the heads of tables, surrounded by aristocrats—all these dinners where Richard Wagner had hobnobbed with King Ludwig II. If you harbor any illusions about inspiration, about divine afflatus, get rid of them straightaway. In the years of his youth, when he was lucky enough to spend time with—he pronounces the name of a famous pianist, a friend of his parents (Rachel nods, the rest give no sign of recognition)—he was instructed to be quiet around the genius, not to make a peep, as if the man were terminally ill. God forbid he should bring up the last concert, or—worse yet—the next concert, or even talk of music. But now, with these young fellows, some of whom are genuine masters, like his neighbor Vadik (he mentions his surname), things are different. You ask: How did it go? Did people show up? And he just mumbles: Went fine. Or says: Played as well as I could, now let's go tie one on.

The students grow quiet. Lydia jots something down in her notebook. His phone vibrates in his pocket. Let's have a look—no, he doesn't recognize the number—and he moves on to the fact that the visual arts, cinematography first and foremost, are increasingly displacing literature and music. He doesn't know why, exactly—maybe it's a lack of imagination? But these days he himself prefers to listen to music with pictures, video. And so, dear colleagues, the ability to write for the screen, to make movies, is a useful thing—although, with the situation being what it is, he has to warn them that their prospects are not at all rosy. If they wanted a recipe for quick success, well, they were out of luck. There were no recipes for success, quick or otherwise:

"No one will shoot films based on our screenplays. From now on, we'll have to work like architects: our boldest, grandest constructions will exist only on paper—in magazines and in printed volumes. They'll never make it to the screen."

A knock at the door. One of the young women from the office.

"You're wanted in Human Resources."

Doesn't she see he's in the middle of class?

He has to fill out a registration form, list all the foreign countries he's visited in the last ten years.

"Can't I just put down 'all of them'?"

"What do you mean, 'all of them'?"

He begins listing countries: Austria, Belgium, Croatia, Denmark...
He feels awkward in front of the students.

"Stop by Human Resources," the young woman interrupts. "No later than Tuesday. Bring your passport."

He follows her out into the corridor: What's this about?

"Your file was requested."

Why was she whispering? They had a file on him? Why hadn't he been told?

"We have files on everyone."

So who had requested it? Had they requested all of the files—or just his?

She shrugs her shoulders: What's the point in asking? Then, with a look of sympathy: "Maybe you wrote something? Said something? Give it some thought."

What could he have written? His heart pauses, then gives a strong jolt. Again and again—a pause, then a jolt. He knows his heart won't stop, that these are just so-called extrasystoles, nothing serious, but it still doesn't feel good. He takes a few breaths, walks back into the classroom: Well, time for a movie?

Motes of dust in the projector beam, the white screen, semidarkness; one doesn't watch serious films on the TV screen. He would show them Iosseliani's *Falling Leaves* and then explain the picture's structure. He tells them what to look for: the family photos, the clatter of billiard balls, the out-of-tune piano in the director's office, the close-ups (infrequent), the Russian words coming from the radio, the fact that almost every event happens twice, has its reflection, like when you close a notebook and the fresh ink leaves its trace on the facing page.

"Georgian girls all have those little mustaches," one of the Olyas says with a sigh.

Let's not laugh at Olya. Any other impressions? He, for instance, finds that *Falling Leaves* never fails to restore his sense of harmony, never fails to reconcile him with reality. By the way, Iosseliani had also spent several years studying mathematics before he made films.

So what's it about? Almost nothing happens: a minor industrial incident. But it's inscribed in an eternal context—by the scenes of peasants, by the photographs, by the tolling of the bell at the end. From his point of view, the film is about the forging of an individual character, about dignity.

"Would you say it's about rootedness?"

Yes, thank you, Rachel. As for the name, he himself doesn't really understand it: leaves don't fall in August.

"The vegetative cycle of grapes. First the berries ripen, then the shoots dry up, and then the leaves fall. The plant is preparing for winter."

That's it. Rachel is a botanist, in the truest sense of the word: she has a degree in biology. Scientific knowledge can come in handy for anyone, but for an artist it's an invaluable source of metaphor.

"An anti-Russian film, through and through," lovely Lydia suddenly declares.

He smiles: "Perhaps anti-Soviet?"

She furrows her little forehead: "Same thing, no difference." He disagrees. There is a difference.

"Andrey Georgievich, what are your feelings about the current government? Yes, our government," Lydia asks in the manner of someone who has the right to know, looking straight into his eyes.

He remembers the conversation with the young woman from the office. Should he make a joke? Why did he have to show them *Falling Leaves*? He responds firmly: "My feelings aren't good. We'll leave it at that."

Rachel claps her hands a few times: she's the only one to applaud.

"I've given you your assignments."

He and Rachel walk to the metro station together. Until recently, she had been working at a school. Then her job became unbearable—for obvious reasons.

"I'm so glad we have you for a teacher, Andrey Georgievich. You're not only a wonderfully talented person, you're also very brave. And you can't have one without the other, wouldn't you say?" She shakes his hand as they part.

Once he's on the train, he remembers the phone call. It turns out he's missed six calls, from the same unknown number. He reaches the Sparrow Hills station, steps onto the platform. "Connection cannot be established." Strange. He's paid his bill. Problems with the network? He tries again—same thing. Back into the train, to the Southwestern station.

He always visits the twins, his good friends, alone. Tonight he expects to see them, Ada and Glasha—short for Adelaide and Aglaya (that's what a love for Dostoyevsky does to people)—and their husbands, Alexander and Alexey, whom he still has a hard time telling apart. Both men are cheerful, slightly boring engineers—you don't meet many engineers anymore. Their children, already in their teens, will be there too. And maybe three or four other couples.

Ada is the elder sister, born ten minutes before Glasha. "What's it like, having an exact copy of yourself?"

"We're used to it," they say, "what's it like not having one?" And they live side by side, on the sixteenth floor—two apartments with a shared balcony. He had known them at Moscow State. They studied chemistry but, like him, preferred the theater. "We had a lot of fun, didn't we, Andryusha?" Memories: everyone smoked back then, and the sisters always smelled of cigarettes—their hair, their dresses. What fun it was. They sewed all the costumes themselves, and built all the sets. Twins can always find roles to play: for example, Ada and Glasha put on a very funny production of *The Canterville Ghost*. But for them the theater remained just that, playtime. It never turned into a profession. Good thing he never got involved with them romantically. Well, there was that one time. With Glasha. Just a momentary fling, many years ago.

The only guests so far are a married couple, whose names he can never remember. Where, he asks, are such and such? "Moved to Georgia." Is that right? He hadn't heard.

"Of course; you're too busy…" Is Glasha mocking him? Doesn't seem so. The usual topics of conversation: the end of summer, parents ailing and—in more detail—being difficult, the relative merits of home-care providers from the former republics of the USSR. He has nothing to contribute on that last topic: his parents aren't yet in need of nurses.

"Andryusha, you're out of focus today." The sisters want him to stop snacking and tell them a story. He's ruining his appetite. They have a pheasant in the oven. He should tell them about his new crop of lady screenwriters.

He runs through the events of the day in his mind. Fairly frightening, really: the sudden request for his file, the question about the government. And the silence—not a wary silence, but a hollow, dead silence—that met his response. Then the lonely applause, the isolated claps—they didn't help at all. It would have been better had the group argued with him, shouted. In previous years, such things had at least led to screaming matches.

"Same as always: two Tanyas, two Manyas, two silent sons-in-law, one aggressive idiot—but also one kindred soul." There's nothing to laugh about, but he feels he should strike a more cheerful tone: "So I'm feeding them my favorite ideas, one after the other, steering clear of politics, and then, suddenly, she pipes up," he remembers beautiful Lydia. "You know the sort, a nasty little guttersnipe—thin lips, small mouth."

His audience exchange glances: Andryusha is surprisingly observant. To be honest, he doesn't remember what Lydia's mouth actually looked like. He brings his narrative to a close by mentioning Human Resources and the office, then thinks to himself: Every story, no matter how simple, requires a climax and a denouement. Now, having finished, he waits to be comforted and consoled, to hear them say that there's nothing to worry about, that they have checkups at their institutions and businesses too, that it's just a formality, that everything's planned out now, including checkups, nothing to be afraid of, these aren't the bad old days. But no one says a word.

"Things are what they are." One has to end on the proper note. "If you've decided to stay, you've got to be ready for anything."

The talk takes off on its circuitous route again, getting tangled, shifting to the past, then to children. After some time the wine is gone and the pheasant's bones are picked clean, and he's thinking out loud about our mistaken notion of justice—the notion that justice is ever present and always wins: "Nothing can banish this childish delusion. In the end, they'll come for us, and all we'll be able to ask is: 'But why?' I myself am spoiled. For instance, I never got lower marks than I deserved. I did well at school, though I was really a C student at best."

"With me it's the opposite," Alexey breaks in.

Alexey has a different notion of justice. If you were given more than you deserve—how can you call that justice? He has a more modest claim. And now Alexey, who hadn't uttered a word all night, relates how last spring he and his friends went down to the courthouse to protest the latest wave of political arrests—to stand outside and protest, since they weren't allowed into the building.

"We stood out there for an hour or two, shouting this and that, but, more than anything, just shifting our feet. It was cold, and I had to go relieve myself. Then I came back and stood some more. I lost track of my friends. There were a few hundred people by then. Then I see buses blocking the road on both sides. We hear an announcement: 'Citizens, do not interfere with the movement of traffic.' But we're all on the sidewalk. Then the police show up—with shields, helmets—and start grabbing people out of the crowd, one by one. They target the people doing the shouting, and anyone with a distinctive feature—a poster, a bright hat, a red beard. I don't really mind being thrown onto the bus—so they'll take me to the station, check my passport, then let me go—but I'm not especially eager. So I just stand there and watch. And they keep saying: 'Citizens, please clear the road.' By now anyone close to the road is getting swept up. The buses are almost full, but they aren't going anywhere—and I sense nature's calling again. It turns out I'm not the only one. I hear two intelligent-looking middle-aged women say: Last time they kept us in there for two hours, stewing, but we had our plastic bottles—you can cut off the tops and . . . They laugh: You fellows have it easy—you don't even need to cut off the tops. That's when I took off. I didn't like the idea of urinating on a bus. And I didn't particularly want to see women pissing in bottles, either."

"And that's all?"

"That's all. I just took off. The end of my career as a protester."

"Andrey is a typical professor." For some reason Glasha speaks of him in the third person. "He doesn't like it when anyone talks for longer than he does."

She was right. He had to take the conversation into his own hands: "What it comes down to, I feel, is lack of imagination. Of course, when you imagine the hardships of emigration ... I can stay with ..." He names a mutual friend, who's been living in Brussels for ages. "He has a huge apartment. Or with ..." He names another of their acquaintances. "He's got a big house in Houston. He'll go off to work each morning, then come back in the evening—and ask, What have you created? Any headway with Hollywood? You open the refrigerator, and he frowns. 'Andryusha, maybe you should look for an easier job, just for the time being?' What, delivering pizza? Trimming bushes? Sweeping the street? 'Don't get the wrong idea, no one's trying to force you out. Great, now you're upset...' Your children start pushing you farther and farther away, the threat of alcoholism, depression. We can imagine that, sure—but how about a guard screaming 'On your feet!' at six in the morning? How about sewing mittens in the shop? The stench of unwashed bodies, playing by prison rules, keeping your head down. Should I go on? Fearing for your life every minute of the day. Not enough heat, food, air. It's not just a matter of 'thinking about the children'—we should think about ourselves. Inertia is a terrible thing. Do you know the story of Kissinger's family? They stayed in Bavaria till the very last minute. They very nearly left it too late. Well, we're no smarter than Kissinger, I assure you."

"Houston ..." Ada says thoughtfully. "Andryusha, did you know we got an apartment in Vilnius?"

"When did that happen?"

"After Alexey's crusade to the courthouse. We sold our dacha."

Vilnius, they reason, can't save them from everything. But with an Israeli passport ... Oh, they have Israeli passports too? Only Glasha and Alexander, for now. He didn't know Alexander was Jewish. Just a quarter—his grandmother—but the one that counts, on his mother's side.

"Looks like you'll have to mind the shop on your own, Andryusha..." Pause.

Glasha recites a line from Pushkin: "The feast goes on. The Master of Revels remains, lost in thought."[24]

Cruel. But appropriate. Ada aims an expressive glance at her sister: "It's just in case things go off the rails. We might not even need it." The rest of the guests are already drinking tea and cognac, eating chocolates.

It's stuffy. He rises from the table, goes into the next room, and walks up to the window. A warm Moscow evening. The lights are on all across town. Ada opens the door to the balcony: after dark, the view's even better. It's not the center, of course, but they like the neighborhood. "And if you lean out and look over there..." Ada slides the glass open.

"No, don't do that," he retreats into the hallway. He's developed a fear of heights.

"Afraid the balcony will collapse?"

"I'm afraid to look down. You succumb to the temptation for a second, and..." Ada beckons to her sister.

"Listen, Andryusha, we're worried about you. You've always exceeded the bounds of any given situation. But you also knew when to drop the theatrics and to get ready for exams."

Yes, there was a time... He puts on his shoes. He'll feel better if he takes a walk. Would they mind if he left without saying goodbye to everyone?

"You know what... I don't think I can walk after all. Girls, would you call me a taxi?"

They walk him to the door and give him two kisses, each on one cheek: "Our weakness is our strength."

"And there's no end to our weakness." They smile, wave.

Under different circumstances, their kisses would have been very pleasant—the girls are so beautiful, so familiar—but today they have no effect. Neither the twins nor the wine have managed to cheer him up, much less intoxicate him. He hardly even touched the wine.

"Up your mother's . . ." The driver hits the brakes, rousing him from an uncomfortable slumber. "You see what that bastard did? These," he inserts another insult, "think they own the road. Did you get a look at the license plate? EKX97. You know what that means?"

Why should *he* know? He asks the driver to turn down the radio just a bit—Russian rap, not the worst thing these days, but a little too loud. Now he tries dialing that number again. This time a mechanical voice tells him to enter a personal password. Password? What password?

"Those little gadgets," the driver pokes a finger at the phone. "They use those to keep tabs on everyone. Where you are, what you're talking about. You can shut if off and pull out the battery—but it makes no difference. That's special technology for ya. They've got us all on a leash."

He should have sat in the back. What was that about license plates? The driver tells him about what happened the previous week, at his mother-in-law's funeral. Some guy pulled up at the crematorium, alone, in a Ford minivan, with an EKX plate, and went up to two of the fellows on duty. These fellows helped the guy unload two coffins. The three of them bring the coffins inside, then the guy comes out, turns the van around, and drives off.

"Who was in the coffins?" He tries to keep his voice steady.

"Who the hell knows? Maybe two poor bastards like you and me."

He isn't well—breathing rapidly, heart pounding, vision blurring. How do the windows work? He lowers the glass all the way down, exposing his face to a stream of cold air. Without asking permission, he turns a dial on the radio—raises the volume. He no longer hears the driver—any rap, any crap is better than stories about crematoriums. He reads the English inscription: "Objects in mirror are closer than they appear." And he repeats the phrase to the beat of the music. Are they closer in the mirror or in real life? Read the goddamned manual. Where are they closer? It makes no sense. Objects in mirror…What does that mean?—What? No, he isn't going to puke. One-way street? Just stop the car, he'll get out here. He needs to get home, but he can hardly walk; he is trembling all over. He reaches the corner of his street, almost at a run. He can see it now, the entrance. Another fifty, sixty steps and he's home. But on the sidewalk, next to the entrance—a dark Volvo he's never seen before. The lights are off but the engine is running. And two long shadows beside it. The license plate. What were those letters? The plate is caked with mud, as if on purpose. No, it's just the one shadow, not two. He grips the keys in his pocket—he can use them as a weapon, or throw them at a window, cause a scene. Run? He can't even feel his legs. Here you are, Kissinger. Another step or two and he'll hear: "Hold it, bastard." Then a terrible force will grab him by the shoulder.

A lighter snaps in the shadow's hands and sends up a little flame. My god, Vobly.

Vobly recognizes him too: "Time for some shut-eye, Andrey Georgievich?"

He rushes towards the door and gets a blow to the head. The scaffolding. He had forgotten to duck. He squats on his haunches, presses his hand to his forehead. No blood. He catches his breath. Vobly leans over him, tries to help—no, no need, everything's fine. Everything really is fine, except for the pain in his head.

"A whack for scaredy-cats"—that's what they used to call it at school. He should put something cold on it. He enters the elevator, leans his forehead against the mirror, and stands there for half a minute. Then he presses the button. By the time he reaches his floor, the pain is gone. He steps back from the mirror and examines himself. He hasn't gotten a whack like that in a long time. "A whack for scaredy-cats"—he's forgotten French, forgotten math, but nonsense like that is still lodged in his mind.

He walks into his apartment, making as little noise as possible. First he looks into his bedroom, then he checks on Anyuta. Both his girls are fast asleep, as he had expected. Was it Goebbels who ended up poisoning his own daughters? He goes to the kitchen and stands by the window, gazing down at the dark empty sidewalk. Then he walks into the bathroom, gets soap, a brush, and a bucket of water, and heads to the elevator, where he scrubs the mustachioed bastard's face off the wall. He tosses the scraps down the garbage chute, returns to marvel at the clean, wet wall of the elevator, then examines his reflection once more. So you're back in good standing, are you?

January 2017
Translated by Boris Dralyuk

NOTES

MOSCOW-PETROZAVODSK

1   An ironic expression once popular in the Soviet Union. Felix Dzerzhinsky was the chairman of the Cheka (Extraordinary Commission), the
first Soviet state security force, and its successor organization, the
OGPU, from 1917 to 1926.

THE GYPSY

2   In his memoirs, Alexander Herzen writes that Garibaldi called America
"the country 'of forgetting the fatherland,'" *My Past and Thoughts*, trans.
Constance Garnett (London: Chatto & Windus, 1924), 3: 77.

ROCK, PAPER, SCISSORS

3   All excerpts from Alexander Pushkin's *Eugene Onegin* are taken from
Eugene Onegin, trans. Stanley Mitchell (London: Penguin Classics,
2008).

4   From Alexander Pushkin's "City of splendour, city of poor," trans. Ant-
ony Wood, in *The Penguin Book of Russian Poetry*, ed. Robert Chandler,
Boris Dralyuk, and Irina Mashinski (London: Penguin Classics, 2015).

5   Two lines from an untitled poem by Anna Akhmatova, which begins,
"There is, somewhere, a simple life and light" (1915), translated by Alex
Fleming.

6   The first line of an untitled poem by Osip Mandelstam from 1915, translated by Alex Fleming.

7   Lines from Alexander Blok's long poem *Retribution* (1908–1913), translated by Alex Fleming.

RENAISSANCE MAN

8   From Alexander Pushkin's *Eugene Onegin*.

9   The title of an infamous editorial that appeared in *Pravda*, one of the official organs of the Communist Party, on January 28, 1936. It condemned the "formalist" excesses of Dmitri Shostakovich's opera *Lady Macbeth of the Mtsensk District* (1934).

10   The opening lines of Aleksey Plescheyev's (1825–1893) translation (1861) of Moritz Hartmann's (1821–1872) poem "Schweigen" (1860), set to music by Tchaikovsky as part of his *Six Romances, Op. 6* (1869).

THE WAVES OF THE SEA

11   Fyodor Tyutchev (1803–1873) was one of the most important Russian poets of the nineteenth century.

POLISH FRIEND

12   Emil Grigoryevich Gilels, born in Odessa in 1916, was regarded as one of the greatest pianists of the twentieth century. This remark, supposedly made by Stalin in the late 1930s, reveals the importance accorded to musical performance in the spread of Soviet propaganda.

AFTER ETERNITY: THE NOTES OF A LITERARY DIRECTOR

13   From Mikhail Lermontov's *A Hero of Our Time*, trans. Nicolas Pasternak Slater (Oxford: Oxford University Press, 2013).

14   From Alexander Pushkin's *Boris Godunov and Other Dramatic Works*, trans. James E. Falen (Oxford: Oxford University Press, 2007).

15   From Alexander Griboyedov's verse comedy *Woe from Wit* (1831).

16   From Pushkin's "Sketches for a Project about Faust" (1825).

17   From Alexander Pushkin's *The Stone Guest*, in *Boris Godunov and Other Dramatic Works*, trans. James E. Falen (Oxford: Oxford University Press, 2007).

18   From Sophocles's *Oedipus the King*, trans. F. Storr (Cambridge, MA: Harvard University Press, 1912).

19   From Sophocles's *Oedipus the King*, trans. F. Storr.

20   From Paul Celan, "And with the Book from Tarussa," trans. Joachim Neugroschel, in *Paul Celan: Selections*, ed. Pierre Joris (Berkeley: University of California Press, 2005).

21   Korsun is the Old East Slavic name for Chersonesus, an ancient Greek colony on the Crimean Peninsula. The modern Crimean city of Kherson is named after the colony. During Russia's annexation of Crimea in 2014, Vladimir Putin and others pointed to the legend that Saint Vladimir the Great (c. 958–1015), who baptized Kievan Rus'—which Russian historians see as the forerunner of modern Russia—was himself baptized in Korsun.

22   From Alexander Pushkin's *The Miserly Knight*, in *Boris Godunov and Other Dramatic Works*, trans. James E. Falen (Oxford: Oxford University Press, 2007).

ON THE BANKS OF THE SPREE

23   A song composed by Kirill Molchanov (1922–1982), with lyrics by Alexander Galich (1918–1977). It was performed in the film *Seven Winds* (1962) by Vyacheslav Tikhonov (1928–2009), who would go on to play the Soviet spy Max Otto von Stierlitz in the television series *Seventeen Moments of Spring* (1973), a role that would win him lasting fame in the Russian-speaking world.

OBJECTS IN MIRROR

24   From Alexander Pushkin's *A Feast in Time of Plague*, in *Boris Godunov and Other Dramatic Works*, trans. James E. Falen (Oxford: Oxford University Press, 2007).

OTHER NEW YORK REVIEW CLASSICS

For a complete list of titles, visit www.nyrb.com or write to:
Catalog Requests, NYRB, 435 Hudson Street, New York, NY 10014